SURRENDERING

A REGENT VAMPIRE LORDS NOVEL

K.L. KREIG

To my husband.
My life would be incomplete without you.
I love you so very much.

Acknowledgements and Thanks!

Thanks...how can five little letters ever adequately express the gratitude I feel? The simple answer is, it can't.

So many more than myself are responsible for this book. Yes, I had the concept. Yes, I wrote the words (thank you, thesaurus). Yes, I've made *my* vision of vampire lore and these characters' love story come true in black and white.

But the true thanks goes to those around me who've supported me in my journey to put my story on a page and actually publish my very first novel.

First to my readers: **Thank you** for purchasing my book!! This was a labor of love and many a night I dreamt about the characters, sentence structure, word choices and the twisting turns of the plot. I hope you enjoyed reading it as much as I enjoyed writing it. If you like my book, please tell your friends! The best thing you can do to support an author you love is word of mouth.

To my *girls*: Tara, Kaitlyn, Beth, Sherri, Teresa, Emma and Diane...a million thanks will never be enough for your honesty, your valued opinions and for putting up with me talking incessantly about this book, particularly over the last several months as it finally came together. I'm so blessed to have each and every one of you in my life! (Sniffle, sniffle, get the tissue...)

To my husband: Babe, you are my everything, my inspiration, my very heart. I can write about romance because I live it every day with you. If my girls think I talked to them incessantly, they have no idea what went on behind the four walls at our house! Thanks for your undying support when I was literally consumed with my writing, even when I didn't always get dinner on the table or I forgot to call the table guy or I couldn't tear myself away from the story to order the new sheets we so desperately needed for our bed! You are my rock and I'm so very glad that you're proud of what I've been able to accomplish, because none of it would have been possible without you.

Thanks to my editor for all of your great comments, collaboration and suggestions. I have a better story because of your feedback. And finally a special thanks to Yocla Designs for the absolutely *A M A Z I N G* job you did on the book cover art! You brought my vision of the story to life and a picture really does say a thousand words through your work.

Finally, I want to shout out to all of the amazing romance authors that gave me the inspiration to try penning my own book.

PROLOGUE

Kate

Rough hands gently roam her fevered body as a hot tongue leaves a blaze of fire in its wake. His burning gaze is fierce, but his hands touch her skin with a reverence she's not experienced. Soft lips and sharp teeth nip down her midsection, pausing only briefly before continuing lower to a place she so desperately needed them to worship. When his tongue pierced her sex, she gasped, her hips bucked but he held her tightly to the mattress, devouring her, driving her higher toward madness.

"Come," he darkly commanded, and her body obeys as an unexpected climax takes her crashing over the edge into thick, hazy, fog-filled bliss. Forcing her tightly clenched eyes open, she watched in sated fascination as he wraps her hips around his waist and thrusts into her wet, aching sheath, setting off an orgasm as equally intense as the first. Hips thrust, sweat poured and breaths were choppy. Every time was the same...unbridled passion and fervent coupling. Complete and utter perfection.

He plays her with expert precision, wringing another wave of pleasure from her well replete body before finally seeking his own pained release. They lay together, slick bodies quickly cooling as he worships her mouth in the same reverent manner.

"I—"

A car horn stopped short the words falling from her lover's lips, evaporating them into the atmosphere like a fine mist.

She blinked her eyes open in both confusion and frustration.

Not again.

Dreams of *him* always ended like this. *Without* fail. They had mind-blowing sex so real she could feel her pussy ache when she awoke. But instead of satisfaction, it ached with emptiness. Emptiness she often had to remedy herself or suffer so greatly throughout the day she couldn't function.

It was the same exact dream, with the same exact ungodly gorgeous man and something always woke her at *exactly* the same point. He was getting ready to say something profound, but the words never came. She daydreamed constantly on what followed the word "I—"

Perhaps it was *"I...want to spend the night,"* (only if you cuddle) or, *"I...want you on your hands and knees next,"* (uh...no need to ask twice) or perhaps even foolishly *"I...love you."* (yes, *that* was foolish, Kate).

She may never know. Maybe she should be content with the erotic dream and the unwelcome feeling of surrendering herself to a man again, even if he wasn't real. God knows she couldn't do that when she was awake.

Never again.

She had been naïve. Well...not anymore. Getting your love callously thrown out by guy after guy like a waded up fast food wrapper tended to turn you into a cynical, heartless bitch who would end up in a sad nursing home, old and alone. The nursing staff that drew the short straw would have to take her wing for the day and listen to her pitiful tales of woe. Tales they'd hear until the day she died. The only thing that would keep her company in the years in between life and death would be her twenty-two cats, knitting hats for the homeless and her trusty binoculars, which she'd use to spy on the neighbors.

She'd surrendered her love too easily and too often, but this last time...well, it was like an adage her father always used to say. *"Death by a thousand paper cuts."* You can make it through the nine hundred ninety ninth one intact, but that thousandth one, that's the one that ends you. And John was her thousandth and most regretful paper cut. More like a goddamned ten-inch knife shredding flesh and bone, fatally piercing that small fragile organ held in the center of your chest.

Turning her head, the bright red digital numerals read five fifteen. *A.M.* An involuntary sigh escaped her lips. She'd gotten approximately three hours of sleep and that would be it. Falling back into her dreams could be a godsend, like tonight, or a curse like most. And although she didn't need to be at work for five hours yet, she wasn't willing to take a chance on the torment she might endure should she nod off. Today, of all days, she just could *not* stomach starting the day badly, waking from the throes of a nightmare which she wouldn't be able to shake.

Try as she might to fight against it, her thoughts involuntarily drifted to John and the night one year ago today she'd found him with his secretary in his office. She'd been so cliché. Showing up in garters, heels and nothing else sans a tan, tightly belted trench coat. In the good old heart of god's country, it had been minus twelve degrees that day and she had literally been freezing her tits off under the thin material. The phrase 'colder than a witch's tit in January' surely originated from Wisconsin.

But she'd wanted to do something nice for her fiancée. As a marketing consultant, he'd landed a big new client and had been putting in long, hard hours to meet an unrealistic deadline. Most nights he wouldn't get home until ten or eleven and he'd been too exhausted lately to keep up on their once active sex life. *Cue Simple Plan's Your Love is a Lie.*

With a bottle of champagne and two cheap plastic flutes in hand, she took the elevator up to the eighteenth floor of John's downtown Milwaukee office building. It was after nine and he'd said he had two more hours of work ahead of him before coming home, but it'd been more than two weeks since they'd been intimate and that just wouldn't do.

She made her way toward his office on the east end of the floor, one lone light reflecting faintly through the fogged glass. The rest of space was dim with only soft night lighting and as she'd made her way down the hallway, lined with offices to her left and cubicles to her right, she had been surprised to see his door shut.

In retrospect, she knew what would be found behind a closed, but foolishly unlocked, office door at nine o'clock in the evening. She knew as she closed the short distance between her faltering footsteps and that offending piece of wood, that opening it would ultimately shatter her dreams and harden her heart.

Time slowed as she turned the knob and discovered her boyfriend of two years, fiancé of nine months, husband-to-be in six, fucking his beautiful red headed assistant over the edge of his desk. And since their backs were to the office door, she had the distinct pleasure of hearing the endearments he'd so freely lavished upon Scarlett. Yes, her name was *Scarlett*. She used to love *Gone with the Wind*. Now she'd never watch it again. They'd ruined her relationship *and* one of her favorite movies all in a matter of seconds.

Her only regret as she'd turned and fled while screaming at him never to show his cheating face at their house again, was that the flutes she'd hurled in their direction weren't real glass so they would actually do some serious damage. If either had gotten a shattered sliver of *adulterer* embedded in oh, say in their corneas, well...that would have been called *karma,* bitches.

Curse her luck.

CHAPTER 1

Kate

"Come on, just one more drink, Katie pie. Pretty please," Erin whined. Why, oh why had she agreed to come out with Erin this evening?

"Begging doesn't become you, sweetcakes."

"It most certainly does...in the right circumstances."

Ugh. She did not need to hear about Erin's vigorous and adventurous sex life. She'd been on such a drought her vagina was crumbling to dust. Admittedly, the drought was self-imposed, but self-preservation required it. She'd met too many seemingly nice men over the last several years that turned out to be douche bags. Hell, she'd been engaged to the biggest d-bag of them all. So, no. Definitely time to take her sorry ass home. That, and she *was* dead-dog-tired.

"Sorry, but I need to go. I have an early class to teach in the morning." It wasn't that early, but with Erin, she always needed a good excuse.

"You act like an old maid, Kate. Not a twenty-seven-year-old single, available woman. It's okay to have fun once in a while. It's even okay to bump uglies occasionally."

Sigh. She heard this speech from Erin nearly every time they went out lately, which was why she usually spent the evening in, drinking a nice glass of wine alone and watching mind-numbing TV. Yes, she fully admitted she was pathetic.

So what if she preferred the quiet of her office to the loudness of a club? So what if she preferred her own company to that of a bunch of sweaty men and small dicks grinding into her on the dance floor? So what if she preferred her research to that of a boring, meaningless conversation about the bond market or the latest tweet on Kim Kardashian's ass?

"Don't start, Erin." Kate was a fiercely private person, letting very few people into her inner circle.

She'd met her one good friend, Erin, during undergrad at Marquette University. Erin had been her rock after her failed engagement. Kate had been convinced John was different from the rest of the men she met, but had been proven wrong. So very wrong. The sound of him pounding on their front door begging for forgiveness, that it'd been a one-time mistake—*blah, blah, blah*—still rang in her ears a year later. But Kate was a fool me once kind of girl. And he'd fooled her damn good.

Erin hugged her. "I'm sorry, Kate. I'm just worried about you. You're better off without him and his whoring ways. It's been over a year now. It's time to move on. Your Prince Charming is out there, and you won't find him with your nose stuck behind a computer screen or in a ream of copy paper."

Kate smiled inwardly. She'd already found her Prince Charming. So what if he was a figment of her imagination? He felt real enough when starring in her erotic dreams.

"I know, Erin. I'm just not quite ready yet. I'm getting there." She wasn't *ever* going to get there. She couldn't allow another man to shatter her heart into a million pieces the way John had.

"Great! How about we go to this new club downtown

on Saturday night? It's called Dragonfly and it's supposed to be the shits. I know one of the bartenders. He said he could get us in."

Kate groaned. The last thing she wanted to do on Saturday night was go to a new bar, packed wall-to-wall with young singles trying to hook up. It would smell like sex, sweat, and a nauseating combination of perfumes and cologne. By the end of the night, her shoes would stick to the floor where too many drinks had been spilled and she'd have to fend off the inevitable wandering hands as she refilled hers at the bar because the slutty waitress was too busy with the table of hot, young up-and-comers to check on her.

So she said the only thing she could to get Erin off her back. "Sure, sounds great."

Erin's squeal nearly broke her eardrum. "Oh my God, Katie pie! It will be so much fun. I can't wait."

Yeah, neither could she. Eye roll. She said her goodbyes and drove the short distance to her house. With only two glasses of wine, she felt safe enough to drive.

It was already nearly ten o'clock when she got home and readied herself for bed, turning off the light. She lay there; eyes wide open, dreading the night to come. Because of the often dark nature of her dreams, she didn't slept well, but the last couple of weeks had been particularly difficult, and walking zombie would accurately describe her.

Wanting to come home after her classes today, Erin convinced her to go for a drink instead. She knew her friend meant well. Kate wished she could share her secret with Erin, but she didn't dare. If Erin looked at her the way her parents did, she wasn't sure she could handle it.

Probably because of her curse, she'd been obsessed with dreams and the psychology surrounding them since she was a teenager. She'd majored in psychology in undergrad and was now working on her PhD while she taught several classes at Marquette as an assistant professor. All coursework behind her, only her dissertation remained and her doctorate was finally within reach. So her exhaustion was in part due to her nightmares, but also her obsession with this research project.

She hoped she'd find a *rational* explanation for her dreams and what they meant. No luck so far, but she wasn't giving up hope. They didn't feel like normal dreams in the typical sense. Too often, they felt...real. She felt *part* of them, as if she were there in these strange, often disturbing settings. If she could find a way to stop them, or at least to forget them as most people did when they woke, she would. And sleeping pills didn't help; they only made her groggier the next day.

The only dream she *didn't* want to stop was that of her fantasy lover, the man she couldn't stop thinking about night *or* day. The man she'd been dreaming about for four solid months now. Her very own Prince Charming.

He had dark, hooded eyes and eyelashes any woman would be jealous of. He had rakish, rough good looks; a constant five-o'clock shadow graced his square, strong jawline. His wavy hair curled just under his earlobes and was as dark as the deepest depths of the ocean, or what she imagined the depths of the ocean looked like. His lips were full and kissable, sexy. The baritone deep cadence of his voice felt like melted chocolate when he demanded she come.

He was... Sex. On. A. Stick.

And she wanted a big ol' lick.

She woke up more than once, aroused and wet, with her hands down her panties, trying to relieve the ache. Big Blue, her BFF and constant companion these days, remained at the ready in her nightstand drawer for when her hands just weren't cutting it. Speaking of Big

Blue, she made a mental note to check the batteries in the morning...they seemed low last time.

Sigh.

Men like that just didn't exist in real life, but at least he was good fantasy fodder and that was perfectly fine with her right now.

Settling in, she hoped tonight would bring her fantasy lover instead of the disturbing nightmare she'd had for several weeks now. While strange dreams had plagued her since childhood, one in particular haunted her and she'd spent over ten years trying to bury it. *No, Kate, don't think about that now.* These dreams are not at all the same as that one. These dreams can't possibly be real.

Young women in cells.

Blood.

Evil.

Fangs?

Nope. Not real. This dream made sense. But she couldn't help the gnawing and growing sensation that these women were begging for help. Her help.

If that wasn't scary enough—and it *was* scary—what terrified the hell out of her was the undeniable evil presence she felt. She'd awoken the last several nights in a profuse sweat; panic nearly choking her. She'd taken to sleeping with her bedside lamp on, like she was ten years old again.

Exhausted, but determined to stave off the nightmares as long as possible, she sat up, grabbed the remote and turned on the TV. With any luck, a couple hours of *Duck Dynasty* after the news should lull her into a good, hard sleep.

Reaching for her glass of water, it was almost to her lips when what flashed across the screen caused it to slip from her hand, drenching the sheets. Terror turned her blood to ice. She could only catch every few words the news anchor uttered, as all her senses were focused on the beautiful young face staring back at her. Begging for help.

"...*missing...week...Northwestern...Sarah Hill...notify authorities.*"

Sweet. Baby. Jesus...this *cannot* be happening again.

The missing girl on TV—Sarah Hill—was the one Kate had been dreaming of.

CHAPTER 2

Dev

"Thanks, darling." Dev gave her one last kiss before he ushered her out of the private room.

"It was my pleasure, my lord," she purred. Hmmm...yes, it was her pleasure indeed. He was nothing if not a generous lover.

"Can I service you again, my lord?"

"No, Delia. You know the rules and you know your way out." His voice was unnecessarily hard. He only took a lover once. Human females tended to get attached rather quickly and that was a complication he just didn't need. He only wanted one woman attached to him, but he'd yet to find her. He'd be sure to tell Ronson, the manager of his new club, Dragonfly, to ban Delia from returning. All the courtesans were to be screened thoroughly. Apparently Delia had grander illusions in mind than simply providing her body...and blood.

Devon Fallinsworth was a very successful businessman. He owned a series of fashionable nightclubs and high-end restaurants in the Midwest. Expansion was underway in several more cities, including San Antonio, Texas, and St. Louis, Missouri. His latest club, Dragonfly, had only opened two weeks ago and was already a huge success.

His clubs were his greatest accomplishment and his biggest success. The general area, always located on the main level, provided a traditional bar to his human patrons. The underground, however, provided a much-needed and controlled service to the vampires in his Regent. He offered a very pleasurable and well-paid job to human females and was able to create a safe environment for vampires to feed. Human females were revered in his clubs; they were not used and abused. They were safe and everything that happened in his feeding rooms was consensual or the offending vampire was banned from the premises for good. He'd had few incidents over the last century since he'd opened such rooms.

Dragonfly's underground rooms, or Dragonfly UG as his vampire patrons referred to it, were highly secured to avoid accidental discovery by unknowing humans and looked just like the main level, with two major differences. The entire staff was vampires. And the back portion of all his underground clubs contained small private bedrooms, in the event a couple desired privacy. Many vampires could care less if they copulated in front of others, but some humans weren't quite so open-minded.

"She seems clingy." Renaldo, his lieutenant and best friend of over three hundred years, stood guard outside the feeding room. At six foot six, Ren stood an inch taller than Devon's impressive six foot five frame and wouldn't let him go anywhere without protection. Ren was enormous and strikingly *GQ*'ish handsome, earning him the nickname "Pretty Boy" among his men. Few dared saying it to his face, though. Dev did often.

"Stage eight, at least. She definitely needs to go. I think I might have heard wedding bells ringing in her head as I walked her out."

"I could see the stars in her eyes, man."

"Jesus Christ, that's all I need. Make sure she gets

her last check and isn't allowed to return. I've got a few hours of work to do, so I'll see you back at the house."

"Sounds good. Manny, Thane, and Giselle are there. I'll see you in bit. There's a new little redhead that started last week. I think it's incumbent upon me to determine if she's a *natural* redhead."

Dev laughed. Ren had a weird obsession for redheads. Dev preferred brunettes, himself.

"See you later, pretty boy."

As he flashed, he heard Ren reply, "Fuck off, *my lord*."

Colors of deep rich burgundy, chocolate brown, and opulent gold adorned his office, the favorite space in his house. Overly large picture windows lined the left side of the study and ceiling-to-floor bookshelves spanned the rest of the walls. Shelves were full to the brink with precious artifacts and books, old and new. He enjoyed reading and was well educated. Of course, he also had to keep up with the changing times, technology, and strategies for his many business ventures. He had to admit, he certainly preferred the technology of the twenty-first century. The Internet and his iPhone were invaluable.

As Vampire Lord of the Midwest Regent, the responsibility on his shoulders was immense, heavy and never-ending, but he surrounded himself with loyal and trustworthy friends. A true leader acknowledges and trusts in the value, input, and talents of others, and Dev was a leader to the core. He had been challenged for his position as Vampire Lord many times over the past several hundred years and no one came close to taking what was his. What would *always* be his. He had been Vampire Lord of the Midwest Regent for over three hundred seventy years now. And he planned to be Vampire Lord for several hundred more.

He was well over five hundred years old and, yes, he appeared to have it all. When one was as old as he, one had enough time to acquire everything he desired.

Wealth.

Success.

Power.

Appearances were deceiving though sometimes, weren't they?

Devon did *not* have it all. And it wasn't for lack of trying.

He had yet to find his Moira, his Destiny, the other half of his soul. He knew she was out there. He'd been searching for her a very long time and his patience was waning and Dev was not a patient man.

Oh, he had his pick of willing women, like Delia, and countless, nameless other faces. He had needs after all, but truth be told, he longed for more and had for quite some time.

He often wondered what his Moira would look like. Would she be lithe and athletic or curvaceous and buxom? Would her hair be fairy golden or black as night? Would her eyes shimmer like the sun bouncing off the ocean waves or be dark pools of mystery? Would her personality be soft and submissive or hard and combative? He tried avoiding this game of 'would she' because once he found her he didn't want to draw comparisons to any preconceived notions.

He'd been back about an hour when Ren gave a cursory knock while striding into his office.

Lounging in his luxurious Italian office chair behind his large cherry desk, Dev cocked an eyebrow at his friend's intrusion. "Knock much? I was busy." Though that was true, he'd read the same paragraph three times and still couldn't retain it. His thoughts were somewhere else entirely.

Ren threw the *Milwaukee Journal Sentinel* down his desk and began pacing. "We have a big problem, Dev."

He continued without waiting for a reply. "There is another missing college student. Sarah Hill, age twenty-two, psychology major at Northwestern University.

Parents reported her missing on Monday, after she didn't make her usual Sunday call and they couldn't reach her. Local Evanston police found her car on campus, abandoned, multiple parking tickets on it."

"Shit."

"Right. This brings the total of missing college girls to eleven in the last two weeks alone in our Regent. All are between the ages of nineteen and twenty-two."

Fuuuuuck. Dev grabbed the newspaper and quickly read the article about the local missing woman. He'd had a gnawing concern lately that something was just, well...off. And he always trusted his gut.

Dev looked up, meeting Ren's icy blue eyes. "Have you heard from Thatcher?" Detective Mike Thatcher was a Milwaukee detective with whom they had an...*understanding.*

"Not yet. I have a call into him as well."

Dev sighed, scrubbing his hand over his face. "Have you spoken with Damian and Romaric?"

Damian DiStephano was Vampire Lord of the East Regent and Romaric Dietrich was Vampire Lord of the West Regent. Together, they ruled the United States.

Ren blew out a breath, nodding. "Just got off the phone with Damian. He hadn't heard of anything unusual, but said he'd check it out. I have a call into Romaric as well, but haven't talked to him yet." Ren stopped wearing the carpet thin, leaned toward Dev and slammed his large hands on the expensive desk, the items on the desk rattled, threatening to fall. Dev arched one thick brow in response, but didn't say a word. They exchanged knowing glances, having been through this once before.

"I have a really bad feeling, Dev. I think that motherfucker is up to his old tricks again."

As Vampire Lord, Dev was ultimately responsible for enforcing their only two laws within his Regent. Except in very controlled instances, do not expose their entire race to the human population and do not kill your blood donor. Most vampires lived easily within those two confines and those that didn't were swiftly dealt with.

But it appeared that Xavier, the most depraved offender of both laws, had finally resurfaced. It was almost as if he were taunting them. The question now was, how were they going to find a rogue vampire that had remained elusive for the last one hundred years?

CHAPTER 3

Kate

Kate walked into the Milwaukee Police Department, a sick feeling in the pit of her stomach. She wanted nothing more than to turn, run and forget she knew what she did. She wanted to, but she wouldn't. She couldn't. She should have come yesterday but spent the entire day trying to convince herself the girl in her dreams was just that...another bad dream. She wasn't real. She wasn't the same missing girl that she had seen on the news the other evening.

But she was. And she couldn't deny it any longer.

She'd dreamed of Sarah Hill again last night and the things she witnessed were unspeakable. Horrific. While she struggled to wrap her mind around what she saw, she could not continue convincing herself to sit on her thumbs and take no action.

No. She'd done that once before. Kate couldn't live with herself if this girl suffered the same fate as the last one. She could barely live with herself now. If Sarah Hill ended up murdered, it would break her.

Sarah Hill could end up like Jamie Hallow.

God, it made her physically sick to think about Jamie. How Kate had done did nothing to help her.

Jamie had been twenty-one. Coincidently, she was

also a student at Northwestern. Kate had dreamed of the missing girl held captive in a dark, dank basement, hands and feet tied with rope to a dirty, bare mattress. Eyes covered with a filthy white cloth. Naked. Crying. Bruised. Pleading to go home to her parents and to her little sister.

Kate's parents had dismissed her once again when she tried to talk to them about it. After that, she never mentioned another dream again.

She'd dreamed of Jamie for three weeks straight and then...nothing. When the dreams stopped, she didn't think twice about it. She was sixteen at the time. At sixteen, she wanted to dream about boys, dances, boys, football games. Boys.

A week after the dreams stopped, while doing an assignment on current events for school, she ran across a picture of a fresh-faced, platinum blond beauty in the newspaper, which gave her pause.

It was a picture of the girl from her dream. Jamie Hallow. She was real. And she was missing, presumed a runaway. But Kate knew better.

There were no leads, and to this day, her body hadn't been found.

Kate tried to assuage her guilt by convincing herself she was just a teenager at the time. What could she possibly have done? How could she have known this was real instead of a horrible, wretched dream? Who would have believed her?

But nothing worked. The guilt she felt was immense, both then and now.

She would not stand by this time and do nothing. There had to be something in her dreams to help the investigation. She would just conveniently leave out the part about fangs...and vampires. She had no desire to be labeled as mentally unstable, although she often felt that way.

She knew the missing young women were running

out of time. Each dream was progressively more violent. More disturbing. So she had to take the chance in telling her story and hope they believed her.

This morning she stood resolutely at the front desk of the police station and spoke to the officer behind it. "I think I may have information on a missing girl, Sarah Hill."

"Okay. Your name?"

"Kate Martin."

"Just a minute please," said the officer as he picked up the phone, presumably to call a detective. "Please have a seat and someone will be with you in a few minutes." He nodded to a block of chairs to the left.

Yes, she'd already wasted too much time coming forward. Time she hoped didn't cost Sarah Hill her life.

MIKE

Detective Mike Thatcher ate up the distance between his desk and the front office as quickly as possible. He'd been assigned as the lead detective to the Sarah Hill missing person case and was banging his head against a brick wall with one dead end after another. It seemed like the girl had just disappeared into fucking thin air.

A loner. No boyfriend. No friends to speak of. Her roommate didn't know a damn thing about her, apparently shacking up with a guy instead. Professors said she dutifully came to class, was an excellent student. They knew of her, of course, but none claimed to know her well. Professor Duncan Bailey was the last person to see Sarah alive, and Mike couldn't find any evidence indicating he should be a suspect. Yet. But something just felt *off* about the guy, so he continued to dig a bit deeper into the professor's background.

Sarah did have a close relationship with Henry and Linda, her parents. Talked with them every Sunday evening without fail. Henry was an old college buddy of Mike's, and while they hadn't kept in touch much over the years, he'd known Sarah as a little girl. She was sweet, funny, smart. On a full-ride academic scholarship to Northwestern. Wanted to be a counselor, specializing in youth and child development.

He'd failed one too many times at finding the lost. One case in particular he couldn't forget. Wouldn't forget. To this day, she haunted his dreams. It was long ago, but it fueled the relentless fire inside him to find as many others as he could.

He desperately needed a new lead, so when he heard there was a woman here with possible new information on the case, he was more than eager to speak with her.

Entering the holding area, Mike zeroed in on a young, dark-haired beauty sitting in one of the weathered and torn yellow vinyl chairs that had seen better days.

He slowed his gait. My God...she was *stunning*. Raven black hair with coppery undertones was piled atop her head. Emerald eyes sparkled like perfectly cut gems. Pouty, full lips, and a perfectly shaped button nose rounded out her stunning face. Wow.

Hal confirmed with a nod that this was the woman who had information on Sarah, so Mike approached the black-haired beauty as she caught his gaze and began to stand. He'd put her at about five foot seven, with what appeared to be curves in all the right places, although it was hard to tell with her bulky winter coat on.

"Ms. Martin?" reaching his hand out in greeting. She offered her slim hand in return.

"Yes. Please call me Kate, though."

"Kate, I'm Detective Mike Thatcher. You told

Sergeant Howard that you have information regarding Sarah Hill?"

"Y-Yes. I believe I do," she stammered. Her gorgeous eyes, framed by long, thick, black lashes looked downward. She seemed nervous. Scared, even.

"Why don't we take this conversation somewhere more private?" he said, gesturing down the hallway.

She followed him to one of the interrogation rooms and he indicated she should take a seat.

"Can I offer you something to drink? Water? Soda?" He smiled. "Bad coffee, perhaps?"

She looked up. That garnered him a slight smile in return. "No thank you. I gave up bad coffee for Lent."

He laughed and her smile grew wide. Beautiful *and* witty. He instantly liked this woman.

He settled down into the chair across from her. "So, how do you know Sarah Hill?"

She sat rigid. Spine straight, shoulders set. Her hands, which were in her lap, immediately began to twist, and while she looked him straight in the eye, there was no mistaking how nervous she was. That fact alone piqued his interest. Yeah, his interest was piqued on more than one level if he was being honest with himself.

Down boy, down. She's a potential witness, for Christ's sake.

"It's difficult to explain, Detective. I don't really...*know* Sarah Hill, per se." She quickly glanced down at the table and back up to him. Pausing for a moment, she continued. "I've been...well, seeing her...um...in my dreams."

He just stared at her for long moments, replaying over and over what she just said.

Shit. She was a nut case. And here he thought he might have a solid lead. Or a possible lay. Wrong on both counts.

"In your dreams." Not a question, a statement. "Exactly what does that mean?"

She fidgeted in her chair but held his gaze. "I know it sounds far-fetched. Crazy even. But please hear me out. I can assure you, Detective, I'm not crazy."

That was questionable. However, he nodded for her to continue. Again, she quickly flicked her eyes to the table and back up at him before she spoke again.

"This particular set of dreams began about three weeks ago or so. I...I didn't see Sarah in them until just a little over a week ago. I didn't even know it was Sarah until just the other night when I saw a missing person's story on the local evening news. I knew then that I had to come in and talk to the police."

He didn't believe a word she said, of course, but he'd pretend to listen to her story and then send her on her way so he could get back to the real job of finding his friend's missing daughter. That was his only priority. Not any other case and certainly not his dick.

"Go on," his deep voice encouraged her.

She took a breath and continued. "Well, as I said, it's difficult to explain, but I see her. I can see that she's being held in a dark, plain room with a cement floor. Cement walls. There's a door, but no handle on the inside and a faded blue-and-white striped thin mattress, no sheets. She's not tied down, but she's asleep a lot. A couple of times she's been awake in my dreams and...she calls out like she thinks someone is there. It's like she senses me, but I don't know how she possibly can."

She paused again, biting her full, pink lower lip. Breaking eye contact and looking down at the table, her voice softened and he had to strain to hear her.

"I thought it was just a dream. A horrifying, inconceivable nightmare. Huge men, that I can only describe as predatory, preternatural even, visit her cell. They draw her blood; they give her shots of something. I think they drug her to keep her sleeping most of the time. They've performed exams—*female exams*—on her while she's unconscious."

She swallowed, visibly shaken, and her fair skin seemed to pale even more.

Oooookay. Enough of this shit. "Okay. So where exactly is she being held?"

Kate looked into his eyes and shook her head, like she expected this doubt. "It doesn't work that way, Detective. I only see what the dream lets me see. I'm sorry, but all I can describe to you is the cell where she's being held. I can try to describe the men that I've seen with her as well."

"Can you describe Sarah? Anything unique about her?" He needed to end this. Right now.

"Well, it's very dark. And of course I've seen her picture on the news as well, but she has reddish blond hair, pulled back in a messy ponytail. She's only in white panties and a white cami."

A witness identified her as wearing a turquoise sweater and dark skinny jeans. Shit, she was really whacked. Just his luck. He was just scooting his chair back to escort Ms. Martin out, when the next thing out of her mouth stopped him cold. It felt like ice water was just shot into his veins.

"I can also see she's wearing a silver horseshoe necklace and she has a cross tattoo on her right shoulder blade."

Goosebumps broke out all over his body. Sarah had a silver horseshoe necklace. She loved horses. It was a high school graduation gift from her parents and they said she never took off. And she *did* have a tattoo of a cross, in memory of her younger brother who died of leukemia at the tender age of eight. But none of those details had been released to the public.

As their eyes locked, she whispered, "Sarah's not the only one missing. I've seen others. Held at the same place."

CHAPTER 4

MIKE

Immediately upon closing the door to the interrogation room where the lovely, but possibly loony, Ms. Martin waited, Mike whipped out his cell phone and dialed Renaldo Hargrave, *Lord*-fucking-Devon's half-wit side-kick.

He *hated* dealing with bloodsuckers. Loathed them. In the last ten years since he'd discovered their existence, he'd learned many things. About them. About himself. About the lengths he was willing to go for revenge.

Vampires were the devil incarnate. Devon and Renaldo tried convincing him that most vampires were not evil. Most wanted a peaceful existence alongside humans, albeit their existence unknown to most humans. To live, thrive, find their mates, have a family. They tried convincing him that they would be foolish to kill their life sustaining food source. But he'd witnessed differently. He *knew* differently. Vampires were indiscriminate killers who could turn on you on a dime. Take your life at will, with no remorse. He knew firsthand. He knew in his gut they were responsible for taking someone very precious to him almost eleven years ago.

He had failed her. He could barely live with himself most days. But he would avenge her. That was his life's mission now. After he succeeded, he didn't care what happened to him. Death was constantly on his doorstep, and after his revenge, he would let that bitch cross.

Mike didn't stay alive these past eleven years by not trusting his gut, and based on what Ms. Martin had just told him, his gut was screaming this was the work of vamps. Would this be the one? Could he finally get his revenge? He hoped so, because he was so very weary. Then he would gladly let death take him and spend eternity burning in the pits of hell, where he deserved to be for failing her.

And it couldn't be a coincidence that Renaldo had called him on this very case yesterday. A call that he had yet to return. So like it or not, which he most definitely did *not*, he needed them.

What Kate Martin told him sat like acid in the pit of his stomach. The police had intentionally kept the necklace and tattoo out of the media. The fact that she knew about them meant she knew more about this case than she was letting on. He wasn't convinced about the dreams, but she definitely knew something more than what she was saying. That much he could tell.

When she mentioned that there were others...his blood ran cold. A low curse fell from him lips as a sickening feeling of deja vu swept over him.

Yes, his gut was wailing loudly now. Something wasn't right here and he was damned well gonna get to the bottom of it. And hopefully—*finally*—get his bittersweet revenge.

Kate sat in the small, sterile room, alone, waiting for Detective Thatcher to return. The room had a one-way mirror on the wall directly across from her and she couldn't help the feeling that she was being watched. Or that something monumental was about to happen.

After she'd told her story, he asked her to wait and hastily exited the room. In relaying her story to the detective, she'd conveniently left out the fangs, vampires and evil sensations, which she knew would get her a one-way ticket to the funny farm. Do not pass go. Do not collect two hundred dollars.

She'd carefully watched the expression on his face as she told him her story. He had no idea how hard it was for her to step foot into that police station. And how equally hard it was not to.

He hadn't believed her, of course. At first he watched her with eagerness and keen interest. As her story progressed, she could see his doubt and disbelief. She wasn't an idiot. He was clearly placating her so he could get rid of her. He hadn't even taken one note. She had honestly expected this to happen. She wouldn't believe her either, if she were he.

Upon hearing about the necklace and tattoo, however, his face turned dark and grim and he immediately left the room. That had been nearly forty-five minutes ago.

She should have opted for that bad coffee after all. She hadn't slept well again last night—*surprise, surprise*—and she was dragging ass today.

She still had a half-day of teaching classes ahead of her, plus a long evening of continued research on her paper.

Kate loved research. Craved it. Lived for it. That was all she'd ever wanted to do for as long as she could remember. Probably explained her minimal social calendar and social skills, truth be told. If she were honest with herself, it probably explained why John felt the need to seek refuge in another woman's body.

Enough, Kate. Pity party over. This is exactly why she purposely kept busy all the time. A busy and full day assured she wouldn't have time to think about the gaping holes and loneliness in her pathetic life.

That's it. She'd waited long enough and was leaving. She had done her duty, told the police what she knew. Just as she was rising from the stain-covered gray plastic chair, Detective Thatcher returned.

At several inches taller than her five-foot-seven frame, he was a classically handsome man. Deep brown eyes, dark brown hair, perfectly straight teeth. Great laugh. Nice ass. But even though she didn't know the man, she could tell sadness surrounded him like a protective shroud. She could practically see it.

"Sorry to keep you waiting so long, Ms. Martin...uh, Kate." He stood still in the open doorway.

"That's perfectly fine, Detective." *It wasn't.* "Am I free to leave now? I have a pretty full day." She remained standing, grabbed her purse, and threw it over shoulder. She was anxious to leave.

He shook his head; undeniable regret etched his handsome features. "I'm sorry, not quite yet. I need you to talk to some, uh...special investigators on the case and relay to them what you told me. They'll be here shortly."

"Detective, I genuinely want to help. That's why I'm here, but I don't see how telling the same story to somebody else is going to make a difference. I've already told you all I know and I really do need to get going. I've got a class to teach in a few hours that I still need to prepare for. I can come back later if necessary." She started walking toward him, intending to push her way out. He held up his hand in a stop gesture, which she grudgingly complied with. It was an effort not to roll her eyes.

"These are special investigators, Kate. We really need to review everything again and I know you want to help.

You wouldn't be here if you didn't. Please. We just don't have time to waste. I'm sorry, but I need you to stay and talk to them." He gestured for her to sit back down. "I'm sure we can get you out of here in plenty of time for your class."

She stared at him and sighed with a slight shake of her head. "Fine. Yes, of course. Anything I can do to help." She took a seat and waited for these 'special investigators' to arrive.

CHAPTER 5

Dev

As Dev and Ren entered the Milwaukee Police Department, Dev decided they should observe Kate Martin behind the anonymity of the one-way mirror for a few minutes first before questioning her. According to the phone call Ren took from the detective earlier, he suspected Kate Martin was a dreamwalker and dreamwalkers were very rare. He was only aware of a handful that still lived. He needed to determine how to best deal with her. How to get her cooperation; gain her trust. That would be much easier and preferable than using alternative methods.

No matter, really. He would use whatever means necessary to find Xavier and destroy his vile soul. And after what Ren told him, his gut was screaming in hopes this woman would be a means to that end.

Xavier was an ancient rogue vampire who'd wreaked havoc on the human and vampire worlds for centuries. He'd become increasingly dangerous and deranged and his actions threatened to expose their entire race to the human population.

In his quest to rule both the entire vampire and human races, Xavier had nearly succeeded at doing just that several decades ago. It took months to clean up from that fucking debacle. They thought Xavier had perished in the explosion that took out his underground compound, but later found he'd escaped. Dev still could not fathom how. He only hoped Xavier had suffered significant losses of his rogues during the explosion.

Dev had talked to Romaric and Damian and both were seeing similar patterns of abductions in their Regents. It was clear Xavier was experimenting again. Trying to procreate using human females. It couldn't be done. Only human females who were bonded to vampires could bear vampire children, but that didn't stop the evil rogue from slaughtering young, innocent women in his quest to try.

He must be stopped. They were out of time. Devon would make sure he killed the demented vampire himself this time.

The vampire he once called "brother."

If Ms. Martin was truly a dreamwalker, her world was about to change. Drastically. Forever.

Not his problem, though. He would delegate her care to his staff. He had to make difficult decisions every day in the best interest of his Regent and all of the vampires under his care who relied upon him.

So as Dev stepped into the closet-sized observation room, he had no qualms, no compunction whatsoever, about using Ms. Kate Martin as a means to his selfish end.

Until he laid eyes on her.

He froze. "Jesus H. Christ."

She was *The One*. The woman he'd been looking for.

His Moira.

His *Destiny*.

He stood frozen, drinking in her every perfect, exquisite feature from head to toe. Wearing her dark, glossy hair in a twisted, messy bun atop her head and dressed in incredible curve-hugging, dark jeans with a fitted ivory sweater that bared just the top swell of her luscious breasts, she was simply...*breathtaking.* Her striking green eyes shone like emeralds. She was the most exquisite, desirable creature he had ever laid eyes on in his very, very long existence.

And. She. Was. *His.*

The desire, the possessiveness pulsing through his body and soul was so fierce, so intense, he nearly crashed through the flimsy barrier that stood between him and his Moira. His cock was hard as granite. His fangs had burst through his gums. He only had a single-minded intention of getting inside that sweet, hot body. *Now.* The savage need to mark her as his was all consuming and unlike anything he'd ever felt. It took every ounce of his stalwart control to stand there, taking no action.

Fuck. This changed everything.

CHAPTER 6

Xavier

Xavier relaxed with a tumbler of fifty-year-old Dalamore Scotch in his hands. He lounged in his overstuffed black leather club chair, made from the finest available Italian leather in a dark maple frame. His one luxury piece of furniture in this hellhole he called home these days. At least he could have a good Scotch.

Rage always seethed just beneath the surface. Vampires were meant to rule the world, were the superior species on this planet, yet he spent his days in hiding, like vermin. His plans constantly thwarted by his former brethren, who dubbed themselves Lords. They were why he was in this hellhole, cowering like a petulant child. They'd completely destroyed his last compound. He was lucky to escape with his life. Lesson learned.

He fingered the ragged scars marring the left side of his previously perfect face, courtesy of his last encounter with the *Lords*. A sinister smile played across his thin evil lips as he reflected on his current plans in motion. Plans that *would* come to fruition. Devon and the rest of the insolent Lords may have won the last few battles, but he would be victorious in the war and that was all that mattered in the end. They had no idea how close he was. A low, harsh laugh escaped.

Successful procreation of the vampire race was something he'd been working on for over five hundred years. That, and the diametrically opposed views he had with Devon and the others regarding the superiority of their race, had led him to where he was today. When he'd parted ways with Devon, he'd gone into hiding and needed an army of his own making if he was going to fulfill his ultimate plan. An army born of his own ideals, dedicated to serving him. Dedicated to his objective of world domination. Doing what he alone commanded. And while he was making progress, it wasn't fast enough. It was difficult to have world domination without enough vampires.

For vampires to reproduce, however, they had to be bonded with their Moira's, their destined mate. And finding one's Moira was not an easy task, so he'd had to use other means to build his army.

The doctors in his employ had made progress in creating a therapy allowing for *any* human female to conceive and carry a vampire babe, not just a vampire's Moira. So far, the concoction only had a five percent success rate, but that was a vast improvement over the tenth of a percent they had just a few short years ago.

Unfortunately, that also meant they went through a lot of females. He made sure to get them young, while they were in prime childbearing years. If they couldn't conceive after three years, they were disposed of. After they were thoroughly used, of course. They were only a means to an end. Nothing else. When their usefulness ended, so did they.

He'd been very careful over the last decade to keep a low profile, taking only the minimum necessary women for his experiments and keeping the kidnappings spread out, so as not to draw attention to himself. He'd managed to stay under the radar while still continuing his work. But his patience was at an end, so at the risk of being discovered lately he'd taken more women than usual.

About a decade ago, in a lucky grab, he discovered something he thought was long extinct. A dreamwalker. And he was desperate to find more.

Dreamwalkers possessed invaluable skills. They upped the ante to help him find and destroy his enemies. With them, and the loyal army he'd spent centuries creating, he would be unstoppable.

His strategy in locating potential dreamwalkers was brilliant and had yielded him several new recruits over the last ten years. He was *partnering* with many psychology professors across the country, whom he'd convinced to start very particular dream studies within their universities, sharing the results with him. Xavier's team monitored the study participants, inviting those who met certain qualifications to join him. Most hadn't come willingly. Well...none had. No matter.

Yes, his plan was well in motion. Soon. Very soon his army would be big enough and strong enough to move his plan into its final stages. Then all the world, vampires and humans alike, would bow to him.

Beg for mercy.

Wish for death.

CHAPTER 7

Kate

Detective Thatcher stepped fully into the room, and she heard footsteps approach behind him. The special investigators must be here. The detective looked a little angry, his jaw was clenched tight and his lips were drawn in a tight, thin line.

Her gaze swung to the man walking through the door behind him. The first thing she noticed was how very tall and muscled he was. The second thing she noticed was how amazingly gorgeous he was. Like, *GQ* gorgeous. This guy was some sort of detective? What a waste!! He should grace the cover of magazines...preferably *Playgirl*. Yum.

"Hi, I'm Renaldo Hargrave, but please call me Ren," he said, extending his hand. She was mesmerized. She couldn't look away from his eyes long enough to grab his hand, which she noticed in her peripheral vision was waiting for hers.

He ended her embarrassment, taking her hand in his.

"H-Hi. Uh...Kate. I mean, I'm Kate. Kate Martin." She gave her muddled head a brief shake. Crap. She was a blathering idiot.

He laughed and it was one of the most sensuous sounds she had ever heard.

Until she heard the man behind him speak. He'd shoved Ren out of the way to introduce himself, causing Ren to stumble several steps to the left.

She tore her gaze from Ren to look at the man pushing his way into the room.

Holy. Mother. Of. Pearls.

She felt the blood drain from her face. She was suddenly light-headed and her knees almost buckled, forcing her to take a step back, steadying herself against the table. She knew her mouth hung open, but couldn't force it closed.

It was *him*...her dream lover. Or his doppelganger. Desire pooled in her belly, flowing through her veins, engorging her in all the right places. Her panties became most uncomfortable in their dampened state.

"And I'm Devon Fallinsworth. But you can call me Dev." His nostrils flared slightly as he watched her intensely.

She continued to stare at him...unable to believe her eyes, unable to move, unable to catch her breath. He was absolutely everything she had dreamed, and more. Much, much, much more.

Tall.

Dark.

Handsome.

No...handsome was too bland of an adjective. He was devastatingly sensuous. Mind-blowingly sexy. His black suit, which looked custom made, draped his perfectly formed, muscular body like a glove. A crisp white dress shirt was unbuttoned just enough that she could see a dark thatch of hair adorning his perfectly tanned chest. Yowza. He was edible.

His dark eyes held her gaze and the room narrowed until it was just the two of them.

He moved toward her until he was standing so close she could feel his body heat radiating into her skin. His masculine scent enveloped her and caressed her like a lover. He smelled like spices, mint, and sex god. She never wanted to look away. She could literally drown in his black, liquid eyes and it would be a happy, welcome death.

"Pleased to meet you, Kate." His voice wrapped around her like a soft, silky blanket. She wanted to cuddle under it next to his warm naked body. She hadn't realized he held her hand until she felt him rubbing small circles on the webbing of her thumb. He held on longer than she thought appropriate, but shorter than she wanted. His penetrating eyes never broke with hers.

"Uh...yes." she breathed.

She was in a desire-induced fog. *Had she spoken? She couldn't remember.*

Detective Thatcher interrupted. "Why don't we all have a seat and you can tell these...special investigators what you know about Sarah Hill. What you told me."

Pulling her gaze away from the sexy beast in front her, Kate retook her seat. Detective Thatcher and Ren sat across from her at the table, but Dev took the seat beside her. She couldn't help her surreptitious glance to see if he was wearing a wedding ring and was happier than she should have been to see none. It took everything in her not to reach out and touch him again. Or scoot her chair closer. Was she dreaming?

She pinched the back of her hand. Ouch. Very much awake.

"Kate, please tell us what you can." Dev's voice was encouraging, but his eyes were smoldering, like he was hungry. For her.

What the hell? Get a grip, Kate! Getting her brain to formulate a coherent thought was challenging.

After several moments, Kate pulled it together and spent the next fifteen minutes relaying everything to Dev and Ren. They listened with rapt attention, asking questions, taking notes. She took care to look at Dev as little as possible, as every time she did, she seemed to stumble over her words and all thought escaped her.

They genuinely seemed to believe her, which was a relief. Maybe she could help Sarah Hill after all.

Dev

As Dev listened to Kate retell her dream, he had a hard time concentrating on her words. He was in awe of her. Her scent was driving him out of his damned mind. The soft thud of her pulse beneath her fair, porcelain skin was mouthwateringly enticing. He had to fight with his entire being to keep his fangs from descending. And the fact that she wasn't looking at him nearly enough was driving him absolutely fucking crazy. He wanted to stare into her mesmerizing eyes forever.

She was more than he'd imagined his Moira to be. She was stunningly beautiful, deliciously curvy in all the right places and her skin softer than the finest silk. All he could think about was being inside her sweet body. His dick was as hard as steel and he'd had to reposition it many times throughout the conversation. He wanted to possess her. Completely. Thoroughly. *Now.*

He warred with himself on how to handle this situation. It was delicate. Not that she was delicate. He had a feeling she was going to give him a run for his money. He was actually terrified of scaring her off. *Him—terrified.* Never thought he would see the day. The man in him knew he needed to take it slowly with her, court her, gain her trust. The pure animal in him, however, vowed he would never let her out of his sight. Ever. Her wants and feelings be damned.

After she'd described the whole dream in detail, he

asked, "Is there anything else you can remember about the setting or her captors, anything unique at all that you haven't told us?"

Kate's eyes shifted toward the floor. "No, no...that's everything I can remember."

Ohhhh, his Kate was holding something back. *His* Kate. She was nervous. He needed to gain her trust so she would confide in him completely. *Give herself to him completely.*

Two things were crystal clear.

This exquisite woman was his and she was a dreamwalker. She didn't know how special that made her. Or how much danger that put her in. Dev made a swift decision.

"Kate, based on what you've told us, I think you're in grave danger and will need to be remanded into protective custody until we can locate Sarah."

Detective Thatcher started to protest and Ren looked at him as though he'd grown two heads. Kate simply gaped at him for a moment before a stubborn look crossed her beautiful features and she did exactly what he thought she would.

"That's not necessary, Detective."

Okay, let's try wooing. "Dev. Please call me Dev."

"Okay. That's not necessary, *Dev*. In fact, that's about the stupidest idea I've ever heard. Why on earth would I need to be in protective custody? I can assure you I am in no danger." She laughed.

Detective Thatcher abruptly stood, a violent look on his face. "She's right. That isn't necessary, *Detective*." Snarly much?

Asshole was living a little too close to the edge. He mentally shrugged. Oh well, his death. Dev didn't even acknowledge Thatcher, keeping his gaze locked with Kate's.

Right, animal instinct it was. "Oh, I assure you, love, it's quite necessary."

"What the hell are you doing, Dev? Police custody? Love?" Ren spoke to him telepathically.

"Fuck off," Dev growled and continued.

"Kate, I'm afraid this is a serial kidnapper and murderer we're dealing with and we've been trying to catch him for years. I don't want you to be in his crosshairs once he discovers you have come forward with information that may help us track him down. He's dangerous. He's left too many bodies in his wake. I don't want you to be one of them." He wouldn't let her be one of them.

She visibly paled. "He's done this before? I don't understand how he would even find out I've been here?" Now she sounded a bit panicked. Good. He would use that to his advantage.

"Trust me, as much as we try to keep this under wraps, this is a high profile case. Young, beautiful college girls are being snatched. It's a media frenzy. Someone will find out you were here and leak it to the press. It's only a matter of time. And when that happens, a bull's-eye will be painted directly on your back. This guy will consider you a threat he may act to eliminate."

He'd tried pushing a little compulsion her way. She regarded him for a moment, her eyes narrowing.

"Thank you, Dev, but I promise you I'll be just fine. I have a good security system at home and I have a concealed carry permit. I practice twice a week at the range. Plus, I've been training in Jeet Kune Do for the past eight years. I'm good." She had the most infuriating smirk on her gorgeous, full lips. Lips he wanted wrapped around his cock. Now.

Well...shit.

He glanced at Detective Thatcher and Ren, and they had the same smirks on their faces, Ren clearly containing his laugh. He pushed a bit of his power toward them. Wiped the smirks right off...at least the human. Ren looked at him with a knowing laughter in his glittery eyes. *Paybacks are a bitch, pretty boy.*

Now what? She wasn't leaving here alone. Over his dead body.

Okay, onto Plan B... Plan B...what *was* Plan B?

"How about compromise, man?"

"Compromise?"

"Yeah, compromise. The act of negotiation, concession, finding a middle ground? I know it's a foreign concept to you, Dev, but pulling alpha won't work on this chick."

Compromise definitely wasn't his best skill. But to keep Kate safe, he would give anything a try.

Dev pleaded—*groan*—pleaded, "Kate, please let us keep you under protection for just a few days. If nothing slips to the press, then you can go back to your normal life. Business as usual." Yeah, no fucking way that was happening. Ever. But she didn't need to know that now. He just needed to get her with him and the rest would fall into place.

She sighed heavily, clearly contemplating his latest offer.

Ren could barely contain his laughter now. His shoulders were shaking. Goddamn pretty boy wasn't gonna be looking so pretty very soon.

"Can't you just post a patrol outside my house?" she asked.

"A safe house would better, Kate. It's just a few days. Come on...just think of it as a much-needed vacation. You do look a little tired." He quickly added, "Beautiful, but tired."

She frowned at that statement, brows creasing, wrinkling that smooth, delectable forehead. He definitely liked it better when she smiled.

"Where exactly is this safe house and who will be with me?"

A small smile played on Dev's lips, knowing he was

making progress. He'd better not too get too cocky. "I can't tell you exactly where the safe house is, for your own protection, but it's just right on the outskirts of Milwaukee." Dev glanced at Ren and back to Kate. "And Ren and I will be protecting you. I promise you, Kate, we won't let anything happen to you." Nothing, but the most intense pleasure you can handle.

"Look gentlemen, I sincerely appreciate your concern, but I'm not in any danger. If you feel better, send a police car by my house once in the evening for a few days, but going into protective custody seems pretty excessive. Now, I really do need to be going, as I have a class to teach in just a few hours."

She grabbed her coat and purse and stood to leave.

"Kate, I really wish you'd reconsider," he pleaded.

There was no goddamned way he was letting her out of his sight for a single, solitary moment. It went against every single protective instinct in his body to let her walk out that door without him. His body vibrated with nearly unrestrained need to pull her into his arms and flash her the hell away from here and he needed to rein himself in quickly before he did something stupid.

"At least tell us where you teach...*please*." That word tasted bitter too. He had a feeling he'd better get used to saying it. A lot. But only to her.

She turned and gifted him with the most brilliant smile he'd ever seen. It was brighter than a thousand suns and more beautiful than any word he knew in any language. What was this poetic shit filling his brain? He was whipped after less than an hour in her presence.

"I'm an assistant psychology professor at Marquette University." And with that she walked out the door.

Dev was out of his chair in a flash. "She doesn't leave our sight. Let's go."

It was a myth that vampires couldn't go out in the daylight. Younger vampires had to temper their exposure to sunlight as it made them weak, but once a vampire came into their full powers at age one hundred, they could withstand the sun just as well as any human could.

"Dev, slow down and think for a minute," pleaded Ren. "Nothing will happen to her."

"You're fucking right nothing will happen to her, because we're gonna be like white on rice. Now get your ass moving or I'm going without you. We're wasting time."

Ren tightly nodded. "Yes, my lord."

"Don't call me that, asshole."

"You touch one hair on her goddamn head and I *will* kill you, leech," gritted the detective.

Dev laughed. "Good one, human."

CHAPTER 8

Kate

Kate could hardly concentrate on anything as she prepared—or *tried to prepare*—for her class, which started in fifteen minutes. What the hell had happened this morning at the police station? So many thoughts and questions swirled in her head.

Giddiness bubbled up inside...her dream lover was *real*. And he had a name. Devon. Dev. How was this possible? It's like she just conjured him up and suddenly he stood in front of her in the flesh. She thought back to a movie she'd seen about two teenage boys who cut out parts from a magazine to make their dream woman. *Weird Science*. That's exactly what this felt like. Weird.

Nothing about her dreams should surprise her, yet it continually did. She'd found lost pets. She'd been witness to those that were ill taking their last breaths. She'd seen more adultery that she could recount. But she never dreamt about herself, it was always others. Except for this one thing. This one man.

Why?

She blushed furiously, remembering what his corded, sinewy muscles felt like under her hands. How his skin tasted, masculine and salty, under her tongue as she ran it across his neck. His jaw. His lips. She touched her fingers lightly to her tingling lips as though she could feel his on hers.

Would the real version match the dream one? No doubt. Did she want to find out? Hell yes. Should she? God no. She already knew it would be far too easy to fall madly in love with him and she simply could not do that. He had unmistakable heat in his eyes, yes, but no one who looked like him would be satisfied with someone who looked like her for long. And then she'd be right back where she was a year ago when she'd caught John cheating.

Lonely.

Depressed.

Heartbroken.

She almost felt like she was having an out-of-body experience, floating twelve feet in the air, watching herself. This could not possibly be real. She didn't *feel* real at the moment. She was just going through the movements.

She knew she wasn't in any danger. What a crock. Did Dev really believe she was, or did he just want to get closer to her? He'd looked at her like she was the most decadent of desserts and he couldn't wait to indulge. Just thinking of him made her heart race.

And the crazy thing was, against her better judgment, she'd *wanted* to agree. To be locked in a safe house with Devon Fallinsworth for two whole days? For the love, what woman wouldn't want that? Only those who batted for the other team, because he was McDreamy and McSteamy, with a dash of McDanger all rolled into one delectable package. Walking out of that police station had been one of the hardest things she'd done in a very long time and wasn't that just stupid?

He radiated danger. Yet strangely enough, she wasn't afraid of him. Au contraire, she felt unbelievably safe with him...odd that. She had just met him, yet she felt like she'd known him all her life and if she *were* in any real danger, she'd unequivocally trust him to keep her safe. He was powerful, seductive, sexy...and formidable.

She'd not been attracted to, or even thought of, another man since John. Well...that wasn't entirely true. She'd been attracted to Dev in her little fantasy world.

But he was real and life was not a dream. And what she needed to do was banish any thought of this man, because he was not long-term boyfriend or husband material; any fool could see that. He was a love 'em and leave 'em kind of guy, of that she was sure. Panties probably fell off of women any time they got within one hundred feet of him. They were wet, at minimum. Hers certainly were. She'd had to change them once already today and she'd probably be changing them again when she went home.

In some ways, she wished she'd never met him. Now that she knew he was real flesh and blood, it would be harder to concentrate on anything *but* him. Her obsession with him before was steeped in fantasy, like that hot guy you see at the grocery store every other week that you wonder what it would be like to bang, but you know it will never happen. But in Dev's case...it *could* happen. And that was a very bad place to go. It could leave the door open even the slightest crack that something *would* happen between them and she knew better than travel down that road again where the only thing that lay at the end is a deep pool of bitterness and despair.

And there was no real life scenario that she could dream of happily ever after, a white picket fence, and 2.5 kids with Devon Fallinsworth. That would be emotional suicide. She was so not going there again.

Kate had her life and her career neatly and precisely mapped out and it didn't include a domineering dangerous man, no matter how much he made butterflies take flight in the pit of her stomach or how moist her core became simply by remembering the way he stared at her with molten hot eyes.

She needed to finish her dissertation, apply for professorship and begin her grant work to fund her archetypes and the collective unconscious study, so it didn't matter anyway. She had no time for a boyfriend or a boy toy or even a fuck buddy. She'd probably never see him again anyway, so instead of dwelling she stuffed him back into the box of things that could never be and sealed that baby up tight with an entire roll of packing tape.

Kate pushed everything to the back of her mind as her students rolled into the classroom and got settled, focusing instead on one of her other passions. Teaching. This semester she was instructing a course on the Psychology of Human Sexuality. It was always well attended. Go figure.

"Good afternoon everyone. I hope you're ready for a lively discussion on the subject for today's class...understanding random hookups."

After the clapping, whistling and whooping subsided, she started her lecture.

Ironic topic, because even though she tried not to, hooking up was all she could think of doing with Dev. Only he didn't feel so random to her. Not by a long shot. And that possibility scared her more than anything else.

CHAPTER 9

Dev

Dev was going out of his everlovin' mind. He could not stand to be away from the one woman he'd waited so long for. This was absolute torture. He'd followed her all over the damn city. She went home first, then to the gas station, picked up dry cleaning, and finally went to Walgreen's before she ended at the university campus to teach her class. Which he found out was the Psychology of Human Sexuality. Interesting. A grin curved the corners of his mouth. Very interesting indeed.

"How are you doing over there, boss?" Ren asked.

"Peachy. You?"

Not true. He wasn't peachy at all. He was in hell. He'd been wracking his brain trying to figure out how he was going convince Kate to come with him. In all his wildest dreams, he never thought he'd have to woo his Moira, although that had been downright naïve. And he wasn't exaggerating the danger she was in. She was a dreamwalker and now his Moira. That put her directly in harm's way from any number of people who may want to get to Dev, including Xavier.

"Couldn't be better." Ren cleared his throat. "You know...I can arrange a security team to follow her.

Watch over her. She'll be protected. You can't follow her around indefinitely."

Ren had been restrained enough not to say anything about Dev's out-of-character reaction to this woman. He knew it wouldn't last. Ren was the only one with enough cojones to challenge him. Pissed him off sometimes, but that was why he trusted him implicitly.

Dev slowly turned his head toward Ren, with barely contained menace simmering underneath his skin.

"No one else will go near her. Do you understand?"

The thought of someone else, anybody else, watching her voluptuous body move, doing even the most mundane of tasks, nearly turned him feral. He'd better figure out a way to get her with him quickly or he could be a serious menace to all those around him.

A knowing, shocked look crossed Ren's face. Dev could almost hear the gears click. "Holy shitballs. She's your Moira. That's the only reason you would be acting like some deranged lunatic, who isn't taking his safety into consideration at all."

Dev stared at Ren for several moments, tightly nodded once, daring his friend to say anything else.

Ren held his gaze. A genuine, full smile spread across his face as he slapped him on the back. "Well, I'll be damned. Congratulations Dev."

Finding a vampire's Moira could take centuries. Some never found theirs and his hope at finding his one perfect match had been waning of late. Vampires were not made, contrary to popular belief. They could not be bitten and turned. That was simply preposterous. A fallacy. Vampires were born of a union between vampire and their bonded human female. And a vampire couldn't bond with anybody except their Moira.

"Don't congratulate me yet. I think the fair Ms. Martin is going to be a hard one to reel in."

"You didn't try to compel her, did you? You know you can't compel your Moira."

While vampires could compel humans, they couldn't compel their Moira's or other vampires. When he first laid eyes on Kate, he knew without a shadow of a doubt, she was his. Yes, he'd tried to compel her at the precinct, but only because he'd actually forgotten that one couldn't compel his Moira. He could hardly contain his sheer joy at finally finding her.

"No, I could not compel her. I tried when she refused to go into protective custody." He laughed. "I think she knew I was up to something because she gave me a funny look when I tried." Yes, she was going to be a challenge. One he was very much looking forward to.

"Don't worry, man. You can charm the panties off of any female, compulsion or not. I have no doubt you'll have her with you within a matter of hours."

Dev knew it would take more than that. The need to be inside her was visceral. He simply had to explore her body, feel her, taste her. He knew had to rein in this overwhelming need or he would send her running for the hills. Not that he wouldn't follow, drag her back and lock her in his house. He would never let his Moira go. Strangely enough, though, he didn't want to imprison her. He wanted her to *want* to be with him, to need him, to love him.

Ren glanced at his watch. "Her class should be just about over."

"Thank Christ." Hopefully she'd just go straight home. He had Thane posted at her house right now to ensure nothing was disturbed while she'd been gone. As soon as she was settled for the evening, however, he intended to pay his Moira a little visit.

And begin his covetous and relentless pursuit to win her.

CHAPTER 10

Xavier

"You'd better have some good news for me, Marcus," Xavier growled. He was tired of living like this. Tired of hiding. Goddamn Regent Lords. He couldn't wait to slaughter each and every one of them. Personally. His hatred for them was so intense; he felt it burning through his gut every second of every single day. He was so close to his goal, he could taste it. Feel it in every cell of his body. Finally, after hundreds of years of experiments and preparation, he was on the brink of world domination.

"I do, my lord." Marcus kept his eyes averted toward the floor. Marcus was a good slave. He was exceptionally brilliant and had been able to make the most progress in the drug that increased successful conception and live births of their vampire babies. His growing army.

"Get on with it, Marcus."

"We took the most recently acquired female into the insemination room this morning, as blood tests showed she was ovulating."

"I don't need these mundane updates. Anything else of actual importance?"

"Ah, we lost another baby and female this morning. Another female likely won't make it until tomorrow.

"Well, we can always get more. Anything else?"

"Nothing else my lord."

Marcus looked deathly pale and he was breathing fast. The human was scared. He was always a sweaty mess when in his presence.

An evil grin ate up Xavier's entire hideously fire-scarred face. Another memento, courtesy of those self-righteous lords. Another wrong to right. While vampires healed from most other grievous of wounds, they could not heal from fire. He would be forever disfigured. He wouldn't allow mirrors anywhere in the compound, as he didn't want a constant reminder that his looks were taken from him, in addition to his freedom. Where his looks once drew females like flies, now it repulsed them.

"That will be all."

"Yes, my lord."

"Oh, and, Marcus...I'm quite hungry. Bring me a female."

"Of course, my lord." Marcus quickly fled the room.

CHAPTER 11

Kate

Kate walked through the front door and straight to the kitchen. It wasn't even five o'clock yet, but she desperately needed a drink. Pouring a glass of Zinfandel from a half-empty bottle, she thought that simply might not cut it tonight. Within fifteen minutes, she was emptying the rest into her stemless glass. Sitting at the kitchen table in silence, she watched the bitter winter wind violently whip fluffy light snow around the yard. It looked like someone had shaken up a snow globe and she was reminded of the Beauty and the Beast one she had as a child. Goddamn Disney and the dream of happily ever after they push on young, impressionable girls.

So desperate for the mind numbing effects of the alcohol, she hadn't even bothered to take off her boots and now there was a puddle of melted snow spreading out beneath her on the cold tile floor. But it didn't matter, because she seemed to have a singular focus.

Try as she might, she simply could *not* stop thinking of Dev. Of his eyes or his smell or his touch. She was obsessing like a fifteen year old with her first real crush and it was just plain pissing her off. The only thing Kate was obsessed about was research.

Until now.

Until *him*.

Now she could think of nothing else. Maybe it had just been too long since she'd had sex and now her lady bits were begging to be used. And used hard. Maybe Erin was right and one amazing sweaty session of the wild thing was what she needed to get refocused. And maybe she was so full of shit that the whites of her eyes were turning brown.

Sighing heavily, she unceremoniously finished her second glass of wine and opened another bottle. She had a paper to write, she had homework to grade, she had a grant to think about. But all she wanted to do instead was sit and daydream, like a lovesick puppy about a man she could never have.

Jesus, Kate. Get a goddamned grip.

Pouring her third and what *should* be her final glass, but probably wouldn't be, she headed into the bathroom and filled the Jacuzzi tub with steaming water and lavender vanilla aromatherapy bubble bath. Lighting some candles and turning on Michael Bublé—*don't judge*—she quickly disrobed and eased slowly into the scalding water, groaning with relief. Bubble bath, wine and a sultry crooner...what more could a girl want?

Why...one very tall, very erotic, very virile man with onyx eyes peering up at her from between her thighs of course.

Kate spent the next thirty minutes sipping wine and reliving her carnal dreams with this incredible man—like she hadn't done that hundreds of times over the last four months. She ran her hands over her nakedness, wishing they were his. Unable to stop, one slipped below the water and stroked her slick center. She remembered Erin telling her how quickly she'd gotten off from the jets of her tub and at the time that had sounded ridiculous. But now, badly needing to take the edge off, Kate stretched her legs, positioning her sex perfectly between the maximum speed stream of water and *Oh. My. God.* Within thirty seconds, an incredibly hard orgasm tore through her, sending warmth spiraling throughout her body. Head falling back, she reached for the controls and turned off the pulsating water, recovering slowly from the quick rush.

Damn. Erin was definitely onto something.

Glass long empty, water cooled, and feeling a bit less tense, Kate decided it was time to leave her wallowing and soak up the alcohol she'd consumed with some food. Except she didn't have much in the house, so she'd either have to do take out or run to the store. And since she'd consumed three very substantial glasses of wine in the last hour, take out it was.

Forty-five minutes later, long hair pulled into a messy bun and dressed in black yoga pants and a ratty yellow Golden Eagles sweatshirt that had seen better days, the doorbell rang. Expecting to see a delivery boy from the *Jade Garden*, her favorite Chinese restaurant with *the* best cashew chicken and egg drop soup to ever to pass her lips, she quickly opened the door without checking the peephole.

And immediately regretted it. *Oh God.* Breathe Kate. In, out...in, out.

Instead of the deliveryman, standing on her front porch was the man of her dreams. Literally and figuratively. And in one hand dangled her food.

"Hello Kate," he drawled, full lips turned up on one corner.

He stood there in the same breathtaking suit she'd seen him in earlier, but with a heavy, long black overcoat shielding him against the elements.

"Hi." Her voice was breathy. Lord, he was just sinfully good-looking.

"I think I have something you want."

There was no truer statement *ever* made than that one. She wanted, all right. Oh, how she *wanted*. He laughed as she stood quietly gaping at his sheer perfection.

"I was talking about the food, but by the way you're devouring me with your hungry eyes, I can see maybe food's not all that's on your mind."

He strode confidently through the door, but not before leaning down and running his nose seductively along the unencumbered expanse of her neck, inhaling deeply. A sexy, low rumble sounded in the back of his throat.

"Mmmm, you smell good, Kate."

Good god. Cue the fan.

He stood back, his burning eyes roaming over every inch of her body. Her *hideously* clothed body. *Go her.*

Finding her voice, she finally asked the question that had been burning in her mind for the last sixty seconds.

"How did you know where I live?"

He smiled mischievously and sauntered quietly through the living room into the kitchen. He was as comfortable as if he'd been there a dozen times before. Having no choice, she followed him but stopped in the doorway and watched as he efficiently found a plate and silverware and set them on the table before dishing up her food.

"What are you doing?"

He looked up from his task, confusion clouding his face. "What does it look like I'm doing? I'm feeding you."

She couldn't help the small smile that passed her lips. She should be irritated and in truth she was, but irrational delight overrode any other emotion she felt. But that didn't mean she was letting him off the hook. He seemed very good—*too* good—at dodging her simple questions.

He gestured for her to sit, but she wasn't about to fall in line that easily. "You haven't answered my questions."

He walked toward her, but gliding would have been a more accurate description. He moved with such stealth and grace, it was almost unnatural. Stopping only inches from her, his piercing gaze pinned her so firmly in place so she couldn't move even if she'd wanted to.

"Really? Because I was certain that I had," he said in a low, deep voice that went straight to her loins.

Unable to speak, she could only shake her head in disagreement.

Leaning down so close his breath feathered her lips, he reached up and drew the back of his fingers lightly down her cheek.

"Where you live is public information, Ms. Martin and as for what I'm doing here? I haven't been able to get you out of my head since the moment I laid eyes on you."

"Oh," she whispered, her mouth suddenly dry as the Sahara. She felt dizzy and didn't know if it was the wine or his scent affecting her. Probably both. His evident desire for her was heady and she found herself making excuses on why it might not be so bad after all to sleep with this man.

Just when she thought he'd lean down to kiss her, he took a step back taking his body heat and unique scent away with him. Disappointment stabbed deep. She wanted his mouth on hers more than she'd ever wanted anything else. Even more than she'd wanted that little electronic Barbie car as a child, the one you could sit in and drive around your neighborhood. And she'd wanted that a *hell* of a lot.

"Now, why don't you take a seat and eat before your food gets cold," he motioned as he pulled out the chair like a gentleman.

Not knowing what to make of this bizarre encounter, she walked to the small round table and took a seat. He sat just to her right and all of a sudden she wished she hadn't drank so much wine. While the haziness clouding her brain was absolutely in part due to him, it was also undeniably the alcohol. A woman didn't face a man like

Dev without a very clear head unless she wanted to end up underneath him in short order. And while she *so* did, she worried with her inhibitions lowered she'd make a mistake of epic proportions and end up hating herself in the morning.

Because nothing had changed between this morning and now, saying *no* was exactly what she needed to do, but she was wound so damn tight that she wasn't at all sure she'd be able to.

Chapter 12

Dev

She was as affected by him as he was she. He could smell her arousal the second she opened the door. It was intoxicating. Unfortunately, he could also see her internal tug of war. She wanted him but she didn't want to want him and that was messing with her head. He needed to put her at ease, while letting her know he intended to pursue her...hard. Dev had a lot of work ahead of him in a short amount of time. He loved a challenge and he won every single one of them. And he fully intended to win this one.

So let the games begin.

They sat in silence while she picked at her food. Unlike the myths, vampires didn't live on blood alone. It was their main sustenance, yes, but they also enjoyed food just as humans did. Dev's tastes ran a little higher-end than MSG filled Chinese food, however, and the smell of the sickly sweet chicken concoction Kate pushed around on her plate unpleasantly assailed his nose.

"Am I in danger?" she asked tentatively as she placed her fork down and looked in his eyes for the first time in several minutes.

"Yes," he said plainly. She *was* in danger and he would not lie to her about that.

She looked slightly taken aback, as if it wasn't the answer she'd expected.

"Has there been a threat or something? Did you see someone outside my house?"

"No. There has been no direct or indirect threat, but it's only a matter of time. You're a threat to him. Once this monster finds out about your special skills, Kate, he *will* come for you."

She looked truly frightened for the first time and while he felt bad about that, he didn't feel bad enough to back down.

"So...are you patrolling outside my house then?"

He regarded her silently for several moments. His stubborn Moira was not going to be easily convinced to come with him. He answered her as honestly as he could without revealing too much too soon.

"I won't let a moment pass that you're not protected, Kate." He'd follow her all over the goddamned city for days if he had to.

At his response, her shoulders relaxed slightly.

"Thank you."

"My pleasure."

She picked up her plate, having hardly eaten a thing, walked to the garbage and deposited the bulk of it in the oblong, plastic lined container. He couldn't stand being more than a few feet away from her and didn't want to be ushered out the door yet, so he poured a glass of red wine from the open bottle on the counter, took her hand and drew her back into the living room. He could smell the fruity potion on her breath when he walked in and knew she'd already imbibed in a few glasses.

"Sit," he waived her toward the couch and handed her the cup when she surprisingly complied without a flippant comment. He took his rightful place right next to her.

Glancing shyly between her glass and his face, he was surprised at the tender feelings that rose up out of nowhere. Dev was not tender anything. He was hard, demanding and passionate about many things. No one would—or could—ever accuse him of being tender. Now, however, as he observed his future mate that's the exact sentiment he felt.

"Do you want to talk about your dreams?" He asked quietly. He wanted to know everything about her. Her hopes and dreams and deepest desires.

She smiled sardonically. "Not particularly, no."

"Okay. Then tell me about your teaching."

Quite frankly, he didn't care what the fuck they talked about. He just wanted to spend time with her. And since he wasn't about to take advantage of a woman who'd clearly had a little too much to drink this evening, spending it talking to her was the best he was going to get.

At that question, her eyes lit up and she spent the next hour telling him about her current PhD studies and her love for teaching and research. He hung on every word she said, drawing it in and tucking it away for future reference. She was passionate, like him. And he knew without a shadow of a doubt that passion would extend to the four walls of the bedroom. Just thinking about it made his stiff erection throb with anger at being kept from his Moira. He'd kept his hands in his lap for most of their conversation because he couldn't control his bodily reaction to her.

Guilt ate at him for how much her life would change after they bonded. Because she would be the mate of a powerful Vampire Lord, she could not be allowed to continue teaching at the University and that gutted him. She would be crushed, so together they would have to find something else that could replace that passion, but where she'd also be safe from harm.

"Well, I should be going to bed. I have an early day tomorrow."

She yawned and he could see how tired she really

was. While he was loath to leave, he couldn't come up with a plausible reason to stay, either.

He rose, as did she, and she walked him to the front door. While he may walk out of the house, he wasn't going any further than that. Against Ren's wishes, he would personally keep watch over her.

"Well...good night Dev. Thanks for stopping by," she said softly as she held the open door, signaling it was time for him to depart.

Leaving without tasting her was probably the second hardest thing he'd done today. Watching her walk out of the precinct without him was the first. He wanted to taste her mouth, her skin, her pussy. He wanted her blood running in his veins. He craved anything and everything that she would give him.

But instead of doing any of those things, he leaned in and gently touched his lips to her forehead. "Goodnight, love."

Then he turned and walked out door, already strategically planning for tomorrow evenings visit.

CHAPTER 13

Xavier

Xavier thrust ruthlessly into her quivering body again and again. She was a tight little thing, and a virgin, if the blood smeared between her pale thighs was any indication. Of course, he'd ravaged her for the last several hours, so it was just as likely he'd ripped up her tender flesh. She was almost useless now. Her broken body was half drained of blood and she was just lying there, taking his abuse. Eyes vacant and glassed over.

They weren't nearly as much fun when they got to this stage. Her screams and sobbing had died down to whimpering and occasional pleading. He would prefer her screams, so her succulent bloodstream was flooded with the sweet aphrodisiac of adrenaline. He bared his fangs to her once again, which started her hoarse, half-hearted scream back up. He struck at her carotid like a rattlesnake, sucking the remaining lifeblood from her young, weak body.

Just as he was finishing, a soft knock came at the door, forcing him to stop suckling at her vein, though he held his fangs tightly in her flesh.

"*If I have to open that door, you're only going to wish you were dead, Rodney.*"

"*I'm terribly sorry to interrupt, master, but there is*

an urgent phone call for you. It's Bill from the Milwaukee PD. I believe you'll want to take it, my lord."

He had minions at police stations all over the country doing his bidding. Unfortunately, this could be important. *"Just a fucking minute."*

He drained the girl in record time, dropping her lifeless body on his bed. He rose, wiping the last few drops of her blood from his scarred, hideous face. He opened the door not caring about his nakedness, taking the phone from Rodney. "Get rid of her." He nodded back toward the bedroom.

"Right away, my lord."

Xavier stepped into his office, grabbed the phone and barked, "What the *fuck* is so important that I had to be interrupted?"

"My lord, I have some news I thought you would want to hear immediately. Several days ago, a woman by the name of Kate Martin showed up at the station asking to speak to a detective about the local missing girl, Sarah Hill. What caught my attention was that in her statement, she mentions dreaming of the missing girl. I also think the Midwest Regent Lord was here interviewing her, based on the rumors around the station."

"Why the *fuck* am I just hearing about this *now*?"

"I'm sorry, my lord. I've had the last three days off. I called as soon as I found out."

Xavier tried to rein in his temper. He needed answers. "Who's the detective that this woman talked to?"

"Detective Mike Thatcher."

"I want the female. Go to her house and pick her up."

"Yes, my lord."

"And Bill..."

"Yes, my lord?"

"If you fail me I *will* kill you. You'll be begging for the sweet mercy of death. But only after I fuck, drain and gut your wife and two lovely daughters while you watch, will I grant you your wish."

He could almost hear the human shitting himself, his fear palpable. Good. It wasn't an idle threat. In fact, he may do that anyway, and leave the human male alive to live with his anguish. "Y-Yes, my lord." He disconnected and flung the phone on his desk.

"Fuck!"

Did the dreamwalker know where to find him? He wasn't going to just sit around, waiting to find out. He hadn't managed to stay alive these last few centuries by being complacent. Finding her and adding her to his collection was his number one priority. As surprised as he was that she'd gone to the police, unfortunately for Ms. Kate Martin that had been a fatal fucking mistake.

And she would be his shortly. He smiled. His day was looking up.

CHAPTER 14

Kate

For the last several days, they'd fallen into a similar, comfortable routine. She'd arrive home between 4:30 or 5:00 in the afternoon and Dev would show up around 7:00 in the evening, dinner in hand and stay until she was so tired she couldn't keep her eyes open any longer. She hadn't gotten a damn thing done all week and for once, she didn't care.

It was both a blessing and a curse, though, because...nothing had happened. Absolutely nothing. Not a kiss, not an ass grab, not one salacious suggestion.

Not.

A.

Damn.

Thing.

Well, except for his perfunctory kiss on her forehead at the end of each evening.

And as annoying as that was, it was also confusing, because the sexual tension arched between them like a live wire. His dark eyes were constantly alight with desire for her, and she knew hers reflected the same. He'd tried hiding his perpetual hard on, but not very well. It was difficult to conceal that much manhood behind a tight, body-molding pair of dark blue jeans. And *daaaamn* if he didn't rock a pair of denims.

But he'd kept his distance, even choosing to sit on the chair tonight instead of on the couch with her as he'd done the three nights before. She'd almost pouted like a five year old who'd been stuck in the corner for misbehaving.

Out of sheer sexual frustration, she'd darn near answered the door tonight wearing nothing but a towel, which would oh so conveniently blow to the floor when a gust of wind would happen to catch it as she scrambled to close the cold squall out.

She was acting and thinking completely out of character.

The thing was...she *liked* him. *Really* liked him. She was drawn to him sexually, yes, but there was far more going on here than just that wanting to get in each other's pants. She was drawn to his dry humor and his passion and even his innate danger. And he really seemed to want to get to know her as well. Against her better judgment, she could feel herself starting to fall for him. And her mind was in a constant battle over that.

All night she'd waited for him to make a move. Once again...nada. When he left tonight, she'd almost grabbed him by the shirt and hauled him back to her bedroom, where she would have promptly removed every offending article of clothing and rode him hard until they both screamed their pleasure.

Now, lying in bed alone, she recounted their earlier conversation and how she'd actually *wanted* to respond.

Any more dreams? Of Sarah, no. Of him? Every. Blessed. Night.

How was your day? Sexually frustrating. Yours?

What would you like to eat this evening? Ahhh...your cock?

If his intent was to drive her mad with desire and want, he'd hit that one way out of the park. She'd taken more goddamned baths in the last four days than she had in the last twelve months. Unable to slip into sleep until she assuaged the burning fire between her thighs, she grabbed Big Blue and went to work. She was nearing the peak when a noise startled her. Flipping the switch off on her battery-operated boyfriend, she lay deathly still, straining to hear where the noise originated. All was quiet, but something felt off.

Dev insisted she was still in danger, but nothing unusual had happened over the past few days, so she'd relaxed a bit. She felt safe, especially with him hanging around so much. Convinced she'd imagined the sound, she was just about to turn back on her BOB and finish what she'd started, when she heard the loose floorboard in the kitchen creak.

Her pulse raced.

Someone was in her house and she was quite sure it wasn't Dev because he would never scare her like that. If he wanted in her bed, he'd simply demand it, not sneak around.

Dev had given her his cell number, saying he'd never be too far away and could be here instantly if she needed him. Unfortunately for her, she'd left her phone charging on the kitchen counter so now she was completely defenseless. She was just reaching for her gun in the nightstand drawer when Dev called her name from down the hall.

Oh thank God.

He came storming in her room, throwing open the door so hard it bounced several times off the wall.

"What—"

"We need to leave immediately. Pack a bag for several days. Quickly." He was efficient, sharp. All business.

"Dev, what's going—?"

"Kate. We have no time," he said as he pulled open her closet door and grabbed the small rolling suitcase that sat in the corner. "There were several men lurking outside. Now pack your stuff. No more excuses. You're coming with me."

"O-Okay," she replied with a shaky voice.

Kate quickly packed, adding only the essentials. Anything she'd missed they could surely get for her somewhere. Stopping quickly in the kitchen, she grabbed her phone, her computer and finally her purse before they swiftly left through the front door.

Shit. She'd have to call her boss and make up some story about why she wouldn't be into work for the next few days, but she'd worry about that tomorrow, when she was somewhere safe.

They piled into the back of black Range Rover, which she'd seen sitting outside every night and was surprised to see Ren in the back seat. The tension was so thick she could practically see it swirling in the air and each man radiated barely unchecked fury.

The driver put the car roughly in reverse and they hightailed it out of there; her house growing smaller and smaller in the rear view mirror. It was a good fifteen minutes before any of them spoke.

"What happened?" she asked, unable to keep the question in any longer.

"Exactly what I told you," Dev snipped.

Why the hell was he mad at her? It wasn't her fault some psycho came hunting her. Except...that it was. She should have listened to him days ago and they wouldn't be in this mess right now.

"Did anyone get hurt?" She wasn't sure why she asked, because someone was clearly there to do her harm, but she simply had to know.

Even in the darkness of the car's interior, Dev's stare was so wholly intense, so consuming, it sucked all of the oxygen out and she could barely breathe. He waited so long to respond she didn't think he would.

"No one that matters."

There was so much unspoken meaning behind those words, he might as well as just said what she really heard. *Not you. No one matters but you.*

When Dev reached for her hand, she nearly wept. She was trying to be strong, but in truth was barely holding it together. They drove the rest of the way in silence and after another thirty minutes or so they were turning onto a road that she hadn't even seen. The driver slowed at a security gate, which was heavily guarded, before the wrought iron doors swung opened. They proceeded up a long, winding, densely wooded driveway before a large estate came into view.

Holy. Shit.

She could only gape at the expansive mansion and grounds in front of her. It looked like it should be on the cover of *House and Home* magazine. The place was massive.

"This is the safe house?" She turned to Dev with a confused look on her face.

CHAPTER 15

Dev

He was close to losing his shit. When he saw the rogues creeping around the perimeter of Kate's house, he'd almost gone nuclear. Ren, Manny and himself quickly and efficiently handled the low-level vermin, but things could have ended very badly and the thought of Kate anywhere near Xavier had him seeing red. The only thing that had set him right again was touching Kate. When he grabbed her hand and she held on for dear life, he almost breathed an audible sigh of relief. What he'd wanted to do was haul her into his lap and not ever let her go.

As they pulled into his driveway, he'd already decided how he was going to explain his extravagant home. Be honest. He would have to tell her shortly of his true nature and the least amount of lies he had to build before then, the better.

"No. It's my home. But you will be safe here, Kate. I promise. I won't let anything happen to you. This place is heavily guarded and very secure. No one will find you here."

"Wow. I have a hard time believing that." She looked at him incredulously. "You could spot this house from the space shuttle."

Dev laughed. He loved her wit.

"It's not as easy to spot as you might think." For security purposes, they had a shrouding spell cast around the estate that made it invisible, appearing only as a cornfield to passersby.

Kate mumbled. "Yeah...I noticed the driveway kind of came up out of nowhere."

Wow, she was very perceptive. Amazingly, though, she let it go.

They pulled up to the large circular drive and the car came to a stop. Dev opened his door and exited the car, holding out a hand to assist her. Their eyes locked. She took his hand and gracefully exited the car, without breaking eye contact. Adrenaline levels were still high from the short battle and he could hardly control his raging cock. Just the simple act of holding her hand in the car caused the beast to pound incessantly on his zipper, demanding escape from his metal prison. He wanted to pull her into his arms and devour her full berry-colored lips. The lust in her eyes, the smell of her arousal and the increase in her pulse all validated she would welcome it, but now was not the time.

He tugged her hand. "Come on, let's get you inside and settled. I'll give you a tour of the house tomorrow."

"Dev." She pulled on his arm, stopping their forward movement.

He turned to face her, running his free hand up and down her arm.

"Yes?"

"Thank you," she responded, tears brimming in her spectacular shining eyes.

Dev smiled softly and pulled her into him. "You're welcome, love."

Kate

Love...he'd called her that for days. Why did it send electric tingles through her body? She wondered if that endearment was for her or if he called all women that. The thought had her frowning.

Ren had grabbed her bags and they all headed up the marble staircase to the maple French doors encased in beveled glass. Dev had now set his hand on the small of her back and it turned her insides to mush. Her body was an inferno of lust. Maybe that was the adrenaline rush they always talked about when you were put in a fight or flight situation, but even as she thought that, she knew it wasn't true. She'd been an inferno of lust for days now.

As they approached the house, the door opened and the next thing she saw made her stop short. Stepping out from behind the door was an exquisitely beautiful and very tall, lithe woman. Goddess was probably a more accurate description. She had to be at least six feet tall, but she had the most striking pixie features, perfect nose, bright blue eyes and creamy skin. *Inferior* popped into Kate's head. She was definitely inferior compared to this stunning creature.

Who the hell was she and what was she doing in Dev's house?

Dev introduced them. "Giselle, this is Kate. Kate, Giselle." *Giselle?* Wow, she even had a killer name.

Kate held out her hand in greeting—and was surprised when Giselle just looked at her hand and back to her face. No change of expression, no greeting. Nothing.

Dev glared at Giselle and it felt like something passed between the two of them. Giselle then smiled tightly and extended her hand toward Kate. "Nice to meet you." And she didn't sound *at all* like she meant it.

What the hell? If anyone shouldn't like someone here, it was Kate. Giselle was the type of woman that every other woman hated on principle alone. She made all other woman in the immediate vicinity look like a fugly frog.

"Nice to meet you, too, Giselle. What a beautiful name." Giselle didn't even acknowledge that Kate had spoken to her; she simply turned and walked back through the entryway, disappearing into the house.

Yikes, what crawled up her ass? Guess she would be avoiding her for the next few days.

"I'm sorry about that. She's not always the friendliest person. I'll talk to her."

Kate burst out laughing. "That's okay. No need. She's probably just having a bad day." Or maybe she didn't like seeing Dev with a hand on another woman's body. She knew the green-eyed monster when she saw it and jealousy was oozing from every pore of that ice queen.

"No, it's not and it will be taken care of. You've done nothing to earn that sort of treatment."

"Don't worry about it, Dev. Really." She just knew if he said anything, it would make it worse. Like bullying in fourth grade when her mom tried to intervene. Yes, that earned her some extra pushing, shoving and tripping on the playground. No thank you.

Ren took off down the hallway with her bags, leaving the two of them alone.

As Kate stood in the enormous entryway, she was in complete and utter awe. She had never seen a house so exquisite in all of her life, except on *Cribs*. Her whole house could probably fit into the entryway alone.

"Wow," she breathed. He afforded this on a police salary? Something wasn't adding up here, but she'd table the question until tomorrow. She simply wanted to crawl into bed and forget the last hour had happened.

"Come on, I'll show you to your room and get you settled."

"Okay."

Kate followed Dev up the grand staircase. She followed him through a maze of hallways, turning left and right. Good grief, she needed exit signs to find her way back out. Finally, they stopped at a bedroom and Dev opened the door. Her bags had been neatly deposited onto her bed already.

"I hope this is to your liking." Dev stepped aside and motioned her in.

The bedroom was huge, but homey. It was warmly decorated in soft browns and taupes. There was a raised four-poster California king bed in the middle of the room, with a chocolate brown paisley comforter and massive amounts of matching pillows in neutral and red accents.

She walked a bit further into the room and looked back at him flirtatiously over her shoulder, smiling. "Oh, I don't know. Do you have anything a little nicer? A little bigger, maybe?"

He stared at her for just a second before he burst out laughing. God she loved that sound. It flowed through her body like warmth from a roaring fire.

"Minx."

Dev walked up to Kate, stopping only inches away from her. The way he walked, one may think it was ego behind his steps, but she knew better. It was confidence. It was power. It was determination. And it was unnerving. He was so close that she had to crane her head back to look in his eyes. Her heart raced and she broke out in a light sweat. Sweet Lord, he was breathtaking.

"We're going to be attached at the hip for the next few days." His eyes became darker, hungrier. His voice thickened and lowered, sounding gravelly. "I'm very much looking forward to it."

Her breath quickened. She felt a rush of moisture between her legs. "So am I," she whispered. She shouldn't be encouraging him, but she was done being coy. He dropped his hungry gaze to her lips and she unconsciously licked them.

Kiss me. God, please just kiss me already. She'd been dying to taste his lips. Taste his tongue. Taste his skin. Her body was ablaze as Dev took in her every movement.

"Will you be okay alone?"

"Yes, I'll be fine. Thanks."

What she really meant was stay, *but why couldn't she say just it?* Her mind had been a jumbled mess for days, but one thing was perfectly clear. She wanted this man before her even if it was just sex and even if it was just for a short period of time.

"Okay then. I'll see you in the morning. If you need anything at all, just yell for me, okay?"

"So...ah...which bedroom are you sleeping in?" *And why isn't it mine?*

"The one next to yours." Dev watched her lips appreciatively. "To ensure your safety, of course."

"Yes, of course." She could hardly breathe. Neither broke eye contact. Neither was willing to say goodnight.

He took several steps toward her, causing her to back up against the bedroom wall. "I'm curious, love. Do you ever have any *good* dreams?"

Not at all what she was expecting him to say. His voice lowered an octave.

"Pleasurable dreams, perhaps?" He had a knowing glint in his eye, like he knew she'd had dreams about him. Heat crept up her neck, into her face. This was a more dominant side of him she'd not seen yet and she loved it. She'd *craved* it.

"No. I mean, not all my dreams are bad, no." No way would she reveal that she masturbated to him regularly and had for months.

"I'm glad." His smile was so amazingly beautiful. She could definitely fall head over heels for this man. *Just sex, Kate. Just. Sex.*

Kate cleared her throat. "Well, thanks for protecting me."

His possessive response sent shivers of desire running up her spine.

"I will always protect you, love."

He closed the small gap between them, their chests almost touching now. He ran his index finger down her cheek, stopping underneath her chin. Their eyes held as he leaned in and did what she'd silently begged him to for days. He kissed her gently on the lips. He wrapped one arm around her waist, pulling her flush against him. Her eyes closed as the gentle kiss turned deeper, his longing for her evident. He coaxed her lips open, teasing her tongue, exploring her mouth. She wound her arms around his neck and tried pulling him closer.

His lips left hers, grazing an erotic path down her jaw. He held her tight as he whispered, "Good night, sweet Kate. Tonight I want you to dream about my cock inside your sweet body."

Winking, he turned and walked out her bedroom door. She just stood there and watched him walk out, mouth hanging open. She raised her fingers to touch her tingling lips. *Holy hell.*

Before he closed the door, he turned back to look at her, his eyes dark with lust. She knew hers were mirrors. Had he decided to throw her against the wall and take her right there, she would have let him. The word 'please' nearly slipped from her stunned lips.

She quickly dropped her hand. "Uh...good night."

He smiled and quietly shut the door. She stood there, rooted to that spot for several seconds. Or minutes. She wasn't sure.

Her emotions were a jumbled mess. She was disappointed, confused, relieved, and horny. She wanted him in a way she'd wanted no one else. Every emotion was ten times more intense with him than with any other man. Why did he stop? Why did she let him stop?

It was evident he wanted her and she couldn't have come off any easier if she tried. That kiss—and his erotic words—had her body on fire, the ache she'd fought for days now fueled with a vengeance.

Damn him! Damn him for being so irresistible that she'd thrown all caution to the wind and was seriously considering sleeping with him, a virtual stranger for God's sake.

She made her way to the bathroom, which was as exquisite as the bedroom, with a dark brown speckled granite countertop and an amazing tiled walk-in shower with multiple showerheads. In the far corner of the room, there was an oversized sunken Jacuzzi tub. Well, at least if Dev wouldn't make a move on her, she'd have her watery jet friends to keep her company, since she couldn't leave with anything from her nightstand drawer.

Once again she wondered what on earth Dev did for a living to be able to afford such extravagance, because she was no fool. This didn't come from a police or detective's salary. She had twenty questions lined up for tomorrow.

She quickly changed and got ready for bed. Snuggling under the thick covers as soon as her head hit the pillow exhaustion overcame her. The emotional toll of the last few days had reached a crescendo and as she slipped into darkness, despite Dev's erotic words to dream of his cock, she actually prayed for the opposite.

For the first time in months, she hoped she *didn't* dream of the one erotic man that, in addition to haunting her dreams, now consumed her every waking hour.

CHAPTER 16

Dev

Dev sat in his office with the most painful hard-on he'd ever had in his very long existence. He'd never wanted a woman more than he wanted Kate. Ever. These last several days of being with her without touching her or taking her was hard enough, but walking away from her after kissing her sweet, soft lips was just excruciating. What he wanted to do was rip off her clothes, push his aching cock into her hot, luscious body, and lose himself in her softness right there.

But he knew he had to walk away. He already knew that his sweet Kate was not the type of woman to have casual sex. Oh, he could've had her tonight if he'd wanted. Her desire for him was potent. When he left, her honeyed scent was so powerful it was as if his nose was buried directly in her pussy. And it was driving him out of his damned mind. He had to escape to his office to keep from knocking down her door and fucking her senseless.

By the second night they'd spent together, he could have had her, but he already knew how her complex mind worked. She would regret it, and surprisingly he didn't want her to. He laughed to himself. He hadn't given a shit about what anyone thought of him in so long, he'd forgotten what it felt like. He was a ruthless son-of-a-bitch, making all decisions swiftly and decisively, without regret, without remorse, without emotion.

Today, though, he was a mess of emotions. Fierce possessiveness. Hot jealousy. Extreme frustration. Unimaginable fear. Unparalleled desire. All feelings he was unfamiliar and uncomfortable with. He had known her only a short time, yet she was already changing him in ways she didn't even realize.

She was his. The fates had already determined that. But damn if he didn't want more from her than just simply *being his*. With a yearning that took him by complete surprise, he realized what he really wanted from her was...*love*.

He wasn't expecting to crave her love in return. Need it with every breath in his body. Now it was all he could think of. And he was pulling out all the stops to get it, which is another reason he hadn't moved their physical relationship faster.

He never thought he'd find her, the one person on this earth made specifically for him and no other. He knew once he found her there would be an undeniable passion between the two of them. There was that, yet there was also so much more. He knew he wasn't imagining it; she felt as strongly for him already as he did for her. But his sweet Kate was surely playing this off as just lust, nothing more, which was why he couldn't take her tonight. He longed for her love and affection with a deep ache that was difficult for him to comprehend.

He was falling hard for her. He had no idea his woman would be so intelligent, sexy, passionate, and witty. She was all of those things and so much more. She was compassionate, loyal to her family, and passionate about many things in life, including her academia.

Ren strode through his office doors. "Damian and

Romaric will be here tomorrow evening, but we've got a video conference with them in ten."

He'd been completely remiss, putting off his business problems while following Kate all over Milwaukee and keeping a 24/7 protective watch over her and now he was very far behind. Now that Kate was in his life, finding Xavier was paramount. He posed an unacceptable threat to her.

"Good. We need to find Xavier and eliminate him once and for all."

"True that. Were you able to get any more information from Kate?"

"No."

"Work your charm, Dev. Just fuck her and she'll tell you anything."

In the next second, Ren was slammed up against the wall, a large hand holding him by his neck, one pissed off vampire in his face. "You will *not* talk about her like that again, understand?"

"Jesus, Dev," he croaked. "Lighten up. I have nothin' but respect for your Moira."

Dev let him go and started pacing. "Fuck! I know I'm being completely irrational. But if anyone looks at her, touches her, or talks to her I want to rip out their throat. You included."

"It will get easier when you bond with her, Dev. At least that's what I've heard."

"I don't know, Ren. I hope so. I can't go around slaughtering everyone in my Regent just for looking at my Moira."

Ren slapped him on the shoulder. "I'm happy for you, man. You deserve to be happy after the hell you've been through."

He *had* been through hell. His entire family was slaughtered. Even after all these years, it was painful to think about. He idly wondered what his parents would have thought of Kate. There was no question—they would love her. It seemed like everyone was drawn to her. Well, except Giselle. But she hated pretty much everyone.

He let his thoughts drift back to a time long ago.

1559

He'd been due home hours ago, but the female companion he'd found tonight was just too delicious to tap once. He could tell she'd been thoroughly used, as her pussy wasn't as snug as some he'd come across, but she blew him like no other and her blood was as sweet as the blackberry jam his meme made. He rarely used a woman more than once, but perhaps he'd return to her, while he kept up the search for his Moira. She'd been one of the few women he'd found that knew about vampires and was more than willing to give freely of her body and blood in return for the indescribable pleasure she'd receive. Dangerous that, but to each his own.

Vampires lived among humans, most humans never knowing they were anything other than what they pretended to be. They were peaceful and wanted to live and thrive as any human does. They were not to kill their prey and they were not to expose their race, for even as powerful as they were, they would be no match for thousands of humans gunning for their heads. There were some of his kind, however, like Xavier, who didn't believe in their chosen lifestyle, desiring total power and killing indiscriminately.

Xavier was like the brother he'd never had. At four, Xavier had been left in the middle of their village, abandoned by his parents, and Dev's parents had adopted him as their own. They'd had an idyllic childhood and were as close as blood brothers. Now both in their early twenties, they'd drifted apart and Xavier was around less and less. Xavier's actions lately had become more and more erratic, more totalitarian and the distance that grew between them saddened Dev.

Then last month, nineteen people went missing from a village down the road. Entire families had just vanished without a trace. This was the third such occurrence in as many months and panic was quickly spreading among the villages. The elders knew a rogue vampire was to blame and there was an all-out hunt to find him and dispose of him before the rogue exposed them.

When Devon discovered Xavier was the one behind the kidnappings and had been keeping humans locked up like animals, he had no choice but to tell the elders, one of which was his father. The depraved things Xavier did to these humans sickened him. Violating small girls in front of their fathers; torturing young boys while their mothers were forced to watch; bleeding wives dry in front of their husbands until their bodies were nothing but shriveled husks.

He'd known Xavier's moral compass was questionable lately, but that he wasn't aware of the depths of his brother's wickedness ate at him every day since. He could have prevented this had he only chosen to speak to his father sooner. When he confronted Xavier, he simply stated this was how it should be. Vampires were not the weaker species. Vampires should rule humans, not live alongside them as equals when they were clearly superior. Humans should be treated like the cattle they were, waiting for their slaughter, while making themselves useful in the meantime by serving a vampire's every need.

Xavier had not been seen in over a month. Hunters had been sent to find him but had been unsuccessful.

Dev should have flashed home, but he'd taken his horse that evening and needed to return it. Flashing such a big beast was not only taxing on his powers, but it would also raise suspicions among the humans in his small village, so he settled for the long ride home instead. Dawn was nearing, but he expected to arrive shortly afterward and, with his medallion, he'd be fine. He was well sated and in a fine mood, making plans with the same female for night after morrow.

As he neared the village, still over a mile away, the scent of blood and smoke overwhelmed him. Forgetting the horse, he flashed to his small cottage, and the sight before him dropped him to his knees in agony. The stench of death made his stomach heave.

His baby sister's body lay in the doorway, her still beating heart lay beside her lifeless body. The look of horror on her face would be etched into his retinas forever. The curtain concealing his parents' bedroom was on the floor and the entire small area was engulfed in flames, but he could clearly distinguish their dead bodies lying in the small bed.

The attack was so fresh he must have just missed the slayer. His family had been murdered minutes ago and he'd been screwing some whore when he should have been home to protect them. He bellowed in grief and guilt and was forced to flee the house as the fire quickly spread. What he saw outside his cottage was more than his mind could comprehend.

Slain bodies lay everywhere. Most of the homes were on fire. Destruction was all around. His entire village had been slaughtered, but the sight that he couldn't wrap his grief-stricken brain around was the one of his friend, his brother, walking out of one of the few homes not on fire. His clothes were drenched in blood and he had a smile on his face. When Xavier spotted Devon, he simply saluted before vanishing.

How his parents didn't know their attacker was upon them until it was too late was a problem that took Dev decades to solve. His dad was an elder and one of the strongest vampires alive.

After that, hate and revenge became Dev's only friend and he'd spent the last five hundred years trying to exact that revenge, but Xavier remained elusive— and that fucking pissed him off.

The memory was painful, as always. He agonized every day that he hadn't been there to save his family, his village, from Xavier's wrath. After he discovered Xavier's special ability, he knew he would have also been killed had he been there, but it still didn't stop the guilt. He was surprised to find the grief felt slightly less today and smiled inwardly. Kate was already healing him in more ways than she even knew.

The webcam rang at the same time Giselle walked into the office, pulling him out of his reverie. He answered, projecting the images of Damian DiStephano and Romaric Dietrich on his computer screen. Marco and T were with Damian. No one, not even Damian, new what T was short for. Circo was with Romaric, as usual.

Both the other Vampire Lords were as striking as Dev. He knew neither had a shortage of willing women spreading their legs, but he was surprised that neither man had found his Moira, either. While he'd yearned to find his, he hadn't realized how truly lonely he'd been until he laid eyes on Kate. That deep dark hole had now been filled with a woman whose essence shined brighter than the stars. He was a lucky bastard.

"Gentlemen." He nodded.

Damian spoke first. "Devon, Ren. Good to see you both. Giselle, you're looking bitchy, I mean beautiful, as always."

"Bite me, asshole."

"Hmmmm, I think I'll pass, babe. Wasn't so great the first time."

Dev jumped in. "Knock it off. We have more important matters to discuss here than whatever the fuck went on between you two that neither of you will let go."

Damian just laughed. If he were here in person, Dev was sure he'd be on the floor with a dagger in his heart about now. Bastard better watch his six when he gets here. Giselle was the meanest bitch he'd ever met. But she was also one of the most loyal.

Romaric spoke up in his usual get-down-to-business manner. Dev liked and respected Rom, but the guy needed to get the cob dug out of his ass. Or get laid more. "Let's move this along. I have business to tend to before I am to be there by tomorrow at nightfall."

They spent the next half hour rehashing what they all knew about the missing girls in their Regents. In total, twenty-eight girls had gone missing in the last three weeks. There were likely more they weren't aware of yet. They'd all come to the same conclusion that Xavier had resurfaced, ramping up whatever sick plan was rattling around in the twisted gray matter that functioned as a brain.

"One more thing you should know before you arrive tomorrow. I have found my Moira. Her name is Kate Martin. She's here at the house and she doesn't know of our kind yet, so keep your mouths shut. I'll see you all tomorrow evening." He cut the video before anyone had a chance to respond.

"Giselle, a word," he said as everyone made a move to depart.

When they were alone, he continued, "You will give Kate the respect she deserves. If you treat her like the dirt under your boot again, you'll answer to me. Understood?"

She nodded curtly. "Yes, my lord."

"That's all." She left without another word.

He was looking forward to tomorrow when he'd spend as much time with Kate as possible before he had to spend the night strategizing on how they could find Xavier this time. Find and destroy. It felt even more urgent now that he'd found his Moira. If Xavier found out about Kate, she'd be in even more danger.

He was even desperate enough to bring in Esmeralda and he and the witch weren't on the best of terms. His rejections of her advances over the years had bruised her pretty, fragile ego. Never trust a witch. Use them, yes. Trust them, hell to the no. And while Esmeralda was stunning, regardless of what anyone thought, he had more discriminating tastes than that. Esmeralda probably wouldn't take too kindly to Kate, so he planned to keep her as far away from Kate as possible. Better safe than sorry.

Dev's urgency to kill Xavier now had much more driving it than revenge. He had a new family to protect and he wouldn't fail—*couldn't fail*—this time.

CHAPTER 17

Kate

She woke feeling refreshed. The gods had blessed her, because she'd thankfully had a rare night of dreamless sleep. She looked at the clock to see she'd slept until 8:30 a.m. Crap! She had class to teach in an hour, which she'd yet to find a replacement for. She quickly grabbed her cell and called into the office. Ten minutes later she'd posted a cancellation for today's classes and due to a 'family illness' found replacements for the next several days, just in case. She really had no idea how long it would be before the threat to her safety had passed.

Not knowing what the plan for today was, she decided to shower and was half way to the bathroom when a knock sounded at her door. Looking down at the skimpy tank and shorts she generally slept in, she wished she'd thought of bringing a robe.

When she opened the door, famished eyes raked her slowly from head to toe. Her nipples pebbled underneath the thin fabric. Dev's eyes lingered on them for what seemed like minutes before they traveled further down her bare legs. His perusal back up was just as agonizing and deliciously slow.

His eyes finally met hers. The desire engulfing them was palpable.

"Good morning," he rasped.

She fought to catch her breath. "Hi."

"Sleep well?"

"Yes, thank you." She suddenly remembered she'd just rolled out of bed. Frantically running her fingers through her hair, she attempted to tame her long locks.

"Morning looks good on you, Kate," he said.

Needing to put a bit of distance between them so she could gather her wits and thoughts, and rid herself of toxic morning breath, she asked, "So what's the plan for today?"

His smile was easy, gentle. "Breakfast first, then a tour. How long do you need to get ready?"

"Thirty minutes is sufficient."

"Thirty? I think I'm falling for you harder every minute I'm in your presence, love."

And with those parting words, he turned and walked down the hallway, leaving her brain to swirl those confusing and terrifying words over and again for the next half hour.

Dev

Thirty minutes to the second later, Dev knocked softly on Kate's bedroom door. As he waited for her to answer, he thought of her in the shower. Water sluicing down her succulent, naked curves, made his groin tighten uncomfortably. He envisioned the droplets beading up on her fair skin. How her nipples would tighten from the cold once she shut off the tap. He ached to get her underneath him. He'd had a painful, never-ending hard-on for days that needed remedying. He hadn't had to resort to using his own hand since he was a young boy but he was getting pretty fucking close to going there.

Kate opened the door, dressed in a long-sleeved, black clingy cowl-necked shirt and faded, well-worn blue jeans that molded perfectly to her shapely body. He couldn't wait to get a view from the rear. Her raven hair spilled in soft waves around her shoulders and she'd put on a little makeup. She was simply exquisite.

She smiled up at him. "Hello again."

Christ, she took his breath away. "Hello to you too. You look absolutely breathtaking, Kate. Are you ready?" At his compliment, he watched a blush quickly creep up her neck, onto her beautiful face.

"Yes, I'm ready. I hope jeans are okay? You look so nice and I'm afraid I didn't bring any nice clothes."

He grabbed her hands and took a step closer. "You look spectacular, love. Don't give it another thought. Come on, let's go." He stepped aside to let her go first, admiring her voluptuous ass, beautifully molded by the denim fabric.

She was perfectly proportioned, but like most human women, she probably thought she was too heavy. He liked a woman who looked like a woman should, with curves in all the right places. Kate had them in spades.

"Would you like a tour before or after breakfast?" He led her down the hallway with his hand in the small of her back. He couldn't be near her and not touch her.

"After, I think. I'm starving!"

"After it is, then." Dev led her toward the dining room. He usually had breakfast brought to him in his office by his longtime butler, Leo, but he'd asked Leo to prepare a light meal and serve it in the smaller of the two formal dining rooms, so as not to overwhelm Kate.

He was starving this morning, but it wasn't for human food. He had a bone deep need for Kate's blood. Older vampires needed to ingest blood less frequently than younger vampires. A vampire Devon's age could go a week comfortably without feeding. Two was doable, but pushing it. It'd been almost a week since he'd fed and while he could go another week with some discomfort, he wouldn't even entertain feeding from another woman since he'd met his Moira.

When they reached the dining room, Leo was just placing breakfast on the table.

"Leo, this is Kate. Kate, Leo. Leo's...many things, but my excellent chef is one of them."

Kate smiled and extended her hand in greeting. "Nice to meet you, Leo."

"Very pleased to meet you, ma'am."

"My mother is called ma'am. Please call me Kate."

Leo chuckled. "Yes, ma'am. Kate. Won't you sit and enjoy the breakfast I've prepared?"

"Oh, wow. This all looks so delicious. Thank you Leo." Leo quickly departed, giving them the privacy he craved.

"I didn't know what you liked, so I asked Leo to bring an assortment of things."

She laughed. "Thank you. That was very sweet. A bit excessive, but sweet."

Dev pulled out her chair and gestured for her to sit. She smiled up at him and took a seat.

"Wow, Leo must be quite the cook. This looks absolutely divine."

"He's a great chef. If cooking were left to me, I'm afraid we'd be limited to ramen noodles, grilled cheese and cold cut sandwiches. I do make a mean stew, though. Old family recipe." His mother was a fabulous cook. She'd been gone almost five centuries now. He still missed his family deeply. Xavier had killed them before Dev realized the depth of Xavier's madness. Dev had failed them and it haunted him every single day.

He couldn't think about that at the moment. He needed to concentrate on Kate. He refocused in time to hear her say the tail end of something.

"...sometime."

"Sorry, what was that?" She grinned at him, showing her perfectly straight, white teeth. Jesus, she was magnificent.

"I said, I'd like it if you made it for me sometime." When he looked a little confused, she added, "The stew?"

His eyes flamed. His cock was bursting in his pants. She wanted him to make her a meal. She had no idea what that meant to him. A vampire cooking for his Moira had significant meaning. He couldn't wait. "Sorry, love. I guess I have a hard time concentrating on anything when I'm around you." He got lost in her bewitching eyes.

"And of course, I'd love to cook for you. I'm looking forward to it. Very much." He meant it. He couldn't wait to feed her from his fork, lapping up any stray liquid that clung to her lips. His balls were getting bluer by the second.

"Me too," she replied.

CHAPTER 18

Kate

Me too? What in the Sam Hill was she doing? Like she was going to see him after this all blew over? Who just took over her mouth? Clingy Kate, that's who. Just being near him had clearly scrambled her brains, like the eggs sitting on her plate. She was aroused and completely on edge. She'd never been like this with a man in her entire twenty-seven years. She should have taken care of this constant ache in the shower earlier. Or taken a bath instead.

Her eyes roamed around the opulent room. The table they were sitting at probably cost more than she made in a year. And he had a chef?

"So what exactly is it you do for the police department, Dev."

He leaned back in his chair, crossed his legs and folded his arms across his lap. He looked so damn regal. Almost like a king.

"I guess you could say I'm a consultant of sorts. I handle...*special* cases."

"Special cases?" That sounded intriguing.

"Yes," he replied flatly.

"What type of special cases?"

"Unique ones that no one else can solve."

"Oh." She looked around the room in confusion. "So, I don't mean to be rude, but you must charge a hell of a lot for your services to be able to afford all of this."

Laughing, he said, "I have several very successful nightclubs and restaurants that are my primary source of income. Consulting with the MPD is simply a...side responsibility."

"Do you have any more leads on finding Sarah?"

"I'm afraid not, no."

"Do you know how long I'll have to stay here until I'm safe to go home?"

A pensive look crossed his face. "No."

"Oh." She looked back down at her cold eggs, not sure how to feel about that answer. She was scared for her safety, of course, but the longer she spent in Dev's presence, the harder it became to separate fantasy from reality. And the reality of the situation is that if they did sleep together, *when* they slept together, this could be nothing more than a fling. Nothing more than casual. And she was surprised at the hurt that caused her heart.

They'd spent the last several days talking a lot about her, but every time she asked a question about him, he hedged, answering on the surface, but never going too deep, especially when she asked about his parents. All he would say was that they'd been gone for a long time and that he missed them greatly. He quickly moved off the subject, so she didn't push. She could tell it was painful for him.

He had lost a sibling as well, so it was only him now. That made her sad for some reason. He was well educated, understanding her passion for academia. They both loved to read and exercise. They had much in common. Every second spent with him not only did she want him more, but she also liked him more.

After they finished eating, Dev asked, "So, was there anything else that you remembered about your dream that you think might help? Anything at all?"

He'd asked this question several times, and she was starting to feel like she wanted to tell him. She trusted him. She started to fidget, trying not to. "No, not really. I'm sorry, I wish I could tell you more."

Elbows on the table, he leaned forward clasping his hands. He spoke in a gentle, coaxing voice, not breaking eye contact. "Kate, I really admire that you came into the station at all. It took a lot of guts and not many people would put themselves out there like that. You did, and you should be proud of yourself."

She relaxed a bit.

"I believe your dreams are real. And I'll believe anything you tell me, Kate. Anything at all. I've seen a lot of crazy shit, so trust me when I tell you nothing, and I mean nothing you can tell me will surprise me. We need to find this bastard." He paused, adding, "And I need your help to do that, Kate. So please, do you remember anything else that maybe you were afraid to share before?"

Should she tell him? She warred with herself. She didn't want this beautiful, sexy man to think she was ready for the funny farm.

"You can trust me, Kate." She sighed heavily, decision made. Guess it was best he thought she was crazy now before she got too emotionally invested.

"It's hard to believe it's real, Dev." Her voice lowered. "I've had strange dreams my entire life. Some are so unimaginably terrifying they couldn't possibly be real. When I was younger, I would wake in a panic and run into my parents' bedroom in the middle of the night. Eventually they got tired of hearing about them, so I stopped talking about it and convinced myself they were just dreams, nothing more.

"In high school, I had a difficult time. My dreams really intensified and I wasn't getting much sleep at night. My grades suffered. I had constant headaches. I was more moody than a normal teenage girl." She gave a small laugh.

"So my parents took me to a doctor. A psychologist. I told her I was stressed with the pressure of school and she gave me a few low dose sleeping pills." Kate closed her eyes, tilting her head toward the ceiling. "For a short time, it was...heaven. I actually slept through the entire night without dreaming. No faces. No sadness. No blood. No death. It was blessed relief. Then even those stopped working.

"You have *no* idea what it's like to see the things I've seen. I thought they were just dreams. Sick and twisted, yes, but still just dreams. When I was sixteen, I realized differently."

Dev waited patiently for her to continue, which made it easier. Getting the next part out was harder than she'd thought. He gently coaxed her, "What happened at sixteen, love?"

The corners of her mouth turned slightly up at the endearment. Her stomach tightened in hard knots. She couldn't do it.

"I can't talk about that right now. I'm sorry. It's not relevant anyway." He looked disappointed. She felt guilty, but she just couldn't bring herself to talk about how she'd failed Jamie Hallow by denying her dreams were real.

"That's all right. Was there anything more you remember about Sarah, Kate? Even a feeling you may have had during the dream?"

"Yes," she whispered. "Evil."

"Evil?"

She nodded. "I know it sounds crazy and you probably think I'm am, but I'm telling you, Dev...I felt evil seeping into my pores. It was terrifying." She just couldn't tell him about the fangs and vampires. That was just too unbelievable, even for her.

He grabbed her hands, holding them in his. "I believe you, Kate."

"You do?" Relief coursed through her.

"Yes, I do. We're going to find Sarah. With your help, we *are* going to find her."

"I hope we find her alive." Tears welled in her eyes.

He stood and pulled her into his arms, tucking her head under his chin. "Me too, love. Me too."

As Dev held her in his strong, muscular arms, she felt safe. Cared for. It felt like home. *Whoa*...where did that thought come from? His next question broke the spell he had somehow woven around her.

"Hey, how about that tour now?"

"Sure. That sounds like a good distraction."

He pulled away slightly to look at her, his face purely carnal. "If it's a distraction you want, love, I'm sure I can find something more pleasurable than a tour."

Liquid immediately flooded her core. She felt him begin to harden against her. She felt hot all over.

Since they'd arrived at his house, he'd significantly upped his seduction efforts and while she'd been silently begging for it the last several days, it suddenly made her extremely nervous. She quickly stepped back, out of the safety and comfort of his arms.

"Tempting, but maybe we should just stick to the tour for now." But damn if she didn't want to find out what sort of pleasures Dev could lavish on her body. No doubt he'd ruin her for any other man.

"Hmm. That's too bad. It would be an immensely enjoyable way to spend the day," he winked. Every sensual word he uttered chipped away at the thick defensive layer she'd built over the last year.

He grabbed her hand, tugging her along. "Come."

Kate was in awe; each room was more splendid than the next. The entire manor was decorated in traditional home decor, but with an old-world feel. It had warm neutral colors and felt cozy and inviting, despite its expansiveness. The color scheme was earth-toned and while it had masculine undertones, she noted plenty of throw pillows, decorative lamps and colorful matching throw rugs to give it a pleasant, homey feel. Oddly enough, it felt like Dev.

They walked through a great room, media room, a formal ballroom and a game room with an enormous bar, where she met two other very attractive men that worked for Dev playing pool. Ren was also there, lounging in an oversized black leather chair, but it fit his large frame perfectly.

"Kate, this is Manny Juarez and Thane Jensen. Manny, Thane, this is Kate Martin. Manny and Thane work for me."

She shook each of their hands. "Pleased to meet you."

"Pleased to meet you too, ma'am," Manny quipped. Thane just nodded. He seemed like a man who could get his point across without even talking. "Please, call me Kate. Ma'am is reserved for my mother."

Manny graced her with a gorgeous smile in return. Wow, she was the ugly duckling in this group.

She turned her attention to Ren. "Hi, Ren. Too bad you couldn't join us for breakfast. Leo's a fantastic cook."

Ren patted his stomach, smiling. "Don't I know it. Didn't Dev keep you entertained enough, doll? If you're bored with him already, I'd be happy to keep you company."

Thane snipped, "Come on, ladies. Stop flirting with Dev's woman and get back to the game. I need to finish whooping your ass, man."

Dev's woman? What the hell?

Manny laughed. "Dream on, asshole. You just wanna wind this up so you can tap that sugar you found last night."

"Fuck you."

"No thanks. You're not my type, dickhead."

Kate suddenly felt a weird pressure in the room, like the other day at the police station. Dev glared hard at Thane and Manny.

"No one leaves tonight." Both men straightened, all playfulness gone. They both spoke at the same time. "Yes, my...sir."

Manny whispered to Thane, "Looks like you'll be doing the ol' five knuckle Olympics tonight, dude." That earned him the bird.

Dev directed his next comment to Ren. "And you...fuck off. My company is perfectly entertaining." Ren shook his head, smirking.

Ooookay...time to lighten the mood. "Hey, I'm not too bad at pool. Maybe one of you would like to take me on later?"

Manny's shit-eating grin returned. "Just say the word, babe." His eyes flicked to Dev's and the grin quickly faded.

Tension immediately crackled in the air and something significant seemed to pass between the two. Dev might as well have pissed in a circle around her. Asshole. She was unreasonably attracted to him, yes, but he didn't have any ownership over her and she certainly wasn't his "woman," as Thane indicated. If she wanted to play pool with them, she would. Hell, if she wanted to do anything with any one of them, she would...if she were attracted to any of them. Sadly, she wasn't.

"You're on, Manny. See you tomorrow. Anyone else have the gonads to take me on?"

Ren laughed hard. Manny joined in and Thane just gaped at her.

"Come on, love. We aren't through with the tour yet." Dev placed his hand on the small of her back, gently ushering her out of the room. Before exiting, she stopped, turning back to the guys.

"Oh, and I expect you to bring your A game. Don't go easy on me just because I'm a girl." Dev stiffened beside her. Guess he didn't want her playing with his employees. Well, tough shit. She would do whatever the hell she wanted.

"I wouldn't dream of it," Manny replied, his smile widening once again. Oh...this was gonna be fun!

They resumed their tour. The whole house boasted tall ceilings and large, expansive windows that spilt in a vast amount of sunlight. While they didn't go in them all, Dev also told her he had seven bedrooms and eleven bathrooms. There were two dining rooms, one larger than where they ate, and a massive kitchen with granite countertops, all stainless steel Electrolux appliances, a subzero refrigerator and a twenty-foot island. A suspended hanging rack full of copper pots and pans completed the look. She loved to cook. Maybe she'd get an opportunity to do it tomorrow in a kitchen that would make even Giada jealous.

She loved the entire house, but her favorite room was an office with three walls full of books from floor to ceiling. There was an eclectic mixture of genres both fiction and non-fiction, from poetry to fantasy. She noticed even a couple vampire romance novels, which she thought was rather funny. There were the classics, like *Twenty Thousand Leagues Under the Sea, A Tale of Two Cities,* and *Dracula* and many books she'd never heard of before. She could spend days on end in there. Dev allowed her ample time to wander around each magnificent room, never making her feel rushed.

They ended in a gym that was nicer than most public ones and she was dying to try out the state of the art treadmill. Since she'd been spending so much time with Dev this week, she'd been very remiss in keeping up with her workouts.

"Like what you see?" Dev asked as she gawked around.

Yep, in more ways than one. "Yes. Would you mind if I worked out for a bit?"

"Not at all. I have some work I'm behind on anyway."

They made their way silently through the maze to her bedroom where they stood scrutinizing each other. Her heart beat faster when he leaned over and placed his soft lips on hers.

"I'll send Ren to help you find your way back to the gym," he whispered.

"I think I can find my way just fine," she replied softly.

"All the same, wait for him." At her furrowed brow, he added, "Please."

"Sure. Fine."

His eyes turned positively molten as he backed her up against the wall and threaded his fingers through her hair. This time his kiss was anything but soft and gentle. It was rough, passionate and ripe with unfulfilled promises. Her legs went weak and her hands came to his taut biceps to steady herself. This...*this* is what she'd been waiting on for four days and by god, he did not disappoint. But all too soon he pulled away, leaning his forehead to hers, her head still bracketed in his strong hands. His penetrating dark eyes, which seemed brighter than usual, bore directly into her soul.

"Fuck, I want you, Kate."

Her already erratic breathing hitched and she couldn't speak through the constriction of her throat.

"You will be mine, love. Very soon." His lips crashed to hers and before she knew what happened he was striding quickly down the long hallway, leaving her to watch his fine ass walk away.

She let her head fall against the wall and thought about his cryptic words this morning. *'I think I'm falling for you harder every minute I'm in your presence, love.'* And *'You will be mine, love. Very soon.'*

This was not how a fling was supposed to go. She didn't normally do casual, but she knew that's all this could ever be and she'd accepted it. So why was he saying things that made it sound so much more permanent?

And what the hell was she supposed to make of it?

CHAPTER 19

Kate

A workout would do her good. Get rid of some of the sexual tension Dev had built in her all morning. She didn't understand her insane attraction to him at all. She felt inexplicably drawn to him. Like she'd known him her entire life. Was it those erotic dreams of him—or of a man that looked just like him?

She planned on running, lifting, and practicing her martial arts until she was ready to drop. That ought to chase away the urge to jump Dev's bones every time she was around him. Maybe for today. Rinse and repeat tomorrow if necessary. She would be too tired to think about kissing him, about running her fingers through his dark locks, holding his head to her breast as he licked and sucked her nipple. *God, Kate, stop it already!!*

She'd changed into her gym clothes and was just pulling her hair into a ponytail when a soft knock came at her door.

"Hey, gorgeous, getting settled okay?" Ren's hundred-watt smile had to draw women like moths to an open flame. He was unreasonably good-looking and she really liked him, but in a brotherly sort of way. She smiled in return.

"Yes, thanks."

"Is there anything I can get you? Anything at all you need?"

"No, I think I'm all set, but thanks. I appreciate it."

She hesitated a minute, not sure if she wanted to know the answer, then casually asked, "So...what's the deal with Giselle and Dev? Are they an...item? She looked like she wanted to scratch my eyes out yesterday."

Ren let a smirk curl the corners of his lips. "Jealous, eh?"

"No, of course not. Don't be ridiculous. Why would I be jealous? I was just curious, is all. She looked like she'd sooner scorch my face off with a blowtorch then let me in the house. I just assumed it was maybe because they were a couple or something and she didn't want another woman anywhere near her man."

God she hoped that wasn't the case, but wouldn't it be just like a guy to try to have his cake and eat it too. At least the men she'd dated did. And if Dev fell into that adulterous category, it would shatter any last shred of hope she knew lie buried deep within her that there *was* a decent man waiting out there...she just hadn't found him yet.

He studied her for a moment before answering. "No, they are not a couple. They have never been a couple. Giselle is his employee. I'm quite sure jealousy wasn't the issue."

She let out a breathe she didn't realize she'd been holding, her relief tangible. "Oh, so she's just a bitch, then."

Ren laughed, loud and deep. "I like you Kate." He wiped the tears leaking from the corner his eyes as he caught his breath. Kate couldn't help laughing along with him.

"So, you ready to hit the gym?"

"Ready. Just let me get my music."

She grabbed her iPhone and headphones and headed down to the gym with Ren, making comfortable small talk the entire way.

———————

She'd been working hard for over an hour and a half now. She'd run five miles, deciding to forgo weight lifting in lieu of spending more time practicing her Jeet Kune Do. She hadn't practiced much lately, and with the possibility of being in danger, she thought it'd be a good idea to practice.

She'd secretly been hoping Dev would make an appearance, but so far he was a no show. She missed him, and how stupid was that? It had only been a couple hours since she last saw him.

Thinking back to the other men she'd dated since high school, she could resolutely say that none of them affected her mind, body and soul the way Dev did. When they were in the same vicinity, desire fired like sparks through her body and all rational thought fled. Yes, he was the most handsome man she'd ever met, but she couldn't understand her unreasonable attraction to him. It was completely out of her control and she was never out of control of anything in her life. Well...except her dreams.

She'd finished her workout and, true to goal, she was exhausted. She was looking forward to a shower and maybe a bite to eat before settling down for a bit to do some research, then hitting the hay. She wasn't quite sure she knew how to get back to her room, but thought she'd muddle through. Eventually she'd find it. This place needed a map upon check-in. She was trying to remember how they got down here so she could retrace her steps when the door opened and in walked Dev.

Oh, wow. He was mouthwatering. Dressed in cream-colored slacks and a soft, black button-down shirt, he looked freshly showered.

"Hi." Curse her for sounding breathless.

"Hi yourself. Did you have a good workout?" He walked across the gym toward her.

"I did." She held her hand, palm facing him. "You probably don't want to get too close, though. I'm sure I smell pretty rank at the moment." Her face was probably red as a beet, too. Lovely.

"Oh, I doubt that. You always seem to smell good to me." At his compliment, she felt herself blush. He ushered her out of the gym, starting their way back to her room. "Join me for dinner."

"I don't know, Dev. I have a lot of research to do." Dinner together had become their 'thing', but was it smart to spend any more time than necessary with him? That would be a big fat N-O.

"Come on. You have to eat. We can't break tradition now," he winked.

"I don't know—"

"Please, Kate. You can catch up your research tomorrow."

Unable to say no, she agreed. "Okay...twist my arm."

His winning smile zinged directly to her sex. Good god...she was in so much trouble.

CHAPTER 20

Kate

Kate tossed and turned, unable to let sleep take her. After dinner, they'd talked and even played a game of pool, which she'd won fair and square. He'd given her another soul-sucking kiss before telling her goodnight and once again, she'd been disappointed. She wanted his hands all over her. She wanted his cock pushing into her body. She wanted his mouth on her. She wanted him to take her completely. She wanted that in real life, not just in her dreams, and it was right in front of her for the taking. All she had to do was *let* herself have it.

She felt like one of those wishy-washy females she *always* made fun of. Kate was not flighty. She knew what she wanted—at least up until a few days ago. Now she felt like she'd been playing a very bad game of Atari, watching that tiny blip ping back and forth between two sides, the paddles too small to keep the stupid thing from slipping by.

Sleep with him, not sleep with him. Sleep with him. No. Ahhhh!!! If she slept with him, a broken heart was inevitable. She got emotionally attached. As much as she tried to convince herself otherwise, she just didn't know if she could do casual. But other women did it, so why couldn't she? She hoped to god they caught this kidnapper soon so she could just be on her way and then she'd be fine. She could then get Devon Fallinsworth back into her dreams where he belonged.

Exhaustion finally took her. She fell sleep hoping for another dreamless night, but it wasn't meant to be. Instead, she dreamed of Sarah Hill. Sarah was tied down spread eagle to a steel table in what appeared to be a surgical room of some sort. Her feet and hands were bound. She was naked and appeared to be sleeping, but Kate knew better. She had an IV in her arm, with tubing that led to a bag filled with clear liquid. There were several naked vampires in the room with her. *Oh my God.* She was going to be sick. Who would do such a horrible thing to such a young, beautiful girl?

She bolted up in bed, screaming and crying. Before she knew what was happening, Dev was there, pulling her into his arms. "Kate, love, what's the matter? Are you hurt?" She couldn't speak, sobs racking her body.

"Talk to me, love. What happened?" She continued to weep on his shoulder, soaking his shirt. "Kate, please. Talk to me. You're scaring me."

"Th-They h-have her tied d-down. L-like, l-like an animal. I think she might have b-been, been—"

"Who? What are you talking about, love? Did you have another dream?" He held her trembling body tightly.

"I think she might have been r-raped."

"Ah, Jesus. Sarah?"

"Yes. I don't know if she's even alive!" She sobbed even harder.

"It's okay, Kate. It's going to be okay."

Dev held her until she started to calm. A short time later, a soft knock came at the door. Dev answered. "Come in."

"Your tea, sir."

He nodded toward the nightstand. Leo set down the tea and quietly left the room. Dev continued to stroke her back, whispering reassuring words in her ear. "Here, love, have some tea."

She sat back and took the cup he handed her. How did Leo know a cup of tea was just the thing she needed? He must have heard her scream.

"Thanks."

"Tell me what you saw, Kate. Try to remember all of the details, okay?"

She shook her head. "I can't. I can't think about it."

Dev put his finger under her chin and gently lifted it so their eyes met. "Kate, I know this is hard and I'm so sorry. I wish you didn't have to go through this. I would do *anything* to take it away. Anything. But you have a very special gift. One that I think will help us find Sarah. And the others. And the son-of-a-bitch that took them." He placed a soft kiss on her lips. "Please, tell me what you saw."

She took a deep breath. "O-okay." The horrible words tumbled out and she told him everything she could remember.

"Were there any other people in the room? Could you see a window or anything that would tell us where she's being held?"

She shook her head. "No, I don't remember seeing anyone else in the room. I couldn't take my eyes off her to see anything else. I'm sorry. I'm not much help."

"It's okay, love." He took the tea and set it back down on the nightstand. He lay down on the bed and pulled her to him, settling her into his side. Her head lay in the crook of his shoulder. "Go back to sleep, love. I'll be right here." He kissed her temple and gently stroked her back.

As much as she didn't want to accept his comfort, his kindness, she simply couldn't turn it away. It felt too good. *He* felt too good.

"Thank you," she whispered.

"For what?"

"For staying with me."

"No thanks necessary, love. Honestly, there's nowhere I'd rather be."

CHAPTER 21

Kate

Kate woke up with a hard body spooning behind her and a steel arm around her waist. *What the...?* It took her a minute to clear the morning fog from her brain and remember where she was. And who shared her bed. When she did, a plethora of feelings ran through her. The fear and sadness she felt for Sarah. The comfort and safety she felt in Dev's arms. Lust and desire for the man who held her tightly against his chest burned through every cell. She could feel the evidence of his desire for her pressing against her backside as well.

Dev nuzzled her neck and lightly bit her earlobe, letting it slip gently through his teeth. "Good morning."

"Morning." She looked over her shoulder to see him staring hungrily into her eyes. It was a look he had often, but she could hardly get used to the fact it was for her.

"How did you sleep after your dream?"

"Good, actually. Dreamless."

"I'm glad." His eyes flicked back and forth between her eyes and her lips. He closed the short distance between them to kiss her and she quickly threw hand over her mouth to stop him. He frowned at her.

"Morning breath," she mumbled.

He reached up and removed her hand. "I don't give a

shit about morning breath, love. I want to kiss you. Now."

He didn't wait for a response. He held her head in place and took her lips in a hot, heated kiss, invading her mouth with his tongue, exploring every inch of it. She moaned and turned to face him fully, bodies glued together from chest to thigh. She wound her arms around his neck and tilted her head for a better angle to attack his lips. His hard length was pressing into her stomach and she reveled in her feminine power to bring a man like Dev to such an aroused state.

He growled and ran his hands down her sides to the bottom of her tank top. He slipped a hand inside and slowly ran it up her torso, over her ribs to the curve of her breast. He cupped her breast, kneading it but avoiding her nipple. She broke the kiss. She moaned and her head fell back as he traced her puffy areola lightly with his long finger. "Oh, God."

He continued to avoid her nipple as he kissed, nipped and sucked his way along her jaw, down her neck. "Don't tease, Dev."

She felt like that's all he'd been doing for almost a week now. Teasing, tempting her with the pleasures he could lavish on her.

"Tell me what you want, love." He scraped his sharp teeth along her neck. She could hardly breathe.

"You know what I want."

"No, I don't. Do you want me to touch your nipple? Do you want me to suck it into my mouth?" He licked a hot, wet path back up to her mouth. "Tell me to suck your nipple, Kate," he whispered against her mouth. *Oh God.*

"Dev—*please.*"

He kissed her with dominating force. "Tell me."

Kiss.

"Say the words, Kate."

Kiss.

"I need to hear you say it."

She'd never had any man say such erotic things to her. She couldn't deny him. "Yes. Please suck my nipple. Please."

She hadn't even gotten the words all the way out before his fingers began plucking her, elongating the hardened nub. He pinched and rolled it between his fingers, while he ravaged her mouth. She'd read of women coming from nipple play, but never really believed it was possible. Until now. She was seconds away from an orgasm and he'd only touched her breasts.

Dev

"Dev, Olivia will be here within the hour."

Fuuuuuck. Of all the shitty timing. All he wanted to do was devour the woman held tightly in his arms. He was ready to snap. *"We'll be down shortly."*

But he couldn't let her go without honoring her request first. That wouldn't be very gentlemanly of him, now would it? And he was nothing if not a gentleman with a woman. *His woman.*

He swiftly lifted her tank and took her ripe, dark pink nipple into his mouth. Kate gasped and her hands flew up to cradle his head, holding him to the finest thing he'd ever tasted. She moaned his name. Sweet Jesus, he did not want to stop. He wanted to lick and suck every inch of her delectable body. He wanted to keep her in bed, naked, for a month straight and even that wouldn't be enough. He knew he would never get enough of this woman. *Mine.*

He reluctantly tore himself away from her sweet, tight nubbin and cupped her cheeks in his hands, kissing her hard and quick on the lips. He put his forehead to hers and groaned. "As much as I really do *not* want to stop, we have to."

She blinked. "What? No, we don't." Her eyes were dilated and glazed with lust. She tried pulling him back down to her kiss-swollen lips.

He groaned. "I'm sorry, love. There's someone coming to the house within the hour that we need to see."

He gently kissed her. He needed to reassure her of his desire. "Kate, Jesus, I don't want to stop, but there is too much I want to do with you—*to you*—to rush this." He rolled his hips, pushing his erection into her mound, eliciting a groan from them both. "I want you more than I want my next breath, but if I don't stop now, we won't be leaving this bedroom all day."

She gazed into his eyes. "You really want me?"

He laughed. Taking her hand, he settled it over his erection. Squeezing, he moved their hands together up and down his impressive length. They both groaned and her eyes closed.

"Look at me, Kate." She opened her eyes, which were still half-mast. "This is just for you, love. Only you. My dick has been granite hard for days now—*for you*."

He stopped while he still could and reluctantly got off the bed. It was difficult to walk away when his cock was like a boomerang...drawn back toward her. "I'll be back in forty-five minutes or so. Is that enough time for you to get ready?"

She looked dazed. "Ah, yes. Yes, that's fine. Thanks." She'd pulled herself into a seated position on the bed.

Dev walked back over to her, leaning over. Cupping her cheeks in his hands, he brushed his thumb over her lower lip. "I want to finish this later. Please say yes."

She didn't even hesitate. "Yes."

"Right answer. See you shortly." He leaned in and kissed her gently at first, deepening the kiss quickly.

They both moaned again. Leaning toward her ear, he whispered, "I can't wait to feel your tight pussy milking my cock when I make you come, Kate."

———————————

Kate

With those parting words, he left her staring after him; leaving so fast she didn't even realize he was gone.

Oh. My. Sweet. Lord.

She flopped back down and lay there for a few minutes wondering what in the hell was happening. She thought she'd been in love with John and was ready to spend her life with him, but the feelings she had for John versus the feelings she was quickly developing for Dev were like night and day. Every look, every touch heated her body more thoroughly than she'd ever known was possible. Dev was like forbidden fruit, once eaten she wanted it all the more. She understood Adam and Eve so much better now.

She threw her arms over her face. She would have to—*hell she wanted to*—surrender to her physical desires for him. No doubt about it. After this hot little episode, she'd be the queen of fools *not* to sleep with him. The question was, while she may surrender her body, how on earth was she was going to keep from surrendering her heart, getting it broken to smithereens in the process?

Of that, she had no damn clue.

CHAPTER 22

Dev

They stepped into his office. On the credenza, Leo had set an assortment of pastries, bagels, and fruit as well as some hot choices, like eggs and pancakes. He also had juices and coffee. He wanted her full and sated—in more ways than nutritional sustenance allowed. Goddamn the luck.

His want for her was burning out of control. He could hardly think of anything else but getting his cock inside of her body. He was getting desperate. His animal instinct to bond with her, marking her as *his*, was fiercely powerful. His sanity was hanging on by the thinnest of threads. If he didn't have her soon, he was worried his animal nature would take the man in him out of the driver's seat, and he could not let that happen. This morning was the second time in the last twenty-four hours that he'd held his sausage hostage and while he'd found release, it was empty and lonely.

"Another big spread?" Kate asked, as she eyed the big feast spread on the credenza. The pink sweater she wore draped her curves perfectly and she wore a different, but equally faded, pair of curve-hugging jeans.

"Only the best for you, love."

She laughed. "Thank you."

As she filled her plate, Dev came up behind her, wrapping his arms around her waist. He kissed her neck. "It's purely selfish, I can assure you. I wanted to be sure you had plenty of energy for the hours upon hours of pleasure I have in store for you later. Did you know that giving oral sex burns about a hundred calories per half hour?"

Kate began choking on the piece of watermelon she'd put in her mouth. Dev slapped her back repeatedly. "Are you okay?"

"Y-yes."

Cough.

"I'm good."

Cough.

After her coughing was under control, she turned, wrapping her arms around his neck, smiling flirtatiously at him. He wiped away a stray tear. Leaning up, she kissed his lips, whispering against them, "Make sure you eat up, then." She kissed him quick and turned back around to continue filling her plate.

It took a second for his brain to register her double entendre. He laughed as she looked playfully over her shoulder, a mischievous smile lighting her face.

Grabbing her plate, he set it down on the credenza. He picked her up in his arms and carried her over to the large leather sofa. He laid her down, draping his big frame over her smaller one, careful to keep one knee on the floor, so his heavy weight wasn't crushing her.

"Why, Mr. Fallinsworth, whatever are you doing?"

"You told me to eat up. I plan on doing that. Right now." He crushed his lips to hers before she could challenge him. His hand snaked underneath her jeans, palming and kneading her rounded ass. She moaned softly into his mouth.

Just then the office door flew open and in walked Ren with a woman in tow. Dev simply turned his head.

"Fucking knock next time." Kate was trying frantically to push him off of her.

"Move," she grunted.

Sighing, he lifted himself off and helped her up, but placed a possessive arm around her waist. She struggled against him, trying to gain her own space, but he would have none of it. She was his and she would stay by his side. He'd watched her face turn about five shades of red since Ren and Olivia stepped through the door. It was...endearing.

"Sorry for the interruption, *boss*." Ren had a wry smirk on his face. Fucker wasn't sorry at all.

Kate was staring at the floor, her face a nice shade of crimson. He loved blushing. It brought the blood closer to the surface of the skin. He gave her a reassuring squeeze while he inhaled deeply, relishing in her intoxicating scent. "Knock next time. *Asshole*." Ren's smirk got wider.

"Kate, this is Olivia Morton. Olivia, Kate Martin. Why don't we sit?"

Kate extended her hand, which Olivia graciously took. "Nice to meet you Olivia."

"Likewise."

---

*K*ate

Kate was absolutely mortified, her entire face burned. Every time Dev touched her, it was like every brain cell flashed a neon sign that said *DO ME*. She knew someone was coming, yet she let Dev feel her up anyway. *Classy, Kate. Real classy.*

She was taken back to the time her mom walked in on her and Alex, her first boyfriend. They had gone to her bedroom to "study," of course making out instead. Her mom opened the door and caught Alex with his hand on her breast, over the shirt, but needless to say, finding your sixteen-year-old daughter getting felt up didn't sit well with her mom. She freaked, lectured, and grounded her for a month. Poor Alex was terrified to come around again and they broke up a short time later.

Strange things were happening to her now, had been since she'd arrived here yesterday. She'd actually sensed someone was coming into the room right before Ren and Olivia had entered. How could she sense someone was coming? And why did she keep hearing words whispering through her head? Like in the bedroom earlier, she swore she heard Dev say *mine*, but since his mouth was wrapped completely around her nipple, that wasn't possible. Add this to the irrationally extreme attraction she felt for Dev and she was feeling a bit overwhelmed.

Dev brought over her untouched plate and handed it to her with a wink. *Jackass.* She watched him walk to his desk chair. Hmmm...make that *sweet ass.*

"So, Kate. Olivia's here because she has a similar...talent as you."

Her eyebrows drew together and she looked at him questioningly. "Talent? What talent?"

"She also has dreams." Kate sat up straight, looking back and forth between Olivia and Dev.

"What are you talking about? What dreams?" She could hardly catch her breath. She was angry, scared and hopeful, all at the same time.

Olivia, who sat on the couch next to Kate, spoke up, gently grabbing Kate's hands in hers. "I have dreams about real events, too, Kate. I've had them my entire life, just like you have. I know what you're going through and I want to help you."

Olivia put Kate at ease and she instantly liked her. She was a petite blonde, with a body that obviously was honed by many hours in the gym. Her piercing blue eyes were framed with long, dark lashes and she looked to be about her age.

"How can you help? The only way you can help is to make them go away. And I haven't been able to find anyone yet that can do that." God, if someone could help her get rid of these horrific dreams, she would be free. Free at last. *Was that even possible?*

Olivia gazed at her with empathy. The hope that had quickly developed was crushed just as fast. "Kate, I know it seems like a burden and honestly, sometimes it is, but you have a *gift.* A gift, which, once you learn to hone and perfect it, makes it extremely powerful. And puts you in control versus feeling helpless. I can help you do that. I can help you control your gift instead of letting it control you."

Kate shook her head. "No. Nope. There's no controlling my dreams. They control me. You have no idea what kinds of dreams plague me, Olivia. If I could control them, I'd make them go away. I'm sorry that you wasted your time, but there's no way you can help me." Tears sprung into her eyes. She could barely speak. "I wish you could."

Olivia grabbed Kate into a tight hug. Over her shoulder, Kate's eyes locked onto Dev's and his were full of sympathy, pain and...*caring*?

"I can help you, Kate. I know you don't know me and have no reason to trust me, but please do. I can't make them go away, but I can help you view your dreams in an entirely different way. I've done it myself. I've helped others do it. I *can* help you."

She pulled away, holding Kate's gaze. "I *can* help you, Kate. Trust me."

Kate shook her head. "I don't think so, Olivia. I'm sorry you've come all this way, but I just don't think I can."

Dev came over, crouching in front of where she sat.

He held her hands in his. "Kate, love, I know this is difficult. Sometimes the easier solution is to bury your head in the sand. But most often the *easier* decision isn't the *right* one. Just give it a try. One day, that's all I'm asking. If you don't feel this is useful, I won't ask her to come back. You have my word."

She'd buried her head in the sand for too many years. Hell, she'd been trying to figure out this dream thing for half her life. Maybe she was going about it all wrong. Maybe trying to stop the dreams wasn't the right answer. It hadn't worked so far. If she was cursed with this problem, at least she should learn how to properly deal with it.

"Okay. I'll try."

CHAPTER 23

MIKE

It was a good day for a road trip. Mike and his partner, Jake, had driven to the Northwestern campus, stopping for lunch along the way. His stomach was revolting against the bacon double cheeseburger and biggie-size fries. He'd been popping Zantac and Pepto for the last hour. He needed to lay off that shit. The combo of grease, pills and alcohol was eating a hole in his stomach. Or was it the job? He was headed for an early grave and he couldn't afford to fill it until he'd accomplished his objective. Maybe he should pull a Jared and eat two meals a day at Subway.

Northwestern's main Evanston, Illinois, campus was really quite picturesque. Along Lake Michigan's shoreline, the vast campus boasted large oak and pine trees, colorful vine-covered buildings and several unique churches. Once parked, Jake and Mike headed to Swift Hall where the Psychology Department was housed. They were going to pay a surprise visit to Professor Duncan Bailey, the last person to see Sarah alive.

As they walked through the snowy campus, Mike's thoughts turned back to Kate. Fallinsworth looked like he wanted to devour Kate on the spot and knowing that he'd followed her, Mike was genuinely worried for her safety. He never should have let that vamp go after her. *Fuck!*

"What, man?"

"Huh?"

"You said 'fuck.' What's up?"

Did he say that out loud? "Nothin'. S'all good." Jake shrugged his shoulders. Mike knew he'd been acting moody lately, but he couldn't help the nagging feeling that something big was about to go down.

They arrived at Professor Bailey's office and he wasn't there. His assistant told them he'd be back in forty-five minutes, so they sat and waited, making small talk with the pretty, young brunette.

Forty minutes later, Professor Bailey walked down the hall toward them studying a piece of paper in his hand. As he spotted them, his steps faltered. He went pale and looked like he was about to be sick. Mike thought for a second the guy was gonna beat feet.

Mike and Jake stood and headed toward the professor. "Professor Bailey, we've been waiting for you. I'm Detective Thatcher and this is my partner, Detective Keller. We're from the Milwaukee PD and we have some questions for you regarding the disappearance of Sarah Hill." They flipped their credentials to the professor. "Do you mind if we take a seat in your office?"

Professor Bailey stood there. He looked nervous, his eyes darting around like he expected someone to jump him at any minute. "I've already answered all of the questions I can from the local police department. I'm afraid you've made a trip for nothing, gentlemen. Now if you'll excuse me, I have a very busy day."

"I'm sorry, Professor, but this isn't a request. We need a few minutes of your time, so we can either do that here or I'll be happy to escort you to the local PD and ask my questions there. Your choice."

A flash of anger crossed the professor's face. "My office is fine," he clipped. The professor headed toward his office. "Mary, hold my calls until we're through here. And call Frank. Tell him I'll be late for our one o'clock appointment."

"Yes, Professor. Right away."

Bailey took a seat, but Mike and Jake remained standing. A little intimidation tactic wouldn't hurt. The bastard was hiding something. He felt it in his gut.

He took out his notepad and pen. "So, Professor, tell us about your relationship with Sarah Hill."

Professor Bailey genuinely looked taken aback. So that wasn't his angle, then. "I don't have a relationship with Sarah Hill, Detective. She was my student, plain and simple. Quite frankly I'm offended you'd suggest otherwise."

"I meant no offense, Professor. We're simply trying to find a missing young girl and you were the last person to see her. As you can imagine, we're trying to put all of the pieces together so we can locate her as quickly as possible."

Professor Bailey gave a clipped nod.

"So, on the sixth of February, the night of her disappearance, what did you and Sarah discuss?"

If it was possible, Professor Bailey paled even more. He cleared his throat. "Nothing important. We discussed a project that she was having trouble with. She needed some guidance. It was a short conversation, that's all."

Jake piped up. "What was the project? *Specifically*?"

"I don't really recall. I'd have to go back and look at my notes and the projects due in class at that time."

Mike raised his eyebrows. "That was two weeks ago, Professor. You can't remember what project was due two weeks ago?" He let his voice drip with sarcasm.

A look of indignation crossed the Bailey's face. "Detectives, I have several research projects underway and I have many students helping me with various aspects of them. In addition, I am responsible for the entire Psychology Department curriculum. You can't possibly think that I'd remember what each and every student was doing. I can barely remember what I ate for breakfast this morning."

Mike wryly smirked, one corner of his mouth turning up. "Personally, if I was the last person to see a girl that went missing shortly afterward—*call me crazy*—but I'm pretty sure I'd remember what the conversation was about."

Jake spoke up. "We'll wait."

Professor Bailey flicked his eyes to Jake's. "Wait for what?"

"For you to look at your notes, Professor." When Bailey looked confused, he prodded, "To determine what the project was about? We'll wait."

"W-Well, that could take a while, Detective. Why don't you come back later this afternoon and I'll have that pulled for you."

Mike smiled, but it didn't reach his eyes. *So you can run, dickhead? Think again.*

"We'll wait."

"Of course, Detectives. My apologies. I do want to help. I've had a lot on my mind lately and even the little things have been slipping my mind. If you'll wait just outside with Mary, I'll check my notes and be out shortly." He pressed the intercom button. "Mary, would you be so kind as to get these detectives each a cup of coffee? They'll be waiting in the reception area for just a bit."

There was only one way in and out of the office, so there wasn't a chance the professor could escape, but he wouldn't put anything past the slimy bastard.

"That's a kind offer, professor, but we'll wait in here. We've got nothing but time on our hands today."

The professor paled even further, but went to work tapping on his computer. Mike sat back patiently waiting for whatever bullshit he was going to spew at them. And now that he'd seen his reaction, bullshit was exactly what it would be.

CHAPTER 24

Kate

Kate and Olivia had been working all day, with the exception of a short break for lunch. She was getting tired. She'd fought Olivia for the first couple of hours, insisting Olivia didn't understand the sickening nature of her dreams, but Olivia had then shared a few dreams of her own. Kate had been confused as to why she dreamed specifically of Sarah, and she saw others being held as well, but her dreams seemed centrally focused on Sarah. Olivia had explained the dreams were random in that way. Even she hadn't figured out how to dream of something specific when she wanted. She didn't think it could be done.

Olivia really seemed to understand what Kate was going through. Wise beyond her years was the best way she could describe her. She felt like a kindred spirit. When Kate questioned her on how she developed her own techniques, she would only say that someone with the same abilities helped her many years ago. It gave Kate enough hope to really try her techniques.

Kate had spent the last several hours meditating and visualizing. Olivia encouraged her to step back from her surroundings and take in the entire picture. Kind of like an out-of-body experience. Remove emotion. View her dreams from a clinical perspective. That way she could see other things—clues—that she would otherwise miss. Even the smallest detail may be a clue, Olivia told her. And when Kate had these disturbing dreams, even the smallest clue could lead to a solution. In this case, it could lead to finding Sarah and the other kidnapped girls.

Olivia had even put her under hypnosis, which before today she didn't believe in. While Dev and Ren had apparently filled Olivia in on Kate's dreams, Kate repeated them in detail, sans the fangs, getting frustrated when she couldn't remember the details Olivia was pushing her to remember.

Was there anyone else there? Describe the equipment? Was there anything that could be considered unique in the room? Emblems? Windows? Were there any weapons? How many entry points were there to the room? Did you hear any noises? People talking?

No!

She didn't know of any of those things! She didn't hear anything. She didn't see anything else. She couldn't tear her eyes away from Sarah tied down to a table.

However, during the hypnosis session, she'd apparently told Olivia some things she wasn't able to consciously remember. Like, where she was being held appeared to be set up like a lab. There were beakers, empty vials and those filled with blood, medical and surgical type of equipment. Disturbingly, there was a row of infant incubators in the corner of the room. Empty. She also remembered there *was* a man in the corner of the room. He was short, heavy and balding with black-rimmed glasses. She couldn't see him completely as his profile was to her, but when she awoke, Dev had called for a sketch artist to draw what she could remember. Unfortunately, she didn't remember anything that would help them find *where* Sarah or the others were being held.

Olivia told her to use the techniques they practiced today next time she dreamed of Sarah. Reluctantly, while she wanted to help further, truth be told, she didn't *want* to dream of this anymore. She just wanted the damn dreams to stop. And then she felt incredibly guilty for thinking that.

Dev came back into the office. "Okay, we're done for the day, Olivia. Kate's tired and she's been put through enough for one day. Thank you for coming on such short notice and for your help. Tell Monti I said hello."

"Anytime, Dev." Turning to Kate, she said, "It was a pleasure to meet you Kate. Keep practicing the techniques. Meditation really does help with this process so try to carve out at least an hour a day to do that. It helps you center your thoughts and emotions." Olivia surprised Kate by pulling her into a quick hug.

As Olivia picked up her purse and coat, she turned back to Kate. "I'm sure I'll be seeing you around, Kate."

"I doubt that. I'll be leaving soon." That thought actually made her sad. "But it was a pleasure to meet you, Olivia, and thanks so much for your help."

Olivia's gaze quickly flicked to Dev and back to Kate. She simply winked, giving her an *oh-I'll-be-seeing-you-again* smile, and walked out the door.

Dev turned his attention to her, softening his voice as he spoke. "You did a really great job today, Kate. I'm proud of you."

"Pfft. I didn't really do anything, Dev. I feel like I could have—*should* have—done more. I don't feel like we're any closer to finding Sarah than we were days ago."

He walked over to her, stopping so close that if either took a breath, their chests would be touching. Her breaths quickened. *Damn you, dampened panties!* Dev suddenly sported a big knowing grin, almost like he knew. Impossible.

As quickly as his smile came, it faded and desire immediately filled its place. His eyes became heavy and hooded and he readied his lips. She wasn't sure which look she liked most...the glow of his smile, or the heat of his desire. Both. She liked both. Equally.

He gently held her chin in place, while he ever so slowly lowered his mouth to hers. Eyes locked on one other. He gently nipped at her lower lip, dragging it through his teeth. *Oh God.* He leaned back in, doing the same to her upper. Finally, he kissed her entire mouth, sweeping inside, dueling his tongue with hers. It was a slow, sensual, panty-dropping kiss. A kiss that promised much more pleasure was coming—*pun intended.*

Holy moly...the man knew what he was doing. That should have sent warning bells off, and in truth, it did. But for some stupid reason she pushed them to the back of her mind.

He wrapped his arms around her, pulling her flush against his hard, sinewy body. The man was sex incarnate. Their mouths worked feverishly against each other's. She thought her entire body would burst into flames. He walked her backwards until he had her pinned against the wall.

"God help me I can't wait any longer, Kate. I need to be inside you," he whispered against her lips. She shut off her mind and surrendered to the moment. Surrendered to what she'd wanted for days. For *months.* Consequences be damned, she was going to have him. She would simply need to reinforce the guard around her heart. This was just sex, Kate. *Just sex.*

Kate wound her hands into his hair, pulling him to her mouth again, meeting his tongue stroke for stroke. His breath was a heady mix of mint, bourbon and man. He tasted like light...and darkness. She never wanted to let him go. His left hand palmed the back of her head, angling her where he wanted. He dominated the kiss, taking, but giving in equal measure. She could feel his arousal, hard and pulsing against her stomach. She was absolutely drenched.

Dev broke the kiss, his breathing as ragged as hers. "Not here, love."

Before she could comprehend what happened, Dev swept her up into his bulky arms and carried her quickly to her bedroom. She'd never seen anyone move that fast. He must be pretty damn motivated. He kicked the door shut, gently set her on her feet, and pushed her against the wall, his body following. While pulling her hips flush against his arousal, Dev ravaged her mouth like a man lost in the desert for a month without water. Like he couldn't get enough of her. She knew the feeling.

Then Dev was laving love bites and open-mouthed kisses along her jaw, behind the sensitive skin underneath her ear, and down her neck. Her head fell back against the wall. She was mindless. Completely lost to him.

Dev

Dev could hardly wrap his mind around how fantastic Kate tasted. How in tune to him she was. He'd heard the link between a vampire and his Moira was intensely strong, even before they became permanently bonded. Once the bonding occurred, that link was even more potent. He'd already started hearing some of her thoughts, though she wouldn't hear his until they'd completed the bonding. *Soaked panties, huh?* He couldn't wait to verify that one.

When her head fell against the door baring her long, sleek neck to him, his fangs dropped and the desire to take her blood, making her irrevocably his was like a freight train on a collision course...almost too much to stop. Making love to her without taking her blood would take every single ounce of iron will he'd gained over the last several hundred years. He willed his fangs to recede.

He grabbed one of her legs, drawing it around his hip. He thickly commanded, "Wrap your legs around my waist." She obeyed immediately.

He kissed his way back up to her mouth, sucking on her bottom lip and tongue before fully taking her mouth in another searing kiss. He wanted to learn every nuance that was Kate. Her hands constantly roamed his arms, shoulders, hair and chest. He loved every second of it. He wanted to do this with her every day and night for the rest of their lives.

He began to grind his pelvis against her moist center and she kept time with him. Fucking hell, he needed to be inside her. *Now*. The scent of her desire had his mouth watering. He could not wait to taste her, to drink from her. *But not this time*. There were so many things he wanted to do with this woman, he was warring with himself on where to start.

Without breaking contact with her mouth or body, he carried her over to the large king sized bed in the middle of her room and gently laid her down on the duvet. He was almost shaking now with the physical and emotional need to claim her.

Laying his larger frame over her smaller one, he forced himself to let go of her mouth and, bracing himself on his forearms, gazed down into her beautiful, unfocused, lust-glazed eyes. He wanted this woman beyond any reason. He wanted her to see his sincerity, his honesty, his overwhelming need for her.

She whispered, "Please don't stop. God, I want you, Dev."

He grinned ear to ear. "How could I say no when you asked so sweetly, love."

He gave her one hard, ravenous kiss and sat up to gaze down upon her gorgeous body. He needed to slow down so he could drink in every creamy inch of her perfection and brand it into his memory. He lifted the hem of her sweater over the slight swell of her stomach and over the generous expanse of her breasts, which were encased in a sexy black lacy bra. They both quickly rid her of the offending garment. Jesus, he could hardly breathe. Words could not describe how perfectly exquisite she was. She was made completely and only for him.

"Fuck, Kate. You are perfection." She gave him a bright, relieved smile and if he wasn't a goner before, he surely was now. She didn't know it yet, but she owned him, heart, body, and soul. He ran his hands up the expanse of her waist, past her ribcage until they cupped her breasts. His thumbs found her taut nipples, pinching them gently. Kate moaned, closing her eyes.

He fastened his mouth on one pert nipple, laving and sucking, flattening it out against the roof of his mouth, all the while stroking the other. Her body arched off the bed closer to him and she held his head to her breast, begging, "Please, Dev. I need you now."

Soon, my love. Soon.

He gave the other breast equal treatment. As one hand strummed her nipple, his other moved down her body to the snap of her jeans. He deftly unbuttoned and unzipped them, pushing the stiff fabric down her legs. He reluctantly released her breast to divest her of them completely. Her took her tiny matching black panties along with them. He'd enjoy her sexy lingerie next time.

Dev ran his hands up both lean legs as he crawled slowly back up her body. When he reached her core, he spread her open, so she was completely splayed to him. Her bare pussy was weeping for his touch. She was so unbelievably sexy he damn near swallowed his tongue. *Mine.*

"Jesus, Kate, you are so sexy and dripping for me. I can't wait to taste you." He took a deep breath. "You smell like heaven."

He felt his eyes start to glow and shut them for a few moments, willing them back to normal. He lowered his head to her treasure and took his first taste of her, taking one long lick from back to front, ending on her clit, where he flicked his tongue back and forth.

"Oh God!" Kate gasped and her hips shot off the bed. He used one arm to hold them in place, while he used the other to keep her pussy fully open to him. His tongue found her secret opening and he plunged in, drinking down her essence. He nibbled and licked his way back up to her clit, thrusting one long finger into her silken, hot sheath, followed quickly by another, pumping in and out. He leisurely savored her like an ice cream cone, ending with a light flick to her most sensitive button. She writhed underneath him, but he held her immobile. He knew he would never get enough of this woman. *His* woman. His cock was painfully hard, like a divining rod that had found its golden treasure. He was going out of his mind with the need to be inside her. But he wanted to savor her taste a bit longer.

She was so responsive. Her throaty moans and pleas were becoming incoherent. Her frantic pulse and tightening pussy indicated she was close to orgasm, even with the lightest of flicks to her clit. Dev couldn't wait to see her come undone, so before picking up the pace, he whispered, "I want you to come for me, love. Come for me hard, so I can fuck you even harder."

Kate

Kate had never been wound this tight before. Dev's dirty talk was unbelievably sexy, pushing her over the edge. His plea to be inside her was her undoing.

"God, Dev!" She flung her head back, squeezing her eyes shut as she shattered into a million pieces. The bolt of pleasure that ripped through her body was unlike anything she'd ever experienced. It was white hot and mind-melting. Goose bumps broke out all over body. She never wanted to come down from this euphoric high.

She wasn't sure how long it took for her to come back into herself. Seconds, minutes...who the hell was counting? Her limbs were literally shaking. Dev was reverently kissing her mound, before laving his way back up her body. When he reached her mouth, he gave her another soul-shattering kiss and she could taste her essence on his lips, his tongue.

He hadn't even been inside her yet and already he was the best lover she'd ever had. She knew this would be a mistake. No one would ever live up to Devon Fallinsworth. She couldn't help thinking...*I want this man for the rest of my life.*

He broke the kiss and looked down at her, with a barely contained heat in his eyes. Eyes that looked almost glowing. He was breathtaking. His voice was almost shaking when he told her, "I want you more than I've ever wanted another woman in my entire life, Kate." As stupid as it may be, she believed every word he said.

"I feel the same way," she whispered.

He was fully clothed and she intended to remedy that immediately. Smiling, she encouraged him onto his back. Naked, she sat astride him, just drinking in his unrivaled good looks. She had seriously never met another man so striking and at the risk of inflating his already big ego, she told him so. "You are quite fetching, you know."

He laughed. "Fetching?"

"Yes, fetching." She kissed his full lips, lightly biting his lower lip. He growled. Actually *growled*. It was heady that she had this power over him.

"Handsome."

Kiss.

"Attractive."

Kiss.

"Beautiful."

Kiss.

She ground her hips slightly against his denim-clad groin.

He groaned. "Kate, you're killing me here. I need to be inside you." He had grabbed onto her hips and was gently thrusting into her, his denim-covered cock perfectly positioned against her bare pussy.

"I want to unwrap you. Slowly. It's like opening your most anticipated present on Christmas morning. You want to savor it."

She smiled sweetly at him. He returned it, spreading his arms wide before hooking his hands behind his head. "Well by all means then, open away, love."

Holding his gaze, she slowly undid each button on his shirt. She parted the halves and only then did she break her gaze to look her fill. Her eyes widened slightly and he moaned when her fingers made their first contact. She snapped her eyes to his and could see his restraint. He wanted her...badly. She couldn't help but tease him just a bit.

Her hands roamed over his defined pecs, his flat, masculine nipples, trailing the thin sprinkling of hair down his washboard abs. He had not one ounce of fat on his perfectly honed body. After she helped him out of his shirt, she shifted back, sitting on his thighs so she could unzip his pants. He was commando. She was breathless.

"Wow." This was the best non-Christmas Christmas present ever.

Seeing him in all his naked glory only confirmed how magnificent he was. He was large, imposing. She quickly shucked off his jeans, taking his impressive cock in hand. She leaned down to lick the pre-cum that had already leaked out of his plum, swollen head, hearing his sharp intake of breath. Sliding him into her mouth, she looked up to see him fisting his hands in the sheets, his eyes closed and head thrown back, tendons in his neck jutting out. He was a splendid male specimen and this was infinitely better than her dreams of him.

As her mouth stretched to accommodate his girth, she had to wonder...*cripes, would he even fit?*

Dev

Oh, I'll fit baby. You were made just for me.

"Jesus Christ, Kate." She was going to be the death of him. He hadn't wanted to look away, but he had to get his eyes under control. Once he did, he forced them open to watch while she licked and sucked him, like he was her favorite Popsicle.

Smiling, Kate ran her tongue along his heavily veined member, from root to tip. Up one side and down the other.

When she finally took his cock back into her hot, wet mouth, Dev groaned and he let his head fall back onto the pillow.

"Ahhhh...Kate."

Kate continued to torture him until he was fighting the desperate need to come. He wanted to come inside her sweet body the first time, not her mouth. There would be plenty of time for that later.

He grabbed underneath her arms, pulling her up his body. He devoured her mouth while rolling her onto her back. She automatically opened her legs, fitting her body to his. *Like a missing puzzle piece.*

He cupped both cheeks with his hands and gently,

reverently kissed her lips, his cock gently nudging her core. She broke the kiss and looked at him.

"I'm on the pill, but maybe we should use a condom."

Vampires did not carry disease. The human birth control pill, however, was ineffective for vampire mates. Vampires could only conceive with their bonded mates. The thought of Kate swollen with their child sent a jolt of unexpected longing through him.

"You have no fear of disease from me, love." He nuzzled her ear and whispered, "No condom. I want to feel every hot, wet inch of your sweet pussy gripping me. Please."

Her breath hitched. "Yes, okay," she murmured.

He touched his forehead to hers. "I feel like I've waited my whole life for you, Kate." He had. "I need you."

"You have me." The words barely left her mouth and his eyes never left hers as he thrust his hips hard, driving himself into her. She gasped and he held still, letting her adjust to his girth.

"Are you okay?" he asked.

She nodded her head. "More than okay."

He pulled out slowly and thrust hard, again and again, seating himself fully within her.

"Christ, you feel so good. So tight. So hot." *Like home.* The fierce desire to take both her body and blood was overpowering. His fangs lengthened and he dropped his face to that lovely place where her neck and shoulder met. He gently scraped her skin with his sensitive fangs, desperately wanting to sink them into her tender flesh.

"God, don't stop. Please don't stop, Dev."

He knew she meant their lovemaking. He wanted her to mean the taking of her sweet blood. He continued to pump into her ruthlessly. He could sense she was near another orgasm when her pussy began to clamp down on him. He wanted her drunk with passion, with lust. Forgetting any other man that came before him. And why did that unwelcome thought enter his mind? Just the thought of another man even looking at her sweet body had him nearly feral. He wanted to mark her as *his* in every way possible, so every human or vampire that came across her knew she belonged to him.

Dev drove her higher and higher until she came apart in his arms again, crying out in ecstasy. Dev pumped ruthlessly into her tight little body.

"Kate, love, I'm going to come." He thrust hard three more times before howling with his own hot release. He pounded relentlessly into her until she squeezed every last drop of his seed from his still stiff cock.

Panting, they lay there trying to catch their breaths, wrapped tightly around each other. Dev showered her face with tiny kisses. No words between them were necessary. He'd never felt more content.

CHAPTER 25

Kate

Best.

Sex.

Ever.

She knew it. She knew this would be the best sex she'd ever have. Dev did not disappoint and she was officially ruined for any other man. This felt like so much more than just sex, though. It felt right, like home. She could have sworn she heard him say that when they were making love. She was definitely losing it.

This was a big mistake. She was already half in love with him, and now she was making shit up. And love? How ridiculous was that. She'd only known him a week. People didn't fall in love in a damn week! Well, unless you were a psychotic, stalker nut-job, maybe. Oh God...she could *totally* see herself turning into a pathetic stalker girl where Dev was concerned. She *so* could.

What the hell had she been thinking? She hadn't been; that was clear. You didn't screw Devon Fallinsworth out of your system, which is exactly what she'd tried to do. Now all she did was fuel an unquenchable thirst. She'd never get enough of this man. Cue the stalker music. She was so screwed. There could be no future with him. The stalker part of her brain asked *Why, Kate? Why couldn't there be a future with him?*

Dev was still lying over her, catching his breath. His face buried in her neck, his arms tightly wrapped around her. She wanted to stay like this forever and pretend she could build a life with this man. Yep, it's official. She was definitely delusional. This...this was why she couldn't have casual sex. She just wasn't a fuck buddy kind of girl. She was emotional. She got attached. The sound of his voice broke her out of her own head. Good. Her head was not a good place to be at the moment.

"That was amazing." His voice sounded raspy and thick.

"I couldn't agree more."

"Stay here, I'll be right back." He gently pulled out, rolled off the bed and made his way to the bathroom. She felt sadly bereft when his body disconnected from hers.

She could see well enough in the dark and enjoyed the outline of his tight ass all the way to the bathroom. Yum. He returned quickly with a warm washcloth and gently cleaned her. He tossed the wet cloth on the floor, settled into bed and pulled her beside him.

"Hungry?"

"Starved, actually."

"I'll call Leo and have him bring us up some sandwiches and fruit. Does that sound good?"

"Sounds fantastic." She didn't feel like getting dressed.

While Dev picked up the phone, Kate took a quick shower and returned to him, snuggling into bed naked. Shortly after, Leo arrived with their food and Dev met him at the door.

They ate smoked turkey sandwiches with goat cheese and mixed greens, along with fresh berries in a sweet glaze. Leo had also included a lovely bottle of chardonnay, and after one glass, she was getting sleepy.

It had really been a long day and she hadn't gotten much sleep the night before.

And she hadn't even thought about her research paper. Strangely, she wasn't feeling guilty over that fact either. She had thoroughly enjoyed her day waking up in Dev's arms and ending the day in the same way, but she could not let him spend the night with her again. Her feelings for him were developing at an alarming pace and the more time she spent in his arms, the harder it would be to leave. Tears stung her eyes just thinking about it.

They finished eating and Dev set the tray on the nightstand. After he had them settled, with her body draping his, he kissed the top of her head. "Go to sleep, love. It's been a long day and you must be exhausted."

She wanted to do just that and she fought the desire to simply nod her head in acquiescence. Instead she said, "You don't have to stay, Dev."

"I'm staying. End of discussion."

She sat up. If he stayed, she was going to fall that last little bit. And she could not allow that. This already felt way too good. Way too comfortable. Way too right.

"I'm not really sure that's such a good idea, Dev. Don't...don't get me wrong; I don't regret what happened at all. I'm just...just not sure it's a smart idea to blur the lines here and make this more than it is."

"And what do you mean by *'this'*, Kate?" Uh, oh. He didn't look happy.

"Well...amazing sex, of course. But we both know it can't be any more than that."

————————————

Dev

His little minx was trying to pull away already. Well no fucking way was he letting that happen. She was his, end of story.

Dev replayed her last comment in his head. *"We both know it can't be any more than that."* He needed to approach this discussion carefully.

"Why not?"

She wrinkled her eyebrows, looking confused. "Why not, what?"

"Why can't this be more than amazing, mind-blowing sex, Kate?" He sat against the headboard, pulling her astride his lap. Hands on her hips held her firmly in place.

"I really, really like you." He more than really liked her, but if he told her that she was his Moira, his destined mate, and he was falling in love with her, he didn't think that would go over too well. "I want to get to know you. Hell, I already feel like I know you. We have a connection that goes beyond just sex and I know you feel it too."

She shook her head and looked down. "Guys like you don't fall for girls like me, Dev. I'll just end up getting my heart broken, and I honestly cannot deal with that." He could see the tears welling in her bright green eyes.

He gently grabbed her chin, tilting her head back up, holding her moist eyes with his. "Guys like me? What exactly does that mean?" Jesus, the sad look in her eyes was more than he could bear and her comment just plain angered him. She was exquisite. How she didn't see that about herself he just couldn't comprehend.

"Are you kidding me?" She waved her hands up and down his body. "Look at you. You're the most gorgeous man I have ever met. Ridiculously good-looking guys like you don't end up with plain-Jane women like me." She quickly added, "And that's okay, I'm not looking for more."

He called bullshit. She was. She was just scared. And her plain-Jane comment pissed him the fuck off.

She continued before he could respond. "But I'm also not looking to get my heart broken either. So...it's best if we just keep this casual and sleeping together after sex isn't casual. At least not to me."

He studied her for a minute. Shit. How was he going to play this so as to not scare her off? Right, straightforward it was.

"You're right."

"I...I am? I mean, of course I am." She looked so disappointed it broke his heart. He was right on calling her bullshit earlier. He needed to take fear out of the equation so she would give them a chance. So she would surrender to him, fall in love with him. So she would want to bond with him, as much as he wanted to with her.

"Yes, sleeping together after sex does complicate casual."

She looked embarrassed, but tried to play it off. "Right. It does. So, ah...I guess I'll see you in the morning then."

She tried lifting off his lap, but he clamped the hands around her hips even tighter. She wasn't going anywhere.

"Oh, you'll be seeing me in the morning, all right. After I spend the night making love to you and *sleeping* in your bed." He kissed her long and deep. "After I wake you up in the middle of the night with my cock buried deep inside you."

He peppered kisses at the corners of her mouth.

"You're anything but casual, Kate. I want you and I always get what I want."

He lay back down, assuming their earlier position with her draped over his body. His arm wrapped around her possessively, tightly, letting her know in no uncertain terms, he was not letting her go. Not tonight. *Not ever.*

He kissed the top of her head gently. "Now, go to sleep, my love."

She gifted him with a small smile and obediently snuggled into his side, quickly drifting off. He might have won this round, but he had no doubt the battle to win Kate's heart was far from over.

Damn stubborn woman.

CHAPTER 26

Dev

Dev extricated himself from Kate's limbs as quietly as he could. He didn't want to leave her, but the other Lords were arriving within the half hour. His plan was a fast strategy session, returning to her as quickly as possible. He was serious about being buried balls deep in her hot, wet pussy in the middle of the night. And she *would* wake up in his arms.

He needed this meeting over with quickly before she woke. If that happened and she found he wasn't there, he knew her mind would immediately think the worst and he'd have much more ground to make up. She was going to make him earn every inch of it too. For some reason, she thought herself unworthy of him and if anything it was completely the opposite. He in no way deserved someone like her. She was sweet, innocent, loving. Everything he was not. He genuinely feared once she learned of his true nature, he would lose her forever. He simply couldn't let that happen.

As he rose from the bed she moaned and turned over but remained asleep. He returned to his room, showered, dressed quickly and made his way to his office to gather a few things.

"Leo, gather everyone in the boardroom downstairs.

Ten minutes. Usher our guests there when they arrive."
"Yes, sire."

There was a whole command center in the lower levels of his home. He'd conveniently left that out of Kate's tour. He would show her eventually, but he'd have some explaining to do if she stumbled upon it and he wasn't quite sure how to do that without being honest with her. He had to do that and very, very soon. How to reveal his true self had been weighing heavily on his soul. He'd figure it out tonight, while he held her in his arms.

Dev grabbed his laptop and papers and headed to the boardroom. When he arrived, Ren and Giselle were already there. "Where are the others?"

"On their way," Giselle answered. "Dickhead and Rom will be here any minute."

Dev glared at Giselle. "Let it go, Elle. Please." That got her attention. He never asked anything of anyone. He certainly didn't say *please*. He *demanded*.

"O-Okay. For you, my lord."

"Thank you." She simply gaped at him. Yeah, Dev didn't say 'thank you' much either.

Manny and Thane breezed in.

"You guys feed?"

"And then some," quipped Manny, his eyebrows wagging up and down. Thane simply nodded. Man of a thousand words.

"Your guests have arrived, sire. I'll show them down."

A couple minutes later Damian, Romaric and several others strode into the room.

"Gentlemen, thanks for coming." Dev said. As usual, Giselle was the only female in the room. And she avoided Damian like the plague. Giselle would never tell Dev what happened between them, but it'd caused some pretty bad blood between the two. Well, mostly on her part, it appeared.

Dev whistled to quiet them down. "All right, let's get down to business. Here's what we know so far. We have a total of twenty eight—"

"Twenty-nine," piped up Damian. "Another went missing in the Philly area yesterday."

"Fuck. Okay, twenty-*nine* girls missing in the last three weeks between our Regents. What I didn't tell you about Kate, other than she's my Moira, is that she's a dreamwalker."

It was so quiet in the room you could hear a pin drop.

"She hasn't seen Xavier specifically, but she's described an evil presence. I know it's him; I feel it in every cell of my body. She said others are being held as well." He described Kate's latest dream and the session earlier today with Olivia. "Hopefully next time she dreams about Sarah she can discern Xavier's location, but we can't wait for her to have another dream. As you know, dreamwalkers can't control them. We know Thatcher was going to interrogate the professor who last saw Sarah Hill. Do we know what went down with that yet?"

"I have a call into him," growled Ren. "Asshole hasn't called me back yet."

Romaric spoke up. "You'd all do well to build a cooperative relationship with the local police versus an adversarial one. It's worked well in my Regent."

"Why, thank you for that observation, Romaric. I hadn't thought of that myself." Ren's comment dripped with sarcasm.

Dev spoke up. "Thatcher has his reasons." He needed to get this meeting back on track. "I think we need to call Esmeralda." That quieted down the room.

Damian pushed off the wall that he'd been leaning against. "Fuck, no. That's a supremely bad idea, Dev." Damian had some strange aversion to witches of any kind.

"What choice do we have, Damian? I'm open to other

ideas here, but we clearly need some help because we're making no progress. You heard Kate's last dream."

Damian took a few steps toward Dev. "Dev, listen. I know this is personal for you man, but we all want Xavier dead just as much as you do. He's a threat to our entire race, to our way of life. We all agree something needs to be done, but to involve a witch, *that* one in particular, is the worst possible idea. She can't be trusted. You know that."

He knew involving Esmeralda was a bad idea, but he was desperate. As long as Xavier lived, there was always a chance he could find Kate. That absolutely terrified him.

"What other ideas you got?"

"I have all of my ears to the ground, as does Romaric, and I know you do as well. From what we've been able to piece together so far, we think that Xavier's new HQ may be out of your Regent, Dev. Fucker is probably right under our noses. Let's wait 'til dusk tomorrow. If we know nothing new from the cop, your woman, or from any of our contacts, we revisit the witch discussion."

Everyone agreed that was the best approach. The idea of those girls spending another minute in Xavier's clutches made Dev physically ill, but patience was required when hunting. He normally excelled at patience, but it seemed he'd left it on the floor of the observation room at the police station the moment he first laid eyes on Kate.

CHAPTER 27

Kate

She woke to a cold, empty bed. It took her a second to get her bearings. She was in Dev's house. And Dev wasn't in her bed, where he said he would be. The sheets on his side were cold, so she knew he'd been gone for some time now, which meant he wasn't just using the bathroom. She should feel relieved that he'd decided to leave after all, but somehow she just felt...*sad*.

She'd foolishly believed him when he'd told her he'd wanted more than just sex. That he'd wanted *her*. She'd fallen asleep dreaming of what life would be like as Mrs. Devon Fallinsworth someday. She was the worst kind of fool.

She'd told him to go, but he'd convinced her there was no place he'd rather be than with her. He made her feel like a completely different person, like she was somehow becoming the woman she always knew lurked deep inside of her. She didn't feel comfortable around most people, but with Dev...with Dev, it was like she was *home*, wrapped in a fluffy robe with matching fuzzy slippers, in front of a fireplace, sipping champagne. She was content for the first time in her life.

She sighed heavily. She needed to get out of here before she fell completely in love with this man. Since it wasn't safe to go home, maybe she could stay with Erin? It was probably for the best. She didn't know if she could stomach seeing Dev again without throwing herself at him, begging him to return the feelings she'd grown for him. Begging him to make love to her again.

God, Kate. Have more respect for yourself than that. She wouldn't beg any man for anything. Ever. She was leaving in the morning for sure. If she had her own car here, she'd leave now. She knew Dev would fight her on it, but she didn't care. She simply had to get out of this house and away from him for good. Get back to her boring, lonely life and work on eliminating him from her head, and heart.

Sleep was elusive, so she decided to head to the kitchen for a glass of water. Or better yet, a shot of tequila if she could find some. She threw on pajama shorts and tank and headed downstairs.

When she reached the first level, the house was blazing with lights, but there was no one to be found. Strange. Why would all of the lights be on in the middle of the night?

Glancing out the front door, she saw several new vehicles that weren't there earlier. At least she didn't think they were. She filled her glass with water in the kitchen. Unfortunately, there was no tequila to be found. She strained to hear any noises in the house. Nothing.

She decided to check out the office. No one was there either, but as luck would have it, a mini bar was tucked in the corner, with an unopened bottle of Patron calling her name. *Hello, darling.*

Trying to convince herself it wasn't because she was drowning her sorrows, she helped herself to a couple of shots to help her sleep—*hopefully dreamless*. While she let the tequila take its effect, she wandered the empty house, ending up in the game room. She'd hoped to get lucky and run into Ren or Manny, but the game room was empty too.

All of a sudden she heard a strange noise, like whooshing. Whoosh, whoosh, whoosh. Rhythmic. Soothing. It sounded almost like blood pounding in her ears when she'd been in the handstand yoga pose for four or five minutes. She frantically looked around to see if anyone was here. Nope. Nada.

What. The. Hell. Was. Going. On?

She left the game room to search the rest of the house, everywhere except the bedrooms at this late hour, but it was empty. And now she couldn't stop hearing that damn whooshing noise, even outside of the game room, but it intensified the most when she was there. Every instinct told her the sound was coming from downstairs, but Dev said this was the lowest level of the house. She searched all over again for an entrance to a basement and finding nothing, returned to the game room.

There *had* to be something here leading to another level. She didn't know why she had such an overwhelming need to figure this mystery out.

She began inspecting walls, pulling books out of shelves, turning off and on light switches. *What the hell did she think she was doing? Starring in an Agatha Christie novel?* Frustrated, she sat in one of the leather chairs by the pool table.

Staring in the direction of the pool rack, she noticed a very slight crack, spanning floor to ceiling on the right side of the rack. It looked out of place but not glaringly so. She walked to the rack and tried fiddling with everything and anything, feeling around for a hidden button. Ready to give up, she leaned on one of the pool sticks and voila! The wall holding the pool rack cracked open and a stairway leading into the dark was in front of her.

With the door open, the noise was clearly louder. As she stood there, staring into the black abyss, she'd transitioned from an *Agatha Christie* novel to *Stephen*

King movie and the audience was screaming, "DON'T GO INTO THE BASEMENT, YOU IDIOT!"

Even though her brain screamed this was a moronic, reckless idea, some unknown force she couldn't resist was pulling her down the stairs. She faltered. Maybe she should stop and wait until she found Dev. No. No...that was a bad idea for many reasons.

Down she went...slowly, stair after stair. Her heart raced. The light from the game room only spilled so far down the stairwell and soon she was enveloped entirely in blackness. But strangely enough, she could see much better than she thought she'd be able to. Her eyes must have adjusted quickly.

As she reached the bottom, the noise intensified and compelled her forward.

She was getting more freaked out by the minute, and not because she was waiting for Freddy or Jason to jump out and go all slasher on her. No. She was freaked out because of the bizarre things that had been happening to her since she'd arrived at this house.

This unholy attraction to Dev. His whispers in her head. This God awful, but oddly intensely pleasurable whooshing noise. Her keen eyesight in the dark? *WTF?*

She'd come this far, so pushing all errant thoughts to the back of her head for later examination she kept moving forward. This level looked like a series of underground tunnels with cold, damp limestone walls and concrete floors. The only thing missing were wall torches. On a scale of one to ten, this ranked at least nineteen on the creepy scale and she had no qualms admitting she was scared shitless. Still, an unseen source pulled her toward the noise. She was unable to stop.

Coming to a fork, instinct told her to turn left. She passed several doors, but had enough sense not to open any. After another left turn, she heard voices and the noise intensified further.

Oh crap. Whooshing, Superman eyes and now voices? She had officially lost it.

She was drawn to a door about halfway down and the noise pulsing in her head was now almost as loud as a jet engine.

Taking a deep breath to calm the swarm of butterflies in her stomach, she slowly opened the door. The crushing noise in her ears muted the voices, but as soon as the door opened, all of the noises stopped. Just stopped. And ten sets of glowing eyes turned toward her.

CHAPTER 28

Xavier

"Bill, you're not lookin' so good ol' buddy. In fact you're looking downright peaked."

A vamp on each arm was physically holding up Bill, as he watched Xavier tie his naked wife and daughters to the kitchen chairs.

"Please, please don' hurt them, master. I gave you what you wanted! Please let them go and you can do anythin' you want to me. They have nothin' to do with this. Please!" Hot tears were streaming down Bill's face.

"Now, Bill. If I were to let them go, that wouldn't set a very good example for the other minions, would it? And I'm nothing if not a man of my word. I told you to get me the woman or you would watch me slaughter your lovely wife here, Camille, and your precious daughters, Becky and Ashley. You failed. I'm afraid this is the consequence for failure, human." His wife and daughters were crying and screaming hysterically, pleading with Bill to help.

Bill sobbed and thrashed, trying to free himself to help his family.

"It's not my fault. There was someone watchin' her. I did everythin' I could. I swear. And you have the woman

153

and Thatcher's addresses. You'll be able to get them. Please let my family go!"

Xavier didn't have to do this. He'd get the woman eventually. He didn't have to do this, but he was a bastard of epic proportions and he *wanted* to. He'd been looking quite forward to it actually.

He never broke Bill's gaze, grabbing his wife by the hair with one hand and a naked breast with the other, he ruthlessly twisted her nipple and jerked her head to the side, before slowly sinking his long fangs into her carotid and drinking deep. The human female screamed out for her husband to help her, sobbing and fighting in earnest. The daughters were screaming and blubbering. They were next. Young blood was the sweetest of all, especially with fear coursing through it.

Yes, he was going to enjoy every second of the long night ahead.

CHAPTER 29

MIKE

Mike lay in the cheap motel room's lumpy bed, eyes fixed on the water stained and crumbling popcorn-style ceiling overhead. He thought he'd have drunk enough to be in a coma by now, but nope...his fucking mind wouldn't shut off. It never shut off. He had yet to figure out that little trick. And yet, each year on this day...he attempted just that.

He desperately wanted to forget. Forget the emptiness inside his shell of a body. Forget the heartache of a love lost. Forget the stabbing pain he felt when he thought about a future that would never be. Forget what he'd lost eleven years ago today. *Eleven years?* How was that possible? It seemed like just yesterday. He dreamed of her often, and while it was comforting, it was also pure hell.

This was his unique brand of torture. His mind wanted to forget; yet his heart couldn't. It *wanted* to remember, but he couldn't quite do that either. He couldn't remember the exact cadence of her voice. He couldn't remember the exact smell of her skin. Or the sound of her laughter. Or the last thing he said to her.

He was alive and she was dead. *Presumed dead.*

Mike took another healthy swig of the nearly empty bottle of Gentlemen Jack. Even the bottle was mocking him. He was no gentleman. He was alive, but he was dead inside. He poisoned his body with alcohol and cigarettes with disturbing regularity. He took untold and unnecessary risks in his job. He fucked women without discretion or emotion, all the while thinking of her. He had a dick after all and it needed to be used, or it would fall off. Or so Johnny, his best friend in middle school had told him.

He simply didn't give a shit what happened to him. He was a walking dead man. He was solely consumed and overtaken with the need for revenge. Hell, he wasn't much better than most vamps he knew. He'd find the one responsible one day. One day soon. He could feel the time was drawing near.

God, he missed her. A tear seeped out of his eye, rolling into his ear. Although intellectually he knew there was nothing he could have done to save her, the man in him thought he should have, and he'd played a sick game of what-ifs for the last eleven years.

What if he'd insisted she go out with him and instead of to that frat party? What if she weren't drinking, would she have been able to better defend herself? What if he'd picked her up after the party and drove her back to her apartment, instead of letting her walk home? What if he'd stopped by after she was supposed to be home? They would have known she was missing earlier. *What-ifs. His life was one big fucking wasted what-if.*

Another swig and the bottle was finally empty. He dropped it on the floor beside the bed and flopped back on the flat motel pillow. As he began to finally succumb to the numbing effects of the alcohol, he thought about his ritual tomorrow. He always took the day off after this particular binge. He'd nurse his

hangover for a good portion of the day, pick up

marigolds, her favorite flower, and make the long drive to northern Wisconsin to visit her grave.

I miss you so much, Jamie. That was his last thought before he blessedly passed out.

CHAPTER 30

Dev

For indeterminable seconds, Dev simply stared at Kate standing in the doorway of the boardroom, not believing the sight before him. How had she found the lower levels? How had she made her way to the boardroom in the pitch black of the tunnels?

Two things happened simultaneously. T, one of Damian's guards, growled and in a lightning fast move, lunged toward Kate. At the same time, Kate screamed and threw up her hands in a protective gesture, stopping T dead in his tracks. Not dead, as in literal, but she had rendered him completely immobile.

What. The. Fuck?

Kate turned and fled, making it half way up the stairs before he was able to flash in front of her. Seeing him in front of her so suddenly threw her off balance and she stumbled backwards, cracking her head on the limestone wall right before he could catch her, preventing her complete tumble down the hard steps.

The minute her skin split apart, her sweet blood pooled to the surface. Involuntarily, his fangs shot down and his dick hardened painfully. *Holy. Mother. Of. God.* Her blood smelled better than a forest full of lilac bushes in full bloom. *Fuck, Dev. That was such an inappropriate thought, you asshole.*

Dev pushed back his involuntary bodily reactions. Taking care of Kate was his only priority. As he cradled an unconscious and bleeding Kate against his chest, he knew he would never forget the confusion in her eyes as she opened the boardroom door. Or the fear in her eyes as T lunged toward her. Or the betrayal in her eyes as she looked up at him on the stairs. *Goddamn it!* He did *not* want her to find out this way. He'd planned on telling her tomorrow, but on his terms.

He didn't know whether she was unconscious from shock or the fall, but he could hear her strong and steady pulse, so he prayed she would be okay. She *had* to be okay. *Please, Kate...be okay. I can't live without you, love.*

"Giselle, keep everyone in the boardroom."

The last thing he needed was a bunch of vamps running around the house while his Moira was bleeding all over.

"Ren and Leo, I need your help in my bedroom. Now. I need some wet cloths and bandages ASAP. Flash in. Be prepared, she's bleeding and unconscious."

"Right away," Leo answered.

Ren's response was a bit different. *"What the fuck just happened, Dev?"*

"I have no fucking idea. Just get up here and we'll figure it out later. All that matters right now is Kate."

He didn't know what the hell happened. Kate had found them. How had she found the secret passageway? She'd immobilized T with a flick of her hands. How could she do that? Dreamwalkers didn't possess powers like that. As powerful as he was, he didn't possess that power and even if he did, they hadn't bonded yet, so she wouldn't be able to access it. He felt like he'd entered the twilight zone, probably much like Kate felt. Shit hit the fan in a matter of seconds.

Dev laid Kate on his bed, careful of the wound on the back of her head. He opened her eyes to see her pupils fully dilated and unresponsive, but everything else seemed okay. Her pulse was strong and steady, her breathing even. Ren and Leo flashed in with some medical supplies.

Leo wanted to help, but Dev shoved him aside, not wanting anyone else touching his Moira. Both men stood to the side, letting Dev care for Kate, knowing better than to say a word or interfere. After he cleaned the blood, he was relieved to find the wound was superficial and the bleeding had pretty much stopped. It had seemed worse earlier. His shoulders sagged in relief, and he let out a breath he hadn't realized he was holding.

Removing his bloodied blue silk shirt, he crawled on the bed, gathering a still unconscious Kate in his arms.

"You gonna tell me what the *fuck* is going on, Dev?" Now that it appeared Kate was out of immediate danger, Ren had started pacing again. Dev was sure the dude had restless leg syndrome. He never sat still.

"First of all, calm down, Ren. And if I knew what was going on, don't you think I would tell you? I have no damn idea. I'm just as confused as you are." Dev kept stroking Kate's back, looking for signs of consciousness. Nothing.

Ren continued ranting like Dev hadn't just spoken, his voice going higher with each word.

"How could she just throw her arms up and freeze a three-hundred-year-old vampire like a fucking icicle? You don't have that skill and even if you did, you two haven't bonded yet, have you? And how did she even *find* us in the first place? Did someone leave the door open?"

Dev sighed. He'd been wondering all the same things. Unfortunately, they were going to get no answers until Kate awoke. He had a feeling she wouldn't be much help in providing the answers either.

"I don't know, Ren. I guess we'll have to wait until Kate regains consciousness and try to get some answers. In the meantime, I need you to help Giselle keep control of the situation down there. By now, the way she and Damian constantly go at each other, one of them may already be dead.

"Tell them as little as you can for now. They'll be demanding answers soon. Answers that we don't even have ourselves yet. And make it clear in no uncertain terms that no one is to touch Kate.

"One more thing. We need to get Big D here. Tell him it's urgent. I want him here ASAP."

"Why do we need the doc? You said you think she's gonna be okay." Ren looked genuinely concerned.

"Because we need some of her blood drawn and analyzed. Shit is not right here, Ren, and we need to find out what it is. I'd prefer to have the blood drawn before she wakes up. I'm quite sure she won't be in such an amenable mood then."

"Right. I'll let you know if I run into any issues." He turned and made it to the door before turning around. He spoke softly. "Do you need anything, my lord?"

Ren and Dev were as close as brothers. They were so close they could feel each other's emotions and that happened in very few vampire-to-vampire relationships. Ren could feel the fear, concern, and confusion coursing through his friend's body and Dev was momentarily touched. Two days ago, Ren would have never asked him such an innocuous question, but even Ren had apparently noticed the subtle changes in him since Kate had swooped into his life. He'd have to be very careful around everyone else. They would perceive emotion as a sign of weakness and he would be challenged for his position as Lord. That was the last thing he could afford at the moment.

"*No, my friend. Thank you.*" Ren nodded sharply once and left the room, Leo on his heels.

Dev had a sick feeling in the pit of his stomach. The skill of stasis that Kate demonstrated earlier was most definitely a vampire trait, not human. But vampires were not dreamwalkers. Only human females were dreamwalkers. And Kate was definitely a dreamwalker. Of that he was one hundred percent certain. So if Kate was exhibiting a vampire skill but was a dreamwalker, what did that mean? He'd never heard of such a thing.

After the brutal murder of his entire village, his only family, he'd tried to figure out how a single vampire could have possibly killed everyone and escaped unscathed. Decades later he discovered Xavier had a very powerful gift that no one was aware of because they didn't know his lineage.

Vampires had many skills superior to humans. All vampires could compel. All vampires had superior strength, speed and agility. And each vampire bloodline possessed a unique skill, passed down only within their bloodline, such as reading thoughts, emotions, flashing or telekinesis. His was the ability to make someone believe an illusion was real.

It couldn't be possible, but he knew of only one bloodline that boasted the particular skill that Kate had demonstrated earlier.

CHAPTER 31

Kate

Kate tried opening her eyes. They felt heavy, the inside of her eyelids like sandpaper against her tender eyeballs. Her head hurt like a mother and she reached up to feel a knot on the side of her skull. What happened to her?

She managed to crack one lid and look around. She was in Dev's house. *Dev?* Oh crap. Everything came hurtling back so fast, she forgot about the wound and sat up without thinking. *Oh God.* Bad, bad idea. A thousand needles stabbed her skull and forced her back down, groaning in agony.

Dev came rushing out of the bathroom to her side. "You're finally awake." *Thank God. Thank God.* He cautiously sat on the edge of bed, like he wanted to touch her, but didn't dare.

Oh no, it's happening again. She was hearing him in her head. He most undeniably had not said *Thank God* aloud. What the hell was happening? It all started when she came to this godforsaken house. Tears pricked her eyes.

"How are you feeling, love?" Dev crooned.

How am I feeling? Hmmm...let's see. Scared, confused, completely weirded out. Ready to fucking lose it. Instead she settled for, "My head hurts a little, but I'll be okay."

Dev's eyebrows creased, his forehead furrowing. "Okay, good. That's good. Are you, uh, hungry, or thirsty maybe?"

"I could use a glass of water."

He reached over to the nightstand to pluck up a glass of water, gently handing it to her. "Thanks," she murmured.

After draining the water, he took the empty glass and set it down. He reached for her hands, but hesitated before actually grabbing them, as if asking for permission. She didn't give it so he dropped them.

They spoke over each other.

"What's going on, Dev?"

"What do you remember?"

They both chuckled. She winced. *Note to self. Don't laugh.*

"Why don't you tell me what you remember first, Kate. I'll try to fill in the holes."

Kate started shaking her head, but the pain made her stop. She had a whopping headache. "Can you get me some aspirin, please?"

"Yes, sure. I'm sorry. I should have offered that." He disappeared into the bathroom with the empty water glass, reappearing a minute later with the aspirin and a fresh glass of water.

"Thanks."

After she'd taken the medicine, he asked, "Okay, let's start with what you remember."

"I'm not really sure I quite remember what I saw, or what I think I saw. It's all a little fuzzy. I think maybe I have a concussion or something." What she thought she remembered didn't make a lick of sense.

"Just try me, okay?" He added with a small smile, "Please."

"Okay. Well, I woke up and you weren't in bed and I

was a little thirsty so I went downstairs to get some water." She left out the hurt feelings and the shots of tequila, as she didn't want to sound like clingy stalker girl, even though she suspected she was leaning that way.

"Then I was kind of awake and all of the lights were on, which I thought was odd in the middle of the night, so I went to the game room to see if I could find Manny or Ren to play pool with." Dev stiffened slightly, his lips drawing into a thin line at the mention of the two men.

"Go on."

"And no one was there. But I...I..."

"You what?"

She looked down at the bed. In a small voice, she confessed, "I heard a noise."

"Okay. What kind of noise?"

"A whooshing sound."

"A whooshing sound. What exactly is a *whooshing* sound?"

"See. I told you I'm not even sure if all of this happened. Just...never mind," she said in exasperation.

"No, I'm sorry. Go on...you heard a *whooshing* sound."

"Yes, I heard a...sound. It sounded maybe like a flowing river or strangely enough like blood pounding in my ears, or something like that. I don't know." Dev jumped off the bed and stood, brows drawn together.

"And I just knew it was coming from below me. I felt, I don't know...compelled somehow to seek out the source of this noise, so I searched the rest of the house for a staircase downstairs and didn't find one. I ended up back in the game room, where the noise was the loudest. I searched until I, quite accidentally, found a hidden entrance behind the pool rack and I followed the noise downstairs. This is where things get really fuzzy."

She paused, and he nodded for her to continue. "That's when I found you, Ren, and others that I haven't seen before. I thought maybe one of them was attacking me, so I turned and ran and then I remember you in front of me suddenly on the stairs. I don't know how you got there so fast. I lost my balance and after that...I don't remember anything."

Dev started pacing at the foot of the bed. "How did you find the boardroom?"

"The what?"

"The boardroom. That's where we were. It was pitch black down there. How did you find it?"

"I...I don't know. I just followed the noise. It was pretty dark, but I could see well enough, I guess. It was kind of spooky how quickly my eyes seemed to adjust to the dark."

Oh Christ.

"Why did you say that?"

Dev looked at her questioningly. "Say what?"

"Oh Christ. Why did you say that? What's the matter?"

"You heard that?"

"Yeeesss? " Her eyes narrowed. "Why?"

Looking a bit somber, Dev came back and sat on the foot of the bed. "Nothing.

It's nothing. Explain the noise more."

Kate threw her hands in the air, frustrated. "I don't know, Dev. It sounded like whooshing. I don't know how else to explain it. I've never heard anything like it before."

"Can you hear it now?"

"No."

"Are you sure? Listen. Close your eyes and concentrate. Can you hear it?" Kate stared at him with her head cocked, an *are-you-serious* look on her face.

"Kate, please. This is important."

"Fine." She closed her eyes and concentrated. "I...I can't hear anything."

"Let's do an experiment."

He stood and grabbed her hand, scooping her up in his arms. "Come."

"Where are we going? I can walk, you know."

He ignored her, carrying her down to the game room. "Do you hear it now?"

"No...I—*wait*. Put me down." Reluctantly he complied. Then she barely whispered, "Yes. Yes, I hear it again. What the *hell* is that?"

CHAPTER 32

Dev

"Ren, is everyone in the basement?"

"Yes. In their sleeping quarters."

Dev shut his eyes and listened, letting everything else fall away. All he could hear was blood being pushed through the arteries and veins of his friends in the lower levels. *Holy shit.* Was that what she heard? If so, how was that possible? Only born vampires had hearing that keen. Bonded mates would not possess that ability, at least not for decades. He didn't hear it anymore as he was so used to the sound after so many centuries.

This made no sense. Keen hearing and eyesight, hearing his thoughts before they were bonded, the super-ability of stasis? Those were all vampire traits...

"I don't know, but I'll check it out after we get you back upstairs, okay?"

"Ren, when will the blood test results be back on Kate?"

"Big D said it'd take a few hours, so it should be anytime now."

"Kate has regained consciousness. Contact him and see if he can speed things along."

"Of course."

Dev put his hand on the small of Kate's back, leading

her back out of the room. "Why don't we get you back upstairs? You took a nasty fall. Do you remember anything else about the men downstairs?"

"No. But why were they here?"

Uh oh. Time for some 'splainin'. "Why were who where?"

Kate laughed, wincing slightly as she grabbed her head. "Dev, for someone so articulate, that didn't make a lick of sense. Why were all of those men in the basement? And for that matter, why is there a secret basement with creepy, medieval tunnels and a bunch of underground rooms anyway?"

He took a deep breath and let it out slowly. "Are you hungry?"

"Are you evading?"

He chuckled. "No, I promise. I just thought maybe it would be a good idea to get something in your stomach first. You didn't eat much yesterday and we have a lengthy discussion in front of us."

"Okay. I guess I am a little hungry. But after that, you need to start talking."

He nodded once and put his hand on the small of her back to usher her toward the kitchen.

Kate

They sat at the kitchen island and ate fresh fruit medley and a chocolate muffin so good it could rival any orgasm. They ate in silence, and while Dev seemed distracted, it was a comfortable silence. Kate liked comfortable silence. Not every minute needed to be filled with meaningless words and it was rare to find someone with whom you could just...*be*.

She was still a little groggy, her head pounding a bit from the fall and the strange noise, but a memory was on the fringes of her brain. Something important about last night was trying to surface but wouldn't quite come. It made her head hurt worse to think about it. She would remember eventually.

After they finished their meals, Dev cleaned up and put their dishes away.

"Let's go back upstairs." He held out his hand to her.

She nodded and took it. The electric charge that was always present between them ran up her arm and through her whole body. She couldn't understand why she was so drawn to him, but it was clear something had changed in her since she'd met him. Things seemed crisper, sharper, clearer. It was odd and unnerving and she couldn't understand it really, let alone explain it. Her senses seemed...supersized. That was the best way she could think to describe it.

They settled in the lounge area of her bedroom, Kate on a leather chair, Dev on the loveseat, and she waited for Dev to start the conversation. She was nervous, as if something was about to happen that would change the course of her life forever.

Dramatic much?

"So..." He looked nervous and was very fidgety. Not at all like the self-assured Dev she'd come to know over the last few days.

"So...just spill it, Dev."

"Okay." He stopped, staring at her with an intensity she hadn't seen before. "I am vampire and you are my Moira, my fated mate."

She frowned at him, her brows and forehead creasing. Then she started laughing. Bend over your arm, belly laughing, until tears leaked out of her eyes. Her head still hurt, but she couldn't stop herself from laughing.

"I'm serious, Kate. This isn't a joke."

She laughed until she couldn't catch her breath. "Oh... Okay. Yeah, right. Good one." *What is he playing at?*

"Kate, I'm happy to give you a demonstration."

Still laughing, she tried catching her breath, gazing at him. "Woooo... Okay."

"Okay, what? You believe me?"

She sat back in the chair, arms crossed over her chest. Still chuckling. "Okay, give me a demonstration."

A slow grin spread across Dev's face and he rose from the loveseat, stalking toward her slowly, like a lion does its prey. God, he moved with such elegance it was mesmerizing.

She stopped laughing, her heart beating fast. The look on his face was pure lust, total desire, and she immediately became wet between her legs. How did he do that to her?

He spoke in a low, gravelly voice. "I can hear your heart beating, Kate. Your pulse has skyrocketed. Your arousal has spiked." Her breaths were coming fast and choppy as he slowly came closer. Of course her pulse had skyrocketed. He was near. He knew what he did to her, so that didn't mean diddly.

"I can smell your arousal, love. I can *always* smell it. It drives me crazy with want." His eyes...they started glowing and she could see that his incisors had lengthened as well.

Oh shit. Last night's missing piece came rushing back so fast it almost knocked her over. She shrank back in the chair, bringing her feet to her butt, curling her arms around her legs.

"Stop. D-don't c-come any closer." He stopped instantly and held his palms up.

"Kate, I'm not going to hurt you. I would never hurt you. You are my Moira."

"Your Moira? That sounds like a made up term. I-I don't believe you." But she did. Deep down inside, she knew what he said to be true. She'd sensed something different about him from the moment he'd stepped into the room at the police station. They were two powerful magnets drawn toward each other, so strong nothing could keep them apart. She knew he was meant for her. Oh my God. This could not be happening.

"What type of special investigator are you?"

"I was truthful with you about that. We work with the police on special cases they can't solve." Still holding up his palm, he tentatively took a couple more steps toward her and knelt down in front of her chair. He reached a hand out to her but lowered it when she shrank away even further.

"Like cases involving vampires?"

"Yes." He nodded.

She cursed under her breath.

"Kate, you do believe me. I can see it in your eyes. I swear on my life I would never see any harm to come to you, by my hand or any other. You have nothing to fear from me. You know this. If I wanted to hurt you, I could have done it many times over by now.

"I'd planned on telling you today and I didn't want you to find out this way, but things are happening to you that we need to figure out...together. Do you remember *all* of what happened last night?"

"Y-yes."

He placed a hand on her knee and she stayed frozen, feeling the ever-present electricity seep into her body. "Tell me what you remember."

Her gaze flicked back up to his eyes, which had stopped glowing. She whispered, "When I walked into the room downstairs, everyone looked at me with...with..."

"With glowing eyes?" She nodded.

"What else do you remember?"

When she just continued to watch him, mute, he softly encouraged her, "It's okay, love."

"I—I... One of them tried to attack me and I screamed and ran. Then...then all of a sudden you were in front of me on the stairs and I fell." Her brows creased. "Wait a minute. Did you push me?"

He jumped up, glaring down at her. "Hell, no, I didn't push you! How could you even think that? I told you, Kate, you are my Moira and I would *never* hurt you. I would die protecting you. I will never give you anything but pleasure, love."

Embarrassment heated her face. Even now, when her head was spinning and she felt like she'd entered a *Twilight Zone* episode, she felt an irresistible pull toward this man—or whatever he was. She was certifiably crazy. She had to get out of here. Now. She needed time to think through what was happening.

She abruptly stood and went to the closet to her get her overnight bag.

"Kate, what are you doing? Put that away."

"I'm leaving."

He was at her side in a second, grabbing the bag out of her hand. Surprise morphed into fury. Emotions were rolling through her faster than an out of control locomotive. It was exhausting.

"Give. That. Back."

"No. You're not going anywhere. It's too dangerous."

"Is that so? More dangerous than being in a house full of vampires? I think I'll take my chances, Mr. Fallinsworth."

Faster than she could blink, she was pinned up against the wall by two hundred twenty pounds of lean, muscular, aroused man...er vampire. She had to crane her neck to look up at him.

"What are you doing?" She hated the way she sounded so breathless and needy.

He leaned down so their noses were almost touching, his strong hands firmly gripping her hips.

"First of all, I'm not letting you go anywhere, love."

He tilted his hips into her, grinding his arousal against her stomach. Her breath caught as his mouth slid to the shell of her ear.

"Second of all, I think we're way past formalities here since my cock has been inside that hot, wet, delicious body of yours." When he nipped her neck and laved it with his tongue, she whimpered. Actually whimpered. *Pathetic.*

He looked at her with so much longing in his eyes, she was sure she would spontaneously combust on the spot.

"You are mine, Kate, and you are not going anywhere." One hand cupped her head, as he took her mouth in a searing kiss. He pulled away suddenly, groaning.

"I'm sorry, I have some business to tend to. I won't be long." He gave her another quick peck and he walked to the door. Turning back, he said, "Stay here. Please. We have a lot more to discuss."

She nodded, with no intention of following his instructions like some lovesick schoolgirl, but knowing if she disagreed he'd likely handcuff her to the bed. *Not a bad idea. Stop it, Kate!*

He closed the door and she whipped into action, throwing clothes into her overnight bag. She ran to the bathroom to grab her toiletries and fished her pj's off the floor. She grabbed her cell phone and called her one close friend, Erin, to beg for a ride back into town. She knew they had turned onto the lane leading up to the house from the highway, so she explained as best as she remembered how to get here and told her she'd be waiting for her by the side of the road in thirty minutes. It would probably take her at least twenty to make the long walk to the highway. She also had to figure out how she was going to get past the security gate.

She looked around the room for anything she may have forgotten and slipped out quietly, hoping not to get busted on her way to the front door.

Thankfully she made it unnoticed and, quiet as a church mouse, exited the house. Once she was outside, she felt an inextricable pull to return to Dev. It was a struggle to turn and walk away. That was all the more reason she had to get away from here. She needed some time to breathe and process everything that happened over the last few days. She felt like a dam after a heavy rain, ready to burst at the seams.

She turned, walking further and further away from the one person she knew, deep down in the depths of her soul, was *The One* for her. And it was the hardest, longest walk she'd ever made in her life.

CHAPTER 33

Xavier

"Why do I *not* have that dreamwalker in my possession yet? Do I have to do everything my goddamned self?"

"I'm sorry, my liege, but neither the woman nor the detective have been back to their homes yet. My sources tell me that the detective is not working today and we still don't know where the woman is. We keep rotating new shifts every three to four hours to keep the men at their freshest. We will find them, I assure you."

The rage Xavier kept at a slow simmer at all times instantaneously boiled over and the animal in him took control. He threw his head back and bellowed an inhuman sound that shook the walls of the compound. He immediately ripped out the neck of the vampire standing in front of him, dropping his dead corpse to the ground.

Several of his other men came running at the sound of the vicious attack, ready to defend their lord and master. The first two arriving had the bad fortune of meeting with an untimely death in a similar gruesome manner before he calmed down enough to stop the killing rampage.

"If I don't have that goddamned dreamwalker in my possession by dusk, more motherfucking heads will roll!"

"Yes, sire." The remaining vampires scrambled for their lives.

CHAPTER 34

MIKE

Light spilled through the tattered blinds that wouldn't quite close. Mike woke with the mother of all hangovers. Holy shitballs...he was gonna be sick. He bolted up from the bed in hopes of making it to the bathroom, which was not a splendid idea, as he tripped over a discarded shoe, staggered and fell face first into the hair-strewn motel carpet. Not something you want to walk around barefoot on, let alone face plant in.

He didn't make much as a detective, but he could have afforded a bit better than this *Psycho*-like motel he'd ended up in. *Was that dried blood on the bottom of the mattress?* Thing was, Milwaukee was a small city, relatively speaking, and he couldn't have anyone finding out what he did to himself, especially anyone on the force.

"Fuck."

He failed pushing himself off the floor, landing on the side of his face. At this rate, he'd have a black eye. The second time he was successful but didn't quite make it to the toilet before last night's JD forced its way back out of his body. Thank God the sink was close.

He rinsed his mouth and headed to the toilet to relieve himself of another quarter of the bottle that had managed to make its way through his digestive system. He made it back to the bed without further incident, feeling mildly better. Another few hours of sleep and he'd finish out the day as planned.

While he felt like a shithead for baggin' on Jake, making him run down leads for the missing Sarah on his own, he could not let his annual tradition of self-flagellation go.

He deserved it. She deserved it.

So, as his gut churned from his over-indulgence, he would see the day through, as he did every year, and tomorrow he'd get back to his duties as a Milwaukee PD Detective to find Sarah's kidnapper.

CHAPTER 35

Dev

"Where did she go? She couldn't have just walked home." Dev's head was still reeling from what Big D had told him and now Kate was gone. The little minx promised she would stay. He should have known better and tied her to the goddamned bed. Too much had happened in the last couple of days and he knew she was overwhelmed. He could feel it.

Dev, Ren, and Manny had searched the entire house and the outdoor grounds, all the way to the highway, but there was no sign of her. No cars were missing out front, but her bag and clothes were gone and, clearly, so was she.

"Damn it!"

"We'll find her, Dev," said Ren.

"I swear to God when I get my hands on that woman, I am going to turn her over my knee and blister her ass so she can't sit for a week!" And then make her irrevocably his. He was going to complete the bonding as soon as he found her, so she would never want to leave him again.

He'd called her cell several times and it went straight to voice mail.

He was in a near panic. Nothing could happen to the

woman that he had come to love. And with what he just found out about her, she was in more danger than ever. He was grappling with how to handle the competing emotions rolling through him. Known for his calm demeanor in the face of battle, he was anything but calm now.

"We need to check her house to see if she's gone back there. Manny, you stay here. Ren, you're with me."

Ren furiously shook his head. "Nope. No way, my lord. At minimum, Manny and Thane go with us. Giselle can handle things here until the cavalry arrive. I've called everyone else home in case this turns into a goatfuck. This could be a setup and I won't have the death of one Lord, let alone three, staining my conscience."

Dev walked up to Ren, standing at his full height, which still didn't quite match Ren's frame. They were chest to chest.

"I think you've forgotten who's in charge, Ren. I give the orders, I don't take them."

Ren didn't flinch or break eye contact, even for a second. "With all due respect, *my lord*, my job is to protect you, and now your Moira. So let me do my fucking job. Sir."

Dev shook his head, a smirk curving the corner of his mouth. "Jesus, you are a pain in my ass."

Ren let a smirk grace his handsome face. "I live for it, my lord."

"And I told you to stop calling me that."

He bowed slightly. "Yes, my lord."

"Fuck off."

"Thane, we're flashing to Kate's. Get up here now, you're going with us. Giselle, you're in charge until we return. If Kate comes back, you are to let me know immediately and keep her here under any circumstances. You are to protect her with your life, like you would mine."

"Of course, my lord."

Their hands were all lethal weapons in addition to their minds, but each of them had their special armament they preferred to use as implements of torture against the enemy. When they flashed to Kate's house, they instantly sensed something was very, very wrong.

That's when Dev heard Kate scream.

Kate

Since Erin lived on the north side of the city, it didn't take her too long to get there, although she drove by Kate twice before she saw her, which was odd. Kate was waving her arms and jumping up and down, but she still drove by. Erin finally saw her about a quarter mile from the turnoff to the house.

Kate made up some story about coming out to a party last night with coworker, who'd ditched her, leaving her stranded. If Erin's raised eyebrow was any indication, she didn't believe a word she said, but didn't press her on it either. Kate at a party? Laughable. Erin had to twist her arm to get her to have a drink, for God's sake.

Knowing she was still in danger and couldn't stay at home, Erin readily agreed to let Kate stay at her place for a few days, buying the lie there was a student who'd been a little too attentive and had been by the house several times. Driving by first to make sure no one was lurking outside, they rounded the block and parked in her driveway.

"Thanks, Erin. You're a good friend."

"No problem, Katie pie. Any time."

Erin waited in the car as she ran inside to grab a few extra clothes.

When Kate opened the door to her house, she immediately knew something wasn't right. The whooshing noise was back and it was so loud, it was almost debilitating. *Holy balls.* Somebody was in her house. Several somebody's, in fact. Kate turned frantically to leave, but strong arms grabbed her arms from behind, stopping her forward movement.

"About time you got home, bitch."

She screamed and the body behind her froze, his fingers digging into her tender flesh. Suddenly she heard the snapping of bones close to her ear and her attacker's kung-fu grip was gone. Kate didn't look back, instead running toward the door, escape the only thing on her mind. She stopped short when Dev unexpectedly appeared, blocking her getaway.

"What the—?"

She didn't have time to finish her sentence or thought before he grabbed her and everything went black. Her body tingled and she felt like she was floating. As sudden as the dizzying feeling came, it was gone and they were back at Dev's house.

Dev frantically scoured her face and body. "Are you okay?"

"I think so, yes."

"Did he touch you? Did he hurt you?"

"No, no he just scared me. Dev, what the hell is happening here? How were you at my house and how are we back here? I don't understand what's going on at all!" She knew she sounded hysterical. Each word was shriller than the last. Tears pricked in her eyes. Emotional meltdown, begin.

Dev sighed, his voice softening. "I told you, Kate. I am vampire. I have many talents and flashing is one of them."

"This is not real. This can't really be happening. I—I

need to sit down." Her legs started buckling and Dev reached out to steady her, but she waved him off.

"Let's go up to my bedroom, where you'll be more comfortable, Kate. Please."

He reached for her, but she stopped him. "Erin. What happened to Erin?"

"Ren's taking care of her. Don't worry. She's safe and she won't remember a thing. She'll think she had a strange dream is all."

Thank you God. If anything happened to Erin because of her stupid, careless actions, she'd never forgive herself.

"Good. Good...thanks."

He reached for her, but she held out her hand.

"I want to walk. No flashing." He regarded her for a minute and nodded, reaching for her hand. She took it. She couldn't deny that she wanted his touch. Needed it. Was already craving it like a drug addict. She was ready to come fucking unglued and he felt like the only thing that could ground her at this moment. And wasn't that ironic, since from the moment she met him, her life started going to shit.

On unsteady legs, she made her way to his bedroom. She'd woken in there earlier, but hadn't had a chance to look around and take it all in. It was much larger than hers with the massive mahogany sleigh bed in the middle of the room, complete with an off-white comforter and black, white and beige throw pillows. It was different than she expected, but somehow suited his personality perfectly. Massive matching furniture adorned the rest of the room, which was painted soft beige. It was homey. At every turn, he never ceased to amaze her.

He scooped her up and strode over to the plush bed, setting her down gently. He held her hand as he sat right beside her.

"Are you sure you're unharmed?"

She nodded. "Yes, I'm fine."

"Why did you leave, Kate? I specifically asked you to stay put."

"You really want to scold me for leaving? That's what you want to do right now? I don't think so. *I* will ask the questions, Dev. And you will answer every single one truthfully or so help me god, you will feel my wrath."

He dropped her hand and stared at her like she'd grown a pair. A pair of cojones, to be clear. Kate wasn't a pushover by any means, but this was an aggressive side of her personality he hadn't seen yet. Well, buckle up buddy, because she was just getting started.

She jumped off the bed, pacing. "I have so many questions I need a goddamn pen and paper to write them all down so I can keep track!" He was silent while she continued her rant.

"Let's start with why I'm really in danger? Oh, and how about telling me who the fuck just tried to kidnap me right now? And how you just found me in the nick of time? Oh, oh...and why don't you start explaining this whole 'mate' thing to me again, because I think I missed that during our first conversation about you being a goddamned vampire!"

He tried to speak, but she talked over him, raving until she was practically yelling, wildly waving her arms. The carpet matted beneath her feet as she paced back and forth. She was out of control, but didn't give a shit.

"And next, maybe you would care to explain why I seem to be able to do inhuman things...like, oh...freeze people with just a thought; and hear things in my head, like you talking and whooshing, which I wasn't able to do just a short two days ago before I came to this house."

She stopped and looked at him, her face flush, chest heaving up and down, but at least her voice softened a bit. Unable to hold them back, tears brimmed in her eyes.

"Finally, maybe you could help me understand why

every time I'm around you, I literally can't think of *anything* else besides getting you naked and inside my body. And when I'm *not* with you, why I have this inextricable pull to be with you. I am not that kind of person, Dev. It's making me batshit crazy!"

Her legs gave out and she crumpled to the floor, sobbing. Dev was there in an instant, wrapping her in his arms. They sat on the floor for an unknown period of time. He whispered softly, stroking her back until she pulled herself together and the river of tears slowly dried.

"Feel better?"

"No."

He chuckled a bit. "So...you want me, huh?"

She pulled back in disbelief. "*That's* what you remember? Out of everything I just said?" Shaking her head, she mumbled, "Typical male."

This time he laughed harder and she rewarded him with a small smile in return. She couldn't help herself. He made her happy, even though she was incredibly terrified and angry at this moment. He gently cupped her cheeks and placed a chaste kiss on her lips. "Everything will be okay, love."

"How did you know I was in trouble? How did you get me out of there?"

"I didn't know you were in trouble until we arrived, but I knew you would be in danger by leaving." At least he didn't say *I told you so*. He probably wanted to. "As soon as we arrived, I could sense the enemy and then I heard you scream. When we flashed into the house, I disposed of your attacker and then I flashed you back home."

"Who is 'we'? Who else was there?"

"Ren, Manny, and Thane."

"Are they okay? Did they get hurt?"

"Yes, they are fine, Kate. They are warriors and it will take far more than a few low level vamps to take them out. They've already returned home, unharmed."

CHAPTER 36

Dev

Kate was visibly relieved. Irrational jealousy reared its ugly head once again. Of course she'd fear for his men. His Kate has the kindest heart he had ever known and once again he fell deeper in love with her. That moment solidified she was everything he'd ever wanted and so much more. More importantly, he knew there would be a 'they.' She was strong and determined and she would make an exceptional mate. He only hoped he could measure up.

"Why am I in danger, Dev?"

It was his turn to get up and start pacing. He knew he had to tell her this part, about Xavier, but he was dreading it. In the short time he'd known her, she'd demonstrated how inquisitive and intuitive she was and she wouldn't stop until she had the entire truth pulled from him, like a rotten tooth.

So instead, he said, "You haven't asked many questions about my revelation earlier...of being a vampire."

"No, I don't suppose I have."

"Why?"

She grinned, shaking her head. "Nice try, but I'm the one asking the questions, Dev."

"Kate, I promise I will tell you everything, but I need to know why you haven't pressed me for any answers relating to the biggest myth you've probably ever heard."

She took a deep breath, letting it out slowly.

"You know, when I dreamed about Sarah I knew I saw vampires and I tried to pretend they weren't real. I'm sorry I didn't tell you before. So, I suppose it's because from the minute you told me, I...I knew it was true. Even when I told you I didn't believe you, I did. It just clicked, I guess. It probably explains why I'm so drawn to you. You have some sort of vampire spell on me or something."

That made him laugh. "No. I have no spell on you, my love. It's the mating bond that calls to us both, drawing us together like a moth to a flame. You are the flame, my dear. A light so bright I'm blinded by your goodness. I can assure you, a vampire has no compulsion ability over their mate. I knew you were mine from the moment I laid eyes on you, but the fact that I couldn't compel you only confirmed what I already knew."

She frowned. "You tried to compel me? When?"

He simply stared at her, waiting for the pieces to fall in place. She whispered, "You tried at the station, didn't you? I remember feeling a weird pressure in my head. What were you trying to get me to do?"

"Agree to come with me. It's true that you are in danger Kate. For more than one reason, but I'll get to that."

That determined, stubborn look that he'd come to know so well emerged. "Tell me everything. Start first with why I'm in danger." Her eyes pleaded. "Please. I have a right to know."

He nodded. "You're what's called a dreamwalker—"

"A—"

"Let me get this out before you ask questions, okay? I

promise that you will know everything that I do when I'm finished."

Her lips formed into a thin line, clearly displeased. She nodded anyway and he couldn't help but grin. She was magnificent.

"As I was saying, you're a dreamwalker, which is a special human female who can either enter another's dreams or witness events that are happening in real time while in a dream state. Only human females can be dreamwalkers and they are very rare."

Kate couldn't help it...she interrupted anyway, raising her hand like a schoolchild, which earned her a big sigh from Dev.

"Olivia is a dreamwalker, isn't she?"

"Yes. That's why I had her come. There is much you can learn from her. You haven't even begun to tap into the full capability of your gift, Kate."

"Curse is more like it," she mumbled. He ignored that comment, as it wouldn't do any good to argue with her until she experienced the good her gift could do.

"As I said, dreamwalkers are very rare and, in the vampire world, they are revered and protected. In the human world, they are misunderstood and often labeled psychotic. Olivia is the bonded mate of one of my club's general managers, Monti Morton. She's had many, many years of experience honing her skills. As I said, she can teach you much."

Interruption number two. "How many years of experience has she had?"

He thought for a moment. "I believe well over a hundred."

Kate started laughing. "I think you need your eyes checked, Dev. She doesn't look a day over twenty-seven. Thirty tops."

"I'm sure she'll be pleased you think so. But she has been bonded to Monti for over ninety years and I believe she wasn't quite thirty when that happened."

She blankly stared at him, her eyes blinking rapidly.

"If you'd let me finish without all of the interruptions, I'll get to all of this." She cocked her head to the side gifting him with a *fine-I'll-shut-up* look.

"Vampires only bond with humans, not other vampires, especially since most vampires are male. Only bonded human female mates can carry a vampire babe. When vampires do bond, their human mate stops aging and will live the same longevity as their vampire mate."

"And I'm *your* mate, like...your wife?"

Dev's eyes were instantly glowing with desire. He no longer tried to hide his true nature or how much he wanted this woman. He answered thickly, "Yes, but a Moira is much more than just how humans define a wife or husband."

Electricity cracked like lightning between the two of them. "How do you know I'm your Moira?"

"I already told you, a vampire knows when they've met their Moira. Instantaneously. You're mine, make no mistake about that."

"And how old are you?"

"Five-hundred and thirty-five years old." He waited for her to freak out, to run screaming for the door. Instead, she continued to surprise him.

A slight smirk turned up the corner of her mouth. "Don't you think you're a little old for me? I mean, over five-hundred years is a pretty big age gap."

He stalked toward her, grabbing her hand to pull her close as she squealed and tried, unsuccessfully, to scoot around him. Leaning down so their lips were inches apart, he whispered, "Ah, but I bring with me a wealth of experience, love."

"Hmmm...I'll just bet you do. But I'm not sure you'll be able to keep up with a youngster like me." She winked.

Dev laughed loudly. "I look forward to showing you—*multiple times a day*—that I most certainly can keep up with you. It is you who will have a hard time keeping up with me, love." He grabbed her mouth in a hungry kiss, grinding his erection into her stomach as he pulled her hips to his.

Jesus, he wanted her. The adrenaline from the events of the last two hours hadn't waned and the only cure was to fuck it out. He needed to be inside her hot, always-wet pussy. Ensure she was safe, even though he could see with his own eyes she was. Know she accepted him for who he was and that she wanted him all the same. But she broke their kiss instead.

"We're not done talking, yet. No kissy until we talky."

He chuckled. "You are very strange, woman."

"So get to the part about why I'm in danger."

He told her about the call from Detective Thatcher and their arrangement with the local police. He explained that, as his Moira, he wanted her close to him, but also because of the types of dreams she was having, it truly did place her in real danger.

He finally told her about Xavier, who'd gone rogue and, in retribution for Dev ratting him out, killed Dev's entire family, along with their entire village before he disappeared. He told her about Xavier's sick obsession with wanting to rule over the human and vampire worlds and that he'd been kidnapping young women for centuries. They'd been trying to stop him, but he'd remained mainly elusive. He explained his role as Vampire Lord, their hierarchy and that each lord maintained order within their respective Regents. Even vampires had laws to live by.

"The other lords are here at the house and I'll introduce you. What you walked in on last night was a strategy meeting we were having to track Xavier down once and for all."

He knew the instant she figured it out. "But I can help with that, can't I? I can help find him with my dreams. That's what Olivia was trying to teach me."

"Originally when we were called to the station, yes, we were hoping your dreamwalker skills could help us track down and kill him once and for all, but once I found out you were my Moira...well, no. Hell no. I've waited over five hundred years for you." His voice hardened. "No fucking way am I putting you in any danger, so don't even ask me. We'll find another way to get the girls back and stop Xavier. We already have a couple of leads."

They didn't yet, but he didn't want her anywhere near this debacle or this very dangerous vampire.

Kate

Kate knew that wasn't the right moment to argue, but there was no way in hell she was going to sit back and do nothing while young girls were being slaughtered by some psychotic vampire with a God complex. She may not have any fighting skills, but the least she could do was locate this Xavier person so those more skilled could stop him. For the first time in her entire life, she was grateful for her ability to dream.

And she knew with every fiber of her being that she was meant to be with this unbelievably gorgeous man, er, *vampire*, in front her. She'd known it from the second she laid eyes on him.

Information overload was knocking at the door, but she had a few more questions that needed answering now. Everything else could wait until later. "So...the whole blood thing?"

Smirking, he replied, "Are you asking me if I want your blood, Kate?"

Heart racing, scared of the answer, she could only nod.

He swallowed hard and his eyes shifted to her neck before locking on hers. "Fuck yes. More than you know. But I promise you it's the most pleasurable sensation you'll ever experience."

Oh. My. Subject change.

"So what about these new abilities I seem to have?"

A weird look crossed Dev's face. "Well, that's a bit of a puzzle, love. After a vampire and his mate complete the bonding, she takes on his skills, as long as they regularly exchange blood. We haven't bonded yet and even if we had, I don't possess the skill of stasis, so I had the doc take some blood while you were unconscious from your fall earlier."

Stasis? She didn't understand at all what was happening. He must have seen the confused look on her face, since he continued explaining.

"The results came back this morning. That's why I left you in the bedroom. I had to go talk to Big D, the doctor."

She visibly paled. Her voice was barely audible. "And what did the results say?"

He hesitated for several beats, and she could tell this was going to be bad. Very bad. "They indicate you are part vampire."

"What?" The words came out on a croak. There was no way Kate could have heard Dev correctly. She definitely wasn't a vampire. Just the sight of blood made her a bit nauseous.

"You have vampire DNA, Kate. There is no doubt. Doc ran the test three times. And since only human females can carry vampire young, that means whomever sired you...is definitely vampire."

Kate jumped off the bed. "That's ridiculous! My father is most certainly not a vampire. I think I'd notice if he were having a goblet of blood with his damn meal sometime over the last twenty seven years!"

"I need to explain something to you. A vampire is

born, not made. As I said before, a vampire can only come from a male vampire and his bonded human female. Unfortunately, our female vampires are infertile, so they cannot reproduce. So we are born as full-fledged vampires, but vampirism has to be activated by drinking blood several times throughout childhood. A small amount at birth, once at age fifteen and once again at age twenty. With each blooding a vampire gets stronger and more vampire abilities are formed, with full vampiric skills by age one hundred. However, if the appropriate blooding doesn't occur, you're just an exceptional human being, not a full-fledged vampire. You may have some underlying skills or senses, but are never able to fully tap into them, like a full-fledged, blooded vampire could."

She stared at him, uncomprehending a word he'd said.

"I'm sorry, Kate. I know the last couple of days have been stressful. But there is no doubt you are an unblooded female vampire. I'm quite sure the man who has raised you as his daughter is not vampire. Just as I'm positive that the woman whom you call mother is not your biological mother. Have your parents ever mentioned you being adopted?"

"Adopted?" She sunk down onto the edge of the bed again, her legs unable to hold her. She whispered, "No. No. That can't be possible. I'm not adopted."

Dev rushed to her side, pulling her close. "I'm sorry, love," he whispered. "But it's the only explanation."

CHAPTER 37

Kate

Kate sat in Dev's office, while he finished up a business call. The past several days had gone by in a haze. Her dissertation paper was all but forgotten. She knew that her research in the area of sleep psychology could be part of the key to solving the kidnapping of these young women, so she made a vow to get back to that tomorrow.

She'd remained dreamless these past several days. Quite frankly, she was pissed, as she desperately wanted to assist in finding Sarah and the other missing girls and she finally had some new techniques to try. Kate hadn't dreamed of Sarah in many nights and knew she couldn't make herself dream of specific things. She just had to learn to make the most of her dreams when they happened. Maybe tonight would be different.

It was clear she couldn't return to her home, as it was too dangerous. She'd taken a leave of absence from her teaching job and found a replacement for her classes for at least the rest of this semester. She spent her days working with Olivia honing her dreamwalker abilities. She spent her evenings talking with Dev and falling asleep in his arms after hours of sweaty, mind-blowing sex, but she'd wake every morning alone. She hated waking alone without him. Dev explained he didn't really need sleep as a vampire and nighttime was when he got much of his work done.

She'd even been able to take Manny up on in a game of pool. While she'd lost, she held her own. He only won because she scratched on the eight ball. She couldn't wait for a rematch.

Dev had introduced her to the other lords in the house. They'd talked in detail about his businesses. She was surprised to learn that he owned the new club Dragonfly. The same one Erin wanted to drag her to a couple of weeks ago. Because of this whole debacle, she couldn't go with Erin as planned and she was disappointed, but Kate promised they would go another time. Now...she didn't know how that would pan out. A problem for another day.

She'd managed to avoid Giselle for the most part, but when they did cross paths, Giselle had at least been civil. It was a start, but she suspected that was Dev's doing. Kate could tell that Giselle still didn't like her and she wasn't really sure why. It bugged her. While she and Dev had yet to complete the bonding, Kate planned on being around for a very long time and hoped they could be friends. She was the only other woman in the house, after all, and it would be nice to have a close girlfriend. She wasn't sure how Erin would be able to fit into her life now that things were so different. She wasn't sure about a lot of things, but she'd take it day by day for now.

Dev hadn't mentioned bonding again since he rescued her several nights ago and she suspected he was trying to give her space to absorb everything that had happened over the last week. That was just fine with her, because there were so many facts to understand.

Fact: She was adopted.

Fact: She was a rare dreamwalker.

Fact: She had vampire DNA.

Fact: Vampires *were* real. (And man, were they easy on the eyes.)

Fact: One of those smokin' hot vampires belonged to her. *To her.*

Fact: Her life was forever changed.

She had a feeling the fact-finding wasn't over yet either. Over the last few days as she'd thought about her parents, they'd been nothing but loving toward her, but truth be told, she never really felt like part of the family. She always felt like an outcast, and she thought it was just because of her dreams. Now she wondered if it was because she wasn't their biological child.

She was an only child and when she asked her parents why they didn't have any more children, her mother said it was because she'd tried, but couldn't have any more. They told her they were happy God had at least given them her. She knew they loved her greatly. It was apparent they had sacrificed much to have her.

Both of her parents were only children as well, so she had no aunts and uncles and her dad's parents had died before she was born. Her mother's father had passed away when she was too young to remember him. Her maternal grandmother had Alzheimer's and was in a nursing home for the last several years. Even before that, they didn't see much of her.

She'd never realized she was different than most people, until she was in first grade. Her best friend, Ellie, was talking about Christmas and how her whole family was coming into town. Aunts. Uncles. Cousins. She didn't know what any of those were, so when she got home from school that day, she asked her mom why her aunts, uncles and cousins couldn't come for Christmas too.

When her mother explained it to her, even at the tender age of six, she'd felt gipped. Robbed. Sad.

She glanced up at Dev, sitting so regally behind his desk, looking so much like the lord he was, and she unexpectedly realized that since she'd met him, all of those feelings of emptiness and loneliness had vanished, and were replaced with belonging. He was her soul mate. The infamous words of *Jerry McGuire*, 'you complete me', ran through her head.

Dev would barely let her out of his sight for a single moment since he'd rescued her from certain kidnapping. Again. When they were together, he constantly touched her, like he couldn't stand to part his skin from hers. A kiss on her temple. A hand on her knee or the small of her back. He even held her hand, which she thought was the sweetest thing ever. She didn't think hand holding fit at all with his commanding, domineering persona, but he didn't seem to care.

She was falling more in love with him each day. If she was honest with herself, she'd completely fallen. He enthralled her. And each day that went by she could envision herself as part of his world—*by his side*. That he didn't pressure her to bond was probably the biggest gift he could have given her and she loved him that much more for it, because she knew he would have bonded her days ago, without question. She needed this time to process everything and was grateful for his compassion.

He had been patient, gentle, soft and loving.

And a big tease. A few times during the day, he'd press her up against the wall with his mouth-watering, sexy body and pillage her mouth, mimicking the same motion with the throbbing hardness between his legs. He had her so worked up just an hour ago she'd practically begged him to take her on the spot, not caring if anyone else happened upon them. The quick orgasm he gave her helped to take the edge off, but she was far from satisfied.

Just thinking about it caused her body to heat and her core to ache. She'd changed her underwear more times in the last week than she did in a normal month. At this rate, she'd need to invest in some new ones. Dev would like that.

At that moment, Dev's eyes connected with hers and a slow, knowing smile spread across his sinfully gorgeous face.

"Just take care of it. I'll call you tomorrow." He hung up the phone, stood, and began slowly sauntering toward her. He was so beautiful it hurt to look at him sometimes. She still had a hard time wrapping her mind around the fact that he wanted *her*.

"It's time." Knowing exactly what he was referring to, she nodded, her eyes never leaving his. She was having a hard time getting used to the fact that he could hear her thoughts sometimes. He explained that was also atypical before mating.

But he was right. It was time. She *wanted* to be his. *Forever.*

"Forever. You're mine forever," he demanded.

She nodded again. Apparently the ability to use the English language had wholly escaped her. As he approached the couch on which she sat, she had to crane her neck to keep his gaze. She couldn't bear to look away.

His eyes glowed with desire, lust and...*love*. Even though neither had professed their love in so many words, she knew he loved her too, all the same.

When he spoke, his voice was low and gravelly. "Say it. Tell me you belong to me. I need to hear you speak the words, love."

"I—" She cleared her throat, unable to speak. She tried again. "I belong to you. Forever." He crouched, bringing them eye-to-eye.

"Please tell me this is what you want, Kate. Tell me you're coming to me of your own free will." His voice bordered on desperation. How could he think she didn't want this?

She grabbed his face with both hands and kissed him, hard. Pulling back, she looked him square in his murky eyes.

"I've never wanted anything more in my entire life. I *never* will."

She heard him mumble *Thank God*, right before he hauled her against his body, savagely plundering her mouth. The next thing she knew, they were in his bedroom. Her back flush with the wall held in place by the gorgeous, hard male in front of her. *Her* male.

His rough hands pushed up her shirt, yanking down the cup of her bra. His thumb stroked and plucked her distended, hypersensitive nipple, pulling a moan from her lips. His mouth never left hers, nipping and sucking on her upper and lower lips. Their tongues dueled, each one trying to gain the upper hand. Dev was winning, dominating her, and she loved every single second of it, but she wasn't about to relinquish the fight quite yet.

She heard a ripping sound and cool air hit her torso and her exposed breast. Before she had a chance to react, his mouth sucked her aching nipple hard, her torn shirt hanging in pieces. Her head, too heavy for her neck, fell back against the wall. Pleasure ricocheted through every molecule of her being.

Winner, round 1: Dev.

She wound her hands into his long hair, holding his head to her breast. She wanted him there—forever. "Dev...please."

"Please what, love?"

"I need you inside of me. Now."

"As you wish."

She thought he would take her to the bed, but instead he literally ripped her jeans down the seams, and, along with her panties, they fell to the floor. She was naked, save the ripped bra and shirt that still hung from her arms.

He'd unzipped his slacks pulling his enormous, weeping cock free. He lifted her leg and with one thrust, seated himself fully inside her. They both groaned.

"Oh God, Dev."

"Kate," he growled. "You feel so fucking good. You were made for me and me alone." His voice was tight and hoarse. His eyes glowed, his incisors sharp and long. She knew how much control he'd exerted over the last several days trying not to scare her, but she was ready for him tonight. All of him.

He pumped his cock slowly in and out of her tight channel. She could tell his control was ready to snap. "You're mine, Kate. Tell me."

"Yes. I'm yours." Her breasts bounced with each slow thrust. She couldn't look away from his mesmerizing eyes. A sudden, intense longing to have him take her blood rushed through her. The need to have his was just as intense...surprisingly.

His nostrils flared. "I'll never let you go, Kate. Ever. You're mine forever, do you understand?"

"Forever. Yes." He picked up his pace, thrusting harder and faster, reaching his hand down between their slick bodies to stroke her sensitive clit.

"I want you to come all over my cock, love." She wanted that too. Her head fell back against the wall, bearing her fine, sleek throat to him. She heard him hiss.

She looked at him under half-lidded eyes, knowing full well what she was about to offer and knowing deep down into the depths of her soul this was what she wanted. What she needed.

"Take me, Dev."

He instantly stilled and she whimpered at the loss of the immensely pleasurable sensations he was delivering with his impressive manhood. No one had ever made love to her so intensely or so sweetly all at the same time.

With extreme effort, she lifted her head from the wall and looked him square in the eye, answering his unasked question.

"I'm sure. I've never been more sure of anything in my life." At his slight hesitation, she whispered, "Please. I need to be yours now."

CHAPTER 38

Dev

Her entreaty was his undoing. He'd wanted nothing more than to take her sweet blood since the moment he laid eyes on her. Every time he made love to her this past week had been hellish torture because he couldn't have her completely. She was *his* and tonight he would make her irrevocably so.

He exercised every bit of control not to sink his fangs into her sweet, milky flesh that second. He wasn't going to bond with her against a wall. She deserved far better than that.

Never breaking eye contact, he carried her over to the bed, whipped off the comforter, and after removing the remnants of her shirt and bra, laid her down on the black silk sheets. Her raven hair blended in with the sheets, so that her ivory skin looked even starker against the darkness. She positively glowed. He could hardly breathe.

"Kate...you are...so...fucking...beautiful."

"You make me feel beautiful, Dev."

He shucked the rest of his clothes before crawling onto the bed. Her eyes roamed over his nakedness and he could both see and smell her powerful desire for him. She reached for him, but he gently grabbed her wrists, pulling them to the headboard.

"Hang on. Don't let go."

At her confusion, he said, "I don't think I can handle you touching me right now. I want to be gentle and when you're touching me, all sane thought and reason completely escape me."

She laughed. "What a coincidence."

His smile was slow and seductive as his eyes roamed her mouthwateringly naked body. If possible, his cock got even harder. And that didn't escape Kate's notice.

His eyes traveled all over her sexy body. "Oh, the things I want to do to you, love."

"What things? Tell me," she whispered.

He lightly drew his fingers down the inside of her arms, which were still securely latched onto the headboard, creating goose bumps in their wake.

"What things...hmmm. Well, first I want to stroke every single inch of your body with my hands."

His fingers continued lightly running down the length of her body, over her collarbone, skirting the outside of breasts, firmly squeezing her hips before he continued on down her thighs. Her eyes were heavy with lust, but she never looked away from him.

"Next, starting with your toes, I want to kiss, lick and suck my way back up the length of your toned, firm legs, spreading them wide open when I get to your pussy, so I can see how pink and creamy you are for me."

He knelt between her open legs, holding them apart with a broad hand on each calf. Her breasts rose and fell with every rapid breath. Her perfect pink nipples were hard and puckered, begging for his mouth. Her honeyed blood was coursing just below her fragile skin, singing to him like a siren's song.

"Then, I want to run my tongue over every curve, mapping every nook and cranny. I want to put my mouth and tongue on—*and in*—your pussy, and make you come over and over again, while I lap up every drop of it and you scream my name until you're hoarse."

Her breath hitched.

"After I'm done fucking you with my tongue, Kate, I'm going to fuck you with my cock. I'm going to take you hard and fast first. Then I'll make love to you slow and sweet. While I make love to you, I'm going to make you mine permanently, by sinking my fangs into your neck, taking your life essence into my body. I will bring you pleasure like you've never known."

Her heavy eyelids closed as he heard her say, *"Yes. God, yes."*

"I want you every way possible and then we'll make up some new ones. I want to take you in every single room of this house, Kate. I want to play strip pool and when you lose to me, I'm going to fuck you on the pool table that you're so fond of. I want to make love to you on the chaise out on our balcony and hear your screams of pleasure reverberate in the night sky. I want to own your body, your heart and your soul."

"You already do."

"I will never get enough of you, love." It was true. He could hardly focus on anything other than the intense need to be buried inside of her.

"Neither will I."

His slow, gentle intentions vanished like dust, his tongue ravenously licking the length of her slit. She tasted better than the finest wine he'd ever consumed, better than the sweetest chocolate that ever crossed his lips. He slid his tongue into her tight pussy, thrusting several times before moving to her clit, lashing at it with furious intent.

She came apart within moments, chanting his name over and over. His chest swelled in pride that he was able to elicit such responsiveness in such a magnificent woman.

Mine.

He grabbed her under the shoulders and pulled her astride his lap, taking her mouth with bruising force.

She met him stroke for stroke. His throbbing cock was nestled right outside her hot, wet pussy and he rocked against her, wanting to gain entry, but needing to be absolutely sure she was ready for this.

He caressed her face, his forehead against hers. She blinked her eyes open, slowly. Desire clouded her sparkling emeralds.

"This can't be undone. Once I make you mine, you will be mine forever. Do you understand?"

"Yes."

"There is no such thing as vampire divorce."

She grabbed his face in her hands and looked at him fiercely. "Yes, this is what I want. Stop asking me and just do it already, damn it!"

He laughed. "Who am I to deny my woman what she wants."

He shifted his hips and thrust into her hard. A gasp escaped her lips; her head fell back on her shoulders. He began a slow punishing rhythm.

"Oh God, Dev. Don't stop. Don't ever stop."

"Nothing could make me, love."

Her creamy, milky neck beckoned him. Her blood sang to him, practically calling his name. His teeth ached something fierce. He scattered hot, open-mouthed kisses up and down her neck, his teeth grazing, nipping, all the while his hips pumped, driving them both higher. With each kiss, nip and thrust, her moaning got louder. So did his.

He stopped at her carotid and sucked hard, drawing a low moan from her. He couldn't wait any longer. He gently pierced her silken skin quickly with his sharpened teeth and at his first pull of the world's sweetest nectar, Kate's hands flung to hold his head to her, as she broke apart in his arms, chanting, "Oh God, Oh God, Oh God."

He had never tasted anything sweeter. Her blood was an aphrodisiac and in ten lifetimes, he'd never have enough.

CHAPTER 39

Kate

Kate had never felt anything like the pleasure currently coursing through her body. She even felt like she could feel Dev's pleasure, which of course couldn't be possible. Reality had vanished and she was floating outside of herself. Dev's bite, while fleetingly painful, was the most pleasurable thing she had ever experienced. With each mouthful of blood he took from her body, her pleasure ratcheted up another impossible notch.

She never wanted this to end. She was officially an addict to the pleasure Dev could deliver.

She vaguely realized that he had sped up his thrusts to a frenzied pace, his fingers digging into her hips, and she felt another rush of euphoric pleasure as he stiffened and released his seed inside of her. He withdrew his fangs from her neck, crying out her name. Every cell in her body felt like a live wire. The feel of his tongue across her sensitive skin when he licked the wound was intensely erotic and she wanted his tongue on her entire body from head to toe, like he said he promised earlier.

They were both still breathing hard and he held her tight, whispering in her ear, but everything sounded like Charlie Brown's mother at the moment...*wah, wah, wah, wah, wah.*

They stayed fused together for an indeterminable amount of time, and she was finally coming back into herself, when she felt him twitch inside her. His cock was still as hard as granite and he was beginning to slowly, ever so slightly, rock his hips back and forth. He was insatiable and she loved every minute of it.

Abruptly a hunger hit her that was so painful, so severe, so undeniable, she knew it would mean certain death—*her death*—without Dev's blood running through veins. She actually felt her incisors lengthen in anticipation.

She felt desperate. She felt terrified.

She felt empowered.

She was still sitting on Dev's lap, his head buried in her neck. Going on what she could only later describe as instinct, she grabbed his hair with one hand and yanked his head backward and to the side, barely registering the surprised look on his face before she sank her teeth into his neck.

With the first drop of blood that passed her lips, she felt rapture like she'd never known. She knew this would be her life's sustenance. Everything became clearer, sharper, crisper.

She felt strong.

Powerful.

Invincible.

Dev moaned in pleasure. He shifted their positions, so he was lying on his back and she riding his stiff cock. He held her head tightly to his neck with one hand and her hips in place with the other, as he ruthlessly thrust upwards into her wet, slick body.

"Christ, Kate," he growled. He barely sounded human. Well...he wasn't, was he?

Their pleasure mingled until she didn't know where hers ended and his began. As they quickly fell over the precipice again together, their shared orgasm shattered them into a billion pieces. She had never known such ecstasy or eroticism even existed.

She felt a sharp tug on her scalp and heard Dev tell her to stop.

"Stop, baby. You've had enough."

No. She didn't want to stop. But as she was taking another pull, he grabbed her head with both hands and pulled more forcefully, extracting her teeth from his neck.

"Lick the puncture closed, my love."

She had a single-minded focus. Blood. As she started back down toward his neck, he stopped her, forcing her to look at him.

"Kate, that's enough. Lick the wound shut, love. Okay?" Her mind was in a haze. She heard him talking, heard the words he said, but the only thing that mattered in that moment was getting the sustenance that was being denied her. She was like a babe to her mother's breast.

His blood was paradise. It was powerful. It was hers.

He shook her slightly. "Kate. Listen to me. If you take any more, you *will* hurt me. Is that what you want?"

Yes. No. No...she didn't want to hurt him. But surely taking a bit more wouldn't hurt such a strong vampire, would it?

He threw her to her back, restraining her. Keeping her from what was rightfully hers. Damn him! She began to struggle in earnest.

"Kate, love. This is a blood high that's got you, baby. Shake it loose. You can fight it. Come back to me. Please."

She wanted to heed his words. She wanted to, but she couldn't. Something way beyond her control was pulling at her to take, take, take. A burst of strength flashed through her body and she lunged toward his beckoning flesh.

CHAPTER 40

Kate

She was crying. She looked beaten down, hopeless. Kate could actually feel Sarah's despair run through her as though it were her own.

She saw Sarah get up and pace around the room. Her eyes didn't look as dull as the last time she'd seen her. The crooks of her elbows were no longer bruised and she had different clothes on from the last time she'd seen her.

Kate felt utterly helpless. How was Sarah ever going to escape? Suddenly she remembered Olivia's training and she felt a little less helpless. She pulled herself back from the scene at hand to study her surroundings closely.

White, nondescript walls. No windows. Metal framed, twin-sized bed with dingy yellow sheets. Concrete floor. Steel door, no handle on the inside. Security camera in the ceiling corner. Nothing else.

Crap! How was this going to help? *Concentrate Kate.* There has to be something here.

Kate shut her eyes and used all of her senses. Did she hear soft crying? She did, but when she opened her eyes, it wasn't Sarah. Her crying had died to a few hiccups for now. There was someone else close by, in another room.

She closed her eyes again and listened hard. She heard the crying again, only louder this time. Kate concentrated on the source of the crying, willing herself to the source. The sobbing now sounded like it was right next to her. When she opened her eyes, she was in another room, exactly like the one Sarah was captive in, except this wasn't Sarah.

It was another young woman. A natural blond, with the most beautiful baby blue eyes she had ever seen. And sweet Jesus, she was pregnant. About seven months, Kate thought.

Oh God.

She quickly looked around and found nothing that would help identify where these women were being held, so she closed her eyes yet again and concentrated, sending out all of her senses.

More quiet sobbing. She concentrated on that sound and like last time, was drawn to it. She found it belonged to yet another young woman, only this time she was not alone. Two very large, very scary men were forcibly taking her from her room.

Correction...*vampires.*

Kate froze. Yes she was invisible, but she didn't know if vampires had different senses when it came to her kind. A few seconds ticked away and they didn't appear to notice anything out of the ordinary. The girl was now crying hysterically, begging them to stop, as they dragged her from the room.

Kate followed.

They took her to the same surgical room she'd seen Sarah in a few nights ago. They strapped her to the same horrific table and injected her with the same IV fluid bag, which stopped her struggling after a minute. Several more vampires entered the room, lust clouding their faces. As gut wrenching as it was to know this girl was going to be violated by these animals, she had to do her job if she was going to help save their lives.

Before turning away from the horrific scene in front of her, she looked carefully at all of the vampires and memorized their faces, so she could describe them later. Next, she looked around the room for anything that could identify where they were being held.

She noticed a small window in the left corner of the room. She noted the window looked to be at about ground level, which meant the majority of this building was underground. Excitement bubbled in her. She went to the window and, though it was dark outside, her senses were sharpened, so she could easily make out an old, decrepit barn, complete with a windmill and a forest of trees in the background.

She also noted the nearly full moon was off to the left and hope that would help give her placement of this spot. She felt herself awakening, so she took one last look around the room to see if she thought anything else would help before she was pulled away. She so wished she could prevent what was occurring in front of her, but couldn't and couldn't bear to watch it unfold either.

She closed her eyes and willed herself back to Sarah. She was now lying in bed with her eyes closed. She pushed all of the hope and calmness within her toward Sarah.

I'll be back as soon as I can, Sarah. You're not alone.

CHAPTER 41

Kate

Kate woke with a start. *Sarah.*

The dream with Sarah was so vivid and she wanted to tell Dev about it as soon as possible so she wouldn't forget one, minute detail.

She tried to sit up, but couldn't. Restraints held her wrists and ankles.

"What the—?"

Panic rose as she tried frantically to escape, but she quickly pushed it down. Panicking wouldn't do a damn thing to get her loose. She was good and securely hog-tied.

What happened? Why was she tied down? Where was she? Her eyes roamed around her dark surroundings, but she could see with full clarity, as if it were daylight. Just like in her dream with Sarah.

She forced herself to take stock of her surroundings. She was in a small room with nothing in it but four walls and the hard surface she was lying on. The door was closed. Oh God! Had the evil vampires discovered her after all?

She began to struggle in earnest. She felt power humming beneath her skin, like a strong electrical current, but as strong as she felt she couldn't break free. She called out for Dev.

Dev. It all came rushing back. Making love and...*oh shit*. As she remembered taking his blood, a severe hunger hit her hard and fast, followed closely by shame. She couldn't stop taking his blood and if he would come to her now, it mortified her further to admit she wasn't sure she'd be able to restrain herself again. She sucked ass as a mate already.

How could she do that to him? She loved him. She would do anything for him. Anything to protect him. Her lover. Her mate. Were they actually bonded now? Had she ruined that with her lack of control?

She felt him before he entered the room. Felt his anguish. She could hear his strong heartbeat. Hear the sweet sound of lifeblood rushing through his veins. She groaned and closed her eyes.

He opened the door and stepped through, locking eyes...never looking away. His expression was unreadable. Holy hell...he was so very sexy in his body-hugging black jeans and black cotton T-shirt stretched tightly across his broad chest and biceps. A severe desire to mount his cock and sink her teeth into his neck assailed her. She disgusted herself.

"I'm sorry Dev," she whispered.

He didn't speak, didn't make any apologies for restraining her, just walked slowly toward her. He should leave her here forever. Probably a good idea, as the hunger quadrupled the second he walked in.

She had to give him an out, so she rushed to speak before he did.

"I understand if you want a divorce already. I did try to kill you, after all." She turned her head, breaking eye contact. She knew what was coming, and while she couldn't bear to be let go by this beautiful, sexy creature, she didn't want to see the look on his face when he told her to get out. She would try to retain a little dignity. But she would tell him of her latest dream before she left.

"You told me you understood." His voice was a little hard and right next to her.

"Understood what?" She still couldn't make eye contact with him.

Instead of answering, he ran his finger lightly down the inside of her arm. She was dressed in a strappy, bright blue silky nightgown that hit mid-thigh. The expensive outfit was quite a contrast to the bleak surroundings she found herself in. Dev must have put her in it, because she didn't own such an exquisite piece of lingerie and the last she remembered, she was naked riding his cock. He'd bought her so many beautiful things this week to replace all that was left at her apartment.

At his touch, her nipples pebbled to hard points, which were visible through the thin material. Her body immediately readied itself for him, as it always did whenever he was around. His gaze and finger traveled to circle the closest nub and she closed her eyes in pleasure. All thoughts of anything else vanished.

She could feel his desire, mingling with hers. For the first time since he walked in, she realized what a vulnerable position she was in. She was restrained, wearing little clothing and her new vampire mate was standing beside her, touching her erotically. God help her, but she wanted more. She was so very turned on.

"You can never leave me, love. Nor I, you. That's what forever means. I thought I made that clear before we bonded."

She sucked in a breath when Dev leaned down and bit her nipple—*hard*—through her negligee, before sucking gently to soothe the hurt he'd inflicted.

"Ahhhnn...more." She couldn't form the words, but she didn't want him to stop. Even if this was the last time he touched her.

In one smooth swipe, he ripped the nightgown from her body, the back half left underneath her still-

213

restrained torso. He caressed her now bared breasts, testing the weight in his hands.

"Forever, Kate. I'll always give you what you want, my love. I'll always give you what you need."

"I want you. I need you, Dev." It was the agonizing truth. She'd never wanted or needed anyone more. She felt like a completely different person than she was just a week ago. It was exhilarating and terrifying at the same time.

He shed his clothes in seconds. After he'd climbed on the hard surface, his head faced her feet and he carefully straddled her face, his erect cock bobbing just inches away from her mouth. She could barely remember to breathe when he grabbed his beautiful member and slowly began to stroke it, so close to her lips, yet so far away. She wanted to lick the pre-cum off the tip. She wanted him to sink that purple, swollen bulbous head between her lips so she could suck him to completion. Correction...she *craved* it.

He chuckled, lowering his head to her opened and bare pussy. With his other hand he opened her nether lips, tested her readiness.

"You are so wet for me, my love. That's so very sexy." His low voice reverberated in hot waves over her body.

He speared his tongue into her wet, slick channel. Over and over. He pushed her to the edge, pulling back again and again, denying her the orgasm she so desperately wanted.

She tried to push her hips closer to his mouth and raise her head to capture his manhood between her lips, but her restraints kept her from moving like she wanted. She needed him to let her come. She was beyond frustrated.

"Dev..."

He chuckled, but never stopped working his gorgeous cock or driving his tongue into her pussy.

"Patience, my love. All good things come to those who wait."

He flicked her clit again, while he thrust a long, thick finger into her pussy. One or two more pumps and she'd explode. Instead, he withdrew his wet finger and slowly eased the digit back to her forbidden hole, pressing in slightly before sinking it slowly to the last knuckle.

"Oh, God," she moaned, tightly closing her eyes.

"Do you want me to stop, Kate?" His voice sounded thick with gravel.

"Stop and you die."

He laughed. "That's twice you've threatened my life in the last twelve hours, my love. You definitely need to be punished for those indiscretions."

"I'm sor—"

Her apology was cut short when several things happened simultaneously. He slammed his mouth on her clit, thrust his finger to the hilt in her backside and two into the depths of her pussy, all while stroking his cock. Talented guy. She was overwhelmed with sensation, both physically and visually. It was an erotic experience like nothing she'd ever imagined.

He was strumming her body like an expert guitarist. She was bombarded with so many sensations, she couldn't think straight, so she gave up trying to and just let herself *feel*. Pre-cum dropped onto her lower lip and she greedily licked it up.

He raised his head from her clit briefly, commanding her to come. She couldn't deny him and screamed his name over and over.

"Open your mouth, love," he softly groaned.

She did as instructed and his hot semen splashed all over her lips and chin, some landing in her mouth. She devoured as much as she could. She was desperate to touch him, but that thought vanished when she felt the telltale prick of his fangs in her fleshy mound, which kicked off yet another blinding orgasm. He withdrew his fangs all too soon and they lay there for a moment, regaining their breath. He was careful not to get too close to her mouth, or more appropriately, her fangs, with any part of his body.

He turned around and must have seen the hunger in her eyes, for he looked at her with such love and longing she thought she would melt on the spot.

"Do you think you can handle a little snack without trying to drain me, love?"

"I—I don't know, Dev." She wanted his blood so badly, she wasn't sure she could stop herself again. He would have to keep her locked up forever at this rate.

"You can do it, Kate. Just take it slow."

"I don't want to hurt you."

He smiled, such tenderness in his eyes. She didn't deserve it. "You won't hurt me, love."

After cleaning her face with the shredded nightie, he lowered his wrist to her open mouth and she bit carefully, relishing his taste on her lips. This time it was different and while she wanted more, she was able to stop herself after just a few swallows, when she felt sated. He encouraged her all the while with a low voice and soft words. She did not deserve him.

"That's it, love. Now seal the punctures closed with your tongue." She did as directed.

"Good girl. Better?"

She nodded. "Yes."

"Good. I'm going to untie you. You're not going to lunge for my jugular again, are you?" He said it in a teasing voice, but she could hear the underlying concern. She felt like a slug. No, she felt like the dirt beneath a slug.

"No. I'm sor—"

"Don't say you're sorry again, Kate. It was completely my fault. I'm the one who should be apologizing. In my haste to make you mine, I completely forgot about the blood high. My blood is very powerful and your body needed time to adjust. I should have been more prepared."

He leaned down and placed a gentle kiss on her lips, and she tasted herself on him. It was undeniably sexy and in that moment, she wanted him inside her more than she ever had. She loved him and she wanted to tell him so, but she was scared. They were bonded for Christ's sake...it was stupid not to tell him. Yes, she was a chicken shit, admittedly. She was bonded to him forever and he should know the depth of her feelings for him went beyond the fact that nature had fated them to be together and they couldn't keep their hands off of each other.

"Please forgive me, love."

She couldn't speak, so she just nodded. He gently released her wrists and ankles and rubbed them both to restore the blood flow. She was stiff when he helped her sit up, and when she glanced at him, his eyes were roaming up and down her naked body. He wanted her. Again.

Good. She wasn't alone in her unquenchable thirst that never seemed to be slaked around him.

"What is this place?" she asked, looking around.

He looked sheepish. "It's where we keep rogue vampires that need restraining."

"Oh my God. Am I rogue?"

"Hell no. But I didn't have anyplace to keep you safe where you couldn't escape and potentially harm others. I'm sorry." He turned and walked to the other side of the room, affording her a view of his amazing tight ass.

"You are strong, Kate. Too strong for this to be the effect of just the bonding. I had Doc come take some more blood while you were out to run additional tests to see what may have changed in your DNA since our mating."

She should be mad that he took her blood, yet again without permission, but at this point she needed some answers and they were beyond her. His face looked grim.

"It took immense effort for me to restrain you. And as a lord, I am the strongest of our race. Hell, you shouldn't even have had fangs until I gave you my blood. You shouldn't have been able to take it on your own like you did. It has to be the vampire DNA, but it still makes no sense. That's probably what caught me off guard and why you ended up being a bit out of control."

"What...what does that all mean?"

In two strides he was enveloping her in his warmth. "I don't know, love, but we *will* find out. I promise you, everything will be okay. Everything will be okay."

She could do nothing but hang onto him. He was her lifeline in this vortex that had now become her life. Her head was spinning. She had a sinking feeling that something was very wrong with her. Something that would threaten to tear her and Dev apart. *Dramatic much, Kate?*

She reluctantly pulled away from his heat.

"Dev, I had another dream about Sarah. This time I have some details that may help find her."

CHAPTER 42

Dev

He couldn't shake his intense guilt for overlooking something so significant as blood lust, which was akin to human drug addiction. Too late, he'd recalled that mating rituals involved small amounts of blood given over a longer period of time to avoid blood lust.

The thought of making her his had been his entire focus only hours ago. He was an ancient vampire and he should have known better. He *did* know better. That was the problem with Kate, however. He completely lost all common sense and rational thought around her. Most especially when he was inside of her.

He almost needed help restraining her, but the thought of someone else seeing her beautiful naked body stopped him cold. He'd managed to drag her away from his throat and restrain her in the dungeon. Not a place his beloved belonged, but he'd had no other choice at the time.

He was baffled at her strength and her developing abilities. He should have easily been able to control her, but he was serious when he told her it took all of his strength to pull her away. Bloodlust makes you temporarily stronger, but it shouldn't give her that much power. Now that they were bonded, she would gradually gain his same abilities, but it happened over a period of years, not minutes.

Of course, with Kate, everything was completely up in the air. He should learn to expect the unexpected, because every time he turned around, something new slapped him in the face.

His index finger rubbed back and forth as he admired his mating mark spanning the circumference of his left thumb. A matching one graced the same finger on Kate, confirming the bonding was complete. He had to admit he felt shamelessly possessive and virile at the sight of his permanent mark on her and vice versa.

While he was intensely proud of her strength and capability, the thought of his mate being anywhere near his nemesis had ice running through his veins. He loved her beyond his comprehension and could hardly breathe at the thought of anything bad happening to her. Reluctantly, he also knew she was their best hope at taking down a vampire that was once his closest friend. And the reality was he was helpless to stop her dreams, so he might as well use the information she saw to find him.

"Let's get you back up to our bedroom so you can get dressed. As much as I'd love to keep you permanently naked, we have a rogue vampire to catch and some girls to save. You can tell me the details of your dream after we've showered."

"Okay."

The smile lit up her entire face up like a Christmas tree. A tidal wave of love washed over him and he knew he'd give this woman anything her heart desired. He was a complete and total goner.

And he'd never been happier. He only hoped that happiness didn't come crashing down around him.

CHAPTER 43

MIKE

Mike's head falling forward startled him awake. Jesus H, the older he got, the harder it was to shake off his annual night of stupidity. He would do it for Jamie, though. She deserved that much. Coming right to the station after his graveside vigil, he'd managed to catch a few hours of restless shut-eye on a worn-out sofa, broken springs digging into his back.

He hurt like hell today and was dragging ass. Even the shitty coffee wasn't helping this morning. They'd need a few more pieces of information from Professor Bailey, but the bastard didn't show at the scheduled time yesterday. Jake had an arrest warrant out on his ass since, according to his assistant, he'd taken an unexpected and indefinite leave of absence.

"Man, you look like shit," Jake said as he strolled into their office. "Hard night?"

No way was he gonna spill his secrets to his partner. That was his cross to bear and his alone. Jake knew something was up, but he had to give the guy credit. He never pushed for an explanation. It made him a great partner.

"Something like that. Any word on the wily professor?"

"Nah. We're watching his house. I have a feeling he'll show up."

Mike nodded in agreement. *Damn*...even that small action had his head protesting. A two-day hangover was hell. He'd already swallowed half a bottle of aspirin and not only did it *not* help his headache, now he felt like fire ants were eating a hole in his stomach too. He was probably getting an ulcer. Just his luck.

He pushed all that shit and wallowing aside. They had a job to do and it didn't matter how bad he felt, he would do it.

On his desk were a dozen new 'leads' on Sarah's disappearance that he had to wade through to determine what was shit and what may be valid.

Pushing back his splitting head and sour stomach, he got to work. He wouldn't fail his friend. He wouldn't fail his friend's daughter. He would find Sarah even if it meant putting himself in the ground.

CHAPTER 44

Xavier

"Sire, I have good news. Another successful delivery occurred this morning. Two more are progressing nicely and should deliver within the next few weeks."

Xavier lounged in his office, his favorite Scotch in hand. He was sated for the moment, having recently devoured three, lovely fresh meals several nights ago at the human male's house. He'd decided to leave the human male alive, for that was far more fun than relieving him of his heavy burden—the guilt of knowing it was *his* actions, or lack thereof, that resulted in the demise of his entire family.

Yes, he was a sadistic bastard. *Smile.*

"Good. And the new female?"

"Ah, progressing nicely. We've completed three rounds of inseminations and are monitoring her daily. We should know within the next couple of days if it took. If not, we'll need to wait until the next cycle to try again, but all test results indicated she's strong, healthy and fertile. I'm hopeful."

His weakness cut him to the quick and generated an almost uncontrollable rage every time he thought about it. His breeding rates were off the charts successful, save one small fact. He had a goddamn genetic mutation where he spawned only females. He'd quit participating in the actual breeding many years ago, telling his lieutenants they had earned the privilege of helping him grow his army.

Other than breading, fucking, and feeding, females were useless, and since female vampires couldn't breed, naturally they had to be disposed of. He didn't share his former brethren's reverence of female vampires.

Only two people knew of this genetic flaw and if his good doctor spoke of it, Xavier would quickly tear his throat out. Or draw out his torture painfully. Either way, he'd sign his own death warrant.

"Anything else?"

"No, my liege."

"Then get the fuck out. And bring me a female. I'm hungry all of a sudden."

"Right away, sire."

CHAPTER 45

Dev

"We need to put that cocksucker in the ground and yesterday!" A round of expletives abounded. The noise level in the room was nearly deafening.

They were in Dev's lower level boardroom; a thirty-foot, hand-carved cherry wood table was the centerpiece of the room and could comfortably seat forty people. It was nearly full.

"Quiet!" Dev yelled. You could instantly hear a pin drop.

"No need to state the obvious. Let's go over what facts we've all been able to gather in the last few days. Ren, start with your conversation with Detective Thatcher."

Ren stood, his loud voice echoing off the walls.

"Apparently one Professor Duncan Bailey was the last person known to see Sarah Hill alive. He tried to run and is now in custody. It seems the good professor was in bed with a *Master* Vampire"—Ren air-quoted *Master*—"who threatened his family in exchange for his cooperation. Apparently this Master Vampire had recently acquired the professor's daughter as collateral for his continued *assistance*."

The usually quiet Romaric spoke up. "What type of *assistance*?"

"I'm getting to that. Bailey's the head of Northwestern's psychology department, and was running several sleep studies that focused on the dream state. Sarah told Bailey she was having some unusual and very realistic dreams and he asked her to be part of his little research project.

"Seems this vamp was looking for candidates for his own little experiments. In exchange for Bailey's cooperation in handing over candidate names and the sleep project results, his family lived. He was also paid handsomely, I might add. Oh...and one more thing. Sarah was the second such young woman this asshole served on a silver platter to Xavier."

Damian slammed his hands on the table as he flew out of his chair. "Son-of-a-fucking-bitch. That motherfucker is now looking for dreamwalkers?"

"It would seem that way, Damian," Dev answered. Dev knew Xavier was a sick son of a bitch, but even he had been surprised at Xavier's depravity. It seemed his former bestie was back to his old tricks of kidnapping women and callously killing them, but according to Kate's dreams, one was pregnant. How could someone keep their Moira in that depraved situation? So many questions and not enough answers.

"You mentioned Xavier. Have we confirmed it's him, or is there possibly another player?" Romaric's deep, ever calm voice interjected.

"The professor claims not to have seen this *master* vamp personally and Thatcher believes him. But they all refer to him as...*my liege or lord*, so, yes, we think it's Xavier."

"Fucking-A!" Damian shouted. The room erupted in shouts and curses.

Dev spoke calmly to Giselle. "Elle, tomorrow morning I want you to go down to the station and personally interrogate this asshole. Use *whatever means necessary* to extract all information from him." Giselle was ruthless. The perfect vamp for the job.

Giselle smirked and nodded in his direction. She lived for this kind of job. A wolf in sheep's clothing was a euphemism that fit her to a "T".

Dev looked at Kate and his entire demeanor changed. His voice softened. His hard eyes filled with encouragement.

"Love, will you tell the others of your most recent dream?"

She looked nervous, and he was immensely proud when she stood confidently and recounted her most recent dream where she saw Sarah and two other females. One, noticeably pregnant; the other being raped. She recounted every little detail she could remember, including the landmarks outside the small window. Her description of the vampires and hostages was detailed and thorough. Too bad she hadn't seen Xavier in her dream.

"So..." Damian began, rising up to his full six-foot-six-inch frame. "Let me get this straight. Are you saying in addition to Xavier tracking down dreamwalkers, some psychotic motherfucking rogue has actually let their Moira be used to help Xavier create his army?"

Dev sighed heavily. "It would appear that way, yes."

"Well, fuck me runnin'. This is worse than shitting fire and falling in it."

Ren burst out laughing, shaking his head. "Where do you get this shit, bro? Do you troll the Internet now to come up with new sayings?"

Damian smirked. "You're just jealous of my timely and inventive wit, fucker."

"Suck it."

"Whip it out."

"You couldn't wrap your lips around it."

"I can get my lips around a tootsie roll just fine, asswipe."

"Children," Dev loudly interrupted. "We have more important things to worry about than whose cock is bigger. Jesus. Damian, why don't you and Ren go *talk* to some of the *visitors* you brought back from Kate's and see if we learn anything enlightening. They should be nice and hungry by now and amenable to provide assistance. If you can keep your hands off each other, that is." Dev hadn't told Kate they'd brought back a couple of prisoners from her most recent kidnapping.

A simultaneous "fuck you" was uttered by both men.

"Elle, visit our professor and report back to me ASAP. Rom, don't you have some contacts in the medical community that we could use to track down information on others who may also be on Xavier's payroll?"

The man of many words that Romaric was, he simply nodded.

"Good. You work that angle."

"Of course. I also have an excellent computer technologist. I will contact her straight away and see if we can't glean a new lead using that method." Rom stood to leave, along with his men. He was one of the most uptight vampires Dev knew.

"Perfect. Let's all meet back here tomorrow night at midnight and see what new information we all have."

As everyone left to attend to their respective tasks, Dev added, "Oh, and gentlemen, it's no contest. My cock wins."

Consensus was not reached on that point.

CHAPTER 46

Dev

Hours later a hard knock reverberated on his office door before it opened. Dev looked up from the papers he was reviewing as Big D's large frame took up almost the entire doorway. And he looked grim.

"What did you find, doc?" asked Dev, as he stood and walked around the front of his large cherry desk.

Big D nervously cleared his throat. "Well, I have run several tests on the two blood samples I took from Kate, cross-matched them with all of the blood samples we have in the database and I come up with the same results. Every single time."

Big D hesitated for several beats before he continued. He looked positively sick.

"As you know, we've already determined from her first blood sample that she has vampire lineage and has to be adopted as both the parents are human."

Dev nodded. The doc was stalling and he was afraid his worst fears were about to be confirmed.

"Yes, I know that already. What else did you find out?"

"Her lineage has been traced back to the Illenciam bloodline."

A roaring sound rang in his head, getting louder and

229

louder so he couldn't think straight. His vision turned fuzzy. He sunk down onto his leather couch in a fog. He'd suspected, but to have his fears actually confirmed...that was another thing entirely. His voice was barely a whisper. "How can that be?"

Big D looked directly into Dev's eyes with sympathy. "I'm sorry, my lord, but they are not wrong. I have repeated them countless times. They are conclusive. There is no doubt that Kate is Xavier's daughter."

This could not be happening.

Holy. Christ.

This.

Could.

Not.

Be.

Happening.

Big D was talking, but he couldn't hear any of the words. Nothing made sense. His world had just gone black. Blown to smithereens right out from underneath him.

Dev had been trying to justify Kate's unusual display of power by convincing himself they didn't know Xavier's background. Being abandoned by his parents it was certainly likely there were others out there with the skill of stasis.

But...a *daughter*? His daughter? Did he know she lived? He must. Was this whole thing a setup to get close to him? How could it not be? Had Xavier somehow known Kate was his Moira? Had the rogues at her house simply been there to get a report back to Xavier? This made no sense, but what other explanation was there? Xavier had finally found a way to gut him. And gutted, he felt. He *loved* her. She couldn't possibly betray him like this...could she? Xavier had taken away everything good in his life, now including his mate.

He could barely breathe.

Jesus, he had been completely blinded by lust...and

love. He'd been led around by his dick from the moment he laid eyes on her, which was probably all part of the plan. Kate was one hell of an actress; he'd give her that.

Fuck! He'd put his entire Regent in jeopardy, not to mention the people he cared about most in the world. Those that had stood by his side for centuries.

The love of his life, *his mate*, was the daughter of the devil himself. *His* Kate was the daughter of his most abhorrent enemy, Xavier Illenciam.

Fate was a crazy, fickle bitch.

He was utterly destroyed. He wasn't sure how long he sat there, but it was so long that doc had left, Ren taking his place. Ren didn't say a word. Just stood by the door, in case he was needed. Dev couldn't even look at him. The last thing he needed to see was compassion in his friends face. Or worse...pity.

Dev finally pulled himself together and went in search of Kate. Ultimately he was a Vampire Lord and his responsibility, first and foremost, was to protect all those under his reign and he could not—*would not*—let Xavier subvert that. He would ascertain if Kate was a traitor. God help her if she was. He may be bonded to her already and his life now inextricably woven with hers, and while his soul would die a thousand deaths being parted from her, he would do anything to protect those that relied on him for their safety and their very lives.

He would get to the truth. By any means necessary. But deep inside he fervently prayed to a God he didn't really believe in that this was just some giant, unbelievable cosmic fucking coincidence.

Kate

Running on the treadmill, Kate just started her fifth mile at the twenty-one minute mark, while Dev caught up on work. She glanced at the beautiful intricate mating mark gracing her left thumb and butterflies took flight in her stomach. He was hers. That magnificent man was hers for all of eternity. It was both a terrifying and comforting thought.

She could hardly wrap her head around how different she felt now. How powerful she felt, after bonding with Dev. The changes she'd felt happening after she'd met Dev were now more noticeable, more pronounced after their bonding. She was getting used to her speed and agility. The constant loud pounding in her head had finally diminished and she could only hear it if she concentrated. She hadn't tried flashing yet. She was petrified where she would end up. Dev said he would teach her when things calmed down a bit.

As she ran, she berated herself for the lack of work on her dissertation, as that's really what she should be doing with her downtime, but she'd been unable to concentrate. So many crazy things had happened over the last several days, she felt like she was on a merry-go-round and couldn't get off. And this merry-go-round was going at warp speed.

If anyone had told her a week ago there were vampire sex gods, freeze frame abilities, flashing, eternal mates, a vampire sadist, and dreamwalkers, she would have suggested a good psychiatrist and a nice big dose of Prozac. And maybe some much-needed time off of work—in an inpatient mental institution. At times, she wondered if this whole thing was a very long, very strange dream, from which she could not wake.

But one look at Dev and she knew all was right with the world, she was where she was supposed to be, even as messed up as things were. She was completely lost in her own head when she glanced up and noticed Dev standing in front of the treadmill. Something was wrong.

She hit stop on the treadmill and jumped to the sides while it slowed down, pulling her ear buds out. She was barely winded. Being a vampire mate definitely had its advantages.

She couldn't help but smile when she saw him. "Hi."

He didn't reply.

She frowned, her brows drawing inward. "What's wrong, Dev?"

"Come with me." His face was completely impassive. Completely unreadable. Not at all like the Dev she'd come to know.

He held out his hand, which she gladly took as she jumped off the treadmill. She loved touching any part of him and it never failed to deliver a large dose of lust straight to her core.

"Okaaay. You're scaring me. What's wrong?"

No response.

He pulled her close and she felt the telltale dizziness that accompanied flashing. *What the hell?*

She was just getting her bearings, when she realized they were back in the underground room he'd held her in the night of their mating. She was already strapped down on that horribly hard table.

"Dev, what the hell are you doing?" she yelled. Something was terribly wrong here. She tried to struggle free, to no avail. Even her enhanced powers didn't help her.

Then he simply stepped back and exited the room. He didn't look at her or utter a word.

"What the hell is going on?" she screamed. "You can't leave me like this! Dev, why are you doing this? I don't understand!"

She continued to yell for several minutes into the complete silence of her barren prison. Dev didn't return.

CHAPTER 47

MIKE

"What the fuck are you doing here?" Mike said, pulling her into one of the interrogation rooms. He'd only met Giselle a few short months ago and she might be the most beautiful woman he'd ever laid eyes on, but the fact remained that she was a predator, just like the rest of them. Except, possibly even more deadly and volatile.

"Now, Detective, is that any way to treat a woman?" Giselle purred.

"No. But you're not a woman, so the same rules don't apply," he responded, a smirk turning up the corner of his mouth. He was being an asshole, but he didn't care. They hadn't pried any more useful details from the professor in their earlier interrogation, he was still sporting the mother of all headaches, and he'd barely slept in days. So yeah, he *felt* like an asshole and she was the perfect target to take it out on.

She stepped into his personal space, licked her ruby red lips and ran a perfectly manicured fingertip down his chest. Mike was a tall guy at six foot, two inches. And at six feet tall, with her fuck-me heals on, Giselle was looking him straight in the eyes, their noses nearly touching. Her breath mingled with his.

"Hmmm...I can assure you I'm all woman. And it would be my pleasure to show you. After we're done here, of course."

Mike laughed, but it was humorless. The urge to take a giant Simon Says step backward was overwhelming, but he would not show any hint of weakness. What was Giselle doing here anyway? He had one very good guess.

"Not if you and I were the last living beings on earth, baby." As he said it, though, surprisingly, he didn't really believe it. Every time he saw Giselle, his cock was unexplainably drawn to her. And that pissed him the fuck off.

She frowned, her bottom lip pouting. "That's not very original, Detective." She looked in his eyes with undisguised lust. Then she leaned in, speaking directly in his ear. "And I assure you, *baby*, it would be pleasure beyond your wildest comprehension. You'd be begging me for more."

His dick had gone rock hard the moment she'd stepped into his space, and at that comment, it throbbed with anger. Traitorous bastard. He needed to get both of his heads on the same page. A knowing smile broke out across her gorgeous face and she finally took a step back, as if she'd accomplished what she wanted. Another Giselle mind-fuck special. Bitch.

Still not moving, he responded, "And I repeat. What is it you want, Giselle?"

That infuriating smirk remained on her stunning face. "I want to visit our house guest, of course."

"This isn't the goddamn Ritz, sweetheart. Forget it. You can tootle on back home and report to Dev that I don't take kindly to him sticking his nose where it doesn't belong. Nothing about our professor concerns you. Or him."

"Now, now, Detective. Don't be like that. You know this does concern us. We're just trying to help solve a mutual problem, which is in both of our best interests."

Shaking his head, Mike said, "Yeah? How's that?"

Giselle dropped her sultry persona, becoming the ice-cold bitch that she generally was.

"Don't be obtuse. We are both very much aware that this case has crossed the territory boundaries, and you are incapable of handling this alone. If you want to live, that is. So drop the high and mighty act. I *will* see our professor and I only stopped by to discuss it with you as a professional courtesy. Don't mistake this as me *asking* for your permission. I'm not."

"Are you threatening me?" Rage built deep within Mike. He balled his hands into fists, desperately trying to keep from strangling her. Or fucking her. She may be spot on, but he'd rot in hell before he let her know that. He was going to rot in hell anyway, so no more skin off his nose.

She had once again slipped back into her sex kitten act, stepping into his personal space. The rate at which she was able to do that was dizzying. Could vamps be bipolar, he wondered?

"Of course not, Detective. You're a very handsome man and I'm just trying to protect you." She leaned in, her lips whispering over the shell of his ear again. "I'd hate for anything to happen to you before I had a chance to spend hours fucking your brains out."

The way his body responded to her repulsed him. He simultaneously wanted to throw her down and bury himself deep in her, while thrusting a rusty, serrated knife into her heart, ripping it out of her sexy body. Christ, he was one sick bastard. And in desperate need of a vacation. Or another bottle of Jack. And clearly a lay. How he longed for the days of complete ignorance about vampires.

Giselle was no longer at his ear, but stood close enough that he could feel every breath she took on his lips. He knew two things with certainty. One, if Giselle wanted to see the professor, she would...by any means. And two, he wasn't about to let her near him without being present, so he really had no choice but to accommodate her. Besides, this could work to his advantage if he learned anything new. If anyone could get additional information out of this guy, it was Giselle. And she was so smokin' hot she probably didn't even need her vampiric skills to accomplish it.

"After you," he said, with a flourish of his hand.

Her eyes narrowed in skepticism, but she made her way toward the door, letting Mike lead once she'd exited the room. They entered another infrequently used interrogation room toward the back of the station. The intercom wasn't currently working and he needed complete privacy for this conversation.

"Stay here while I get our perp." He turned to leave as she called out to him.

"You'd better not fuck me over, or you'll regret it."

His face hardened as he turned and glided toward her, leaning down so they were nose to nose. "When I fuck you, Giselle, I guarantee I will regret it." He turned and fled the room before she could respond. He'd been dead serious.

Ten minutes later Mike returned with Professor Bailey.

"Have a seat, Professor," said Mike, gesturing toward an empty chair.

"I don't know anything more than what I've already told you. I don't understand why I'm in here again." The professor had sweat dotting his pale balding head, slightly dripping down his temples, as his beady eyes flitted back and forth between Mike and Giselle. They lingered longer on Giselle, of course.

Giselle leaned forward, grinned seductively, and put her elbows on the table effectively shoving together her...*assets*. *Assets* that were simply fan-fucking-tastic.

"I'm afraid I have a few more questions for you,

Professor Bailey. It shouldn't take too long and we'd really appreciate your help."

Mike guessed the professor forgot where her eyes were located as he replied to Giselle's chest...uh, *request*, that is. And for some godawful unknown reason, that supremely pissed him off.

"Y-Yes. Yes, of course. That's fine. I want my daughter found and returned safely, so whatever you need from me, just ask."

She whispered, "That's what I was hoping you'd say."

CHAPTER 48

Dev

"So, to what do I owe the pleasure of being summoned to the great Lord Fallinsworth's residence?" Esmeralda purred as she sauntered toward Dev's desk.

Esmeralda was a stunningly beautiful woman and she knew it. At a tall five foot nine inches, she had voluptuous curves in all the right places. Her olive skin always glowed with a unique golden aura. He thought it was specifically designed to draw in her prey. Her dark chocolate eyes gave you a false sense of warmth and security. Her waist-length midnight, ramrod straight hair rounded out the entire sexy package. As sensual as she was, she'd never once made him hard. Not for lack of trying on her part, either.

Ren growled. Actually growled. There was definitely no love lost between those two. Dev wasn't particularly fond of Esmeralda either, but she was a necessary evil at this point. He didn't have time to track down another witch.

Throwing Ren a glare, Es turned back to Dev. "You really should learn to keep your pets on a leash, darling."

Ren started toward her and Dev held his hand up, never taking his eyes from Esmeralda. He didn't trust her enough to look away for a second. Ren retreated to stand by the door, beefy arms crossed, death glare pasted on his face.

"Enough. Es, I'm in need of your assistance." Damn, it physically hurt to say that.

She regarded him for a moment, her dark eyes drawing him in. A smile curved her full, red lips.

"It will cost you, darling."

Another reason he didn't like to ask Esmeralda for help. She'd wanted to bed him ever since they met more than one hundred years ago. She'd tried just about everything. And since her sorcery didn't work on him none of her advances had been successful. He was actually afraid that the witch might try to harm Kate when she found out about her, which was just about to happen.

"Of course it will. What's your price?"

Esmeralda ambled slowly around the desk, stopping directly in front of Dev. In his personal space, as always. As she reached out to touch him, he grabbed her wrist, stopping her midstream. A flash of surprise crossed her face, but she quickly hid it. To keep a semblance of peace, in the past he'd always indulged her in these games. No more. He had a mate—even if she may be a traitor—and being touched by another female, especially Esmeralda, repulsed him.

Her mask firmly back in place, she seductively purred, "It's not money that I want, Dev."

He smiled, although he knew it looked cruel. "I'm afraid that's all you're going to get from me, Esmeralda. I'm bonded now."

She immediately jumped out of his hold as if she'd been burned, shock forcing her mouth to hang open. "What? How can that be possible?" she shrieked.

"Oh come on, Es. You understand how vampire bonding works. I found my Moira, quite by accident, but found her nonetheless and the rest, as they say, is history. I don't think I need to explain the bonding ritual to you in detail, *do I*?" He was pushing the envelope, but this was just a bit too enjoyable.

She blanched just a little. Her aura dimmed significantly. Wow, she was way more besotted with him than he'd originally thought. Fuck. This could end very badly.

"When?"

He straightened to his full height. "When is irrelevant. In fact, my mate is one of the reasons I need your help."

A smug look replaced the one of shock. The corners of her mouth turned up in a smirk and she took a step back toward him. "Is that so? Trouble in paradise already then?"

Damn. This was such a bad fucking idea. "Never mind. I've changed my mind. Leave." He should have asked Rom, who could sense the spoken truth, but he didn't want the other Lords to find out about this possible subterfuge just yet.

"Now, Dev, don't be like that. I can and will help you, of course. For just a small price. It's nothing, really. And it doesn't involve getting you into my bed. Although if you were willing, I wouldn't turn it down either."

His spidey senses were immediately on high alert. "You haven't even heard what I'm asking of you."

"It matters not. My price won't change, regardless of the ask. But go on. What grave problem causes you to scrape the bottom of the barrel in asking for *my* help?"

He regarded her carefully. She was playing him, he was sure of it. If his instincts were wrong in asking for her help, all that he cherished could be at risk. But if he didn't, all of the lives he was responsible for could also be lost. Goddamn it, he was backed into a corner and this may be his only way out. Esmeralda was the most powerful witch he had ever come across and he'd formed a loose alliance with her as he knew he might need her help from time to time. Unfortunately her services hadn't been useful in uncovering Xavier's home base and they knew he also must be working with a powerful witch to hide his whereabouts. No, he had to proceed with the plan. Whatever her price, he would have to pay it.

"Confidentiality goes without saying. If I find out you've spoken of this to anyone, I will personally tear out your heart and enjoy doing so."

She laughed, throwing her head back. "Good luck, vamp." Chuckling, she added, "I promise to keep your *deep, dark secret*, darling. Spill it. How can I serve *his majesty*?"

He glanced quickly at Ren. He didn't know how much Ren knew about Kate and he didn't want it getting beyond these four walls. He knew her life would be in danger from the other lords, should they find out.

"I recently discovered my mate is a direct descendent of the bloodline belonging to Xavier Illenciam. In fact...blood tests conclude he is her father."

A collective gasp bounced off his office walls. Obviously Big D hadn't told Ren.

"And I need you to determine if there was any ploy on the part of my mate. I need to know if she was sent here by Xavier to infiltrate my Regent and if she's been reporting back to him or anyone under his employ."

A wicked smirk lit up Esmeralda's face. She was so easy to read. She clearly hoped this would end badly for Kate and she'd once again have a chance with him. Little did she know that regardless of what she discovered about Kate, his fate was already determined. As per vampiric mating rituals, he would be tied to Kate until either of their deaths. And if she were a traitor that meant that she would be his captive for eternity. He prayed with his whole being that was not the outcome.

"I'd be happy to help you, darling."

Yes, Dev thought snidely. Of course, she would.

"I'll need to spend some time with your mate, of course."

"Not gonna happen. You will not be in physical contact with her." Having her here was bad enough. There was no way in hell she was getting near Kate.

"I can't do the ritual without being in her presence, Devon."

"Bullshit. You're the most powerful witch I know, Esmeralda. You can, and you will, find another way."

She was quiet for several moments, finally slightly bowing her head in mock solute toward him. "I will get back to you on the specifics soon, then."

"You will do it now."

"Sorry, darling. No can do, not even for the great and powerful Dev. I need to determine what I need and do some cleansing rituals before I can perform the spell. I will get back with you in a few hours with further instructions."

She turned, walking toward the door. Ren didn't budge, looking to Dev for instruction. Dev reluctantly nodded his approval for her to leave.

Fucking witch. This was about the most important assignment he would ask for her help with and it would undoubtedly be the last. He needed to find another witch whom he could actually trust. And fast.

CHAPTER 49

Dev

The lords were all gathered again in the boardroom. The chatter was incessant and he simply wanted to get the update over with. The only thing he could focus on was locked up in a room about fifty yards away from where he presently sat.

Dev had had a bad fucking day. He had to confine his mate in the rouge room this morning and spent the entire rest of it waiting on Esmeralda to get back to him on what she needed to perform her ritual. She was unnecessarily drawing out his agony and when he'd threatened to bring in another witch to help instead, she suddenly came up with the items she needed in order to determine whether Kate was telling the truth or not. Hair and blood. How utterly unique.

She'd given him some bullshit about needing to wait until "the witching hour" to perform the ritual, so while he was in this meeting, he'd asked Big D to collect Kate's hair. They already had some blood in the lab from the previous samples they'd taken. He'd keep this meeting as short as possible, so he'd be done well before midnight and would have a few minutes to talk to Kate alone before Esmeralda started.

He was man enough to admit that he was being a

pussy. He hadn't visited her all day. He'd ignored her pleas. Hearing her begging through their shared connection was agony. She was confused and angry. She had no idea why she was locked up in that room, like some animal that had committed a crime. Had she? He truly didn't think so.

The more he thought about it, the more he believed she had no idea of her heritage. She'd acted genuinely surprised when he told her she carried vampire blood. He just didn't think she could be *that* good of an actress. He could now admit he may have acted hastily in keeping her captive while he figured this out. Did he need to go to that extreme? He didn't know. What if she was lying to him? His whole Regent...hell, *all* of the regents could be in jeopardy. Shit. He should have trusted her more and by not doing so, he felt like a bastard of epic proportions. She would no doubt agree. Would she understand? Jesus, he hoped so.

The sound of Elle and Damian's voices arguing—*loudly*—brought him back to the moment at hand. Goddamn he wished he knew what had gone down between the two of them.

"Elle, what were you able to find out from the professor?"

Elle pulled her attention away from Damian, while they both continued muttering under their breaths. One of the reasons Dev had sent Elle to interrogate the professor was because she possessed a rare skill to memory sift. Alas, it only worked on humans, not vampires.

"He's been telling the truth about never seeing Xavier. I didn't see any interaction with him, but I did see that one of Xavier's lieutenants, Geoffrey, is the go-between, so we can definitively say Xavier is behind the kidnappings.

"Geoffrey would meet with the professor every other week at the university, where he would turn over the results of the sleep studies. That's how they are able to identify potential dreamwalkers. He also had to provide details on the participants that were interviewed for the study but weren't accepted. Occasionally he would be told by Geoffrey to put a particular candidate he'd previously dismissed into the study.

"The sleep study, along with their '*alliance*' has been going on for over a decade, but just a few days ago the professor's daughter was taken. Dickwad apparently grew a conscience and wanted to end the study after the vamps had taken an interest in Sarah Hill. When he tried to get out of their arrangement, they took his daughter as *incentive* for him to continue.

"Sarah is the second participant in the professor's sleep study that was identified with potential dreamwalker ability and so she was also kidnapped. The first girl, a Jamie Hallow, was kidnapped eleven years ago and was never found. The professor seemed genuinely broken up about her, which is why I think he tried to disengage with Xavier after they started focusing on Sarah. He didn't want any more blood on his hands.

"On a side note, when I mentioned Jamie's name to our detective, he looked like he was gonna ralph on the spot. I got the impression this case was very personal to him and just got a lot more so. We should keep a close eye on him and make sure he doesn't do anything stupid, like try to find Xavier on his own and get himself killed."

"And why would you care if something happens to your insolent detective? It sounds like he's a detriment instead of an asset anyway."

Rom could be such a coldhearted asshole sometimes. Dev would rather continue their alliance with Thatcher as opposed to bringing on someone new, but Elle's response peaked his interest. Elle seemed a little too passionate about making sure nothing happened to Detective Thatcher. He decided to let her respond instead of stepping in, as he was quite interested in her explanation.

Elle glared at Rom. She had fear of no one or nothing. Dev worried that was going to be her demise someday.

"Because, as much of a pain in the ass as Thatcher is, he has been somewhat collaborative and he's house broken. Starting over again to train a local police detective takes a lot of time, effort and trust. And we don't have that luxury at the moment."

Hmmm...sounded convincing enough. But he knew Elle like not many did. And there was something she hadn't said in her well thought out explanation. Did she actually *like* Detective Thatcher? Wow...he hadn't seen that one coming. Oh well, that was a conundrum to solve on another day. He had far bigger fish on his plate to fry at the moment.

"Anything else?" Dev asked.

"Yes. Since all of the meetings occurred on campus, the professor does not know Xavier's location. I'm afraid this is all we're going to get from him."

"Thanks, Elle. Good work."

Dev turned his attention to Ren. "Ren, were you and Damian able to get anything from our house guests? Are they still resting comfortably?"

Ren laughed. "Well, they were until little dick over there used his firestarter ability. Damn, I thought the whole fucking house was gonna burn down around us."

"Fuck off, Ren. And it's called an interrogation tactic. And it was only one of them I ashed. Besides, I got the fire back under control...without too much damage." Damian glanced at Dev. "I'll pay for the repairs, of course, Dev."

Christ. Put Ren and Damian together and the two acted like prepubescent children.

"Were you able to learn anything before you burnt him to a crisp?"

"Unfortunately not. He was loyal till the end to Xavier. Now the other one we were able to get a bit of useful information from." Glaring at Ren, he continued, "Of course, it took my *special interrogation technique* to pry it out of him, but he did tell us that he reports to Geoffrey and that, upon Geoffrey's orders, they were there to capture your woman, Kate."

"Christ, Damian, we already knew they were there to kidnap Kate! Tell me something I don't already know." Dev was having a hard time holding it together and everyone else was noticing.

"Chill. Give me a chance to finish."

Dev nodded. "Continue."

"They were to take her to Xavier. They had orders to do *whatever* it took to get her there, short of killing or feeding from her, as they suspected she was a dreamwalker and Xavier wanted her alive. They wanted Kate badly and if they couldn't capture her directly, they thought your detective may be persuaded to help, so they also sent a team to his house as well."

Elle gasped and immediately fled the room. Dev could only guess she was going to check on Thatcher. This was one big clusterfuck.

So they were at her house to do her harm, not get an update on him and the other lords. Based on this new information, he knew without a doubt that Kate was not a traitor, and he felt lower than the lowest scum of the earth. How she carried Xavier's blood, he did not know, but he aimed to find out. He needed to stop Esmeralda immediately, before she started her spell.

"Ren, go find Es and tell her to hold off on the spell until I talk to her. Don't let her out of your sight. I don't care what you have to do."

"It would be my pleasure."

So Xavier knows she's a dreamwalker, which put her in twice as much danger. He also knows she was in the police station. Which meant Xavier also had minions deep within the MPD and likely knew about the lords' involvement in protecting Kate. Did he also know that Kate was his Moira?

Dev needed to wrap up this meeting, but fast. "Rom, were your experts able to find anything?"

Rom nodded once and began handing out papers to the group. "Of course. They were able to uncover seven additional documented sleep studies, similar to the one that Professor Bailey was apparently conducting. Two others in your Regent, two in Damian's and three in mine. We have a list of the universities and professor's conducting them, which is what I just handed out. I've already instructed my people to interview the professors in our Regent, which they will do first thing tomorrow morning. I'm quite certain there is a connection to Xavier here as well."

"That's a great lead, Rom. Damian and I will do the same and we'll reconvene here again tomorrow evening for another update. For now, I simply want them interrogated and watched. Although I doubt it, any one of them may be the key to finding Xavier. Are you in need of Elle's skills?"

"No, I have several sifters at my disposal in my Regent," Rom replied.

"I, as well," added Damian.

"Good. Anything else to add?"

Silence.

"See you tomorrow, then, gentlemen."

Was the tide finally turning their way? He fucking hoped so.

CHAPTER 50

Kate

Kate didn't know how long she'd been captive in this desolate room. She'd cried, screamed and pleaded, but Dev never came back. She had even tried to talk to him through their connection and he ignored those pleas as well. She wasn't sure how that worked exactly, if they needed to be close together or not, so she didn't know if he'd even heard her.

She had absolutely no idea what she'd done to deserve this sort of treatment. Yesterday had been hands down the best day of her entire life. She thought it had been for Dev too. She'd run almost every gamut of emotions possible since she'd been locked up.

Anger.

Confusion.

Hurt.

Despair.

Aaaand...she was back to anger. How could he do this to her without any explanation? That rat bastard! They may not be able to divorce, but there was no way she was putting up with this shit when she was released. She knew she couldn't return home because she was still in danger, and she may be angry, but a fool she was not. However, she was most certainly going to move into one of the other bedrooms. The one farthest away from him. Preferably after a hard swift kick to the family jewels.

Dev hadn't bothered to pop in and explain why the hell he'd kept her locked up like a rabid dog, but Leo, however, had been in to feed her several times. She wasn't hungry, but he pleaded with her to eat something anyway. It wasn't his fault she was in here, so she reluctantly complied and ate enough to keep him off her ass.

She pleaded with Leo to tell her what was going on, but he was loyal to his master and would only tell her that Dev would be in to tell her himself sometime soon. He said that every time he was here, but Dev never came. Leo was kind, as usual, but he'd been a little more distant than he normally was. What the hell was it everyone thought she'd done! Apparently vampires didn't believe in the due process clause of the fourteenth amendment.

She was cataloging creative ways to get revenge on Dev, when the door opened and a man that she hadn't seen before walked in. She was completely vulnerable and immediately on alert.

"Hi, Kate."

"Who are you?" Her pulse skyrocketed, fear coursing its way through her veins.

"Oh, I'm sorry. I forgot we haven't met yet. I'm Doctor Dirk. Most everyone calls me Big D, though."

Big D. Yes, Dev had referred to him several times. He was the one running blood tests on her.

"Why are you here? Where is Dev? Why am I locked up like this? What in the hell is going on here?" She was practically hyperventilating.

"Whoa, there. That's a lot of questions at once, Kate. First, I'm very sorry for these unfortunate circumstances of our first meeting. I've been quite looking forward to meeting the woman who stole Lord Devon's heart."

She just stared at him, not knowing how to respond, so apparently he took that as a sign to continue.

"As for why you are locked up, I'm afraid you'll need to discuss that with your mate. I'm not at liberty to say." He turned around and set down a phlebotomist kit, which she hadn't realized he'd even been carrying.

"What the hell are you doing with that?" She was now petrified.

Instead of a needle, he withdrew a pair of scissors from the kit and turned to approach her.

"I just need a small sample of hair and I'll be on my way."

"Uh, the hell you will."

While she apparently possessed the skill of stasis, actually controlling it was an entirely different story. She'd also been working with Dev on trying to use that ability this week and she hadn't been successful. He'd told her that sometimes it can take years, or even decades, to master the skills a vampire possesses and use them upon demand. And they still weren't sure why she could tap into a power she wasn't supposed to be able to because she'd not been blooded. She would gradually take on the skills Dev possessed, but so far she hadn't been successful in doing anything vampire-like since their mating. Now would be a really good time for that to change.

So as the doctor came toward her, she attempted to use the techniques Dev had been trying to teach her.

Earlier in the week, they had used Ren as the willing victim, him pretending to be an attacker. She could hear Dev's soft, seductive voice in her ear as he stood behind her, coaching her.

Imagine your target as being perfectly still, like a statue.

Imagine he can't move a muscle.

Imagine him frozen to the ground he walks on.

That's it, Kate.

Now, imagine my cock driving in and out of your hot, sweet pussy while your climax makes you cream all over it.

Well, that had been the end of that particular lesson and onto another one entirely. Her entire body flushed and readied for her mate.

Jesus, Kate. Focus.

She concentrated, imagined...aaaand nothing. Shit! He was now at her side, clipping a small chunk of hair and placing it in a clear vial. Damn it. What good were these stupid powers if she couldn't even use them.

After he'd placed the items back into his kit, he turned around and looked at her sympathetically.

"I'm sure Dev will be in very soon, Kate. He loves you very much."

She snorted. He hadn't told her he loved her yet. But in fairness, neither had she said it to him.

"If he loves me so much, then why the hell would he do this to me without any explanation?"

He stared at her for long moments, and she thought he would walk out without answering.

"Because he loves his people just as much." He turned and walked out the door before she could ask any further questions.

What the hell did that mean, *he loved his people just as much*? Did he think she was a danger to his people? How could he possibly think that? She couldn't even *do* anything remotely dangerous!! She couldn't even stop this guy from cutting her damn hair!

She tried calling out to Dev again. Begging, pleading for him to talk to her. To release her.

As with every other time she'd tried...nothing. Crickets.

She decided then and there that a kick to his jewels was probably far less than he deserved.

CHAPTER 51

Dev

Dev stood outside of the room in which Kate was being held, gathering his thoughts. He'd wanted to get to her sooner, but had a few things to handle before he could devote the time necessary to his beloved.

He'd dispatched Manny, Ren, and several others to interview the two other professors in his Regent. He would have dispatched Elle, but she'd fucking disappeared and he couldn't reach her. She'd get a goddamned earful when she returned.

He'd retrieved Kate's hair and blood samples from Esmeralda, but he couldn't be certain that she didn't secret some away before Ren tracked her down. She insisted she hadn't. Of course, he didn't believe her, but he couldn't prove it or keep her here.

Unfortunately he'd put himself, and Kate, in a compromising position by doubting her and jumping to conclusions without first asking or investigating, and that worried him. He didn't usually make careless mistakes like that. Kate had his head all fucked up and he'd better get it back on straight and quick, or he would put his life, and hers, in peril.

He slowly and quietly opened the door, preparing for his mate's ire. He was both grateful and disappointed when he found her sleeping. And it looked like her sleep was fitful, as she was thrashing about.

He quickly undid her restraints and flashed them into his bedroom, where he held her tightly to him on their king sized bed. She had not awakened so she must be in a very deep sleep. Was she dreamwalking again? He was so proud that he had a Moira with such a special ability, but he also knew it was difficult on Kate, and for that, he wished she didn't have to bear that burden.

He held her as she dreamed and thought about what Olivia had told him when he'd asked her opinion on how to handle this delicate situation only a short half hour ago. He had no goddamned clue how to be a good mate and this was an epic fuck-up, so he needed some womanly advice.

"When a woman is wronged, her trust is broken and trust is both difficult and timely to regain. While flowers and gifts are nice, and always welcome, of course, a good bit of groveling goes a long way to repairing the damage quicker. You didn't trust your mate, my lord, and that was a big mistake. She deserved the benefit of the doubt before you jumped to the worst conclusion possible. So in this case, I would advise groveling. Lots and lots of groveling. Kate is a reasonable woman and it's clear she loves you very much. I'm sure she'll forgive you...eventually. Good luck, my lord."

He was a Regent Lord. He *didn't* grovel...to anyone. But in this case, Olivia was right. Groveling was not only the right thing to do, but also probably the only way Kate would forgive his insolence.

He only prayed groveling was enough.

Kate

Kate waited as long as she could for Dev before sleep overcame her. Her last thought before drifting off was that she hoped tonight was a dreamless one, because she could not deal with any more stress than she was already under.

Unfortunately that wasn't to be. As soon as sleep took her, she was sucked back into that horrid place where helpless young women were held against their wills and unspeakable things happened.

Kate was immediately drawn to Sarah, as always. She lay in her bed, staring at the crumbling drywall ceiling, a completely blank look plastered on her face. Kate wondered how Sarah would possibly be able to recover after they rescued her.

Stay strong, Sarah. We're going to bring you home soon.

This time it was easier to pull herself away from Sarah to once again look around the compound. This time she hoped she could get more information that would help save these poor women.

She forced herself out of Sarah's room and into a dimly lit hallway. Down the right side of the hallway were a series of closed doors. She slid into the room next to Sarah's and once again found the fair-haired young woman she had seen before, who was severely pregnant. She looked peaceful in sleep, but Kate knew she was anything but.

She slipped out of that room and into the next and found a very frail, very young-looking Hispanic woman, with stringy, dark matted hair. She wore a torn, faded yellow T-shirt with a giant smiley face on it, *ironic that,* and blood soaked cream panties. Kate noticed how bruised her arms, hips and inner thighs were. Her glassy, vacant eyes were sunken and she could see the outline of her ribs through her minimal clothing.

This was almost too difficult to bear, and as much as Kate wanted to wake up so she wouldn't be witness to any more of this torture, she needed to gather as much information as possible before she was pulled from her dream again.

Kate slipped out of this room and into the next eight rooms, all holding women in similar states and most in various states of pregnancy. She began to distinguish the women that had been there for a while and those that hadn't, not only by the condition of their bodies, but the expressions on their faces. The newer ones had hope and anger. Those in longer captivity were apathetic. Void of any emotion or life behind their dead eyes.

One young woman was clearly near death. Kate doubted she would be alive in time for them to rescue her. This was absolute agony to bear witness to their torture.

The woman in the last room gave Kate pause. She wasn't as young as the other women. Definitely not the young nineteen-to-twenty-two-year-olds that had been kidnapped recently. She suspected this woman had been kept prisoner for quite some time. But what caused her stomach to drop was that she looked strikingly like Jamie Hallow. That couldn't possibly be. Could it? Jamie was never found, but how could she have been kept prisoner for eleven years? Kate couldn't think about that now, as she had a job to do.

Moving on, Kate found the surgical room where she'd previously witnessed two women being raped. Blessedly, there was no activity in that room at the moment, so she kept going. There had been nothing so far that gave her any further indication of where this place was located and she was hoping to find an upper level with more windows.

She stumbled upon a few more rooms with supplies and office equipment. She scanned the offices for any papers lying around that would give her anything useful and found nothing. Nothing, until the last office she came across, which was a bit bigger than the rest.

The office was extremely cluttered and there were stacks of paper *everywhere*. On the desk. On the filing cabinets. On the floor. In the chairs. There was almost no surface she could see without the piles of paper. Only a narrow path on the floor, leading from the door to the desk was devoid of paper.

She quickly scanned those, finding none of them useful, and noticed that the computer monitor had been left on. Unfortunately, she couldn't understand much of anything on the screen. It looked like a bunch of meaningless numbers in a spreadsheet, but she thought it was some sort of master medical document on the kidnapped women. Column headers indicated Subject A, B, etc. She noticed what looked like dates too. She had a fairly good memory, so she'd try her best to remember what was on here so she could tell Dev and the doctor when she awoke. She wished she was able to actually bring things back from her dreams because a flash drive would come in handy about now.

She was about to leave the office when she noticed a newspaper sticking out from underneath the desk, like it missed the trashcan. Upon closer inspection, she noticed that the newspaper was the *Door County Advocate*. Door County was at the end of the Sturgeon Bay in Wisconsin. Her family had vacationed frequently in Door County when she was younger. *Holy shit!* Was it possible that they were really a mere forty miles or so away?

Kate quickly left the office and continued down the series of sterile-looking hallways. As she neared the end of this particular hallway, a feeling of evilness seeped into her pores. She was both drawn and repelled by the door standing in front of her and she warred with herself on whether to enter. She thought of those poor women she saw earlier and quickly decided to forge ahead, before she lost her nerve. For some unexplained reason, every instinct inside of her screamed this would be a defining moment in her life.

She went through the door and was met with stairs that led to a lower level. She was plunged into darkness as she descended down. When she reached the bottom, another series of hallways lay ahead. She was drawn to the left and while she wanted to explore each room on this level, she knew time was running out and she felt an unexplained urgency to get to the room at the end of this hallway.

Kate was outside the closed door and a feeling of terror unlike any she'd felt before passed through her body. She forced herself through, not knowing what she was about to see, and was surprisingly met with an empty room. Empty, as in, no one was currently occupying it, but someone obviously lived here. It was a small sitting room of sorts, with a tidy, nondescript desk and a large Italian black leather chair, which looked luxurious and very much out of place in the sparse room. She took note of a caramel colored liquor in a clear decanter, which sat on a shelf alongside a lone crystal tumbler and a few books.

She didn't get a chance to look any further, as she heard a muffled cry coming from behind a door to her right. Upon entering the secondary room, she was struck still. To her horror, in front of her on the blood-soaked bed, lay a naked young girl, probably not older than fifteen, covered in blood and bite marks on her neck, breasts, and inner thighs. Her skin was frighteningly pale and she was sobbing uncontrollably.

A low growl brought her attention to the butt naked man—*no, correction*—vampire at the foot of the massive bed. He was moving toward the young girl like a lion that had successfully taken down its prey. Kate gasped and his head whipped around in her direction, as he stood tall.

Oh shit. He can't see me, can he? He's not supposed to be able to see me.

Oh my God. Oh God. Kate was frozen with fear.

Standing before her was one of the handsomest and most hideous creatures she had ever laid eyes upon. When she was eleven and in sixth grade, a boy in her class had played with matches and accidentally burned down his parents' house. He barely made it out alive, and was horribly burned on over sixty percent of his body. He survived and didn't return to school until the seventh grade, but he was scarred for life. So she knew all too well what severe burn marks looked like.

The right half of this vampire's face, including his entire nose and right side of his lips, was horrifically scarred and disfigured. Half of his head was entirely hair free, while the other half was clearly shaven clean to the skull. His right ear was almost missing entirely. His entire upper torso and most of both arms, except his upper left shoulder was also scarred. His whole right leg also bore the same painful marring's. Even his private parts appeared scarred. Not that she tried to look. The part of his face that wasn't scarred, however, was divinely handsome and mesmerizing and she instantly knew who stood before her.

Xavier.

"Well, well, dreamwalker," he drawled. "I know you're here. I can *feel* your presence."

He could feel her presence, but couldn't see her? Both pieces of information were good to know.

"Would you like a demonstration of what I'm going to do to you once I get my hands on you?"

No. Nope. No demonstration needed. Thanks for asking, though.

He snarled and grabbed the young, frightened girl by the foot, dragging her to the foot of the bed and rammed himself into her small, fragile body. She cried out as he bit her savagely on the neck, sucking her lifeblood so hard and fast that most of it spilled down his chin and throat. As quickly as he struck, he let her go, throwing her toward the headboard. She landed half way off the bed, unmoving.

He stood at full height again, as he let the blood drip unnervingly off his chin. He talked to the air, while turning in a circle. Comical, really, if the situation weren't so dire and horrific.

"If you give yourself up to me willingly, Katherine Martin, then I promise to let you and your lords live. If you do not, then I will rain hell on your lords, their Regents, and the human race. And every single day I let you live in my company, you will pray for a death that I will never grant."

Holy shit. He knew who she was. By name! This was sooooo not good. Okay, Kate. Time to wake up any time now.

"And you can tell your lords that I will enjoy fucking you, while I drink freely of your blood. Every. Single. Day."

Kate turned to flee when she felt herself waking up. Thank you, God, for small favors.

As she was being pulled back into her body, she thought she heard Xavier say, "Until we meet again, sweet Kate."

So. Not. Good.

Chapter 52

Mike

He was fucking pissed. He was now sitting in Devon Fallinsworth's office, *at his fucking house*, a place he'd hoped he would never see, with an equally pissed off Giselle blocking his escape. Blood was dripping from the cut above his eye and, quite frankly, he was more than a little concerned the bloodsucker wouldn't be able to control herself. He was in a house full of vamps and expected them to circle like vultures any minute.

A half hour ago he'd been headed home, after several of the longest, shittiest days of his life. Just as he'd reached his car, Giselle popped up, blocking his entrance. He hated it when vamps flashed. It was completely unnatural and unnerving. She'd given him some bullshit about being in danger, blah, blah, blah. He couldn't go home, blah, blah, blah. He'd told her to fuck off, shoved her out of the way, started his car and drove off. He hadn't been home in days. Between his binge drinking and sleeping at the station, he needed a good long shower. Even his lumpy mattress sounded good tonight and he hated that old thing.

He'd just turned onto the highway, heading south toward his meager house, when she suddenly flashed in front of his goddamn car, causing him to slam on his brakes and swerve into the ditch in order to miss hitting her. He almost clipped a one hundred-year-old oak. He should have just mowed her ass down instead of trying to avoid her. That bitch was going to pay *every* cent it cost to repair the damages to his now incapacitated car. Maybe it would be totaled and he'd make her pay for a brand new one.

Before his head had even cleared from the impact, she'd had his door open and had flashed him to Devon's house. Where he now sat. Glaring at her. Blood dripping down his face.

"Listen up, Giselle. You get me the fuck back to my car right now or so help me God, there will be hell to pay."

She stood there with a smirk on her face and arms crossed against her bountiful chest, which pressed her quite lovely tits even further above the black lace corset she wore. Christ, if she weren't a vamp, he would have fucked her ten ways to Sunday by now. God knows his dick didn't care what species she was. That bastard wanted a go at her anyway.

"My eyes are up here, detective."

Buuuusted. He started to speak, but she talked right over him.

"Believe it or not, I'm trying to save your pathetic little human life. Why, you ask? I can't even understand that myself. But you are in danger, Detective. If you'd shut your piehole for five seconds, I've been trying to tell you that we received intel this evening that your house is being staked out by Xavier's lackey's, who were sent there to kidnap you. I saved you from certain death, and the thanks I get for that are your futile threats."

Mike began to protest when she cut him off...*again.* Bitch.

"And before you pull your macho bullshit and tell me I'm full of shit and that you can take care of yourself— *yada, yada*—I checked out your place before I came to the precinct and I could smell their stench a mile away. So they are there. They are waiting for you, and they will take great pleasure in killing you once they've tortured you for an indefinite period of time.

"Which means you are going to have to stay here until it's safe for you to return to your home. Like it or not. Unless you have a death wish."

This made no sense. "Why in the hell would they want me?"

"They know you are working on the Sarah Hill case and they know Kate was in to see you about it. They are actually after Kate and will do anything to find her."

His stomach dropped. Had something happened to Kate? "Is she safe?"

Giselle nodded. "She's been here for the past several days, since they tried snatching her from her home."

She added, "And before you ask, no harm has or will come to her. She's safer here than anywhere else."

Well, fuck. They stared at each other for several minutes. Neither wanting to give in and be the first to break their eye lock. Jesus, they were both stubborn as the day was long. He hadn't fulfilled his objective yet, so a death wish was off the table. But sometimes it sounded like sweet relief from the constant pain he carried in his soul.

His memory flashed back to the station the other day when she also mentioned she was trying to protect him. This whole situation confused the hell out of him. Mike couldn't wrap his head around why Giselle even seemed to give a shit if something happened to him. Why not let just him traipse off home and get flayed piece-by-piece? He wasn't exactly their biggest fan, and she knew that.

So what was her angle? Although she was trying hard to throw him, he was getting the genuine vibe that she actually *cared* what happened to him. And why would that be? He knew he'd have to tread lightly or she'd Mrs. Hyde into her usual frigid bitch. Then not only would he get no answers, he also wasn't sure he could restrain himself from trying to kill her. Or fuck her. *Christ.*

Mike stood and slowly made his way across the room toward Giselle. Her challenging eyes never left his. She didn't move, other than to drop her arms to her side and stand to her full, glorious six feet. Instead of her red fuck-me heals today, she had black, thigh high fuck-me harder boots, which ended a couple of inches below her tight, black leather mini skirt. As sick as it was, he wanted to know what she had on under that skirt. The thought almost made him throw up a little in his mouth.

Two could play the mind-fuck game, he thought. But was he really *playing?*

He stopped a couple of inches in front her and could feel her body heat seeping into his. Vampires did have beating hearts and although their body temperature ran a little below that of humans, they still threw off plenty of body heat. And under certain circumstances—like perhaps that which included his cock buried in her hot, wet pussy—he had no doubt Giselle could get even hotter. *Concentrate, Thatcher.*

"And why would you care what happens to little ol' me, Giselle," he whispered.

Her breath caught and he was pleased he'd caught her completely off guard. He leaned even closer. Her eyes dilated, narrowing to slits. Wow...she really wanted him. The thought made his blood run hotter than he was comfortable with.

"I mean, I know you want to fuck my brains out and give me *indescribable pleasure*, as you've already told me, but you're so *fucking* beautiful and sexy, you could have any man you want. Why me?" He inhaled deeply. Christ, she smelled divine.

Her breathing sped up and she opened her mouth to respond, but closed it again, saying nothing. She was completely off her game. Good. Because if he was totally honest with himself, so was he. He had absolutely no idea what he was doing here. He wanted her more than he could remember wanting any other woman in his life, and that terrified the hell out of him. Because of what she was, he could never fuck Giselle, but Jesus, did he *want* to. He wanted to with such ferocity, he almost willed himself to forget she was an enemy. And doing that could get a man killed.

Knowing all of this, he had no idea how his body ended up pressed against hers, pinning her in place against the office wall. He had no idea how his hands ended up on her hips, pulling her closer to his aching cock. He had no idea how his lips started grazing her cheek, her neck, her lips. And he had no idea how to force himself to stop this madness.

His entire concentration at the moment was on getting Giselle's substantial tit out of the top of her corset. He was dying to know what color her nipples were and his mouth watered at the thought of their taste.

So since he couldn't figure out how to stop this madness himself, it was a good thing someone else decided for him before he reached the point of no return. He almost had her breast completely out of its lacy confines, when he heard someone clear their throat. And it was definitely too low and masculine to be Giselle. They quickly pulled away from each other, Giselle straightening herself. Mike didn't turn toward the interloper immediately. He needed to get his raging hard on under control first. And oddly, he needed to make sure Giselle was covered.

After several seconds, Mike finally turned around, only to face a grinning Renaldo.

Fuck. Color him embarrassed. And pissed. That asshole better have not seen an inch of Giselle's creamy skin.

"Did I interrupt something?" If possible, Renaldo's grin widened further. He was really enjoying this, the bastard.

With a quick look to Giselle, he noticed she seemed just as embarrassed as he did, and like ice water to the face, that quickly shook him out of the spell he'd been under. She was embarrassed to be caught with him? Of course she was. He was just a lowly human. A source of nourishment is all.

And now he was pissed for an entirely different reason. He was upset with himself for forgetting who and what she was. How could he let himself get so carried away with her? Because head number two had brainwashed head number one, that's how.

He looked Giselle in the eyes as he responded to Renaldo.

"No, it was absolutely nothing. You didn't interrupt a fucking thing." He almost felt bad when a flash of hurt quickly crossed her face, but he quickly shoved that away. Wow, she was a great actress. And he was an asshole. Good to know they were back to their respective roles.

Neither of them spoke as they stared each other down, the air thick with tension. Renaldo had to be thoroughly enjoying this and would never let him live it down. Just peachy.

"So I see your pet is safe and sound, Elle." She moved so fast, all Mike heard were two bodies thumping against the wall.

"You shut the fuck up, Ren."

Ren laughed, holding his hands up in the universal surrender position.

"Easy wildcat. Just making an observation, is all. No offense intended."

Giselle let Ren go, muttering curses under her breath. She stormed out of the office without so much as a word to him or a glance back in his direction. Yep, Mrs. Hyde was back in full force. He didn't know why and didn't plan to delve too deeply into it, but deep down her disregard cut him to the quick. Wow, what a pussy thing to think. Had he suddenly grown a vagina?

To his surprise, Ren didn't say a word about the compromising position that he'd caught them in. Hell, Mike should be falling at Ren's feet, thanking him for interrupting what would have most definitely been the biggest mistake of his sorry life. Instead, Mike stayed silent while Ren thoughtfully regarded him.

"Glad to see you're alive and in one piece, Detective. What did Elle tell you?"

Mike sighed and walked back over to the couch before sitting down on the plush furniture. Fuckers had a lot of money that was for sure. His head throbbed and suddenly he had a hard time concentrating. He was simply exhausted.

"She told me that my life was in danger and that I had to stay here for the time being. Unless I had a death wish. Which much to my, and probably your dismay, I do not. At least not yet. I have some things to accomplish before I spend eternity in a different kind of hell."

"Wow. You are the most depressing and cynical human I have ever encountered. You need therapy, my friend."

Mike didn't respond. The truth hurt.

"There are a couple of extra bedrooms on the third floor. I'll show you where you can lay low until the danger passes and you can go back home. We're getting close to finding Xavier, and hopefully recovering those missing girls, which I know is both of our priorities."

"Wait. Girls? What girls?"

"The missing girls. You do remember the case you're working on, right, Detective?"

"Yes, but I only know of one missing girl. Sarah Hill. Have you verified other missing girls?" He remembered Kate mentioning there were others, but no other missing young women had been reported recently. At least not in Milwaukee.

"This is really a vampire matter, human, but since you're here indefinitely, you may as well make yourself useful. The short story is there are over two-dozen girls missing around the country that we've linked them to the same possible rogue vamp that took Sarah. How about you get some shut-eye first and we'll bring you up to speed with rest of the details in the morning?"

Mike began to protest, but Ren interrupted. Jesus, were all vampires such poor listeners?

"No, Detective. Not up for further discussion now. I don't know what happened tonight, but it looks like you were injured and you look like death warmed over. You need sleep and a good meal. Only then will we talk about the case. I assure you—we will fill you in completely and let you help with whatever you can. But in the morning."

Mike nodded once, knowing he didn't have the strength to argue.

"Fine."

"Good." Ren ushered him through the massive house to a hallway with several doors and stopped at the third door on the left.

"You can use this room. Has an en suite bathroom. For your own safety, I don't need to tell you to not wander around without supervision. We'll have someone bring you breakfast and fetch you in the morning when Dev is ready to meet."

"Ah. So I am still a vampire's prisoner. Just with a king sized bed and a walk in shower with multiple showerheads."

Ren smirked. "Don't forget the room service."

"Right."

"Hand over your guns."

Mike glared at him. He didn't want to be completely defenseless in a house full of vamps. "I don't th—"

"I don't give a shit what *you* think, Detective. Hand them over. All of them. Now."

Mike retrieved both of his guns. The one strapped in

his arm holster and the other on ankle. He reluctantly handed them over to him and Ren turned, walking back the way they came.

"Fucker," he uttered under his breath.

Mike turned the knob, stepping into his posh prison cell, when Ren called to him from down the hall.

"One more thing, Detective. If you hurt Giselle, I will personally cut out your shriveled up heart, after I first suck your body dry of every single drop of blood. Sleep tight," he said with a wink and a smile.

Mike closed his bedroom door, locking it from the inside. For all the good that would do. If the vamps wanted him dead when he slept, well, then...he would be. And there wasn't a damn thing he could do to stop them. Especially now that he was sans weapons.

He had one thought as he fell into bed, clothes and all, before drifting off to sleep.

What the fuck had he gotten himself into?

CHAPTER 53

Kate

Kate awoke with a start. Instead of the hard manacles that had bound her for the past however many hours, she now had hard, muscular arms binding her to an equally hard, muscular body.

Dev.

He had finally freed her. She was instantly grateful, but anger promptly overrode that emotion. She tried to free herself, but his arms tightened around her, holding her more snugly to him.

"Let me go." Kate squirmed to get free, to no avail.

Dev sat them both up, her legs straddling his lap. His arms locked tightly around her. His hard cock pressed where she desired it most. Unbelievable. He was turned on. Her body involuntarily responded to his closeness. *Traitorous little bitch.* She was livid. With not only him, but also herself for her involuntary reaction to him. How could she be so pissed and wet at the same time? *Ugh.*

"I'm sorry, my love."

"Sorry? You're sorry? What exactly are you sorry for, Dev? Are you maybe sorry for tying your *mate* up without any explanation whatsoever? Or are you perhaps sorry for leaving me there for hours without coming to see me? Or maybe you're sorry for sending in

Doctor Scissorhands to *cut my hair*! Are you kidding me?"

She pushed on his chest, trying to dislodge herself from his lap, but he held on tight.

"Ugh! Let. Me. Go!"

"No. I won't. *Please* hear me out, Kate. I'm new at this relationship stuff and that's not an excuse, but it is the truth. I think I'm going to make a lot more mistakes before I get this mate thing right and so I'm apologizing for not only the many mistakes I've made over the past twenty-four hours, but also for all of the future mistakes I'm bound to make."

Kate sighed. Why did he have to be so damn endearing? She was still angry, but it dissipated slightly with his genuine apology.

"You'll have to apologize again for your future mistakes when you make them. An all encompassing *one time* apology will not be anywhere near sufficient." Yes, her inner toddler tantrum came out.

He laughed. God, she loved that laugh. It sent chills through her entire body.

"Of course, my love. I'll grovel as much as I need to stay in your good graces."

"Good. At least we're on the same page. So...what happened? What ever did I do to warrant being held like a criminal? And even criminals get due process, by the way." Yep, she was still plenty pissed.

Dev took a deep breath before he began.

"Big D came to me yesterday with some rather shocking news and I overreacted. As I said, I've made a lot of mistakes in the past twenty-four hours and for that, I am deeply and truly sorry. What I did was unforgivable, but I beg for your forgiveness anyway, Kate. I didn't trust you and I should have. That was wrong of me and mistake number one. I should have talked to you before I just took action. I shouldn't have avoided you all day." He sighed. "So many mistakes."

She was silent, not giving him any quarter.

"We got the results of your blood test back and...we know who your father is."

Kate had a sudden sick feeling rush through her body. This was not going to be good news. "Who?" she whispered. She could barely get the word past her lips. She already knew what he was about to say.

Dev looked down at their joined hands, which she hadn't realized they'd done. Oh God. He couldn't even look at her. This was bad.

"Dev, who is it?"

He raised his eyes to hers and she saw sympathy. And anger.

"Xavier."

Kate's hands flew to cover her mouth. Xavier? The vampire who wants world domination? The vampire who's kidnapping young, innocent women and using them as baby incubators? The same vampire who wants to kidnap *her* too? The vile, evil creature she'd just dreamt about? She was going to be sick.

Kate jumped up and ran to the bathroom, spilling the contents of her stomach into the toilet. Dev was behind her, holding her hair, rubbing her back, whispering words of comfort. Oh my God. Now it all made sense.

Dev thought she was a traitor. Dev thought Xavier had somehow orchestrated this entire meeting with him.

She vomited again until all that was left was dry heaves; sobs racked her body. How could he possibly think she would betray him like that? She loved him so very much. She would do anything for him. Anything to protect him.

She stood up, brushed her teeth and returned to the bedroom, sitting on the loveseat at the opposite end of the room.

Dev had stood in the bathroom doorway, silently watching her. Probably trying to discern any deception on her part. Nice. Even though she had nothing to feel guilty for, she couldn't even look at him.

She caressed the mark circling her left thumb. The one that magically appeared after their bonding. She thought about that night, how much she loved him, how grateful she was to have found such a fantastic man in her life. Her anger lessened.

"I didn't know," she finally voiced, turning to look him in the eye, so he would see the truth and sincerity in her words. Tears streamed unbidden down her face.

"I know, love." He crossed the room with a tissue and knelt in front her.

"I love you. I would never betray you like that."

He gathered her in his arms and sat them both down on the loveseat. "Oh, my sweet Kate. I know that and as I said before... I overreacted. I was so very wrong and I lov—"

"Oh my God." *My sweet Kate...*

"What? What is it?"

"My sweet Kate," she murmured.

"Kate, what the hell are you talking about?"

"He knows I was there." She had completely zoned out and Dev was shaking her gently.

"Who knows you were where? Kate, you're making no sense."

"Xavier. He knew I was there. He talked to me. He...he—"

"He what? Knew you were where? What did he do, Kate? Look at me." His entire body had gone rigid at the mention of Xavier.

She turned toward Dev.

"I just had another dream. I saw him. And he knew I was in the room with him. He called me by name. He—" She swallowed and whispered, "He killed a young girl in front of me. He threw her across the bed and it looked like she was dead. He told me the awful things he was going to do to me once he got his hands on me. He called me *his sweet Kate*."

"Fuck." He grabbed her arms, turning her fully toward him. "You listen to me, love. That will *never* happen. Do you understand? He will never lay a single finger on you. I would die before I let that happen."

She nodded.

"You have to trust me, Kate. I won't let anything happen to you. We'll kill the bastard and he won't be any threat to you. I promise you."

Kate spent the next few minutes telling Dev about the rest of her dream, including about the newspaper she had found and the numbers she had seen on the computer screen. She described all the young women she had seen held in rooms similar to Sarah's. She explained the way the compound looked and how she'd been drawn to Xavier's room.

Dev surprised Kate with a slow, sensual kiss. She melted into him, her anger completely dissipating.

"I love you. I'm sorry I haven't told you before now. You are an incredible woman. I'm proud and lucky to have you as my mate. I'm sorry. Please forgive me for my mistakes."

She put her finger on his lips.

"I'm plenty pissed with the way you handled it, but I understand why you did it. It's okay." And she did. She understood that, as a Vampire Lord, he had great responsibility for his people and she wasn't sure that she wouldn't have reacted the same if in his position.

He kissed her, slowly, reverently, breaking away all too soon.

"Now, I know you must be tired, love, but we need an emergency meeting with the other Lords. Right now. We need to act quickly on your new information."

Kate looked down at the sports bra and tight running shorts that she was still wearing from yesterday.

"If you don't mind, I'd like to change and shower quickly. I'll be ready in less than ten minutes."

Dev smiled sinfully. He grabbed her hips, pulling her tightly to him. She could feel his hardness throbbing against her stomach. He leaned down to run his nose along her neck, nipping with his sharp teeth along the way. Arousal flushed through her body and the butterflies constantly residing in her stomach took flight once again. Her core clenched. Oh my, she wanted him desperately. She had been without him for far too long.

"Oh, I don't mind at all, love. But I'll be joining you. And we may be a tad longer than ten minutes."

He was right.

CHAPTER 54

Dev

In the boardroom as everyone dispersed, there was a lot of excitement that they may finally be closing in on Xavier. After Kate had given the details of her latest dream, Dev, Rom, and Damian had each called on some of their best men to scout out the Door County area.

Dev knew that Xavier's lair was likely shrouded with magical assistance, but Kate had some very good markers between the two most recent dreams, so he felt positive they'd be able to at least narrow down some areas to investigate further. Plus, he had a secret weapon on his side. Manny had the ability to see through shrouding, but only within close proximity. That was how they located Xavier before and foolishly thought they'd destroyed him in the fire. That was also why they'd been unable to locate him again. Using Manny's abilities without focus would be like trying to find a needle in a haystack. Virtually impossible and highly ineffective.

It would be a difficult task now, as there were certainly lots of old barns, windmills and trees in the area, but if they could get close to Xavier's lair, Manny would find it, of that he had every confidence. In fact, the shrouding actually helped, by acting like a beacon to those very few vampires who possessed the ability to see through it. Not a lot of vampires shrouding. Not many vampires he knew enjoyed getting into bed with a witch. It was a danger to one's long-term health.

As much as Dev didn't want to part from her, after the meeting, he had sent Kate back to bed to get some more sleep. Even though she was exhausted and needed the sleep, his Kate fought him, as usual, but he promised to wake her up in a couple of hours. And since he could hardly wait to take her again, he planned on keeping his promise.

He craved her.

He was addicted to her.

She had only been gone for thirty minutes and already he didn't know if he'd be able to wait the hour and a half more to wake her up. He was hard as hell.

Dev couldn't get Kate's dream about Xavier out of his head. It only solidified Xavier didn't know Kate was his daughter, but how could that be? No matter how he worked it, he couldn't figure it out.

Something about this whole situation nagged him. Why would Xavier let his own daughter out of his sight? She could prove to be very useful to him, not only because of the fact she was a dreamwalker, but because it was clear Kate would be very powerful someday, blooded vampire or not. He couldn't imagine how powerful she would be had she been blooded.

No, he was missing a critical piece to this puzzle. He just couldn't quite put his finger on it yet.

Dev was contemplating that when Ren strode into his office, sitting down in one of the two guest chairs on the opposite side of his desk.

"I need to apprise you of a situation, my lord."

Dev sat back in his chair, smirking. Ren looked nervous and ready for a fight and under any other circumstances he should be. Allowing a human in their house without his permission was an offense punishable by death. Fortunately for Elle, he couldn't do without her and he knew Ren had a brotherly fondness for Elle, protecting her above all else. Well, above everyone else except for him, that was.

He should string this out, but he didn't have the heart to put Ren through it. He was going soft. *Fuck that*. Devon Fallinsworth wasn't soft.

"Oh?"

"Yes." Ren looked a little surprised, but continued. "Well, you know that Detective Thatcher's life was in danger and Elle ran out of here earlier this evening to check on him."

Ren stopped and Dev arched his brow for him to continue.

"When she got to his house, she found three rogues staked out there, but Thatcher clearly wasn't home. She found him just leaving the precinct."

"And?"

"And he was unharmed."

"All right. Is that all?"

"Um...not quite." Ren hesitated.

"Jesus, Ren. Stop pussyfooting around. Spit it out."

Ren stood, resolutely.

"In order to keep Detective Thatcher safe, Elle thought it would be best to bring him back here. Just until we eliminate Xavier. I agree with her decision."

And there it was. Ren was defending Elle by agreeing with her impulsive decision, and by doing so, he would take any punishment that Dev dished out upon himself. Ren had balls of steel. That was why he was his lieutenant and had been for so many years.

Dev nodded. "Okay."

"Okay? That's all you have to say?"

"Yes. Except he's now your full responsibility."

"Of course." Ren turned, walking toward the closed office door, turning back before he left.

"You knew, didn't you?"

Dev laughed. "Of course."

As Ren left, Dev heard him mutter "asshole." Good. Even though Kate made him soft in some ways, he could still be hard when it mattered. And speaking of hard, he had slightly over an hour left before he could bury his cock inside his mate once again.

Sixty minutes never seemed so long.

CHAPTER 55

MIKE

He slept like the dead. It was a dreamless sleep. Thank Christ. He never knew when Jamie was going to invade his thoughts, his dreams. He barely woke when a vamp strode in with his breakfast and a fresh change of clothes. His name was Len, Larry, Leo. Something like that. What-the-fuck-ever. He was a vamp. That was all he needed to know.

After Mike ate breakfast, which was admittedly quite good, he showered and changed into fresh clothes. He had just finished dressing when Ren knocked at his door. Either the guy had a sixth sense or there were cameras in his room. He wouldn't put it past these sick fuckers to watch him sleep.

He only hoped there were no cameras in the bathroom, because he choked the chicken in the shower earlier. He couldn't get thoughts of Giselle's breasts out of his mind. Tits he never got to savor. He'd woken up hard and couldn't walk around with a toddler in his pants all day. He may not actually screw the pooch, but that didn't mean he couldn't fantasize about her and what it would be like to taste her pussy, to take her hard against the shower wall. But fantasize was all he was going to do. He'd lost his mind yesterday when it came to her and her luscious body. His mind-fuck boomeranged back onto him and he certainly didn't intend for it to happen again. His intent was to avoid her as much as possible while he was essentially kept prisoner here indefinitely.

Dev and Ren brought Mike up to speed on everything, at least he thought it was everything, but who really knows? They couldn't be trusted. They set him up in a small extra office on the main floor, complete with Internet connection. While the vamps were on the ground scouting Door County, he was using his police connections in other parts of the country to glean any additional information he could on the other missing girls. With so many missing girls, it was tedious work.

Kate had done a very good job describing the girls she'd seen in her most recent dream pretty well to one of Dev's vamps, who had the skills equivalent to a police sketch artist. He was actually still trying to process the reality of dreamwalkers. Next thing he knew, someone would tell him witches were real. *Jesus, don't even go there, Thatcher.*

Attention turning back to the list of the missing girls who'd been both officially reported as such and who were linked with the psychotic-to-the-millionth-degree vampire, he was down to the last two of twenty-nine pictures. Some of the eleven women Kate had seen in her dream hadn't been officially reported missing that he could find. Conversely, of the reported missing women, only six matched to the pictures the artist drew. So either the rest were dead, or they were held in another part of the compound Kate hadn't seen. Obviously the women he couldn't match were missing women not yet reported. He would get to that task next.

He picked up the last two pictures, pulling them apart so he could study both of them. His eyes drifted to the very last picture, held in his right hand and he instantly lost the ability to breathe.

Staring back at him was...*Jamie. His* Jamie.

Except it was an older version of Jamie. A sad, vacant, shell of the young, beautiful and vibrant Jamie he once knew. This couldn't be right. Jamie was never found, but she was presumed dead, so...*no*. This had to be her doppelganger. It wasn't Jamie. It couldn't possibly be.

But his gut told him another story. Jamie had a small, dark mole on the very right side of her upper lip. He used to lick it when he kissed her. He loved that mole. It was sexy as hell.

And the gaunt face staring back at him had that same dark mole on the right side of her upper lip.

So if this was, in fact, Jamie—*his Jamie*—that meant not only was she *not* dead, but she'd spent the last eleven years in the hands of one sick fuck and Mike had done nothing to stop it. He'd done nothing to help her.

Jamie was alive. He'd been right. Vamps *were* responsible for her disappearance. And she had been in a never-ending living hell on earth, only wishing she were dead.

He promptly leaned over the desk losing his lunch in the wastebasket. Christ, hot wings are a fiery bitch coming back up.

Like a pussy, tears streamed down his face, but he didn't care. And of course, karma being the fickle bitch she was, Giselle chose that moment to stride into the office without knocking, like she owned the place.

Just. Fucking. Great.

CHAPTER 56

Dev

Frustration rolled off him in waves. For three days, they had searched the Door County area for any sign of Xavier, running into dead end after dead end. They had split up into three teams, covering about ninety percent of the area so far. Unfortunately Manny had extra duty, as he would scout locations the other two groups found that were possibilities. So far, nothing, nada, zilch, zip, zero. And it frustrated the fuck out of Dev. His *sparkling* personality was taking a nosedive and most everyone was giving him wide berth. Everyone except his precious Kate, that is. She calmed him.

Kate hadn't had any more dreams and was equally as frustrated, but he was equally as grateful. While she wanted to help, he didn't want her anywhere near Xavier, even if he couldn't actually *see* her. Who knew what that vile monster had up sleeve and if he could trace her to his mansion. He'd called in extra security the past few days. Call him a paranoid SOB, but no one was dying under his watch. Especially not the love of his life. Hell...she *was* his life now.

Rom had his computer wiz research the names on all the property deeds in Door County and the surrounding areas, trying to match any to the known vamps in

Xavier's entourage. Two possible hits, but both turned out to be nothing.

Tonight they should have the remaining areas searched and if they came up short, he wasn't quite sure what his next move would be. And Dev was never without a Plan B.

While they hadn't found Xavier yet, they were making progress in other areas.

The detective had positively matched all but one of the eleven missing women from Kate's dream. Some of them hadn't been previously identified as the original twenty-nine missing, so that brought the total missing women now up to at least thirty-two.

They also had some minor success with the other professors conducting sleep studies around the country, with the exception of two, who were inconveniently *missing*. Looked like Xavier was starting to clean up loose ends.

Elle and the detective were currently sifting through the many files and computer records they gathered from the other five universities. While they were able to get their hands on more information, unfortunately none of the remaining five professors had any more information than Professor Bailey when it came to the whereabouts of Xavier.

He was like a fucking ghost.

Standing beside his bed—*their bed*—he watched his Kate sleep. She was so beautiful, so perfect for him. He still reeled with the depth of emotion he felt for her in just a short period of time. He found himself daydreaming of what it would be like to watch her belly grow ripe with his child. She would be sexy as hell, all round and swollen. He'd always dreamed of finding his Moira, yes, but he'd never dreamed about having a child, a family. Not until he met *her*.

He pictured a little boy, with raven hair and emerald eyes, running his *meme* ragged. Climbing trees, bringing insects into the house, constantly dirty. He pictured that same young boy growing into a warrior, a lord someday, finding his Moira and having a family of his own.

It surprised him to feel sadness at something that would never—*could never*—be. Because of her vampire DNA, she wouldn't be able to carry a child. Probably why Xavier discarded her. If she was barren, she was useless to his experiments. But why not kill her instead? Why find an adoptive family to raise her? How did Xavier not know she was his daughter when Kate was dreamwalking? And he *was* certain Xavier didn't know and that made no sense at all to him.

Unless...click.

The puzzle pieces instantly fell into place. Xavier didn't know because...she wasn't *supposed* to be alive.

"Ren, urgent meeting in fifteen. My office. Bring the detective and make sure Big D is either there or available by phone."

"On it."

He gently woke Kate and told her he'd figured out something very important. She quickly dressed and they made their way to his office. The other lords had headed home, as it was not a smart idea to be gone from your Regent for any length of time, but they had left behind several of their best men to help with the efforts. He'd loop them in after this meeting.

He'd debated the idea on revealing Kate's parentage, but if his theory held water, it was critical to what Xavier was doing.

When everyone was gathered, he began.

"I think I've figured out something important, but let me start at the beginning, because not all of you know that Kate is Xavier's daughter."

You could hear a pin drop, everyone, except Ren, clearly stunned. Kate sat next to Dev, a protective hand on her shoulder as he stood, addressing the group. He'd purposely put her in his chair behind his desk. He would kill anyone who tried to harm her.

"She didn't know until just yesterday and she's not working for Xavier. He wants her dead as much as he does us. Which brings me to the purpose of this meeting.

"I couldn't understand why, if she was Xavier's daughter, would he just not kill her? But I think that's exactly what he intended to do; only I think he sent someone else to do his dirty work. Someone he trusted, who unbeknownst to him, went behind his back and let her live." He gazed at Kate with sympathy before continuing.

"I'm sorry, love, but we need to talk to your parents. We have to find out how they came to adopt you. We have to find this person, as it may be another lead to finding Xavier."

He didn't wait for her consent before continuing.

"Doc, I've also been thinking about these young women getting pregnant and how so many of them could possibly be. We're thinking about this wrong. We all know that a human female cannot get pregnant from a vampire unless she is his Moira and they've bonded. And we all know how difficult finding your Moira is, so how is it that so many females Kate saw were pregnant? It's just not possible they have all bonded, which means they're doing something else to impregnate them. And we need to find out what.

"Xavier must have some sort of research scientist or a team working for him to find ways to impregnate a human female without bonding. Obviously we cannot let this type of experimentation continue, at least not in this heinous fashion, but this mission has become even more critical. Not only do we need to rescue the girls and destroy Xavier, but we also need these scientists alive. And we need their records to determine if there are other female vampires out there who were also supposed to be discarded."

Big D spoke first. "I find it curious that there is a female descendent from Xavier, but no males that we know of. Word would have leaked out by now if Xavier had male heirs. Hell, knowing Xavier, he would have shoved it down our throats himself."

"I was thinking the same thing, Doc," said Ren.

They formulated next steps and Dev adjourned the meeting, after agreement that Ren and Dev would be the ones to meet with Kate's parents, along with Kate. The three of them would head there in the morning. The scout teams were not expected to return until first light, but even if they found something, they needed time to strategize on how best to handle the mission with the least amount of casualties. Dev had no doubt Xavier would try to cut his losses and kill as many girls and other humans he had in the compound, while trying to save his vampires and his own hide.

He had just shut the door to their bedroom when Kate pushed him against the door, kissing him furiously. He groaned, switching their positions so he had the upper hand. Kate may have changed Dev in ways he would never understand, but dominance wasn't one of them. He loved it, he craved it, he needed it. He broke their kiss, searching her eyes to be sure this was what she wanted. His poor Kate continued to be bombarded with revelation after revelation. It had to be exhausting.

"Please make me forget," she pleaded. *Fuck me hard, Dev. Fuck me now. Please.*

He swiftly stripped their clothes and lifted her against the door. "Wrap your legs around my waist." She complied.

She wanted rough and he was more than happy to oblige. With one deep thrust he was buried to the hilt in her sweet, sweet pussy. She moaned, her head falling back against the door. Her pulse beckoned to him.

"Christ, Kate. You feel so good, love." He set a fast, punishing pace, her generous tits bouncing with each hard hammer into her body. She was mesmerizing and he couldn't wait another second to taste her honeyed blood. His incisors sharpened and he quickly struck. Kate's pussy immediately squeezed his cock, and he felt her shatter as she chanted his name repeatedly.

Being inside her was a feeling unlike any he had had in his long life. There were no words in any language to describe the pleasure coursing through his body. He wanted this to last forever, but the way her pussy was gripping and squeezing him, he couldn't hold back more than several more thrusts before he was emptying himself into her, causing her to explode a second time.

At the peak of their pleasure, she none too gently bit his neck, drawing his essence into her. His orgasm went on and on for what seemed like minutes. Every time inside of her was better than before. They clung to each other as they came down from their post-orgasmic bliss, Kate's legs still wrapped firmly around his waist.

"That was...wow."

"I agree," he chuckled. He pulled back to look into her lovely eyes. "Everything will be okay, you know."

"When you tell me that, I believe you. But I'm still scared."

"I know, my love. But I won't let anything happen to you."

"I know. I trust you."

"Come on, let's get cleaned up and get a couple hours of shut eye before our difficult day tomorrow."

"Okay."

As they drifted off, he hoped that tomorrow would bring answers to many unanswered questions. But he didn't have his fucking fingers crossed.

CHAPTER 57

Kate

The meeting with her parents today went better than she'd thought it would. After first profusely apologizing that they'd never told her she was adopted, they explained how she came to live with them and why they'd never told her.

They had been on a waiting list for so long, they'd given up any hope of being granted a child, so when a representative from the agency came knocking on their door late one night, with Kate in hand, they fell in love with her instantly, agreeing to adopt her. The man who dropped her off wasn't one they had worked with before, but he told them the agency would contact them in the next few days with the paperwork to sign. Of course, they thought it slightly odd, but were so desperate for a baby, they didn't question him. When the agency didn't call after a couple of weeks, they followed up, but were told that a man by the name of Tom Cutler, which was the name he had given, wasn't, nor had ever been, employed by that agency.

They panicked and by that time, they simply could not give her back, so they kept their mouths shut, withdrew their name from the adoption agency as potential candidates and moved up to northern

Wisconsin, starting over with a new life, raising her. She came to find out that the birthday she celebrated wasn't even her real birthday. The man had left no paperwork with them that evening, not even a birth certificate, so she had no idea what her actual day of birth really was. That had stung.

Obviously not able to tell the complete truth, Kate explained that Dev was her boyfriend and Ren was a good friend. They seemed very impressed with Dev. They had been after her to get married and give them grandbabies. The married part she'd accomplished. The baby part would never be. But that was okay with her, as she had Dev for eternity and he was more than enough. They left, telling her parents she would be in touch with them and they would try to make it to dinner very soon.

On the long drive back home, Dev and Ren checked out both the adoption agency and Tom Cutler. As suspected, all searches for Tom Cutler were a dead end. Of course it was an alias. Her parents didn't remember much about what he looked like, as they were so taken with her, but they did say he was rather on the short side and had thinning hair. And that was so helpful, as that didn't describe about two million men in this country.

As she sat on the chaise in their bedroom, frustration welled within her. She was not a violent person, but she just wanted Xavier found and killed. She desperately wanted to save all of those kidnapped girls from their daily horrors. She wanted to leave the goddamned house and do something with Dev, like normal people. She wanted to finish her dissertation paper. She wanted to veg out on the couch and watch *Real Housewives* and *Ellen*. She wanted normal.

She sighed. She wanted to go back to teaching. That was probably one of the things she was most sad about. She was literally just months away from completing her PhD and applying for a professorship that would secure her tenure and she knew there was no way she'd be able to go back to that life. So once all of this other stuff was behind her, she'd have to figure out what she could now contribute to this new life. She was not going to sleep in every day, read romance novels and wander around, waiting for Dev to finish his workday.

No.

She had a lot to give, a lot to contribute, and she wasn't about to be a stay-at-home wife of a Vampire Lord.

And what happened when they did rescue these women? Many would need years of trauma counseling and some may not even want to return home under the scrutiny of their parents or loved ones. At least for a while. While counseling was never really Kate's career aspiration, with her training, she knew she'd be able to help these tortured women.

The kernel of an idea started forming. She'd have to give it more thought, work out the kinks, before she talked to Dev about it, but suddenly she was very excited and had something to really look forward to after they'd taken care of the task at hand.

Feeling a bit more refreshed, she rose to find Dev, but was hit with sudden queasiness, and had to sit back down. She guessed the chicken salad sandwich she'd had for lunch wasn't sitting well with her. She knew that damn diner they'd stopped at for lunch on the way to her parents' house was sketchy.

She lay there for a few minutes until the worst of the nausea passed, praying she wasn't going to spend all night worshiping the porcelain god, when she'd much rather make love to her new mate.

Dev

After returning home, Kate said she was a little tired and went to rest in their room. Dev wasn't sure if she was physically, mentally or emotionally tired, and while he didn't want to be away from her for a minute, he wanted her to rest.

So Dev sat in his office, getting the daily update from Giselle and the detective. They'd identified several more missing girls potentially related to the dream studies and they were working on tracking down more leads. He'd asked them to check out other adoption agency registries that may have had potential parents withdraw their applications. If there were other female vampires out there, he definitely wanted to find them. And protect them. He had a feeling there were more out there than any of them knew. He would have Rom's computer wiz help with that request as well, as it was bound to be an arduous task.

Just as Giselle was finishing her update, Ren walked in, excitement lighting up his pretty boy face.

"We have an update from the field." The men had not finished their scout of the area last night, with only a few more houses remaining this evening.

"And?"

"We think we may have found it. Manny found shrouding over a large wooded area on the northeast part of Washington Island, north of the Door County peninsula."

"Get everyone together in here immediately. Get Damian and Rom on the vid com. Tell Manny to leave two men there to watch for any activity and have everyone else return."

As everyone was filing out of his office, Kate walked in. And she didn't look well.

"What's the matter, love? You don't look well."

She laughed, but it lacked her usual cheeriness. "Well that's not something any woman wants to hear."

He gathered her in his arms, kissing her forehead.

"Bad choice of words. You look edible, as always. Just a little on the peaked side."

"I think it was just something I ate. My stomach's a little sour, but I'm feeling better than I was. I'll be fine."

"Manny thinks he found Xavier and we need to strategize. Do you want to go lie down again and I can just update you later?"

"No. I'll be fine. I want to come. But I think I'm out on chicken salad sandwiches for the near future. Just the thought of them makes me want to vomit."

"Well, that's easily solved, love. Don't think about them." He wrapped his arm around her waist, drawing her down tightly on his lap. "Let me hold you until everyone gathers."

"Yes, I'd like that."

CHAPTER 58

Xavier

The dreamwalker hadn't returned for several nights. Too bad, that. He rather enjoyed taunting her last time and looked forward to doing it again. What really made him hard was the thought of taunting her in person. He could sense her goodness, and that needed to be stripped away. And he couldn't wait to be the one to do it.

So, he'd decided to do something he'd never done in all of his years alive. Kate Martin was going to be his special pet, shackled and chained at his side at all times. Even when he fucked and fed. Hell, he might even make her partake.

She'd have her own nice cage in his quarters where he could keep an eye on her at all times. There was something special about this dreamwalker that he couldn't quite put his finger on, and he couldn't wait to find out what it was...and shred it from her until she was a shell of her former self. A mindless slut, doing whatever he wanted, whenever he wanted. The idea had merit. He should have taken a pet much, much earlier.

He looked forward to the day he had Ms. Katherine Martin in his possession. And that day should be this evening. His very powerful witch had done a locating spell, much to the detriment of her health, but no matter. He'd find another witch if she didn't recover. She was going to die anyway, either by her hand or his. Too bad, really. He'd just acquired this particular witch only several short months ago after he'd killed his last one because she'd proven to be as useless as the warning on a pack of cigarettes. This particular one was supposed to excel at locating spells, and she'd tried to bullshit him that she couldn't do a locating spell, saying the witch Devon was using to shroud himself was too powerful. He, of course, made her continually try.

And finally this evening...success! She'd found a hole in the shroud concealing Devon's location. It appeared Devon's witches' power had faded somewhat...much to Devon's misfortune.

Now not only would Katherine Martin be his, but he'd finally get his chance to destroy Devon Fallinsworth for good. *The almighty, self-righteous and powerful lord.* This was the opportunity he hadn't gotten so very many centuries ago when he'd slaughtered the rest of Devon's family.

1559

Devon was supposed to be here. Xavier yearned to cause him immense pain and agony and being unable to stop his family from being slaughtered while he was forced to watch would accomplish just that. Devon should feel the same pain Xavier felt at being betrayed. He had been hunted like an animal for the past month. Unable to return to the only place he'd called home. Abandoned by his real family, he had now been abandoned by his adopted family. And the blame lay squarely at Devon's feet.

Xavier had only recently come into his unique powers, which was how he'd been able to kidnap multiple villagers at a time. He came across it quite by accident. His prey one evening wasn't very amenable, the cock tease. She decided to run. He decided not to let her. Fuck, did he have fun that night. He'd vacillate between mobilizing and immobilizing her in various positions. It was electrifying.

So he decided to test his powers. See how many people he could immobilize at once. At first it was only a few, but as the months went by, his powers grew. The village where he abducted nineteen people was the most he'd been able to do so far. He was overjoyed! He couldn't wait to share the information with his brother, but before he could, Devon started chattering about the kidnappings and how they needed to catch and destroy the rogue responsible. He wasn't a motherfucking rogue! He was vampire! The strongest species that ever lived. Devon was so idealistic. Vampires could rule the world. They were not meant to live alongside undeserving humans, their food for fuck's sake, like they were equals. They were not equal.

No. He could not tell his closest friend, his brother, of his unique ability and now he was glad for that. It would make his surprise all the sweeter when he figured it out for himself. For how could a lone vampire slaughter an entire village? It wasn't possible. But...oh it was.

His plan to make his traitorous brother watch his family be slaughtered had been thwarted. Xavier waited for hours...until close to dawn. Finally he couldn't wait any more. It wasn't quite according to plan, but at least when Devon returned from whatever whore he was buried balls deep in, he'd discover his family, dead. He knew Devon well enough that guilt would suffocate him for the rest of his life. And for now, that would have to do.

The agony on Devon's face as he stood outside his— their—burning cottage was incomparable. This revenge was enough for now, but Devon's punishment was far from over.

Xavier's sinister smile grew. "It's time, brother," he mumbled, readying himself for tonight's battle.

CHAPTER 59

Dev

Ren was displeased with him, but he couldn't give two shits. This was personal and he wasn't going to stay back like some pussy while everyone else had all the fun killing a bunch of rogue vamps. And Xavier.

Fuck that.

He was a Vampire Lord, one of the strongest vampires in the world. Besides, his unique skill of making illusions seem real was going to be critical to their success and Ren knew it. Dev appreciated his concern, but it was misplaced. While he was torn between wanting to stay to protect Kate or fight, he knew this was the place he was most needed.

So Ren was pissed at him and in turn, the women of his household were incensed with him as well. Giselle was fuming because she'd been tasked with the assignment of staying back to keep Kate safe. And Kate was furious because she said she didn't need a *'goddamn babysitter'*. Yeah...he was their least favorite male at the moment.

While Kate's skills had improved quite a bit over the last couple of weeks, she was still far from her full vampire powers and she needed protection 24/7. Elle didn't need more reasons to resent Kate, but Dev simply could not leave her without protection. Who was he kidding? She would *always* have protection. So when he couldn't be around to protect her, he'd already decided that person was going to be Elle, but he'd spring that on them later.

Much, much later.

Right now there were roughly thirty vamps on the outskirts of the rundown Washington Island property, all indications leading them to believe Xavier was here. Most were Devon's men, but several of Damian's and Rom's most experienced fighters were here to help.

And he was very concerned. Because of the shrouding none of them, except Manny, should have been able to see a thing but fields. However, each and every one of them could see the faded, single-story, broken down white shack in front of them and the rusted, weatherworn windmill in the background. The house was so small that it looked more like an outhouse than something that a human would occupy. Let alone a hoard of rogues. Something was very wrong and they needed to proceed with even more caution.

On Dev's command, the vampires surrounded the shack, weapons drawn, with Ren and Dev taking the lead to enter the premises first. For now, four men were to remain outside of the house, unless they needed them.

Empty, as suspected. They walked through the small structure, quickly finding a stairwell leading down. Flashing into unknown territory was dangerous, so they agreed to use that only as a last resort.

They quietly made their way down the rickety wood stairwell, only to enter what appeared to be a spider infested, dirt-floored basement, complete with rotted wooden shelves lined in canned goods. Every one of them could feel the unease in the air, likely another trick of the witch to deter vagrants from the property. It only reinforced to him they were in the right place.

He looked around the small space. Not a door in sight.

But Dev knew better. The door was simply hidden. He gave a single nod in Ren's direction.

Ren closed his eyes, releasing his unique power. He could sense any living vampire or human being within a half-mile radius and pinpoint their exact location. That was one of the reasons he was Dev's personal bodyguard. He was better than any electronic motion detector.

"The door is behind the shelves, my lord. There are ten humans in single rooms directly to the right. There are eight more directly to the left. Those are probably the women. There is a large cluster of vampires, roughly fifteen or so, in a single room at the end of the right side hallway. There are several more humans one level below, some in individual rooms, some in a cluster in a single room, as well as another fifty or so vampires."

"Good work, Ren."

Shit. Those were more rogues than he'd expected. Guess Xavier had been busy. They made quick work of finding the hidden latch, revealing another downward stairwell. This stairwell was made of stainless steel and he could clearly see a hallway at the bottom that went only left to right. They likely only had seconds before rogues were on them, since they no doubt tripped some sort of silent alarm when they opened the secret door. But they had the element of surprise, as they knew exactly where to find what they were looking for.

They put their plan into quick action, splitting up their duties to rescue the girls, detain any other humans and kill as many rogues as possible, most importantly Xavier. Too bad Ren's power couldn't pinpoint exactly where that bastard was.

Chaos erupted the minute they split. The rogues on this floor attacked, but were quickly wiped out, with minimal injuries inflicted on his team. It was clear these were young, low-level, disposable vamps and were no match for him or his men.

They made it quickly to the downstairs stairwell and waited. Adrenaline scorched his veins like wildfire. This was a high like no other, except when he made love to his mate. Dev focused, used his powers to project the images of a fire on the lower level, complete with smoke and heat to round out the realness of it. There was almost nothing a vampire feared more than fire.

Within minutes, rogues stampeded up the stairs. Those that could would likely flash outside, but his men stationed there would take care of them. He wanted a couple alive for questioning and those would be the older, more powerful, more useful rogues.

It was a bloodbath. Rogues were everywhere, like fireflies. While their powers were weaker than his and his men's, his team sustained several injuries in the battle, a couple of them fairly severe. He had several shards of razor like ice stuck in his arm, thanks to a rogue with ice making ability. He took immense pleasure in removing the rogue's head for that little stunt. He also narrowly missed an arrow aimed straight at his heart, barely nicking his underarm instead. By the time they'd slaughtered all the rogues, body parts littered the narrow hallways. Dark blood ran in rivulets down the walls, pooling at their feet. He was covered in it.

He'd kept in touch with his men outside all the while, and about a dozen rogues had flashed out there, but Xavier had yet to make an appearance.

"Ren, do you sense anyone else on the premises?"

"No, my Lord."

They exchanged a knowing look. Xavier wasn't here. Fear coursed through Dev.

Kate.

Something was terribly wrong. He couldn't

communicate with her at this distance, but he knew he'd felt her fear in his gut.

Along with Ren and Manny, he flashed back to his estate and the scene in front of him left his blood running cold. It was déjà vu.

The front door stood wide open, the house completely destroyed on the inside.

"Kate!" he bellowed. He frantically turned to Ren, who sadly shook his head. They weren't here. Or they were, just not alive.

A frantic search of the house turned up no sign of Kate or Elle, but he did find Leo in the kitchen. Or what was left of him. Fuck, Leo had been with him for decades. He was like a brother to him. He wanted to grieve, but he couldn't. The only thing that mattered at this moment was finding his mate. Alive and unharmed.

"What the fuck happened here!" Dev roared.

"I don't know, my lord, but we'll find out." He reached out, putting a hand on Dev's shoulder. "We'll find her, Dev. We'll find her."

"But will we find her in time?"

The noise Dev let out was so loud and long, he feared the entire house would crumble around him. It didn't matter. If anything happened to Kate, he wouldn't make it until sunrise. He would follow her anywhere...even in death.

CHAPTER 60

Kate

Jesus, she was sore. She couldn't seem to think of anything else except how much her body ached, everywhere. And she couldn't quite remember why, but it nagged at the very edge of her memory. Something wasn't right, she felt so very weak, but she couldn't place her finger on why. She couldn't quite shake the fog from her brain enough to put all the puzzle pieces together.

She blinked, trying to focus her eyes on her surroundings, but everything was pitch black. She tried for several minutes, but nothing came clear. She tried to move, but her body wouldn't respond. After several more minutes, her hand finally obeyed her command, reaching in front of her and what she encountered made her nearly paralyzed with fear.

Bars. Cold iron bars.

She felt everywhere her hand could reach and encountered more of the same. She was in a cage. Her vision slowly returned and she noticed she was in what appeared to be a very large dog kennel. She couldn't sit up quite straight, as the top was too low.

And the room she was in looked all too familiar.

Memories of the night's events flooded back.

She'd been in Dev's office working on her dissertation paper, all the more determined to finish it since she'd come up with her new long-term plan. She was so worried about Dev it made it difficult to concentrate, but she needed to do something to get the fact that he was in danger off her mind. This was her world now and her new mate took care of his problems himself, even if that put him in danger. Like it or not, she would have to accept it.

Giselle sat across the room from her, as far away as she could get. She could be across the massive mansion and it would still be too close as far as she was concerned. She'd told her to leave, but Giselle refused. 'My lord's command,' she'd said. 'Bitch', she'd thought.

Giselle scared the shit out of her when she jumped up and rushed toward the open office door. She closed it softly, belying the sudden concern worn on her face.

"Get under the desk," she commanded Kate.

"Get under the desk? What the hell has gotten into you? Just because Dev commanded that you babysit me like some four-year-old does not mean I'm going to—"

"Get under the fucking desk. Now. There's someone here."

Terror had run through Kate. The only ones at the house were herself, Leo and Giselle. Everyone else had gone on the dangerous mission.

She complied, hiding under the massive cherry desk. Now she couldn't see a damn thing. "Who is it?" she whispered.

Giselle gave no response, but she knew she was still there. Giselle may not like her, but she knew that Giselle would never leave her. She would protect her to the death.

Abruptly the door flew open and pandemonium erupted. She heard cursing, grunting and furniture breaking. She could smell blood, which made her incisors involuntarily lengthen. She was terrified for

Giselle, but also, selfishly, for herself. Yet, here she sat, like some stupid, helpless female, letting someone else defend her and possibly get hurt. She was just about to come out when...silence. Everything just stopped.

She strained to hear what was happening, but heard nothing. She slowly rose from behind the desk and was completely shocked by the sight before her. Giselle, who looked badly injured, and the vampire she was fighting were immobile. Frozen in mid fight. Had she done that without realizing it? She didn't think so, but she wasn't sure. She didn't have good control over her powers yet.

Just then she heard heavy footsteps and as she turned toward the office door, a large, imposing figure entered. Covered in blood. The half scarred face was wearing a malicious grin. She would recognize that face anywhere.

Xavier.

"Hello, Katherine."

After a brief struggle, her world went black.

Xavier hadn't been able to immobilize her for some reason, but she wasn't strong enough to fight him on her own, especially without Giselle's help. She'd tried to freeze him, but it didn't work and next thing she knew, she was waking up in this cage. Where was Giselle? As much as Kate disliked her, she certainly didn't want something bad to happen to her. Giselle had fought to protect Kate's life.

The door opening brought Kate out of her thoughts and well into her living nightmare as Xavier walked into what must be his study.

"Well, well, well. I see my pet is awake."

Pet? While she'd rather tell him to go fuck himself, she remained silent.

"Don't feel like talking? That's okay, my sweet. I have more than enough for us to talk about."

He pulled a chair up in front of her cage, leaning toward her after he sat. She could see the fury in his terrifying eyes. What did he have to be furious about? She was the one in a fucking cage.

"Tonight has definitely been full of surprises, sweet Kate. And I don't like surprises. When I finally manage to find one of my greatest nemeses, imagine my surprise when he is nowhere to be found. Imagine my further surprise when the dreamwalker he is protecting is immune to my powers. I don't know how that can be possible. Most unfortunate. And imagine my shock when I return to my compound to find all of my pets gone and my men slaughtered. That made me most unhappy."

Kate internally sighed. At least the mission was successful.

"Where is Giselle?"

He continued as if she hadn't spoken. "But the night wasn't a complete waste, you see. To my utter delight, I was particularly surprised to find that you are Devon's Moira."

Bad, bad, bad. How did he know she was his Moira?

"Ahhhh, sweet Kate. I can see your head spinning. You're thinking...how did he know we were bonded? I'm surprised Devon didn't explain that to you. You see, when a vampire bonds, the mating marks that wrap around each mate's left thumb are not only a symbol of their love and devotion, but also a replica of the male vampire's family crest. That way, any vampire she comes across can clearly identify the female. They all know she's taken, and by whom. It can be both a blessing and a curse for the female. In this case, a curse for you, my sweet, but certainly a blessing for me."

His fowl breath gagged her, as he laughed in her direction. Her nausea returned with such a vengeance, she didn't think she'd be able to hold the meager contents of her stomach down.

"Do you want to know why this is a blessing for me, sweet Kate?"

No. She did not want to know.

"Because if I have you, I will also have Devon in very short order. He will move heaven and earth to save his *lovely* mate. And lovely you are. But alas, all he will do is succeed in getting himself captured as well. And it will be so much sweeter to do what I have in mind with you, if he is forced to witness it all firsthand. Sweet retribution, really. Why this turned out just delightful!" His laugh was maniacal. He really was a deranged lunatic.

He reached his hand in between the cage bars, trying to touch her and she cringed toward the back, trying to get as far away from him as possible. His face turned menacing as spittle flew in her direction with his tirade.

"Yes, he'll have to watch while I fuck his mate so hard you bleed all over my cock. And while I shove my cock so far down your throat, you won't be able to breathe. My come will coat your tongue and run down your chin. He'll watch while I feast on your blood as I take your ass. After I've had my fill, I'll let every one of my vampires have a go with you. There will be no place on you that goes untouched, my sweet Kate. Your precious Devon will watch as I break you piece by piece, bit by bit, until the light fades from your eyes right before him. And once you're gone, that's all he'll want, too. He'll want to follow you into sweet oblivion. But I won't let him. I'll keep him alive, torturing him to within an inch of his life for *years* on end. It's not even near an equivalent price to pay for everything he's done to me."

Holy shit. Her father was one fucked up dude.

He stood up abruptly. "Well, got to go. I have quite a few plans to make before I'll be ready for my next houseguest." Then he vanished.

She couldn't keep the vomit down and barely had her

head turned before she retched everywhere. Great. Now she was a caged animal, covered in puke.

"Giselle," she whispered. Silence. She called a little louder, but there was no response.

Dev, can you hear me? No answer.

Tears now ran down her face. She was petrified. She was well and truly on her own. She didn't know if Giselle was alive and she didn't know if Dev would find her in time. Hell, she didn't want him anywhere near here. She wouldn't risk him being captured. Xavier was more depraved than they had all imagined.

She tried her powers again. Nothing. She'd tried to flash several times while he was talking to her, without success. She'd tried to freeze him while he sat in front of her. Nothing happened...except he continued to run his foul mouth. She'd improved her skills the last couple of weeks, so while not perfect, she was able to pretty readily use her power of stasis.

Except on Xavier. But he couldn't use his power on her either. And that was clearly a conundrum to him. So maybe their powers wouldn't work on each other because they were family? If that was the case, it was both good and bad for her. Good, as he couldn't immobilize her, but bad, because she couldn't protect herself. She was on the verge of a panic attack.

Pull it together, Kate! You are the mate of one of the most powerful beings in the world. Stop being a sniveling little baby and save yourself.

Right. Time to problem solve, not fall apart. She could do that later when she got out of this mess. It was up to her to either live or to die, and by God, she intended to live. She didn't know how she was going to accomplish that, exactly, but she knew she'd rather kill herself than be subjected to anything Xavier, modern day Attila the Hun, just described in unnecessary and nauseating detail.

CHAPTER 61

Dev

Thank God they'd had the foresight to send the detective to a hotel last evening. He didn't need another lost soul burned on his conscience. Thatcher must be pretty taken with Elle, if the broken lamps and furniture were any indication. Apparently Dev would be getting a hefty bill from the hotel for all the damage the detective inflicted. After they told him, Thatcher insisted he be brought back to the house until they found her.

As for Dev, he was absolutely beside himself. A ruthless, cold-blooded killer had stolen his mate. And Xavier wasn't stupid. He would quickly find out that Kate was his mate and use that against him. He was simply waiting for his phone to ring with Xavier's directions. He would do anything to save Kate, even sacrifice his life for hers. No question, no hesitation. He loved her that much.

But it wouldn't come to that. While he knew Xavier had been plotting his capture and undoubted torture, he'd been doing a little planning of his own.

They'd been back to Xavier's compound to see if he'd foolishly brought Kate back there, which he had not. He assumed Xavier had taken Giselle as well, since there was no sign of her. There were, however, definite signs of a struggle in his office, including several pools of Giselle's blood. But none of Kate's, thank God. He wasn't sure he should be grateful for that, but at least that meant she'd most likely been alive when Xavier took her.

And on her way to him was Esmeralda, his traitorous witch. She most definitely tampered with their shroud, allowing Xavier to not only kidnap his mate, but also one of his most loyal vampires, leaving another in pieces. Literally. This was entirely on her head and she was going to help them fix it before he killed her. Xavier clearly had his own witch issues, so with any luck, Esmeralda would find Kate through a locating spell.

Speaking of the devil, the commotion at his door dragged him from his thoughts.

"If you know what's best for you, you will take your hands off me. Right now."

"Not a chance, witch." Ren was barely able to rein in his anger. Dev knew he and Elle had a special bond and her disappearance was killing him. He felt helpless, just like Dev. And Ren was a smart vampire. He knew if something happened to Kate, that this was the beginning of the end for Dev.

"Sit the fuck down and shut your fucking mouth before I shut it for you." He practically threw her in a chair. Yep, holding to control by a hairsbreadth. Exactly how he felt. Esmeralda had enough self-preservation sense to look scared.

Dev came and sat in a chair directly across from her. He never did that.

"What's go—"

"Stop. If the next words out of your mouth aren't the truth, so help me God, I'll rip your black, treacherous heart out right fucking now. No second chances. So...think very carefully about what you want to say."

The look on her face revealed she knew she'd been

SURRENDERING

caught. He could see every emotion pass through her beautifully criminal face.

Remorse.

Fear.

Shame.

She broke eye contact, looking at the floor instead. Just as well. He could hardly stand to look at her without wanting to rip her lying tongue from her rotten mouth.

"I'm sorry," she whispered.

She's fucking sorry? His rage was an out of control inferno.

"Did you think with Kate out the picture that you'd be able to step into her place? That I would want to fuck you instead? Bond with you, instead? Is that it, Esmeralda?" He rarely used her full name when speaking to her and at the sound of it her eyes flew to his.

Dev threw his head back and laughed, but it was laced with disgust, not humor. He stood, looking down at her cowering form. She looked as young and vulnerable as he'd ever seen her. And he couldn't give a shit.

"Get this through your thick skull once and for all, witch. I don't want you. I never have. I never will. I would rather stick my cock into a Venus flytrap than in any black hole in your body. Your actions caused the death of a longtime friend of my family. Your actions caused one of my most loyal vampires to be kidnapped, perhaps even killed. And your actions have caused my beloved mate to fall into the hands of my most powerful and dangerous enemy. And you did this all so you could fuck me? You disgust me!"

He was screaming at her now as he grabbed her by her clothes and shoved her hard up against the wall, feet dangling inches from the floor.

He growled through gritted teeth, "Hear me and hear

me well, Esmeralda. If he so much as harms one delicate hair on her precious head, I will personally take it out of your hide. Tenfold. So you'd better pray that she's unharmed, untouched and healthy, or you're in for a world of hurt, witch."

He released her, uncaring as she dropped in a puddle to the floor, legs buckling beneath her.

"I'm sor—"

"Shut the fuck up! You will keep your goddamned mouth shut and *I* will do the talking!"

He sat down behind his desk, calming himself before he spoke again. The next time he spoke, his voice was even, in control, but menacing.

"You will use your magic to find Kate and you will do it now. I have her hair and blood right here. I have her clothing if you need it." He glared at her, still slumped on the floor.

"And if you don't, I'll kill you."

Esmeralda stared, witnessing a side of Dev she'd never seen before. A side he didn't show many people. Those who did see it rarely lived. But he hadn't decided Esmeralda's fate. Yet.

"Now get the fuck off my floor and get to work, witch." His harsh command had Esmeralda scrambling in fear for her life to do his bidding.

The phone call he'd been expecting all morning finally came. Xavier. He was making him sweat it out, making every minute he was parted from Kate feel like a thousand centuries.

"Yes."

"Hello, brother. It's been a long time."

"Get on with it, Xavier." At the moment, he wished his unique power included reaching through the phone line to gut the son-of-a-bitch and hang his intestines from the ceiling fan.

"Now, now, Devon. Is that any way to talk to family?" he chuckled.

"We are not family. But you have mine and I want them back." He was having a very hard time not letting Xavier under his skin, but he knew if he did, it could be worse for his Kate. And Giselle...provided she still lived.

"Direct, as always. Color me blue when I found out the dreamwalker was your bonded mate. I mean...I couldn't have scripted our little reunion tete-a-tete any better if I'd tried." Xavier's glee oozed through the phone.

"If you've harmed either one of them, I'll slowly rip you apart."

"Ah, Devon. Such strong words when I'm in the omnipotent position."

Dev's jaw ticked back and forth, his teeth grinding so hard, he worried he'd break them.

"I take your silence as agreement. Good. Now, I'll take you in exchange for your lovely mate. You will come alone, because while I'd love to pay you back for my many losses this evening, at the moment, I'm far more savoring the thought of getting my hands on you. If you don't come alone, she dies. If you try to double cross me, she dies." He paused before adding, "I assume you'll take the deal?"

"Of course. But I want Giselle too. The meeting point?"

"Giselle? That would be the female vampire?" It was a rhetorical question, so he remained silent.

"Very well, you can have her. If she's still alive by then. She's hanging on by a very thin thread. She's been an enjoyable plaything for my men. Needs blood to heal her near-mortal injuries. Shame, really. So...we'll meet at the lighthouse at Rock Island State Park. Half an hour."

"Fine."

Too bad Xavier would be the only one there. He would have his mate back by then.

"I'm looking forward to getting re-acquainted, brother."

Dev hung up and turned to Ren and Sulley. "You two are with me. We go now before they move her."

They were already at the old park ranger's station at Rock Island State Park. Esmeralda had located Kate fifteen minutes ago and he would not wait another second to free her from Xavier's clutches. They wanted the element of surprise and had already scoped out the area, finding the secret passageway to the lower compound. Dev silently wondered how many of these compounds Xavier had around the country and how they would find them all.

Ren had already identified one human and fifteen vampires, one with a very week aura. They were hoping that was Giselle. She wouldn't answer when he called her and he would not leave one of his own behind.

To provide shrouding protection, Esmeralda had come with him, Ren, Manny, Thane, and two of Rom's best fighters. He had to leave the rest of his men back to protect the girls and other humans they'd rescued earlier, so he was working with a smaller crew, but they'd be fine. He didn't trust leaving Esmeralda behind, so she was going in with them. If she died, oh well. It would be a quicker death than she deserved.

"Manny, the witch is with you. You will guard the outside and, so help me, witch, if I so much as get a tingle that you are sabotaging us, I will gut you faster than you can take your next breath. Thane and Henry, bring Giselle home."

They headed into action.

Now that he was close enough, he could communicate with Kate. Kate had done a good job at describing her surroundings. The fact that she was kept like some animal in a dog crate nearly made him nuclear. He breathed a little easier when she said she was okay, but until she was safe in his arms, he wouldn't believe it.

"Kate, my love, I'm on my way."

No response. Fuck. His heart beat faster with fear. Why wouldn't she answer him?

As they entered the structure, Dev used his powers to hide them from view. He knew this wouldn't work against high-powered vampires, like Xavier, but it would work against low level vamps. He had a whole litany of surprises in store for the others. Sulley, one of Rom's men, was not only a skilled fighter, he had the power to sense a being's deepest fear, so his skill would be particularly useful, along with Dev's. This way they could personalize the illusion to each rogue to maximize its benefit. They'd just have to make this quick because making those types of illusions drained him of power quickly and that would make him vulnerable.

He continually tried calling out to Kate, but she wouldn't respond. He knew something was terribly wrong. *"Hang on my love. I'm on my way."*

They quickly made their way down the steel staircase in complete blackness. Kate was a level down, but Giselle was straight ahead at the end of the hallway. Thane and Henry had their orders. They would flash Elle home and Henry would return to help them while Thane stayed with her if necessary. If not, he'd return also. Big D was at their new location, ready to tend to her.

In short order they had made it to the lower level without incident. His only thought was getting to his mate. The second was eliminating Xavier, but only after Kate was safe. The fact they had run into no rogues at all was disconcerting. Something definitely didn't feel right. They were feet away from the room that held Kate when all hell broke loose behind them.

Ren was pinned to the ground by an unknown force and Sulley was in hand-to-hand combat with a rogue the size of a lord. There were three more gigantic rogues tearing down the hallway toward them and Dev had a sudden fear for Ren's safety, stepping protectively in front of him.

"Save your mate, my lord."

"Looks like I need to save your ass first."

"I've got it covered, my lord."

"Yes, I can see that."

Sulley and Dev made quick work of the rogues in the hallway, freeing Ren, only for more rogues to rush them from either side. A feeling of vertigo assaulted him and he had to fight to remain upright.

"Go, my lord. We can take care of this."

His men could handle this, so Dev didn't waste another second. *"Kate, I'm coming."*

Dev swiftly closed the gap between him and where his mate was being held, kicking the door open.

What he saw inside was completely unexpected, freezing him in place with terror.

Kate stood before him in the middle of the room, clothes torn to the point of barely covering her. She was covered in bruises, her right eye completely swollen shut. Tears streamed in rivers down her red face. If all of that wasn't bad enough, what paralyzed him with fear was the fact that Xavier had her completely pinned to him, one arm around her neck and another around her midsection. The arm around her neck forced her head to turn at a grotesque left angle.

Dev had been completely unprepared for this. Ren hadn't sensed any vampires with Kate.

"You broke our deal, brother," Xavier sneered.

Dev focused solely on Kate. *"Are you okay, love?"* She wouldn't answer. *"Kate, answer me, please."*

"If you're trying to talk to your luscious mate, I'm afraid Katherine can't really communicate at the moment. You see, I have some tricks up my sleeve too, *brother*."

"*Kate, blink twice if you can hear me.*"

Two blinks. *Thank God.*

"*I'm going to figure a way out of this. Hang on, love.*"

How could he rescue her without causing paralysis? One wrong move and her head would be severed from her spinal column. Snapping a vamps neck didn't cause death, but it did cause permanent paralysis. And throwing an illusion wouldn't work when Xavier literally held Dev's entire life in filthy hands.

"I've spent the last five hundred years fantasizing about the day I would end your life, brother. The same way you effectively ended mine when you ratted me out like the slimy traitor you are."

Dev remained silent, never taking his eyes from Kate.

"We could have ruled the world together, Devon. We are among the strongest, oldest and most powerful vampires alive. We could have had it all. We could have been kings. But you had to have a fucking conscience. How can you stomach living side by side with humans? They are animals! They are our food!"

Dev continued to ignore Xavier's rant. He had to figure out how to get out of this mess. "It's going to be okay, love."

"Hmmm, I'm not so sure it *is* going to be okay, my sweet," Xavier whispered in her ear. He licked her cheek, studying Dev the entire time.

Dev saw red. How *dare* Xavier touch his mate in such a manner. Dev made a slight move toward Kate and Xavier jerked her back toward him more firmly, making her wince.

"You'll never make it in time before I snap her neck. And I'm not sure how much fun I would have fucking a vegetable. Never tried it before, but it could definitely be worthwhile. But I really do like my bitches to put up a fight."

Kate looked terrified and she started sobbing softly.

"I won't let him hurt you, love."

"You are one sick motherfucker." Dev was trying to keep his cool, but he felt himself falter slightly. It was clear Xavier had the upper hand at the moment.

"I thought we'd already established that, Devon."

"Me for her. That was the deal." At this point, he just needed to get Kate away from Xavier. The fight outside of the room continued to escalate and Dev had the first twinge of real concern. He wasn't sure either of them would make it out alive of this FUBAR situation.

"Me for her, Xavier." He had to keep him talking...distract him.

"Yes," Xavier sighed. "That was the original deal. Until you broke it by trying to sabotage me. Now I'm afraid there is a new deal on the table. Well...the *only* deal, really."

"And what might that be?"

"I have been forced to spend the last five hundred years living underground like a lowly sewer rat. All thanks to you. My body has been ravaged beyond any repair, also thanks to you. I have spent the last half a millennia waiting, plotting, anticipating my revenge. And I couldn't have written a better ending to our rivalry if I'd tried. I am going to relish watching you suffer as I fuck and bleed your mate right in front of your eyes. I will let my men line up and use her over and over again. You will watch the life slowly leave her body, unable to save her. And when her body finally gives out and you watch her die, I will enjoy torturing you to the brink of death, only to bring you back again so you can suffer her loss in perpetuity. I will show you no mercy."

He had to get Kate away from this psychopath. He just needed to get him to release her. If he could get her out of his grip, he had a chance at saving them with a powerful illusion, but he couldn't risk it while Xavier held her life so precariously in his hands. He obviously had no idea Kate was his daughter and that was definitely a secret they needed to keep.

Dev felt the power Xavier unleashed. This had been his worst fear—that he would be immobilized, unable to help his mate. So while he could feel Xavier's power—*nothing happened*. He still had the ability to move. And, he realized, so did Kate. She'd been struggling in Xavier's arms from the moment he walked in.

He could see the confusion could Xavier's eyes, but Xavier quickly recovered. Dev was confused as well, but wasn't about to reveal that little fact to him. The upper hand may just have shifted to him slightly.

No sooner had that thought crossed his mind when the unthinkable happened. He watched helplessly as Xavier sunk his fangs into his mate's neck, but just as Dev was charging to free her, Xavier wailed and threw Kate across the room, where she landed in a still heap on the floor.

Dev only had seconds to react, as Xavier stood clawing at his throat. He threw the illusion that he'd turned his back on Xavier to tend to Kate, who still lay in a crumpled pile bleeding on the ground, when instead he already had her safely in his arms, and unable to flash inside for some reason, ran outdoors where he flashed them the hell out of there and back to the safety of their new home.

CHAPTER 62

Kate

It had been over a month since Dev rescued her from Xavier's clutches, who still remained alive unfortunately. They never did understand why Xavier threw her across the room after he bit her, but she recalled him hissing, like he was hurt. Big D had enlisted the help of the scientists they'd recovered to help figure it out. They were also trying to determine why Xavier's powers didn't appear to work on either her or Dev. None of them had ever run across this before. Whatever the reason, they were grateful or there may have been a very different ending.

She was devastated to learn of Leo's death, but thankfully everyone else had returned safely, albeit a little worse for the wear. Ren and Thane had completely recovered from their injuries within a couple of days.

Giselle, on the other hand, had been in very bad shape and it was touch and go for a week. So while she'd finally recovered physically, she was still recovering emotionally. She wouldn't speak of what was done to her in the short time she was in captivity. She'd been very withdrawn.

Giselle and Detective Thatcher had apparently gotten close in the weeks before holy hell erupted, but now

Giselle wouldn't even speak to him. He called her constantly, even trying to get Dev to intervene, but nothing would sway her. Kate felt sorry for the detective. He seemed like a nice guy. She actually found herself wishing the ice queen would reappear. At least that would mean she was getting back to normal.

She'd talked to Erin by phone a few times in the last month. The only thing she could tell her was that she'd met someone and was spending all of her free time with him. She knew eventually she would have to end their friendship, as she couldn't reveal anything about her new life. That saddened her. Her one consolation was that Kate and Olivia had become quite close. She'd also talked to her parents several times by phone and because Xavier was still loose, Dev had put some protective detail on them, for which she was grateful.

After their ordeal, Kate talked to Dev about her desire to offer a women's shelter to the women they had rescued, so they could acclimate back into society before returning to their homes, if they chose. He supported her one hundred percent and they devoted a whole wing of their new estate to the venture. Even thought she wouldn't technically need a license or anything to provide counseling, given the vampire world was different than the human world, she'd still submitted her final dissertation paper and waited on comments. She hoped to defend next month and graduate with her Psychology PhD at the end of this spring semester. She'd come so far and put in so much effort, quitting so close to the goal line didn't feel right, whether she needed those little three letters after her name or not.

She walked down the halls of the shelter, checking on the girls, as she'd done daily since they'd been brought here.

"How are you doing today?" Kate asked Sarah softly.

"Better. Each day gets a little better."

Kate had been thoroughly confused when Sarah had

told her she hadn't been raped. When they talked about what Kate had seen, Sarah said some powerful looking vampire walked into the room right before anything happened and shooed everyone else out, telling them he had the privilege that day. And then he simply unstrapped her, covered her in clean ratty clothes and carried her back to her room. Untouched. Unharmed. And that's where Sarah stayed until her rescue. Why would a bloodthirsty rogue protect a woman they'd kidnapped to be a baby breeder? And why weren't the other women that lucky, because none of them were. It didn't make sense.

Kate rubbed her shoulder tenderly. "I'm glad."

"Can we work on the dreams again today?"

"If you think you'll be up to it. I don't want to push you."

"I want to. It's the only thing that makes me feel like I have some semblance of control," Sarah replied, tears in her eyes. Even though Sarah hadn't suffered the same physical fate as the other girls, she'd still been significantly traumatized.

Sarah had confided in Kate that she'd dreamed of a very elusive man, whom she'd dubbed her knight in shining armor and he helped her escape, at least in her mind, when she was held captive. Kate knew what it was like to dream of gorgeous men, so of course she wanted to help Sarah hold on to anything that would help her heal. And giving her control over something— *anything*—would help.

"Of course we can work on them, Sarah. I'll be back after I check on the other girls, okay?"

Sarah hugged her tightly and held on for dear life. Tears sprung into Kate's eyes. She'd formed a strong bond with a few of the other girls after the ordeal, but particularly with Sarah. She was almost like the sister she never had. One other girl was also very dear, but Kate had a very difficult time not letting the guilt eat away at her. She pulled away from Sarah. "I'll be back in a bit."

She walked down the hallway cheerfully greeting the girls who had their doors open. Instead of the dingy, dirty filth they had lived in for weeks, months and even years in a couple cases, their accommodations were plush, homey, safe.

In all, they'd rescued fifteen of the twenty-nine missing girls. They guessed the others were kept at another one of Xavier's hidden locations and while it killed her to know there were still girls out there suffering the same fate as the ones they had just rescued, she had to be content for now that she could at least help a few of them. She was confident they would find the others soon. It had become an all-out obsession of all the Lords.

When she reached the last door on the left, she knocked softly.

No answer.

"Jamie, it's Kate. Can I come in?"

No answer.

Kate could have easily gotten into the room if she wanted to, but that wasn't the point. These women needed control back in their lives and if they wanted to remain locked in their rooms they had that choice. Of course they tried to coax them out daily, if for nothing else but to eat. Jamie would only allow food to be brought to her. She hadn't left her room and hadn't talked to anyone since her rescue, but that didn't stop Kate from trying. Every day.

Several minutes went by. She knew Jamie was at the door, afraid to open it. They'd been through this routine daily since the girls had been rescued. Jamie Hallow, the girl presumed dead eleven years ago, all the while a captive of Xavier's, was among the fifteen girls rescued. Jamie had a very long road of recovery ahead of her and had yet to talk about any of the things that happened.

Kate was particularly surprised to discover Detective Thatcher and Jamie had been dating at the time of her disappearance. Jamie had refused to talk to him as well and he wasn't taking it well. Between Giselle and Jamie, the detective was a mess. He was such a nice guy, she felt for him.

She provided soft words of support and comfort to Jamie through the door, same as she did every day. She hoped at some point, she would trust Kate enough to at least open the door and have a face-to-face conversation with her and that eventually Kate might get her into the on-site counseling they provided. She wouldn't give up.

It was 7:00 p.m. before she left the shelter and she was exhausted as she joined Dev for dinner. She hadn't been herself for weeks, dealing with nausea and fatigue, and yesterday she asked Big D to take some blood and run a few tests. She saw him daily now that he worked with her at the shelter. Her stomach turned at the food sitting in front of her and she finally knew why, but she still couldn't believe it. She was thrilled, but scared shitless.

"Any word on Esmeralda?" Kate knew Dev was upset with himself for leaving her at Xavier's compound, but obviously his only thought had been of her rescue. They hadn't seen her since. Had she been captured? Had she just run away, knowing how furious Dev was with her? Not that Kate was too happy with the bitch either. Trying to get her killed so she could have her mate. If she ever laid eyes on this witch, she wouldn't be held responsible for what she'd do. Kate insisted the next witch Dev partnered with be an old hag. And she was— *smile*—complete with a huge wart on the tip of her nose.

"No. Nothing." He paused, adding, "I don't want to talk about her. How was your day, love? You look exhausted."

She beamed at her wonderful, sexy mate. Ever concerned about her wellbeing. "I'm great. Had a very productive day with a couple of the girls. No progress yet with Jamie, but I hope she'll come along soon."

"Good to hear. Don't think I didn't notice you're not eating again. You really need to talk to Big D, Kate. I'm getting worried about you."

This was it. How would be react? He never talked about wanting kids. She looked at her plate as she spoke. "I did, actually."

Dev dropped his fork, leaping across the table to pull her into his arms. He was so overprotective.

"Something's wrong. What's wrong? I can tell something's wrong."

She couldn't help but laugh. "Wow. Pessimist much? Nothing is wrong, Dev. Everything is...wonderful actually."

"Wonderful? You're sick all the time. You barely eat. You barely have enough energy for making love. That is not fine. That is not normal."

"Actually...in my condition, it is." She watched his face carefully to see if he understood what she was telling him.

"What do you mean, your condition? Vampires don't get sick, love."

She pulled away. Men were idiots sometimes. "Oh my God, you are so dense! I'm not sick, Dev. I'm...I'm..." She took a deep breath and spit it out. "I'm pregnant."

His face would have been funny if she wasn't scared he was going into shock, so she rushed to explain.

"I know we didn't talk about kids, but I'm happy about this, Dev. I think it's a blessing. Big D said it was probably because I was never blooded, but he didn't know for sure. I don't really care how it happened anyway. Say some—"

She squealed as he picked her up and spun her around the room. "You're pregnant? You're pregnant! Holy fuck, I can't believe this. I'm going to be a father. How is this possible?"

"It's a miracle," she mumbled into his chest. "Dev, you're making me dizzy. Put me down, please." He mumbled "sorry" and set her down but didn't let go.

"Are you happy?" She hated how insecure she sounded. Instead of answering, he kissed her senseless.

When he finally broke free, he looked lovingly into her face and spoke the sweetest words she'd ever heard, causing tears to sting her eyes.

"Happy? Oh, my love...words haven't been invented yet to describe how I feel. You have stirred up emotions in me I never knew I possessed. I've never known true love, until you. I never knew true fear of losing something, until you. I never knew what making love was, until you."

Tears now streamed freely down Kate's face as her mate poured his heart out. He gently cupped her cheeks before continuing.

"I'd long dreamed of my Moira, Kate, but my vision paled in comparison to the real you. You've made me wish for things I never imagined possible, including a family. This baby is a miracle and I don't care how it happened; only that it did. You are my entire life, heart and soul, and I don't know what I did to deserve you or this gift you are giving me, but I'll not question it. I love you so much, Katherine Marjorie Fallinsworth."

She had no words, so she settled for something simple, but powerful. "I'm glad I surrendered my heart to you, my lord."

She squealed as once again she was swept into his arms and he swiftly carried her to their bedroom, her back landing on the plush bedding.

"I've told you repeatedly not to call me *my lord*, love. Bad girls don't go unpunished, you know." He began undressing her quickly.

"Good. That's what I was hoping for," she taunted.

As Dev began a most pleasurable form of punishment, Kate couldn't stop the tears of joy stinging her eyes. After trying to push away the best thing that had ever sauntered into her life, she now had everything she never knew she wanted and then some. A mate, a baby on the way, a whole new family.

Surrendering her heart to Devon Fallinsworth was the single best decision she'd ever made.

Epilogue
Three months later...

Damian

"I can't thank you enough for doing this, Damian. I really appreciate it."

"It's not all on me. Rom is helping out as well. But no problem, Dev. I'm happy to be of assistance."

While Damian tended to be more on the selfish side, he actually meant it. Dev and his new mate, Kate, were in desperate need of a vacation. He was happy to keep watch over Dev's Regent while they took their delayed honeymoon. While there was a distinct separation of duties in their Regents, when Damian became Lord of the East Regent a century ago, the three lords agreed collaboration made them a stronger, more united front. This was the first time a need had risen for one lord to temporarily take over for another, so Damian, Dev, and Rom spent quite a bit of time strategizing to ensure Dev's absence wouldn't put any of their Regents in jeopardy.

"Have a great time in Europe, Dev."

"One more favor to ask, though, if I may."

"That sounds ominous."

Dev's short laugh bellowed through the phone, before he quieted, affirming the seriousness of his request.

"Leave your shit with Giselle at the door. I don't know what happened between you two and I'm not asking, but she clearly went through something traumatic when Xavier had her and she's just starting to make a bit of progress. I don't need you setting her back."

Damian was actually going to split his time between his Regent and Dev's, staying at Dev's new estate when he was in Milwaukee, which meant he would inevitably run into Giselle. For protection, Ren and Manny would accompany the newlyweds, along with several other men.

Thane and Giselle were staying back at the estate and Giselle wasn't exactly the president of his fan club. She was the only female vampire he had ever fucked and maybe—*just perhaps*—he took it a little too far with his kink. He'd thought they were having a great time and had been looking forward to Round two when she escaped from her bonds, kicked him, *hard*, in the balls and took off. She would never discuss it with him, no matter how much he tried, so eventually he gave up. In retrospect, he probably should have probed her hard limits a bit further before they started, but in all fairness to him, she said she was into that shit. Lying bitch.

Okay, he could do this. He could occupy the same space as her and be civil. Or at least he would give it the old college try.

"Done."

"Good. And you'll call me if you need me." Not a question. Damian had repeatedly promised to reach out to him immediately if there were any issues. Since Kate was pregnant, they were going to fly in a private jet, as they didn't know the repercussions of flashing on her pregnancy, so it would take Dev some time to return if needed. But there wouldn't be any need. Not under his watch.

"Just go screw your mate's brains out, Dev. Hell, I

might even make some improvements to your Regent in your absence."

"Fuck off, Damian. You don't have enough experience. Or gumption."

"Ouch, that stung." With only a hundred years as Lord of a Regent under his belt, he was the least experienced of the three and he admitted to prioritizing partying a bit more than putting his nose to the grindstone. He had an uncanny ability to play the stock market very well and had devoted much time to that, as opposed to the business side of governing, as Dev and Rom had. Dev had entrusted him with a great deal by asking for his help and he didn't intend to fail his friend.

"Truth hurts, my friend. Truth hurts."

"Okay, I'm ending this conversation. See you in a few weeks."

"Thanks, D." They both disconnected without saying goodbye.

Damian didn't know how Rom felt about finding his mate...they didn't sit around drinking wine and "discuss their feelings" like a bunch of chicks. And while he was truly happy for Dev, at four hundred ninety-nine years, he was still having a grand time and didn't care to find his yet. It was clear Dev was pussy-whipped and no female was going to lead Damian around by his dick.

He'd taken several long-term human lovers over the years, although that was infrequent. They were all beautiful women and great lays, but he was forced to break it off when they professed their love, even though they'd mutually agreed no strings at the beginning. His last long-term lover had been nineteen years ago now and another nineteen would be too soon for him.

He was actually looking forward to seeing what females the Midwest had to offer and planned on checking out Dev's clubs while in town, particularly his new one, Dragonfly. Maybe he could get a few ideas for his own clubs. Between the three lords, they owned over three-dozen nightclubs, with Rom holding the bulk.

They still hadn't found all of the missing girls, and the nine doctors and eight scientists Dev's team recovered from Xavier's lair were now his and Rom's responsibility. Dev and Kate had their hands full with the shelter and the rescued women.

Xavier had done some pretty fucked up shit and Damian still couldn't believe what they'd discovered.

Xavier was running a baby factory, that much had been verified. And they'd found a way to impregnate unbounded human females. That still boggled his mind.

No babies had been recovered, however. So where were they? None of the recovered humans proved to be helpful in that regard...they were all held against their will as well. They only knew, once delivered, the babies were separated from the mother and taken off-site. They were still sorting through the boxes of the paperwork, computers, and flash drives that had been recovered, but the gist of it was Xavier had kidnapped countless young women over the years and had only started looking for dreamwalkers within the last decade.

Their main objective these past few months had been to find the remaining missing girls and babies, so the subject Kate's parentage hadn't received much discussion. Quite frankly, they didn't know if the humans they'd recovered would even know anything about it.

So what he'd found out today had floored him and he'd made the executive decision not to discuss it with Dev until his return. He was sure Dev would cancel his honeymoon and Damian had every confidence he and Rom could piece together more of the puzzle in his absence. Dev and his mate needed some time away from this madness. Unfortunately, it would all be here when they returned.

Damian replayed his conversation with T this morning. Since Giselle had been so despondent lately, refusing to continue her research with the human detective, Damian offered T's services instead. That vamp was wicked good at research. He was also very persuasive during interrogation and they spent hours a day interrogating the humans, but there were so goddamn many of them, it was an arduous task.

"My lord, I have some new information that I thought should be shared with you first. The detective does not know and I thought that best for now."

"What is it T?"

"Dr. Marcus Shelton, Xavier's lead physician and researcher, revealed to me that Xavier is unable to sire male offspring."

"What? How is that possible?"

"According to the doctor, it's a genetic anomaly. No one knew besides Xavier and himself. In his spare time, he was trying to find a cure, but he hadn't been able to yet. And that's not even the best part. Dr. Shelton was the one given the task of eliminating unwanted female vampires. The female babies sired by Xavier."

"Holy shit. Vampires? As in, plural? As in...there are more?"

"Yes, my Lord. During the first ten years that Dr. Shelton was held captive, he indicated Xavier sired at least a dozen females. He hasn't sired any for the last two decades or so because he stopped participating in the insemination process."

"So there are over a fucking dozen of Xavier's female offspring running loose in the world?"

"No, my lord. At first, Dr. Shelton did what he was told and disposed of the babes. He said he couldn't bear to kill any more innocents and began hatching a plan to save them. He is also apparently quite skilled with computers, and found different families on nearby adoption registries that had been waiting many years for infants. He began showing up on their doorsteps late at night, hoping they would accept a child, no

when he ran into issues with the second. The family
was suspicious and called their adoption representative
while he was still at the home. He fled, leaving the baby
there. He doesn't know what became of that baby. He
placed a third successfully a couple years later. After
that child, Xavier gave up the insemination duty to his
other rogues. Obviously if Xavier ever found out, it
would not only put the doctor's life in danger, but that
of the doctor's family."

"So there are possibly three females alive...well, two
outside of Kate...sired by Xavier?"

"Yes, my lord. Three total."

"Do we know where the other two are? Where he left
them? Do we know if they are still alive?"

"No, my lord. He did not keep any records for
obvious reasons and after all this time, doesn't
remember the addresses. He did say they were all
relatively local, within one hundred miles of this area,
as he didn't have time to go too far."

"And their mothers? Are the mothers still alive
somewhere too?"

"He did not believe so, my lord. He said most
females don't make it very long."

"I don't understand why he returned to Xavier each
time he was allowed to leave? That makes no sense."

"Leverage, my lord. They had his family, of course."

"Of course." Damian was silent, letting this new
information sink in. "So Kate may have two sisters, or
half sisters, then."

"It would appear that way, my lord."

"Okay. We need to locate these two other females.
Kate said her parents mentioned that they'd dropped
themselves off the adoption registry. Let's see if we can
take that angle and find the other two. See if the doctor
can at least narrow down a time frame of when he
thinks he dropped them off. Year, time of year? Shit,

anything else would help. And pull out a fucking map so he can help narrow down the locations."

"Yes, my lord."

"And T, this stays between us. Do not tell the detective. I'll talk to Rom and we'll get more resources on this. We'll wait to tell Dev and Kate when they return."

"Of course, my lord."

So, Xavier could only squirt female swimmers? Interesting. And Kate had possibly two other half siblings roaming about. What were they like? Were they from the same mother? Were they also dreamwalkers, or had they inherited their father's demented genes? He needed to find them and quick.

His gut burned. It always did when he got a premonition. Unfortunately they weren't always that clear or very specific...more like a *feeling* instead. But over the years, he'd learned to trust it. It had never failed him before.

They all thought Xavier already knew about Kate being his child. He had to when he bit her. Another reason he wanted Dev and Kate to get away. If Xavier did know, he'd be relentless in coming for her, and his soon-to-be-born grandchild.

And if he didn't find these other females soon, Xavier would. Yes, his gut was on fire. This could turn into the biggest clusterfuck he'd ever been involved in and right quick.

He picked up the phone and called his friend, his mentor.

"Rom, it's Damian. We've got a problem."

~ The End ~

UPCOMING RELEASES

Book 2 in the Regent Vampire Lords series, *Belonging*, is scheduled to be released in January 2015 and will feature Damian's story. Keep reading for a little sneak peak.

Book 3 in the Regent Vampire Lords series, *Reawakening*, is scheduled to be released in March 2015 and will feature Romaric's story.

Also planned for 2015 is a Novella featuring Mike and Giselle's rocky saga and possibly a fourth novel, depending on reader interest.

Please visit my website at http://klkreig.com to keep up-to-date on release dates, cover reveals, etc. I would also love to hear from you, so feel to email me at klkreig@gmail.com.

An unedited snippet from
BELONGING
Book 2 in the Regent Vampire Lords series

Coming January 2015

For the second time in the last several hours she awoke to a gentle touch on her cheek. She was completely disoriented and blinked her eyes open, trying to shake off her dream. She hadn't dreamt of per past in a very long time. Staring down at her with affection—*and desire*—was Damian.

"Hello Kitten. How are you feeling?" His voice was silky soft, like feathers gliding over her sensitive skin.

"Is it morning yet?"

"No, it's still the middle of the night. I just wanted to check on you. How does your head feel?"

"Ummm...I'm not sure." A slight headache lingered, but it was mostly gone. She pulled herself into a sitting position, leaning against the soft leather headboard.

Damian's eyes snapped to her chest. She followed his line of sight, noticing her nipples were as hard as pencil erasers. She could even faintly see the outline of her areola through her thin tank. When she lifted her eyes they connected with his. And just like that, she lit up inside. Her stomach was in a free fall, like every other time she'd looked at him tonight. She was sure the lust on his face was mirrored in hers. Holy guacamole, she wanted him. It was exhilarating and terrifying at the same time.

He swallowed thickly and even his adam's apple was sexy. Movement caught in her peripheral and
looking down, she watched him grow hard right before her eyes.

"Kitten, you'd better stop looking at me like I'm your

favorite saucer of milk or I'm not going to be responsible for what happens next. I'm barely holding it together as it is." His voice was low and hoarse, ratcheting up his sexy status another notch to *'so-fucking-hot-I-dare-you-not-to-touch-this.'*

"I want to be inside you so bad, Analise," he groaned. *God, she wanted that too.*

How could she be so wildly attracted to a man she'd just met? This wasn't at all like her. Was this some sort of vampire voodoo? She'd heard of this type of thing before. Vampires could make humans do their bidding at will. Was that what was happening here? Was that why she could barely resist the urge to climb into his lap and rub her body all over his...like a goddamned cat? Like a *kitten*!

She saw red. How *dare* he try to compel her!

"What are you doing to me?" She grabbed the blankets and covered herself completely, putting a ridiculously flimsy barrier between them.

He actually had the audacity to smirk. "You mean besides making you wet?"

She inhaled sharply, her mouth forming an O. He did not! What an asshole. Of course, he'd already admitted as much earlier.

"I want to know what you are doing to me and I want you to stop. Right now," she spat.

"So...I guess you're feeling better then." *Ooohhh.* Fury spiked her blood pressure higher by the millisecond. He pushed every single one of her buttons. Good and bad.

"Do you really get women with that mouth of yours?"

"Ah Kitten, come now. You wound me." He held his hand over his heart in mock hurt. "It's not my *mouth* that gets women."

"You are the most infuriating, cocky person I have ever met." And sexy and handsome and erotic and...

"God, I love hearing the word cock come out of your mouth. I'm so fucking turned on right now, Analise. You have no idea." Lust and desire clouded his eyes.

When had he gotten so close? Unrestrained hunger tightened his stunning face. He had no issues showing or telling her how much he wanted her. It was unsettling...and a huge turn on.

He leaned closer, bringing their mouths within a hairsbreadth of each other. She had only to lean forward an inch and his soft lips would be hers for the taking. He would let her and she wanted nothing more. He scrambled her brains.

God Analise, stop being such a tramp.

She pushed on his chest, trying to gain some space, some breathing room. He moved only slightly and that was only because he chose to do so. She was under no illusions she'd managed to move someone built like a 747. As she felt the hardness and warmth of his pecs under her hand, she realized touching him was a tremendously bad idea. All she could think of was trailing her fingers down his torso until they reached his greatest treasure.

Whew...was it hot in here suddenly?

This was not going at *all* according to plan. Granted, she hadn't yet hammered out the details of her elaborate strategy, but letting him have control definitely wasn't in it. And right now, he had it in spades.

"What are you doing to me?" The soft words barely passed her constricted throat. Now, however, she wasn't exactly sure what she meant by them.

His eyes never left hers as he closed the gap, capturing her lips gently between his.

"The same thing you're doing to me, Analise," he whispered reverently before he took them again. How could he make her want to commit murder one minute and melt like chocolate sitting in the hot sun the next?

Damian deepened the kiss, scattering her thoughts to the wind. Next thing she knew, she was on his lap, straddling his hips, his erection prodding between her legs. Had he moved her there or had she done that herself? Strong, muscled arms held her tight against an equally sinewy body. Unable to stop herself, she wrapped her arms around his neck and let her body take over. As Damian ate at her mouth her hips rolled, the rough fabric of his jeans rubbing perfectly against her terry-covered clit. Their tongues dueled, their breaths quickened.

She ran her hands over his back, down his arms. She couldn't get enough of his toned, sleek body. He caught her wrists, holding them with one hand at the small of her back. Her pulse skyrocketed. She hated being restrained, but with Damian she became even more impossibly turned on. She was embarrassingly wet if the dampness on her pajamas was any indication.

Damian scattered hot, open-mouthed kisses on her face, her neck. He'd placed his free hand on her hips, helping them keep time with her pace. She was quickly soaring toward orgasm and he hadn't even touched her...at least not in the way that counted. This was all kinds of wrong, but she couldn't stop. Her head felt heavy, falling back on her shoulders. She was so close to soaring.

"Come for me, Analise. I need to see you fall apart in my arms." His soft voice sounded raw, husky and was exactly what she needed to push her over the edge into complete paradise. A white light exploded behind her closed lids. Goose bumps blanketed her body as an orgasm ripped through her setting every nerve ending on fire. She'd never felt pleasure like this.

When she finally came down from ecstasy, she felt Damian's soft kisses at the corners of her mouth, her eyelids, her cheeks. He'd released her arms at some point and placed one hand at the small of her back and one around her neck. His strong grip felt...comforting. Right.

As the last vestiges of her orgasm waned, shame

flooded her. Her cheeks warmed. How could she have just rubbed herself to climax on Damian's lap, like some wanton hussy? She tried, but couldn't help the tears that formed, spilling over her closed lids. Great, the last thing she needed was Damian to think she was easy *and* an emotional head case. Christ, let's just multiply her embarrassment a thousand fold.

"Baby, what's wrong?" Too late. *Uhhhh. Shoot her now.* She kept her eyes closed, wishing the whole thing would go away. She'd done that a lot in her life. Hadn't worked so far. Guess she wasn't a quick learner.

"Kitten, talk to me. What's the matter? Did I hurt you?" He sounded slightly panicked.

Did he hurt her? No, not yet. But he would. Just give him time. Everyone did sooner or later.

"I don't want to be another notch on your bedpost," she whispered, inwardly groaning. Where in god's name had that come from? That's not all what she intended to say. *Get out before I let you fuck me* had been more like it.

"Ahhh Kitten." He pulled her tightly to him, strong arms wrapped completely around her. He stroked her back, her hair. Tears fell quietly, wetting his shirt. Pretty soon snot would be running down her face. Great. *Excuse me, Damian, while I wipe my buggers from your two hundred dollar shirt.*

He held her as he spoke. His voice firm, but full of sincerity. "Listen to me good, Analise. You are *not* another notch on my bedpost. I don't want another woman. Only you. It will only ever be you." He pulled back cupping her cheeks in his strong hands, forcing her eyes to his. "I won't hurt you, Analise. I will protect you. I will protect your heart. I promise."

The ability to speak vanished. She shook her head. That's all she could do. He sounded so sure, so sincere, so possessive. She ached to believe him. Every word he said resonated deep inside, slowing filling each empty crevice in her very damaged soul. Every word created more chinks in her already fragile armor. For the first time since she was ten years old, she longed to be loved by someone. To *belong* to someone. To Damian.

Stupid, foolish schoolgirl thoughts.

He touched his lips to hers one last time before pulling the sheets back. Sliding in, fully clothed, he pulled her body into his arranging them comfortably.

"Go back to sleep, Analise. I'll be right here when you wake." He was staying. She was never more grateful...or terrified. Letting him stay was the single dumbest idea ever, but she was simply too exhausted to fight him.

The walls she'd spent so many years building were crumbling quickly and she had no clue how to stop them from disintegrating into nothingness. And that would be so very bad. Because if she allowed Damian into her life, into her heart and he broke her...well, she would never recover. Damian would literally be the straw that broke the camel's back.

Hope. It was a fool's emotion. It was that tiny light at the end of a black tunnel that kept one going in even the darkest of times, but the inevitable crash that followed was all the more devastating because once you reached the end you realize it wasn't a light after all. It had been a sick, twisted illusion all along. She should know. She was *Hope's* bitch.

Against her better judgment, she drifted off to sleep in the warmth and comfort of his arms, wondering what in the hell she was going to do now. Because in order to find Beth, she needed Damian. And against all that made sense, she couldn't spend much more time with him without falling head over heels in love. But that also meant she could end up eternally broken.

Analise had recovered from heart-crushing devastation and deep betrayal throughout her life, but she knew without a single doubt that she would never recover from loving and losing Damian DiStephano.

He held the power to destroy her permanently.

About The Author

Most authors will tell you that writing is all they've ever wanted to do. I guess I'm one of the few that don't fit in that bucket. Writing a book was never on my bucket list until three years ago. On my list was: Climb the Corporate ladder. *Check.* Go to Europe. *Check.* Complete a half marathon. *Check.* Eat chocolate daily. *Double check. Isn't this on everyone's bucket list?* Catch up on two seasons of Games of Thrones in one day. *Painful, but check.* Lose five pounds. *This will never be checked.* And finally, devouring romance books at an alarming pace like the unashamed book addict I am...*Over a thousand checks!*

Living in Nebraska with my soul-mate hubby, I pen my magic world at night, while paying the bills with an actual compensating job in the corporate world during the day. Writing is just an all-consuming passion for now, but, boy, if I could dream...

My other loves include my simply amazing, incredible and talented children, a steamy novel, great friends and family, and a warm ocean breeze gliding over my sun drenched skin with a cocktail in hand.

If you enjoyed this book, <u>please</u> consider leaving a review at Goodreads or the many various other on-line places you can purchase ebooks. Even one or two sentences or simply rating the book is helpful. If you're anything like me, you rely on reader reviews to help make your determination on purchasing a great book in the vast sea of available ones. Many THANKS!

Finally, if you would like to learn more about me or message me, please visit the following places:

Facebook: https://www.facebook.com/pages/KL-Kreig/808927362462053?ref=hl

Website: http://klkreig.com

Goodreads author page coming soon! Right now you can find me just under K.L. Kreig.

Email: klkreig@gmail.com

Thanks!

~ Kelly